GUS

by
Kim Holden

Published by Do Epic, LLC

ISBN 978-0-9911402-7-5

Cover design by Brandon Hando

Editing by Monica Parpal and Amy Donnelly

OTHER BOOKS BY KIM HOLDEN

BRIGHT SIDE
ALL OF IT
SO MUCH MORE

Dedication

Bright Siders
This book is for you.
You fill my heart to
overflowing.

Dr. John Okerbloom, MD
1952 - 2014

Kate Sedgwick
My hero

Sunday, January 22
(Gus)

Every step I take is heavier than the one that came before it. I don't know where I'm going, only that my destination is a mind-numbing amount of alcohol.

As I step from the grass of the cemetery lawn to the concrete sidewalk, I feel a shift inside my chest. The softness of grief hardens to anger again. It's been this way for days now. Grief. Anger. Grief. Anger. Grief ... Anger ...

I don't want to feel anymore. I'm fucking tired of it.

I've spent the past few days trying to drown death in a shabby motel room on the unquestionably shady side of town. There's a liquor store next door that sells Jack and cigarettes. That's all I need.

Speaking of cigarettes, I'm almost out. I'm smoking my last now. At the thought I hear her voice in my head saying, "You should quit."

I answer, "Don't fucking start with me today, Bright Side."

The woman I just walked past on the sidewalk gave me an exceptionally wide berth, which leads me to believe I said that out loud. I scrub my hand over my face in the hopes that it will erase delirium. It doesn't.

"I need some fucking sleep." Yup, I'm talking to myself again. Whatever. I need a drink.

There's a bar on the next corner. It looks dark and dingy — perfect.

When I open the door, the stench of stale beer, sweat, and cigarette smoke hits me. I'm home. At least for the next few hours.

As I walk toward the bar, I notice the dozen or so middle-aged patrons are sizing me up. The vibe of the place screams that these people are regulars. This is where they drink away their rent and grocery money on a daily basis. And I'm intruding. I glance down and realize the suit and tie doesn't help. I loosen the knot of my tie and slip it off, stuff it in my pocket, take off my suit coat, and undo the top few buttons of my shirt as I take a seat on a stool at the end of the bar.

The bartender greets me with a nod and slides a cocktail napkin in front of me as I roll up my sleeves.

1

I reach for my pack of cigarettes while I order. "Jack. Make it a double." It's habit, the pack is empty. I knew that. "And a pack of Camels."

He doesn't card me and points to a vending machine in the corner before he reaches for a highball glass and the bottle of whiskey. I slide from the stool and buy two packs of cigarettes from the vending machine. When I return my drink's waiting for me.

So is a woman that's probably my mom's age. I bet she was attractive twenty years ago, but the brutality of a hard life and poor choices is etched deep in the creases of her face. I reach around her for my drink. She smells like cheap perfume and even cheaper sex. Before I can escape, she's talking.

I don't want to talk.

"What's a handsome thing like you doin' in a place like this?"

Why not just ask me if I'm up for a fifty-dollar fuck, or a twenty dollar blow job, and skip the chitchat? I don't answer and take a seat three stools away.

She moves one stool closer. "Anything I can help ya with, cutie?" Her hands are jittery. She's looking for money for her next fix. I wouldn't touch her with a ten-foot pole, but I half want to toss some money at her because I can identify with her need to escape reality right now.

Even though I feel sorry for her, I don't have it in me to conjure any genuine compassion. I drop my head and shake it. Usually I'm not the asshole, but today is different. I tilt my head and look her in the eye. "Can you bring back the dead? I could use some fucking help with that."

I guarantee she's never heard that one before. She's blinking at me, a rapid fire, fluttering succession of confusion.

I let my eyes fall to the glass of amber liquid I'm swirling in my right hand and answer my own question, "I didn't think so." I tip the glass back and drain it in two gulps. I place it on the bar top upside down and gesture at the bartender for another before I look at her again. "Leave me alone." It's a demand. Her tight smile tells me she's heard that one before; probably too often for her addiction's liking.

Solitude is my companion and we get along famously, until

sitting upright on the stool becomes difficult. I don't know how much time has passed, but I know it isn't enough to make a dent in my heartbreak. I'm ten or twelve doubles in when the bartender refuses to serve me anymore. I want to yell and throw a full-on fucking tantrum, but the truth is I'm too tired for the drama. My vision is blurry and my limbs are past the point of numb and have moved into a mechanically uncooperative state. Movement is a struggle. I just need to sleep, so I let the guy call me a cab instead.

The cab takes me back to my motel. The walk up the stairs is slow, labored, and clumsy. I'm not sure I even shut the door behind me before I stagger to the bed and drop face first onto the filthy bedspread. It smells dank and musty: a disgusting mix of age, grime, and God knows what else. The room is spinning, sucking me into a vortex of dizzy relief, an escape from the here and now. I don't know if sleep comes for me or if my body just makes the unconscious decision to shut down. I'm grateful either way.

Tuesday, January 24
(Gus)

Have you ever slept a day away? I mean, like fall asleep and wake to find an entire day has lapsed without you bearing witness to even a minute of it?

It's fucking beautiful ... medicinal ... sedative. I don't dream. Well, I probably do, but I never recall them upon waking. I've never been more appreciative of this gift than I am this morning. It was more than twenty-four hours of nothing. Like I said ... fucking beautiful.

I remember Bright Side's mom, Janice, used to hole up in her bedroom for days at a time and sleep. I always thought it was sad ... a wasted opportunity. Now I think I understand. Because the last thing I want to do is get up from this bed, step out of this room, and face whatever life has in store on the other side of that door. I'm not ashamed to admit I'm hiding. I'm *fucking* hiding.

After I take a piss I look for my suit coat, which I find in an unceremonious heap by the door. For two seconds I think about how much I hate this goddamn suit. It's less than a year old and I've only worn it twice—both Sedgwick funerals. I'm burning the bastard when I take it off. I fish through the pockets for my cigarettes, lighter, and phone.

I hesitate with a quick glance around the room before lighting up. I usually don't smoke indoors but the overall degradation of this place practically begs for it.

I power up my phone. I shut it off days ago when I left home because I didn't want to deal with everyone ... or anyone. I checked in with Ma about the funeral via text, but that's it. I'm already cringing before I see the number of missed calls, texts, and emails because I know it's going to be too many.

87 missed calls

72 texts

37 emails

"Dude," I say, exhaling exasperation, or denial, or indifference. I can't decide which at the moment, so I toss my phone on the bed and finish my cigarette, followed by another ... followed by another. It's fifteen minutes of nothing more than breathing through my addiction. I can't stop thinking about her.

4

Nothing specific, nothing I can visualize or recall. It's just pain and emptiness. Darkness. The light, *the bright light*, is gone. I'm fighting to draw calm out of the cigarette with each deep pull; to dispel the darkness.

The calm doesn't come.

So, I pick up my life—my phone—again, and skim through the missed calls first: my mom; my bandmates: Franco, Robbie, and Jamie; our producer, MFDM (the Motherfucking Dream Maker, his real name's Tom, but he loves it when I call him MFDM); and our tour manager, Hitler (not his real name obviously, but it suits him given his tendency toward overall insensitivity. Our next tour's been in suspense. Apparently, in his mind, said tour and the almighty dollar take priority over us dealing with terminal illness and the death of a human being.). The only name I want to see, both on an instinctive and selfish level, isn't here. And it never will be again.

I skip the texts and emails and call my mom instead. She answers on the second ring. "Gus, honey, where are you? Are you okay?"

I hate hearing her worry like this, but knowing my desertion is fueling it makes it worse. "Hey, Ma."

She repeats, "Where are you? Your truck's still at the church."

"Yeah, I know. I've been staying at a motel." My throat feels dry and scratchy as I speak.

"Gus, you should come home." My mom's never been one to tell me what to do. Suggestively guide? Absolutely. But tell me what to do? It rarely happens.

I don't answer.

She sighs, "Honey, I know this is hard—"

I cut her off. "*Hard*? Please tell me you did not just say this is *hard*, Ma, because that's the understatement of the century." She sniffles and I know she's starting to cry, which makes me feel like shit because I know I'm the catalyst. "Sorry Ma."

"I know." The pain that rises out of those two words reminds me that we're in this together. She misses her, too.

I throw on my suit coat and pick up my lighter and cigarettes and stuff them in my pocket. "I'll be home in a half hour. Love you."

"Love—"

I end the call before I hear her finish.

By the time I settle up my bill at the motel, take a cab to the church to get my truck, and drive home, an hour has passed. It's lunchtime.

When I open the front door, the aroma of garlic and caramelized onions assaults me. Veggie tacos. My stomach growls on cue. I can't remember the last time I ate.

I kiss Ma on the forehead on my way through the kitchen. "I need to get out of this damn suit. I'll be right back."

When I return, we eat in silence. Ma's a lot like Bright Side. Or maybe Bright Side was a lot like Ma. They both understood the power of silence. Some people are threatened by silence and try to avoid it or fill it with needless bullshit. Silence isn't the enemy. It can bring comfort and clarity and validation. It's a reminder of time for what it is ... presence. Which sadly doesn't mean as much as it did a week ago.

Eight tacos in and my stomach starts screaming for mercy. "Thanks for taco Tuesday, Ma."

She smiles but it doesn't begin to reach her eyes. "You're welcome." She looks tired. "By the way, Franco's been by every day to check on you."

It's her way of telling me to call him. "Yeah, I'll call him when I get out of the shower."

Two phone calls down (Franco and fucking Hitler), and I'm ready to throw my phone out the window into the fucking ocean, crawl into bed, pull the covers over my head, and forget everything. We're leaving for Europe Thursday morning to begin the postponed tour. Our self-titled debut album, Rook, has done well in the states since its release late last year, but it's nothing compared to how it's blown up in Europe. Hitler can't wait to get us over there. I know I'm an ungrateful, selfish asshole for not wanting to get back out on tour, but the honest-to-God truth is I don't even know how to function anymore. Bright Side wasn't only my best friend; she was like my other half ... the other half of my brain, the other half of my conscience, the other half of my sense of humor, the other half of my creativity, the other half of my heart. How do you go back to doing what you did before,

6

GUS

when half of you is gone forever?

Wednesday, January 25
(Gus)

It's my birthday today. I'm twenty-two. I feel fucking eighty-two.

Ma made me cupcakes. Twenty-two chocolate cupcakes. Each one with a candle in it. It takes me two tries to blow them all out.

Guess I'm not getting my wish.

I knew that.

This is the first birthday I've ever had that I've wanted to skip. I want to rewind time and go back to my last birthday. Bright Side and Gracie were both here. And I don't mean metaphorically. I mean here physically, in this room with us. Smiling and laughing and eating cupcakes until they got sick.

I'm smiling now thinking about them, but my stomach hurts.

I don't want to eat cupcakes without them.

No more birthdays.

No more reminders.

I fucking hate reminders.

Thursday, January 26
(Gus)

I know I didn't pack enough clothes, but it's too late now. Franco's waiting in the kitchen for me, talking to Ma. The record label sent a car, which is waiting in the driveway to take us to the airport. Our plane departs for Germany in two hours. I grab another handful of boxer-briefs and socks and drop them into my bag, where they take up residence alongside two pairs of jeans, three T-shirts, deodorant, toothpaste, toothbrush, laptop, wallet, passport, and phone.

I sling the bag's strap over my shoulder and check the pocket of my jeans for my cigarettes and lighter. I can't step out of my bedroom without staring at Bright Side's laptop that's been sitting untouched on my dresser for over a week now. She left it to me. It houses all the music she ever wrote. I feel honored to have it. My mind's screaming at me to go back for it, but my heart is pulling rank and commanding me to leave without it. I'm not ready. The CD she left for me is lying on top of it. She knew she was dying. I know it's a good-bye and I'm sure as hell not ready for that. I flip off the light and start down the hall toward Franco's voice.

Franco tips his chin up when he catches sight of me. "What's up, douche nozzle?"

I shake my head. "Not much, mangina."

Ma doesn't even flinch. It's how Franco and I have always talked to each other. They're terms of endearment. The truth is, Franco's the only person I have left in my life who will tell me exactly like it is now that Bright Side's gone. No sugarcoating, no blowing smoke up my ass, just straight up honesty. I love him for it. Despite the tough guy façade of shaved head and tattoos, he's a softy ... with a fierce sense of loyalty.

He points to my bag. "That all you're taking, man? We'll be gone for two months."

I shrug. "And my guitars. I can buy more on the road when I need it. Let's roll, dude."

He nods and I'm thankful for his lack of psychoanalysis. He hugs Ma. "Thanks for breakfast, Mrs. H." He's palming two large blueberry muffins wrapped in a paper towel.

She squeezes him tight. "Of course. Have fun over there,

Franco."

"Will do."

When she hugs me I want to fall apart in her arms. To cry like I did when I was eight and I broke my ankle. But I don't. We both hold on longer than usual and hesitate to release. "Make sure you enable the security system every night while I'm gone," I tell her.

The corner of her mouth turns up and I know she's put on her brave face for me. "I always do. Don't worry about me. Go see the world, Gus. I'm so proud of you."

I nod. Compliments have always managed to embarrass me, like I'm somehow not quite worthy of them. The last few weeks I've felt *completely* unworthy. "Thanks Ma. I love you."

She kisses me on the cheek and hands me my own paper towel-wrapped blueberry muffins. "I love you, too, honey. Be safe."

Normally I'd respond with, "Always," but I can't bring myself to say it now. I feel like it would be premature betrayal for the next two months of unknowns. I don't feel like being cautious. Not in the least. "Bye, Ma."

"Bye, Gus."

Friday, January 27
(Gus)

It's officially Friday by the time we touch down in Berlin. I've never traveled outside the United States before and I quickly learn what all the fuss is about — jet lag is a motherfucker.

My ass is dragging from the moment we step off the plane, through customs, and all the way to our hotel. Time is not on my side today. We've got back-to-back meetings before soundcheck this afternoon, and then two interviews before the show tonight.

It's hard to put my game face on. I fucking loath faking anything. I'm horrible at it. So I'm actually grateful when Hitler escorts us everywhere. The dude's in love with the sound of his own voice and I'm more than happy to let him yammer on for us during the meetings. Most of it is stuff he should be dealing with anyway. And I practically want to hug the guy when he instructs both interviewers that all personal questions are off the table. No need to dodge why the tour was delayed or why we've been off the radar for a month. Thank God, because I'd probably take somebody's head off if they mentioned her name. I say Bright Side's name in my head a million times a day. But hearing her real name, Kate Sedgwick, spoken by a stranger who never knew her? Some journalist feigning concern or sympathy? I'd be tempted to silence them with my fist.

Dinner is preceded by, and concluded with, several pints of strong German ale.

There's enough alcohol in my system that when we take the stage my guitar feels comfortable in my hands and the crowd is only a fuzzy blur of color and motion. My memory's teetering just enough to the near side of lost that I need to concentrate with single-minded focus on the chords I'm playing and the lyrics I'm singing. That leaves room in my mind for nothing else for a solid hour. It feels like I've discovered the formula for coping: the combination of excessive amounts of alcohol and live performance.

Magic.

Friday, February 3
(Gus)

We're a week into this tour, and the distraction of drunkenness and performing isn't working anymore. I don't think I've been sober since the day we arrived on this side of the pond. During the first few days, I couldn't sleep enough. These past few days, I haven't wanted to. It's like I can't get enough of just sitting around thinking about her: her ever-present deep but feminine laughter; the faint dusting of freckles on her nose and cheeks and between her shoulder blades; how she loved to watch the sunset; the sound of her voice when she said *I love you*; how beautifully she played her violin. I know I'm obsessing in an entirely unhealthy way, but I have this fear that if I don't keep turning her over in my head, I'll forget. And forgetting scares the hell out of me.

Franco thinks I should see a doctor. Maybe get some sleeping pills, or anti-depressants.

I think that's a pussy's way out. I'm not going to start popping pills to avoid grief. Booze is my only strategy. Some would argue meds would be a better alternative, but I don't like the idea of giving some doctor carte blanche to manipulate me with scripts. If anyone's going to manipulate me ... it's going to be me.

I try not to think about that night with Bright Side. I try not to think about it because everything else pales in comparison. It was the best night of my life. I didn't know it was going to happen. She didn't know it was going to happen. But *goddamn* it did happen. So, while I'm lying on this bunk in the tour bus, in the middle of the night, cruising across the European countryside, I'm going to give into it and replay it in my mind. Closing my eyes, I allow the memories to flood in.

I walk into the guest room from the hallway at the same time Bright Side walks in from the adjoining bathroom. She's brushing her teeth. She always multi-tasks while she's brushing her teeth. Right now she's digging through her duffle bag on the floor.

"What're you looking for?" I ask. The sight of her hunting through her bag makes me sad. She's packed and ready to leave for Minnesota

early tomorrow morning. I don't know when I'll see her next. We've never gone more than a day or two without seeing each other, and even that was rare.

She shifts her toothbrush to the side of her mouth and tries to talk through all of the frothy toothpaste. "Pajamas," she says. At least, that's what I think she said. She turns, runs back in the bathroom, spits out the toothpaste, and returns smiling. "Pajamas," she repeats. "I think they're in my other bag. It's already out in my car."

"Gimme your keys. I'll go get it," I offer.

She shakes her head. "Nah. That's okay, I'll get by without them. Can you get the light?" she asks.

I'm gonna miss this. Our friendship. The familiarity. She's always been here. With me. We do everything together. Since we were kids every time we've spent the night under the same roof, we had to sleep in the same room together. Whether it was in my room, or in the living room on the sofa, or more recently here in the guest room the past couple of weeks. Always together. Hell, I don't know how I'm gonna fall asleep without her in my arms after tonight.

I flip the light off and take off my shorts and T-shirt. I always sleep in my underwear, but I always wait until the light is off to strip down to them, which is weird because in the morning I'll climb out of bed and she'll see me. Nighttime is always more intimate though. The darkness brings with it a certain longing, and damn, I've loved this girl forever. She doesn't know that though.

I slide into the left side of the bed, because she always sleeps on the right. With the moonlight filtering in through the blinds, I can just make out her silhouette as she slips her shorts down her legs. It's a quick movement, but it's playing out in slow motion for me. When they drop to her ankles I feel the familiar tug of arousal stirring. My gaze is trained on her as her hands disappear behind her back and she slides each bra strap down her arms from under her tank top. With straps free, she reaches up under her tank top and magically her bra appears in her hand. Dropping it on top of her duffle bag with her shorts, she walks toward the bed. With the moonlight on her, I can see her little pink cotton panties. Whoever said cotton panties aren't sexy hasn't seen Bright Side in a pair of them. Shit. I may be in trouble. Full-on boner is taking shape and I've got nowhere to hide. Then I peek at her tank top. It's pale yellow and thin from frequent washings. She's had it for years. Her nipples, dark and so beautiful, strain against the worn material. Closing my eyes, I quietly

13

*take a few deep, calming breaths. I'm talking to myself inside my head,
"Get your shit together, dude. It's Bright Side. You've seen her in a
bikini a million times." But goddamn this is different, so I add, "She
doesn't know you can see her, perv. Stop gawking," and then, because
my dick is doing most of my thinking for me at the moment, I add, "at
her gorgeous fucking body."*

*As soon as she's under the covers, she scoots over to my side and
presses up against me searching for warmth. The cool sheets make her
shiver, like they always do, as she drapes her arm across my chest and
rests her head on my shoulder. I wrap my arm that's under her around
her back and rest my hand on her hip, and when I do, all is right in the
world.*

*Her voice is only a whisper when she speaks. It's quiet, but it tears
open the night. "I'm gonna miss you, dude. So much."*

Kissing her forehead, I whisper back, "Me too. You have no idea."

*"You'll have to buy one of those ginormous pillows or an inflatable
doll to snuggle when I'm gone."*

*I laugh, because of course she would make a joke right now. "Think
I can find one that talks and farts in its sleep, just, you know, so it's a
realistic stand-in for you?"*

*She slaps my stomach, but she's laughing. "Shut. Up. I do not.
Gracie would've told me."*

*The logic behind her denial makes me laugh even harder and I
confess, "You don't. I was kidding."*

*With a contented smile playing at her lips, she rolls over to her
other side and I follow suit. The beast in my underwear has calmed
down, so I pull her into me and spoon her. This is how we always fall
asleep. She feels so good in my arms that I would swear God made her
just for me. Pressing my forehead against the back of her head, I can't
help but feel melancholy. And then it hits me again. She's leaving.
Bright Side is leaving. When I kiss the back of her head it feels eerily
final. It's intuition; that my heart quickly pushes aside. "I love you,
Bright Side."*

*She rubs her hand over the back of my hand that's pressed against
her stomach. It's a loving gesture. Just like everything else she does. "I
love you, too, Gus." Bright Side has always known how to make people
feel loved. She's so damn good at it.*

*When her hand stills, I realize that her tank top has shifted up
slightly and my pinkie and ring finger are resting against her bare skin,*

just above the top edge of her panties. I've touched her skin a million times. But not like this.

And dammit, the tug starts in my groin again. It's a rapid ache and it's building fast. To avoid embarrassment and further stimulation, I slide my hips back so I'm not pressed up against her. But I can't help myself and my hand starts moving. It's a bold, but subtle, selfish, but giving gesture meant to sooth us both. Every ounce of concentration I have is laser-focused on that one-inch strip of Bright Side. My fingertips float over her skin, savoring it. She's so soft. After I stroke back and forth a few times, I realize she feels tense in my arms, so I stop. "Sorry," I whisper. But when I lift my hand, she takes it and guides me back, offering permission. Without a moment's thought, I take it. This time I sneak under the hem of her shirt so that my entire hand, fingers and palm, are touching her. Light as a ghost, gliding over her skin but increasing incrementally, driven by spontaneous purpose, until my fingers are spread out in an act of tactile adoration and satisfaction. We're both breathing more heavily now. And though she's relaxed somewhat in my arms, I can feel each inhalation reach her belly. Each breath is slow and measured. Bright Side is only slow and measured when she's concentrating on something.

When I drag my hand across her belly again my thumb traces the underside of her breast. Her breath stutters and my dick hardens instantly. I know she feels it, the tip has breached the waistband and it's straining painfully against the elastic restraint. At the same time I pull my groin back farther, she reaches back over my hip and pulls me into her.

I can't help the deep groan that rushes out of my mouth when I'm pressed up against her ass. It's relief paired with physical stimulation, a need both being met and intensified simultaneously. I feel her sigh under my hand. She's with me. Then, because it feels so damn good, I roll my hips a few times. Jesus Christ, I must've died and gone to heaven.

And I never want to leave.

Her hand slides back until she's palming my ass cheek. My hips are engaged, slow and wanting, grinding against her. When she lifts her tank top over her breasts and directs my hand to her, I don't hesitate. I take her in my hand and stroke her gently before plucking her nipple between my thumb and forefinger. It hardens under my touch and she moans.

Oh fuck. *That moan just killed me. She's the sexiest damn woman* on Earth. That moan was proof.

I can't take it anymore. I whisper, "I need to touch you."

She nods and it's more than permission, it's agreement.

I slip my hand down the front of her panties and tease her with my fingers, which sets her lower body in motion. I answer her physical plea and let my fingers slide lower. She parts her legs and welcomes me. She's so wet. I circle her a few times before diving in and she meets every plunge with her hips. "Gus?"

"Yeah?" My voice is hazy and faint, lost in this mutual attraction.

"I need you to kiss me." I've never heard that voice come from between her lips — it's lust. And it makes me envy every guy whose ears it ever fell upon before mine.

I've never wanted anything more in my life. Slipping my fingers out of her, I shift so she can roll to her back. I'm propped up on my elbow, looking down at her. "You're so beautiful." It's so quiet I don't think she'll even hear me.

The slight smile on her face tells me she did.

Goddamn, I've dreamt about this moment forever. Kissing Bright Side. If I'm gonna do this, I'm gonna do this right. While she's lying on her back, I rise up and climb over her so I'm on my hands and knees hovering above her. I take her face in my hands and I thank God for what's about to happen. And then I close my eyes and lower my lips to hers. Kissing her softly, I part her lips with my tongue. When her tongue meets mine, I know she's right there with me. Kissing has never, ever, been like this for me. I can literally see fireworks behind my eyelids. I love this girl. I love every last thing about her. And what I love most right now is kissing her. How she meets every move I make with one of her own. How when I pick up the pace and intensity, she matches it.

After a few minutes of kissing, I'm so fucking horny I can't see straight. My entire body is humming. I grasp the hem of her tank in my hand and tug, asking between feverish kisses, "Off?"

She answers breathlessly, "Yes."

With the tank top history, all I want is to feel her skin against mine. Rolling over, I pull her on top and she drops all of her weight on me, one knee on either side of my hips. And if it's possible, I'm even more turned on with her in the dominant position. Her nipples rub against my chest, the telltale reminder of her arousal dragging deliciously across my skin, heightening every nerve in my body. They're screaming out in raging pleasure. Pulling her back in for a kiss, I slam her mouth to mine. The *kiss is deep and demanding. She wants this, too. Her body is rocking against me. Reaching down between us I pull the waistband of my boxer briefs down so my shaft is exposed. It's one more barrier down and it feels so good. Then I move my hand to her back and run my fingers up and down trying to mentally ease up and put myself back in the game. I've been out of my mind for the past few minutes and I want to make this last and remember every single second. Every single detail. I only get one shot at this. I know that. I want it to be perfect for her. She's trailing kisses down my neck to my chest now, alternating between gentle, adoring pressure from her lips; to stinging, playful nips from her teeth; to sexy, tortuous teasing from her tongue. Reveling in the euphoria she's creating with her mouth, I run my hand down her back, over her panties, and nudge the thin fabric aside between her legs. When I start stroking her with my middle finger, I can't take it anymore. I need these damn things off. I reach for the waistband with both hands at the same time she reaches for the waistband of mine. Apparently great minds think alike. Without pause, she stands up to take off her panties, and I fully intend to rid myself of mine at the same time — that is until I watch her thumbs disappear inside at her hips and shimmy them down her legs. Now I'm completely transfixed on the naked woman standing over me.*

As she steps out of them, I say, "Don't move."

"What?" she asks softly.

"I just want to look at you for a minute."

I'm staring at her. And she's staring at me. My underwear aren't off, but I'm on full display.

I scan her body one last time and when I meet her eyes there's a need in them that I can feel. I shed my underwear and she drops down to her hands and knees over me and when she kisses me I know we're both way beyond ready.

"I need to grab a condom if we're gonna do this, Bright Side." She wants to. I can see it all over her face, but I still feel like I need to give her an out.

She takes me in her hand. It's the first time she's touched me there.

"Ah shit, Bright Side. Don't ever stop what you're doing."

"Ever?" she asks devilishly.

"Never, ever," I answer.

"I can't get pregnant, Gus. No plumbing, remember?"

"But —" Goddamn, if she's suggesting what I think she's suggesting ...

She interrupts, "Have you ever been with anyone without a condom?"

That's exactly what she's suggesting. I shake my head. "No. Never."

"Neither have I. If you want to use one ... " Her voice trails off and she just stares at me for a few seconds before she continues. "But if you don't ... "

I finish her thought, "I don't." I fucking don't.

She's looking at me for the go-ahead.

I nod, begging her with my eyes.

I'm still in her hand when she guides me to her wetness and lowers herself down around me.

And I lose my fucking mind when I glide inside. She's tight around me. I've never felt anything like it. No barrier, just skin on warm, wet skin. This is intimacy. I get it now.

I take her hips in my hands and help guide her up and down, back and forth. We move together and I can't take my eyes off her body sitting up on top of mine. Riding me. She's sexy as hell.

Holding her close, I roll us over. When I'm settled between her legs, I touch the tip of my tongue between her breasts and slowly run it up, sucking gently at the base of her throat as my hips begin to move. She pulls back when I do and meets every thrust with one of her own. I knew Bright Side was graceful. I've watched her surf. I've watched her dance. I've watched her play her violin. But none of that compares to what I'm watching her doing beneath me right now. What she's doing to me? It's mesmerizing; I can't take my eyes off her.

And then I decide I need more of her. I take her knee in my hand and push it back toward her so I can go deeper. She gasps when I do.

"You okay?" I ask.

"Yeah," she sighs contentedly in her lust-filled voice.

Fuck. I pick up the pace because it's building. I feel it in both of us. She's moaning now, tightening around me. Wringing every last wish, and every last craving, and every last ounce of passion out of me; I willingly and hungrily give it all to her.

My lips find hers one more time and she responds like the world's about to end. This kiss is the precursor to a euphoric detonation.

And then she completely shatters underneath me and it's the most beautiful thing I've seen in my life. I explode along with her. "I love you," I gasp.

She's panting beneath me and smiling, but suddenly she looks bashful as she bites her bottom lip. And she looks tired.

I kiss the tip of her nose and pull out of her. And then we just stare at each other for a long time. And even when the shyness fades, we don't say anything. I think we're both trying to process what just happened. And me? I'm trying to commit every second of it to memory because I know in my heart this will never happen again. I was just given a gift. And I will treasure it for the rest of my life.

My eyes flash open when I hear Franco cough in the bunk beneath me. It brings me back to the shitty present. I hate the shitty present. I want to rewind time. I want to go back. That's why I don't think about that night. It amplifies the fucking disaster that is my current life.

Sunday, February 5
(Gus)

Last night it seems I was impaired two or three lagers beyond the ability to function. I honestly don't remember any of it. I guess they cancelled the show due to my sudden "illness." It will be rescheduled and tacked onto the end of our tour. Everyone's pissed at me and I know I should care, but I don't. How fucking sad is that? Robbie yelled at me last night. He told me to, "Pull my selfish, fucking head out of my ass." In the five years I've known Robbie, I've never heard him yell. It should've had more of an impact on me, but it didn't.

The logical part of me knows I'm letting them all down.

Every other part of me doesn't care.

Tuesday, February 7
(Gus)

It's afternoon, and I've been sleeping off another long night. I wake up to the sound of Franco's voice coming from the front of the bus—and he's talking with a woman. This intrigues me because the bus is moving, which means we haven't reached our destination yet, which means there shouldn't be any females on this bus. The longer I listen, I learn that Hitler is gone due to a personal matter back home. Which sucks for him, but is fantastic for me because his constant fucking condescension was getting on my last frayed nerve. He's left us with a stand-in, a new tour manager. I can hear her listing off her credentials to Franco. Based on what I can make out, she's fairly new to the game, but she sounds legit. Like she knows her shit, or at the very least is a great bullshit artist. Either one works for me. And she sounds ambitious, saying something about how she's "committed to helping us succeed" and "keeping this crazy train on the tracks." I almost laugh to myself—good luck with that.

I roll out of my bunk and stagger toward the sound of their voices. The stand-in is sitting at the table behind the driver. Her skirt is so short it's almost non-existent. Thin, mile-long legs are crossed at the knee and presented like an exhibition out in the aisle. They're the first thing I see. The second thing I notice is her blouse. It's strategically unbuttoned to frame her impressive cleavage. The third thing I notice is ... nothing, because I'm still fixated on her legs and breasts. It's February and we're in Sweden (I think) and it's snowy and cold as hell outside—she's definitely not dressed for the weather.

Sex. I'm not gonna lie, it's all I'm thinking about at the moment. Sex with that body. Somewhere in the back of my mind I feel like an asshole for immediately going *there*.

Sex, for me, used to be about exploration of a woman's body, an appreciation of the act itself, a mastery of my craft, and, well, intimacy. Watching a woman come unhinged with pleasure and passion as a direct result of my touch, my body, is fascinating and hot as hell. I've never been in a relationship, but I've been with plenty of women. I lost my virginity when I was fourteen—to a seventeen-year-old, no less—and the train's been in motion since. I

21

wouldn't say I'm good-looking, but I'm decent in the looks department and the ladies seem to like my body. I'm six-foot three, and I used to surf a lot, which kept me in good shape. I'm a big guy. Muscular. Chicks dig big guys.

But everything I knew about sex changed when it happened with someone I loved. Last August—Bright Side. We'd known each other our entire lives. She was my next-door neighbor—my best friend. I was *so* in love with her, but she never knew it. She was funny, smart, talented, and fucking gorgeous. The most perfect creature God ever created. And that one night was all about exploration, appreciation, and intimacy. She's the most responsive lover I've ever had, but it was so much more. It was *emotional*; the best fucking night of my life. Period.

How do you follow that up? The answer is: you don't. At least not with any kind of honest effort. Every woman I've been with since is just a fuck. Plain and simple fucking. I'm in it to get off and that's it—quick and dirty. Selfish? Absolutely. Does it make me feel like a dirtbag? Absolutely. For all that, it's still astonishing how many willing participants I get. It's sad how anxious and indiscreet they are—no shame ... no pride. But you know what? It's not my job to parent a twenty-five-year-old woman just because someone else has clearly failed in that department. So, yeah, I let them accommodate me. I turn my attention back to the stand-in, and let my eyes drift up to her face. It's commercially pretty: big, dark eyes; high, prominent cheekbones; and full lips— all aided by a heavy coat of makeup. I'm a fan of natural beauty myself, but these days I can overlook that kind of thing. She's probably in her mid-thirties given the smile lines that frame her mouth. She's staring at me with her heavily lined eyes. She's stopped talking to Franco now that I'm here, and her expression is like an open book—easy to read.

She excuses herself from the conversation and stands to meet me in the aisle, extending a hand. "You must be Gustov." She's talking to my bare chest.

I shake her hand. "I must be," I say, not embarrassed in the least by the fact that I'm standing here in my underwear on the verge of an erection.

From my peripheral, I catch Franco out of the corner of my eye behind her. He's shaking his head slowly and he's wearing his serious face. He rarely brings out his serious face. It all adds up to say, *Don't do it.* He's been my wingman for years and he has an uncanny gift for spotting batshit crazy a mile away.

She's still holding my hand and her eyes have dropped to my midsection.

I follow suit and let my eyes drop to her chest. I don't want to look at her face. This isn't going to be personal. Eye contact makes everything more personal.

Now she's urging me backward. I oblige and when we reach the bathroom door I open it. It's an invitation that she accepts without hesitation when she follows me in.

I'm unbuttoning the rest of her blouse before the door shuts behind her. And by the time she manages the lock on the cramped quarters her shoulders are bared and her bra straps are pulled down to her elbows freeing her huge, obviously silicone tits. Again, I prefer natural, but once they're in my hands, my mouth, I'm not complaining. She's theatrically moaning. I tune it out.

When she starts wiggling out of her micro-skirt and panties I stop her, "Save it. I don't have a condom in here."

She whispers in my ear, "It's okay, I'm on the pill." Her voice is husky. It's not sexy. It's needy. I hate needy.

Now she's trying to kiss me.

That's not gonna happen either. It's too intimate. I haven't kissed anyone since Bright Side. I turn my head. "Not okay. The way I see it we have one option here—"

I don't even have to finish my ultimatum before she's dropped to her knees and my underwear have been tugged down.

When she takes me with her mouth I can't hold back, "Ah shit, that feels good."

She's aggressive. It's obvious this isn't her first rodeo. There's no fooling around with just the tip, she's taking me all in. And I'm a big guy; this is full-fledged, deep throat, porn material.

She's got my ass in her hands and is holding me tightly against her. I'm worried I'm hurting her so I pull out. She literally begs me to continue. Well shit, you don't have to ask me twice. It's not long before her hair is knotted in my hands and I'm full-on thrusting.

Release isn't what it once was. It's momentary blinding satisfaction, followed up too quickly by reemergence into bleak reality.

I reach down and pull up my underwear as she's standing, wiping her lips and chin with the back of her hand. Her eyes are dilated and tell me that though I'm finished ... she isn't. "I'm Clare, by the way."

I nod absently. "You have quite a way with introductions."

She runs her finger down my chest. "So do you. I look forward to working with you." The look in her eyes tells me "working with" in that sentence is interchangeable with "fucking."

I release the lock on the door behind her, "See ya around," and leave her alone in the john to her own devices.

When I emerge from the bathroom, Jamie is sitting with Franco at the table playing poker. Jamie raises his chin in greeting. We aren't talking much lately. Franco shakes his head. I know he's disappointed in me. He tried to warn me. It's strange, because I used to be the one that looked out for the band. I used to be our leader. Now it's Franco. Maybe it makes sense; he's the oldest at twenty-five. Or maybe it's just inevitable given that I'm failing miserably at life.

Thursday, February 9
(Gus)

Our producer, MFDM, called me today. He said he's been talking to our record label and the label wants to re-release our album in a few weeks and include a bonus track. The bonus track is a song called "Finish Me" that Rook recorded last December with Bright Side. I wrote the song in the days following the bombshell — the bombshell being the discovery of Bright Side's terminal cancer diagnosis. The band flew to Minneapolis and recorded it in a studio there about a month before she died. Bright Side wrote and played the violin arrangement and sang with me. The song is our best to date, but it's also personal. Too personal. There's no way I'd be able to perform it live, which is what would be expected after an album release. Hell, we only started playing "Missing You" live again this week, and that was only after I wrote a new guitar arrangement for it and we picked up the tempo. It's morphed from a sad ballad to a hard-driving angry screamer. Because I'm *outstanding* at angry these days.

I know the label will get their way. It's about time to release a new single. What a coincidence.

Saturday, February 11
(Gus)

Clare has turned into a welcome distraction. In between phone meetings, assisting us with interviews, interacting with venue staff, smoothing over the day-to-day fuck-ups I create, and whatever else she does, frequent doses of sex—whenever and wherever—have become routine. I may have to start buying condoms in bulk. She seems happy to do her part in our one-sided exchanges. I know, I'm a huge asshole, getting bigger by the day, but no one's twisting her arm. Aside from taking smoke breaks together we don't spend any significant amount of time in each other's company, which is ideal. When we talk it's strictly business, and that's kept to a minimum since Franco's handling most of that these days anyway.

Sunday, February 12
(Gus)

"Gus, can I be straight?" Franco gives me a hard look, and I know I'm in trouble. I used to hate being in trouble with Franco. Still do a little bit I guess, but not enough to change my ways.

"Of course." I don't really want to hear it.

"Dude, we've been on the road for two weeks now. Though I love the man bun and hobo beard—" I try not to laugh, but it sort of comes out like a snort. "Seriously, you're rockin' the hipster, mountain man, homeless look like a champ," Franco continues. "But you need to shower. Like, every day. This bus is small, man. Hygiene is priority one. You smell like road kill."

I nod. "Point taken, dude."

Nothing is a priority.

Saturday, February 18
(Gus)

Tonight we play our biggest show yet. It's in London at an arena called O2. Twenty thousand people. *Twenty fucking thousand.* That's a far cry from playing Joe's Bar in San Diego in front of two hundred just two years ago.

Sometimes I wish we were still playing Joe's.

I'm nervous. I never get nervous, but my hands were shaking all through soundcheck. Maybe I need a drink. What am I thinking? I *definitely* need a drink. I haven't had one since last night. There wasn't any beer on the bus. I suspect Franco has begun his attempt at a passive intervention.

I already resent passive.

And intervention.

With two hours until the show starts, I need some grub. I'm walking back to the bus to grab a pack of cigarettes, when Clare runs up behind me. I don't know how she runs in five-inch stilettos, but she does. She's panting. She's always out of breath, probably because she's the only person I've ever met who smokes more than I do.

"Gustov," she gasps. Even my name is a pant.

I slow my pace but don't stop to wait for her. I turn my head to address her, but not enough to meet her eyes. I have trouble looking her in the eye. Every time I do I see a disappointed Bright Side staring back at me, like a ghost haunting me. I can't face it. Bright Side would've hated Clare—polar fucking opposites. "Clare." That's the extent of my greeting.

"I noticed you seemed a little off during soundcheck," she says matter-of-factly.

I'm not insulted. It's true. "I need a drink," I respond.

She's next to me now, leaning in so her mouth is near my ear. "I have something better than alcohol."

At that I do turn and face her because this woman is insatiable. "Jesus Christ, we fucked an hour ago, Clare," I say, exasperated. "I'm good for a few more hours. Thanks anyway." She irritates the hell out of me and I don't try to hide that fact from her.

She smiles seductively. It's flirtatious. It's also my cue to look away. She giggles. Her giggle is annoying on many levels: it's high pitched, which is in stark contrast to her low, husky voice; it's given too freely when it's not earned, maybe it's a nervous tick; and it's fucking loud. "No, love. Although that sounds like a *fabulous* idea, I'm thinking of something else."

By now we've reached the bus. I follow her up the steps before I join back in on the exchange. "Well, what is it?"

She reaches into her overcoat pocket and pulls out a small glass vial of white powder held between her pointer finger and thumb and waves it in front of my face.

My initial reaction is *hell no*. I don't say anything though.

She's grasped my wrist and is pulling me to the back of the bus and into the small bedroom she claimed on the first day she joined us. "Come on. Just do one line with me. It'll help you get through the show."

This is where I should stop and actually articulate the words, "*Hell no*," but I just keep following her like a goddamn dumbass.

While she's dispensing the powder onto a Vogue magazine that's lying on her bed and efficiently forming it into two small lines, I look at her face closely for the first time. There are shadows under her eyes that I can still see through her heavy makeup. Fine lines feather out from the corner of each eye. She's more haggard than I realized. I blurt out, "How old are you?"

She sniffs like her nose is already two steps ahead of her in its need, and looks up at me with wild eyes. "Twenty-five."

That's what I thought. Coke has aged her. I guessed her ten years older. I size up the powder lined up in front of us. "This isn't your first time, is it?"

She's rubbing her nose with the back of her hand. Her hand is twitchy. It reminds me of the prostitute that propositioned me at the bar back home the day of the funeral. "No. You're going to love it. It'll make you feel like Superman."

In spite of everything I'm looking at, which is at the very least a glaring anti-drug campaign and at best just plain sad, my mouth makes the decision for me. "Okay."

She goes first. She's quick. A pro. It makes me wonder how long she's been doing this.

I go next. I'm slow and it takes several passes. An amateur. My nose stings and my eyes are watering.

As the drug infiltrates my mind and body, I'm silently apologizing, "I'm so sorry, Bright Side. It's just one time. I won't turn into Janice." Bright Side's mom was a cokehead.

I'm justifying it away. I smoke weed on occasion and have taken pills a few times. I tell myself that this won't be any different.

Except that it is.

Clare goes with me, uninvited, to a pub around the corner. I eat, even though I'm not very hungry at this point. She smokes. She never eats. It weirds me out.

By the time the show starts I'm still flying high. I'm not lethargically going through the motions tonight. I can't say that I feel completely in control, because I'm sure as hell not, but there's this force driving me from the inside out. It amps up my anger and channels it into a fierce performance. Amazingly, the crowd eats it up. It's the strangest fucking experience of my life. It's like watching everything play out from somewhere outside myself, while at the same time feeling it so deep inside me that I swear it was never there before. It's completely surreal.

Time is inconsequential, irrelevant. Before I know it the band is telling me that's all we've got, the show's over, it's time to leave.

Franco stays behind with me while I smoke a cigarette before we get on the bus. "I'm not sure what that was tonight," he says, "but the crowd loved it."

They did. So did I. "It was the new Gus."

He squints at me like he's trying to solve a puzzle. "You okay, shithead?"

I smile at him. That's right, *I smile*. I haven't done that in a long time. "Fan-fucking-tastic, dude."

Tuesday, February 28
(Gus)

The past eight shows have gone off like clockwork. Clare has come through every night and fueled Superman. An unexpected perk of being Superman is that I don't think about Bright Side much anymore. I mean I think about her, but I'm not obsessing.

Sleep is an elusive motherfucker, though. Clare gave me some pills last night after the show. I don't know what they were, but I slept like a baby.

Monday, March 6 – Tuesday, March 7
(Gus)

No show tonight.

A free day.

It's a goddamn miracle.

I'm more and more tired these days. The yo-yo of alcohol and cocaine during my waking hours and pills to sleep is messing hard with my constitution. But I'm functioning. I'm killing it every night on stage.

We're in Amsterdam now. Yup, that's right—the land of hash bars and the Red Light District. It's like Christmas. I've talked the guys into taking a field trip. They were surprised because I haven't gone out with them the entire time we've been in Europe. Clare's pissed at me because I didn't invite her. Whatever. Just because I've been, *for the most part*, sleeping with her exclusively doesn't mean I'm going to take her out. We're not in a relationship. We have an arrangement. Two totally different situations.

After walking along the canals and feeding the pigeons in Dam Square, we eat an early dinner to get in out of the cold. Everyone we come across is so friendly and most of them speak English, which surprises me for some reason. After dinner we venture out in search of all things uniquely Amsterdam. When we step inside the first "coffee shop" we come across, it takes no coaxing to entice Franco, Jamie, and Robbie to join me, even though they rarely partake in pot.

Thirty minutes later we're all stoned off our asses, reminiscing about how our band got together and how god awful our first few shows were. I haven't laughed in a long time, and it feels good. I'm relaxed, just living in the moment. It's exactly what I needed.

Hours pass before we leave and move on to the Red Light District. We're all blissfully stoned as we pass by and watch window peep show after window peep show. I can't talk the guys into going into an actual brothel, so we settle on a live sex show. It's real-live porn, just a guy and chick going at it. It shouldn't be funny, except that for some reason it is. It's funny as hell. And none of us can watch with a straight face. We're all laughing like we're thirteen years old and have never seen boobs or a dick

32

before.

We got kicked out before the show even climaxed. Dammit.

It's around midnight when we get back to the bus. Everything is quiet. We're still laughing about the sex show when Clare steps out from her room. We must have woken her up. She looks fucking murderous when she slides the bedroom door open and scowls at us. "I'm trying to get some sleep." Up north she's wearing a paper-thin tank top and down south she's wearing a thong. She's oblivious to the fact that four sets of eyes are on her.

"Somebody's in a bad mood." I laugh, because even she can't ruin my mood tonight.

She narrows her eyes at me, then exhales bitterly. "So, how was the hash, anyway?"

I smile. "Fucking. Excellent." This is the first time I've smiled at her.

She notices. Suddenly her anger seems to have disappeared, and her lips curl into a smile. It's her seductive smile. It's the only one she ever wears. It's basically safe to say that her smile is a proposition. "Excellent," she purrs as she takes a handful of my T-shirt and pulls me into her room.

She slides the door shut behind me and just like that she's on her game. "Did you fuck anyone?"

I laugh. "Excuse me?"

She's direct as she pulls my T-shirt over my head. "I said, did you fuck anyone? Prostitutes?"

I'm a little slow on the uptake. "Oh, no. We watched, does that count?"

Her smile returns and her dark eyes look possessive. "Good. You ready to have some fun?"

Fun always includes drugs and sex. "Hell yes."

She begins digging through her side table drawer and pulls out a plastic baggy filled with several different colored pills. She sifts through them and pulls out two identical capsules. She pops one in her mouth before handing me the other.

"What is this?" I usually never ask her anymore.

"Does it matter?" She playfully challenges.

"Probably not," I answer, because it really doesn't matter.

She's removed her tank top and steps out of her thong. She's unbuttoning my jeans when she says, "That pill is going to make what's about to happen in this bed the most intense thing you've ever experienced."

I toss it in my mouth and swallow. "Sounds good, dude."

"Did you just call me dude? I am not a dude." She looks down at her breasts. "Obviously." She's insulted, but not enough to finish stripping me bare.

I've never called her dude. Dude is usually a term of endearment for me. It's something I generally save for my closest friends. She's not my friend and there's nothing endearing about her. I wish I could take it back. I feel like I've shared a personal piece of me. "I didn't mean it."

"That's better." She's consoled.

If she knew, "I didn't mean it," was more an insult than an apology she'd be pissed, but the drugs are starting to cloud my mind. Suddenly I don't care about anything else but getting her into this bed.

Sex with Clare is always rough. It's the only way she likes it. She's like some kind of fucking masochist. She wants to be dominated. And she's into some way kinky shit. Sometimes it's cool. Sometimes it's not. But tonight is different. Everything's playing out in slow motion. Everything's softened. It's vanilla sex compared to what we usually do, which should be boring with her, but it's not. I'm into it. I'm taking my time. I'm kissing. I'm touching. I'm pleasing her. And she's pleasing the hell out of me.

When we're done she doesn't want me to leave her bed. So I don't.

I didn't know it then, but that was a mistake. The culmination of many, *many* mistakes.

When I wake up several hours later, my head feels like a fucking marching band is playing at full volume inside my skull. I stretch and my entire body aches. Then I feel a warm body next to me.

There shouldn't be a warm body next to me.

Please let this be a stranger in bed with me, I think. But I know it's not. And I know I've just fucked up royally. I sneak a peek and sure as shit Clare's next to me. "Shit." This I do say out loud.

Her eyes are closed. "What?" she says. Her voice is still half asleep.

I roll my eyes. "Nothing." I slide out of bed and start looking for my pants. I find them by the door and pull them on. I'll look for my underwear later; I need to get out of here.

She's watching me now, and I can't figure out how she could possibly be smiling at me like that when she took the same shit I did last night. Why doesn't she feel like hell? "Last night was hot," she says. "You're sweet when you want to be. When you let your guard down."

Shit. *Shit.* This just keeps getting worse. I'm racing through my fuzzy memories of last night and can't come up with much after we got in bed. It's like my memories aren't related to anything physical, but instead take on this dream-like quality. And they're completely unattached to Clare, completely separate. They're hazy and vague, but warm and tender. Like I was some place totally safe. Somewhere I never wanted to leave. I felt love and loved.

Her voice breaks my trance. "I've never had someone make love to me before." She looks like she just won a prize and it makes my stomach churn because for some reason that I can't explain, I know she's right. I didn't fuck her, I made love to her. I'm so confused. I need to get out of here.

I slide the bedroom door open and am about to escape when her next words explain everything. "You called me Bright Side last night. What does that mean?"

I feel bile rise in my throat and there are tears stinging the backs of my eyes. That name from her mouth is desecration. I can't think of anything worse right now than hearing Clare say *her* name. I turn on her instantly and am standing over her pointing my finger an inch from her face. "Don't you *ever* fucking say that name again!" I'm yelling.

Her face has flipped from triumphant to shocked.

Franco's out of his bunk now. He's got ahold of my arm and is pulling me out of the room. He sits me down at the table near the driver, and hands me a cigarette and a lighter while he tells our driver, "Pull over, Ed. Gus needs to get out and cool down." My hands are shaking so badly I can barely light the cigarette.

Ed, our driver, pulls the bus to the side of the road and I slip on my Vans and coat, not bothering with a shirt or socks. I step off the bus into the snowy shoulder of what I assume is Dutch countryside. I'm pacing next to the bus and almost done with my first cigarette when Franco joins me.

"What's up, punk ass?" He's wearing his concerned face: brows furrowed and lips tight, turned down in a slight frown. It's the same face he wears anytime something bad happens.

I shrug as I inhale more nicotine into my body. It isn't calming me down like it usually does. My head is throbbing, my heart is racing, and the whole of my body is shaking inside and out. "Did you hear the whole conversation this morning?" The walls are thin; if he was awake, he heard it.

He nods apologetically. "And last night."

I squat and bury my face in my hands. I'm not just embarrassed, I'm lost. I rub my eyes and my hands come away wet. I light another cigarette. I'd rather cut off my right arm than hear the answer to this question, but I force myself to ask it. "What did I say to her last night?"

He eyes me. "You don't remember?" It's not really a question, he knows I don't. He's stalling.

I shake my head.

He scratches his bald head. He doesn't want to answer me, but I know he will because that's what good friends do. They give you the bad news even when you don't want to hear it. "I'm not going to get into all the details, but you kept calling her Bright Side ... while you were having sex. You told her you loved her, dude."

I turn around and scream with everything I've got in me. It feels like my head is splitting open. The pain is excruciating, but it only makes me want to scream longer and louder. When the screaming dies out I can't catch my breath, and before I know it I'm doubled over retching into the snow. I don't remember what I ate last night but it's all over the ground and my shoes now. My stomach empties quickly but my body doesn't relent. I keep heaving. It makes my eyes fill and spill over. And when the heaving stops, I realize that I'm bawling. I'm on the ground now, knees wet with vomit and snow. I bury my face in my forearms and crouch down on the wet, snow covered ground. I'm crying like I cried the moment she died. Crying like my fucking world is about to end. Franco kneels down beside me and puts his hand on my back. "My heart hurts so fucking bad, dude," I gasp. "I miss

36

her. I miss her so much."

"I know, big man." No judgment.

I'm thankful it's Franco here with me because he knows how to talk to me. I couldn't do this with anyone else right now. Not even Ma.

"I don't know how to be Gus without her, dude. I'm fucking lost as shit."

"I know."

I rise up on my knees and look at him.

He hesitates like he was going to say something and thought better of it. And then he says it anyway, "Listen, I know it's none of my business, man. If you're into Clare that's on you, but—"

I interrupt. "I'm not. I don't know what the fuck I'm doing with her."

He raises his eyebrows. He's calling me out.

"Okay," I huff, "I know what I'm doing with her. I'm fucking her. Using her. She's a meaningless distraction. That's it."

"But she's been helping you with your meds, too."

That was way too casual for Franco. "Is that what you call it? Meds?"

His eyes narrow. "Yeah," he says cautiously. "I talked to her a few weeks back about you. I didn't go into personal specifics, but told her I thought you needed to see a doctor. She told me a few days later that she'd arranged for a doctor to come by the venue while the rest of us were at dinner and that you got a prescription for anxiety and sleep meds."

"Doctor? I didn't realize Clare had a fucking license to practice?" I don't like the fact that she's been keeping Franco in the dark. But the truth is that I've been lying to him, too.

There's a shift in his features, a vein in his forehead begins pulsing and his eyes turn dark and intense. I know what's coming. "What have you been taking?"

"Coke, pills, whatever she could get her hands on."

He's on his feet in a flash and flying toward the door of the bus. I surprise myself by jumping up after him, and soon it's me holding him by the arm trying to keep him out of her bedroom. He's a strong fucker when he's angry. He doesn't get angry like this often; I've only seen it once or twice in five years. He can be scary as hell when he's pissed like this. He isn't budging. Clare is standing by the bed, wrapped in a thin robe. Her face is pale but unyielding. Franco's screaming at her. "What have you done to him?" When she doesn't answer and stands there defiantly with her arms crossed over her chest, he explodes again. Louder this time. She flinches. "I said, *what have you fucking done to him?!*"

A smirk emerges and her eyes shift to mine. "Nothing he didn't want, right love?"

I have a grip on both of his biceps from behind now. His arms are shaking violently with rage. "You *fucking* lied to me!" I don't know how he keeps getting louder, but he does.

No response.

He's pointing at her. "Stay away from him, do you hear me? Stay *the fuck* away from him. You don't give him anything. You don't talk to him. You don't even look at him."

She looks at me and there's fear behind the icy façade. I know she hasn't been doing this job long, and she knows it could be in jeopardy. "Gustov is a grown man, Franco. I never forced him to do anything. He wanted it."

I don't like Clare, never have, but I have to admit I feel a little sorry for her right now. She's in the direct path of hurricane Franco and it should be me. "She's right, dude," I huff. "She never forced me. If you're gonna be pissed at anyone, it should be me."

Franco turns, breaks my grip, and faces me. His eyes pierce me and I know I'm in for it. "Oh, I am pissed, Gus." I can tell, because he rarely calls me Gus. "*Fucking* pissed. What in the hell were you thinking? Listen," he pauses, glancing at Clare like he wishes she wasn't within earshot. He turns back to me and continues, "I know everything is shit right now. *I know that.*" He lowers his voice. "We all miss her, dude. But this is no way to deal. Do you know how disappointed she'd be if she was standing here watching this whole goddamn debacle play out?"

She'd hate it. I fucking know that. "Well, she's not here, is she?" I can't have this conversation. I don't need the reminder. I live it every second. "She's fucking dead." I'm not listening anymore. I walk away toward the mini-fridge and pull out a beer.

Franco turns back to Clare and points at me sitting at the table. "Stay the fuck away from him." It's a not-so-subtle reminder. Then he looks and me and points at Clare. "Same goes for you. Stay away from her. Find a new fuck buddy."

Clare closes the door to her bedroom. She's on the inside and I feel some relief having the buffer.

Franco slides into the seat across from me. He looks spent and has calmed down. "Sorry, dipshit. I shouldn't have brought up Kate in front of her."

I throw back half the can before I come up for air. "The cat was already out of the bag, dude. Sounds like I did a stellar job of that last night." I run my fingers through my hair and hold it back in a ponytail. "I can't believe I did that."

He raps his knuckles on the table. "You pretended the person you were with was the person you wish you were with instead. We've all fantasized. No shame."

I look him in the eye. "You don't fantasize about dead people."

"You were higher than a fucking kite." He exhales and stares at me for a while, his eyes begging for honesty. "You loved her, I know you did. Don't play the 'best friends' card with me, man. Do I blame you? *Hell no.* Kate was the most incredible woman I've ever met. All of us sorry fucks will be lucky if we end up with someone who's half the person she was."

I nod and sit back and finish my beer.

Franco lets me.

End of discussion.

Monday, March 27
(Gus)

As the plane hits the tarmac at San Diego International Airport I let out a sigh of relief. I feel like I've been holding my breath for two months. I know it's totally irrational to think that geography will change what's going on in my head, but being so far from home and everything that's familiar didn't help matters. The European leg of the tour wrapped up last night in Paris. I'm tired as hell and all I want to do is sleep for the next three weeks straight before the US tour starts up again.

Franco elbows me when the aisle frees up enough to squeeze out into the flow. After retrieving my bag from the overhead compartment, I trudge through the airport to baggage claim. I'm following Franco. He's not talking. I know he's as beat down as I am from the clusterfuck of the past two months.

Though I haven't done any drugs since that night shit went down with Clare, I haven't been sober for the past sixty-something days. My blood's been holding steady at 80 proof. It's wearing me out if you want to know the truth. I did it to hide from life, but now I just feel buried alive.

Clare stayed on for the rest of the tour and finished her job. She didn't talk to me after the big blowup. And I didn't talk to her. With the distance came a newfound clarity—she might be even more fucked up than I am. I don't know what made her the way she is, but there are definitely some issues behind her tailspin. If I had a guess, I'd say she's going to crash. Hard.

Tuesday, March 28
(Gus)

MFDM got them to hold off on the album rerelease until today.

He knew I couldn't deal with "Finish Me," and playing it while we were on tour was out of the question.

I love the dude for fighting for us.

Wednesday, April 19
(Gus)

I've spent the past three weeks avoiding everything. Sleeping as much as possible. I eat dinner with Ma every night, but that's the extent of my contact with the real world. It's the only part of my day that I look forward to—time with Ma, even if we don't talk much. It's comforting for both of us.

Thursday, April 20
(Gus)

I'm holding my phone in my hand looking at it like I have no idea where to begin. Or maybe I'm second-guessing making the call at all. I haven't seen or talked to Bright Side's boyfriend, Keller, since the funeral. But during the past few days I can't stop thinking about him and his daughter, Stella. Wondering how they're doing. He's a good guy and Bright Side loved the hell out of him, so I hope he's keeping his shit together better than I am.

I dial his number. Before it starts ringing, my heart is pounding so hard I feel like I'm going into cardiac arrest. I hang up.

I guess I'm not ready for this.

Friday, April 21
(Gus)

The tour starts tonight in Vegas. It's early, eight o'clock in the morning, and Franco's in the kitchen talking to Ma. We need to leave soon but I haven't packed yet. I grab my duffle bag out of my closet and toss it unzipped on the bed. I throw in a few T-shirts, jeans, socks, and underwear, along with my laptop, toothbrush, toothpaste, and deodorant. I check my pockets for my wallet, phone, cigarettes, and lighter. Throwing the bag's strap over my shoulder, I glance back at Bright Side's laptop. It's still sitting untouched on my dresser. *Goddamn*, I want to take it so bad. To open it up and dive in. Dig through everything she left behind. To have her back in my life again. But it's not that easy and it's so fucking intimate that it almost makes me cry thinking about it.

Instead, I snag my guitar cases from the corner and shut the door behind me. I shut the door on Bright Side. Again.

Ma and Franco are talking. I hear them from the hall. But when I step into the room there's instantaneous silence. Coincidence? Nope.

"It's okay, don't let the fact that I'm actually standing in the room with you stop you from talking about me."

Harsh? Yeah.

Do I care? Yeah, with Ma and Franco I do.

Can I stop acting like an asshole? Nope.

Ma frowns and hugs me.

I hug her back. It's an apology. "Morning, Ma."

"Good morning, Gus." She's forgiving me.

I love her to death for it, because she shouldn't forgive me.

The flight is short and we've landed in no time. A cab drops us off in front of some monstrosity of a hotel on the strip. It's eleven o'clock. I'm ready for a few stiff drinks and a nap, but Hitler met us at the door and wastes no time ushering us through the masses to an elevator.

It's not until we're tucked away inside a shiny elevator that he starts talking at us. "Jamie and Robbie arrived about a half hour ago. The two of you have ... " he pulls back the cuff of his dress shirt to get a look at his Rolex knock-off, " ... twenty minutes before the photo shoot begins."

Jamie and Robbie have been in Vegas for a few days. A mini-vacation. Good for them.

I look at myself in the mirrored wall in front of me. My clothes look like I slept in them. Come to think of it, maybe I did. My hair hasn't been washed in a couple of days and it's pulled back in a ponytail. It's getting long again. I'm thankful for the sunglasses because I can't see my tired, bloodshot eyes staring back at me. Admonishing me.

Hitler doesn't say anything else.

Neither do we.

The elevator stops on the fifteenth floor, and when the doors open we follow him out. Everything in Vegas is opulent and over-the-top. I've always hated it. It's pretentious and fake, just a lot of smoke and mirrors. Hitler stops a few doors down and opens the door to what we soon discover is a suite, like a house inside a hotel. The furniture has been cleared from one end of the living room and a crew is setting up backdrops, lighting, and cameras.

Franco and I drop our bags and Franco walks over to sit on one of the numerous leather sofas with Robbie and Jamie. I walk over to the bar and pour myself a glass of whiskey. Three gulps and the glass is drained. I fill it up again and take it with me to sit with the guys.

I must have started to drift off, because minutes later I'm roused from near sleep by a cute blond in tight jeans and a black tank top. "Come with me, Gustov." Her voice is hypnotic. Or maybe it's her ass. Or her small but unbelievably perfect breasts.

"Gladly," I respond. And just like that the two of us are behind closed doors and she's pulling my clothes off.

"We don't have much time," she says.

Damn right we don't. I need you right fucking now.

She hands me a pair of black jeans. "Put these on."

I'm confused. "Wait. You want me to put these on?"

She blinks her doe-like brown eyes at me. "That's what I said. Hurry up, we need to do something with your hair before they come in to do your makeup."

Dammit. She really does want me to get dressed. I thought shit was about to go down. Now I'm standing here in my underwear, hard, and she wants to fix my hair.

I don't miss the fact that her eyes flit down to my manhood standing at full attention before she turns her back on me to sort through a pile of shirts on the bed.

I slip into the jeans. They fit well, despite the bulge.

"I'm Lindsey, by the way," she says as she turns toward me again. She shakes my hand before handing me a shirt.

Now I feel like an idiot because she seems pretty cool. "And I'm an asshole, by the way."

She laughs at my admission.

"Sorry about that." I wouldn't usually apologize for something like this, because she didn't seem offended and I still have the feeling that we might hook up later, but she just seems ... nice.

"No worries. I've done this job for ten years. I've heard and seen it all." She looks older than I am, but I never would've guessed that she's been doing this job for a whole decade.

It's my turn to laugh and it feels like a weight's been lifted off my chest. I shrug on the shirt.

"Sit here, please," she says, gesturing toward a chair. After tugging the elastic band out of my hair, she rakes her fingers through it a few times. It's tangled.

"Hmm." She's thinking.

I look back at her over my shoulder. "It's a fucking rat's nest. I didn't know a photo shoot was in the plans today. Sorry." I'm apologizing again. I feel bad, like I'm making her job harder.

She smiles and it's friendly. It makes me want to stay in this room forever. "Never doubt me," she says. "There's a product for everything." She starts finger combing my hair again. "Even this."

Five minutes later, my hair looks better than it has in months. I guess I shouldn't have doubted her.

Lindsey hangs up the shirts and folds the jeans that weren't used while someone applies makeup to my face. Usually I hate it when they put this shit on me, but I'm not paying attention because I can't take my eyes off Lindsey.

When the makeup artist (I didn't look to see if it was a man or woman) leaves the room, I blurt out, "Are you going to our show tonight?"

She laughs again and it's like music to my ears. "No. Though

I've heard some of your songs on the radio. You're good."

"You should come. I can get you in." I sound ridiculous. And desperate. Of course I can get her in; I'm in the fucking band.

"I can't. Have to catch a flight back to Seattle tonight. Thanks anyway, Gustov."

"How about dinner? Before you leave?" Goddamn, it's almost embarrassing how hard I'm trying here. And it's not even about the potential of sex with her that's got me so wound up. It's just ... her.

She blinks a few times and I already know she's going to turn me down. "Gustov, I'm flattered. Truly." She smiles to soften the rejection, I suppose. "And you're not an asshole," she adds quickly. "But I have a boyfriend."

I nod. Understood. And if it's possible, I have even more respect for her. I don't get in the middle of other people's relationships. End of story.

Someone clears her throat behind us. I turn and there's a woman standing just inside the doorway. Her stance tells me she'd rather be anywhere but here. For the most part, her attention is focused on the doorframe in front of her. I can only see the left side of her face, and it looks tight, not friendly. I wonder how long she's been standing there. Judging by her posture, it's been a while. She shifts her weight to her right side, and she's holding a legal pad of paper tightly in her hand. She looks impatient. Impatient, like it's her middle name. Like she eats, sleeps, and breathes impatience. I already don't like her.

"Gustov, if you're done here ... " Her voice is quiet, and her eyes flit in our direction without turning to face us. The hasty eye contact tells me she heard everything. She's judging me. "They're ready for you." The tone of her voice is total annoyance.

Without taking my eyes off Lindsey, I hold up a finger in Impatient's direction asking her to give us a minute. She turns and quickly disappears.

Closing the gap between me and Lindsey, I offer my hand again. I'm nervous. I hate being nervous.

She shakes it. She's calm. The calm bleeds in through the contact and I welcome it.

Meeting her eyes, I say, "He's a lucky man, Lindsey." I mean it.

Smiling, she nods and winks. "Thanks Gustov. And just so you know, if I wasn't completely, madly in love with the guy, I would've said yes to dinner."

I smile like a schoolgirl, release her hand, and walk out the door.

The photo shoot, an event I usually loath, isn't as miserable as I expected. And I'm not even drunk. The photographer, Jack, isn't the type we've worked with in the past. They usually take themselves too seriously and wear the title, *artist*, like it somehow elevates them to a state incapable of communicating with the lowly "talent." Jack has a sense of humor *and* humility. It's a nice pairing, one of my favorites. He gets all of us to loosen up and act natural. Hell, I don't know what natural *is* anymore, but I'm doing it.

By the time I get out of the shower and change into some clean clothes from my bag after the shoot, Lindsey's gone. I kinda wanted to see her again, but I know that's a little too stalker for my style. It just felt good to be attracted to someone so normal, but she's taken and that means it's time to put her out of my mind.

I'm startled back to the present by the sound of Hitler barking at me from the living room. "Gustov, join us. We've got a few things to go over before soundcheck." He says it like he's *involved* in soundcheck. I'd be surprised if he's ever touched an instrument in his life. I walk to the bar and fill a glass with whiskey before taking a seat on the sofa next to Franco. My ass barely hits the cushion when I realize I can't listen to Hitler sober. So immediately I rise again, grab the bottle from the bar, and set it on the coffee table in front of me before settling in.

He gives me one of his looks. It's the degrading, I-don't-get-paid-enough-to-tolerate-your-shit stare. "Anything else you need before we get started?" Pure sarcasm.

Which of course I meet with a little of my own, because I can't keep my mouth shut. "Lunch and a hooker? We are in Vegas, you know."

He shakes his head in disgust. He's so over me it's not even funny.

Shrugging, I take a swig from my glass. "Had to try."

Franco shoots me a warning look to shut up, but his smile is seeping through. The smile's winning.

Hitler ignores my retort and clears his throat. "As you know, I'll be with you for the duration of the tour. And though Europe was successful, despite a few rescheduled shows," he says, glaring in my direction, "a lot is at stake with your return to the United States. The US tour last year was good, but your album is really taking off in the states now. 'Finish Me' is in the top ten on the alternative charts this week. You can't afford any mistakes now." He's staring at me as though he's waiting for an answer to a question he didn't ask. When I don't respond, he continues, "Management has a few requests."

"Requests" means "demands." I drain the rest of my glass.

"First, you *will* start playing 'Finish Me' at every show."

Franco, Robbie, and Jamie are all looking at me. Their expressions tell me this is the first time they're hearing this, too. Shaking my head, I huff, "That's not gonna happen."

More throat clearing. Hitler knows he's in for a fight. "Gustov, this is non-negotiable."

I reach for the bottle and take a long swig. Fuck the glass. "Come on, this is America, everything's negotiable," I say. I'm going to try humor because I am so close to losing it and throwing this bottle of whiskey across the room.

He smiles aggressively. "As I said, you will play 'Finish Me' at every show."

"We'll see about that, motherfucker," I say under my breath before I steal another drink from the bottle.

Franco heard me. He takes the bottle out of my hand and drains some himself before handing it to Robbie and Jamie, who both do the same before handing it back to me. I've been so wrapped up in my own shit that I forgot what solidarity felt like. I love these guys for sticking with me on this. This is why we're a band.

Hitler's quiet. Taking that as my cue, I stand. "I need a cigarette."

Apparently he's not through with the ultimatums yet. "We are not finished here."

I sigh and sit—I'm not defeated. I'm irritated. And he knows it.

"This tour is going to be more demanding than you're used to. Back to back shows almost every night from one end of this country to the other. For these reasons, *among others*, Gustov, we feel it's in the best interest of the success of this tour, and this album, that you have a PA for the duration."

I squint my eyes and look around at the guys. They all look confused, so I turn back to Hitler. "A PA better not be what I think it is." At this point, humor is not going to cut it.

"Scout MacKenzie will be joining us on the tour bus. She will act as your personal assistant in all matters related to this tour, but her main tasks will be scheduling, communication, and PR. She is to be treated with dignity and *respect*." The emphasis he put on respect and the way he's looking at me tells me he will castrate me if I touch this woman. And now even though I'm pissed, I'm curious.

"Scout," he calls loudly over his shoulder.

Impatient, from earlier, walks into the room. My eyes don't even make it up to her face before I stand. "Oh, hell no," I say, striding toward the balcony. The cigarette's already between my lips.

Hitler's angry and his voice booms from behind me. "This is non-negotiable, Gustov."

I light my cigarette, inhale, and with the cigarette clutched between my fingers, I point at him. "I don't need a fucking babysitter."

His pompous laugh resounds behind me as I rip open the sliding door leading to the balcony. He's practically shouting now. "I'm afraid after your behavior in Europe, you certainly do."

Shutting the door on his condescension, I slump into a deck chair.

I'm lighting a second cigarette when Franco joins me. He opens his mouth to speak, but I beat him to it. I'm irate. "They can't fucking do this," I say bitterly. Then I look up at Franco. "*Can they?*"

He shrugs. "I don't know, dude."

Snubbing out my cigarette, I huff. "The next few months are going to be a nightmare. What good is a personal assistant, other than to narc back to fucking Hitler?"

His eyebrows rise in agreement. "I'm not sure what to make of this either." He chuckles a little, apparently amused. "She's definitely not a new fuck buddy. He made sure of that. She's all business, man."

I'm staring at the ground lost in my own rage, but his laughter pulls me out of it. I shake my head. "Have you talked to the girl, dude? She's rigid as fuck."

He laughs harder. "Yeah, I get that. We all got introduced after you left. Go easy on her though, I think she's just shy. And maybe a little uptight," he adds.

"*A little*? She was completely disgusted with me earlier when she heard me hitting on the stylist." I look him in the eye and can't help laughing with him. "This is a goddamn nightmare."

He slaps me on the shoulder before he walks away. "Welcome to Hitler's hell, twat waffle."

Nine weeks of hell.

Nine more weeks and I'm home.

Nine more weeks.

Home.

Saturday, April 22
(Gus)

The show last night was probably the best one we've played since last year. I was on the uncomfortable side of sober by showtime, but it worked. The crowd was loud and their energy was easy to feed off of.

We didn't play "Finish Me." Hitler was furious. I'm beginning to take some serious pleasure from seeing that vein in his forehead throb.

I went to sleep as soon as we got on the bus after the show and didn't wake up until noon today. I've never slept so hard on the road. I feel almost human.

Before I open my bunk curtain, I tug on a T-shirt. There's a decency line I'm pretty sure I shouldn't cross this time around. The last thing I need is Impatient calling sexual harassment on me.

It isn't until after I use the bathroom that I realize the bus isn't moving. And I'm the only one on it. After putting on some jeans, socks, and my shoes, I grab the essentials and make my way out into the bright sunshine. We're in Phoenix and it's hot. I don't mind the heat; it beats the hell out of the cold. I've had enough cold this winter to last me a lifetime.

While I light the first of many cigarettes for the day, I survey the surroundings. We're parked in the back lot of the venue. There's a taco joint across the street, and my stomach starts growling at the sight of it. This boy *needs* tacos.

The place is small inside and cleanliness doesn't seem to be high on the list of priorities, but it'll do just fine. And when I see veggie tacos on the menu, I know I'm home. I order a six-pack of tacos and a bottle of water and take a seat at the booth by the front window. The tacos don't taste like Ma's, but they're damn good.

When I'm done, I find that I don't want to leave. The sidewalk outside isn't crowded but there's a fairly steady stream of people. I love to people watch. I could sit here all day and try to guess people's stories. Or make up their stories in my head. I can get creative, and it's entertaining. So I sit back and watch. The blinds are closed except one that's bent open. I feel like a spy peeking through it.

About five minutes later I spot a tall, slim brunette wearing a loose red hoodie and shorts. The shorts aren't obscenely short, but they show off her spectacular legs, long and lean. She looks like a runner. She's talking on a cell phone. Some people walk around, especially when they're distracted by something like a phone, and don't pay attention to what's going on around them, but even with her hood pulled up, I can tell by the subtle movements she's making that's she's looking at everything around her. She'd be a brilliant witness to a crime; I'm betting that nothing gets past her. It's fascinating. At one point she stops moving and leans up against the wall. She seems intense and focused. She doesn't talk with her hands. The hand that's not holding the phone is tucked in her front pocket. And even though she's standing still, she can't stand still, like there's a nervousness that she can't shake. Or maybe it's impatience kicking in. I feel for her. Calm is elusive most of the time; I miss it.

She's still on her phone when she pushes off the wall and crosses the street. She's walking toward me. The closer she gets, the more I can't look away. I don't know if it's those damn legs or the natural grace with which she moves. She's like the human equivalent of a gazelle.

I'm fixated on her until I realize who she is. It's Impatient. And my eyes instinctively jump away, but only momentarily before they bounce right back to her. She's probably twenty feet away when I realize I'm staring.

I shouldn't be staring. Especially when she can't see me through the blinds.

But I am. I'm not trying to be rude. I'm curious.

There's scarring on her right cheek. It looks like she was burned severely. Her hair falls around her face, but I can still make out the scar tissue. It looks like it starts below her eye, just missing her nose and mouth, and continues down her cheek and neck, disappearing into her shirt. I wonder how much of her torso is affected since her legs are unblemished. How did I not notice this before? I've been around her for two days. I'm usually a little more observant. Now it's obvious that I really have been ignoring her and the job she's supposed to be doing.

She's coming in this restaurant now. Luckily, my seat keeps me obscured by a plant. I can't see her, but I can hear her. Her voice, though quiet, is anything but meek. It's the kind of voice that holds authority, but presents it to you in hushed, soothing tones. And there's a slight accent I didn't notice yesterday — East Coast, maybe. I decide to listen in.

"Yeah, it's only for nine weeks. I really need this money. I can do anything for nine weeks, right? ... I haven't really talked to Gustov yet, but he seems pretty rock star cliché ... " She sounds a little bitter. "His ego seems to project out in front of him. You know, you run into it before you even meet him. Honestly, he seems like a jackass ... Listen Jane, I need to grab something to eat before I dive into day two. Do me a favor and go outside today. Take a walk. Get some fresh air ... Okay. I'll talk to you later. Bye."

Well, that's unfortunate. I was kinda hoping I could ease into friendship or at least roll with the whole PA idea. You know, if you can't beat 'em join 'em? Yeah, that. I know I judged her hard, initially. It's just the whole idea of her as my PA that I don't like. My first impression of her rubbed me the wrong way, but I may as well not fight it. I mean, hell, I don't need another obstacle. Guess she's not open to friendship, though. She's right about one thing: I am a jackass lately. In my opinion, she's out of bounds with her "rock star cliché" assessment. I've always kinda prided myself on not being cliché.

After hearing her less-than-stellar characterization of me, I decide it's best if I slip out of the restaurant while she's ordering so we don't bump into each other.

I don't see Impatient until later that afternoon. I'm sitting in my bunk on the bus when she approaches. And I know it's immature, but I'm a little hurt by what I overheard her saying about me earlier and I've been stewing on it. And maybe a little mad at myself because I'm starting to question who I've turned into. I don't want to be a cliché. Whatever the reason, I don't even look at her when she starts talking. It's rude, but I can't help myself. She meets my evasiveness with a little of her own and stands facing away from me while she talks. Touché. Head turned slightly, she's side-eyeing me, but she's direct and to the point. The conversation goes something like this:

Scout: "You need to blah, blah, blah. And when you're done with that we need to go over blah, blah, blah."

Me: Ignore, but nod as if I'm listening.

Scout: Silence. My rudeness has been met with irritation. She's pissed and doesn't try to hide it. At least she doesn't embarrass herself and kiss my ass. She just flat out doesn't like me and has no qualms about it.

I'm discovering more and more that people in this business have no pride. They'll sacrifice morals, ethics, hell, even their own mother if it means getting ahead. It's fake. Everyone wants to be your friend. Everyone wants a piece of you. It disgusts me and warps my sense of reality. I'm almost happy this girl so blatantly doesn't like me. It restores my faith in humanity.

Sunday, April 23
(Scout)

I may not have many friends, but I try to give everyone a chance. I try to give them the benefit of the doubt. Probably because people have never really done the same for me. But lately, these past few months, my patience is shot. I make split second judgments on people and rarely go back on them. And they're usually negative. I've been around Gustov Hawthorne for a little over forty-eight hours now. He's an ass. My first impression was dead-on. I walked in on him trying to hit up the stylist. The fake, easy-going charm oozing out of him like some kind of toxic playmaking trap set for his next conquest. Men are pigs. Gustov may be one of their leaders. Not to mention that sobriety doesn't seem to be on his agenda for the next two months. He's going to live up to the "rock star" title if it kills him. And it just might. What a waste.

I'm here for the money. That's it. I've got a job to do. And I'm going to do it if it kills me, because I can't go back home. I can't. Okay to be fair, I'm here for two reasons: money *and* escape. Maybe leaning more toward escape, the opportune but temporary variety. I'm finishing up my two final online classes to graduate and get my degree next month. A degree and the money I make will hopefully allow me some permanent escape when this job is done. I know I'm running away from my problems. I know that. *And I hate that.* But being home reminds me of him. It makes me feel ugly inside. It makes me feel used. It makes me feel like a failure. And I hate failing at anything.

So, when I was offered this job very last minute, I jumped on it, even though it's not ideal. It boils down to the lesser of two evils. And this evil provides an exit from the other evil.

And so far, Gustov is fairly low maintenance — at least for me. I don't need his input for the majority of my daily tasks, and when we do need to communicate, I use a passive approach. Direct doesn't seem to work with him. I'm great at passive, and I prefer it; it's how I've lived most of my life. People respond better to me when I'm passive. And anyway, I don't think Gustov likes me either. That's fine. It's better this way. He's just a job. I'm here as a buffer between him and management because they don't want to deal with him. Honestly, I can't blame them. I want this job to be over with, but I've got this. That's my pep talk ... *I've got this.*

Nine fucking weeks.

God.

Fucking.

Help.

Me.

Wednesday, April 26
(Gus)

Scout is a big fan of sticky notes.

And she's kind of a smartass.

I just came back to the bus to grab my phone, because I forgot it. It's sitting on my bunk with a sticky note stuck to it that reads: *You forgot your phone. Again. It was dead. It's charged now. You're welcome.*

I can't decide if I love it or hate it.

Pretty sure I hate it, which is why I've resorted to equal opportunity sticky note torture. Two can play at this game.

I turn the note over and write on the back: *I didn't forget it. It's a cranky bastard when it doesn't get time to snuggle in my bunk. It was napping, not dead.* I drop the note on her bunk before I leave.

Thursday, April 27
(Scout)

It's been one week.

I've discovered that Gustov drinks a lot.

He drinks all day long.

I thought it was all part of the rock star act, but I get the feeling now it's how he gets through the day, like he needs an aid to deal with reality. At first, I didn't like him. Now that's coupled with feeling a little sorry for him. For the most part, I try to avoid him. When I can't, I tolerate him. Although, I have to admit his sticky note replies are pretty witty. He's kind of a smartass, which is fine because smartass is my second language.

The rest of the guys, Franco, Jamie, and Robbie seem okay. I don't talk to anyone much. This isn't anything new. I've always been a loner. I try to keep to myself, but they're all polite. And sober most of the time, which is a bonus for intelligent conversation. I haven't watched any of their performances. I don't plan on it either. I sit on the bus reading while they're playing and when the chaos settles post-show, I go back in and play damage control if it's needed. It's usually not needed. The only thing I seem to run across is Gustov being pawed at by some overly enthusiastic groupie. He disappears into dark rooms with them every night.

Eight more weeks to go.

I've got this.

Friday, April 28
(Scout)

Now we're in Kansas City, Missouri. I've never been to the Midwest. It feels comforting and stable in a way I can't explain, like the people here have life figured out. No one's in a rush and that's nice. I wish I could live that way. My brain never turns off. Maybe that's what happens when you grow up in New York, in a city that never shuts down and reboots. Sometimes I wish I could turn my mind off altogether, but I can't. That's just stupid and unrealistic. Life is a fight. And I'm a fighter. And I'm good at fighting. I'm good at protecting myself when I have to.

I'm standing outside the bus when my cell phone rings.

"Hi, Jane," I answer with relief. It's been a few days since we talked last and I've been worried. I need to know she's okay.

"Hi, Scout." She sounds happy. It makes me glad, because it's rare that I hear genuine happiness in her voice.

"So, how's it going today? Anything exciting on tap?" I ask. It's how we always start off our conversations. Even though I don't want to be home, I still want to know what's going on. And that Jane's okay. So we talk every few days. I don't miss home, but I miss the feeling of home. I miss security, or the illusion of security. I'm a creature of habit. I miss having a routine.

"Paxton's home this weekend. We're going out to lunch in an hour. I'm meeting him at Pasqual's Deli." Now she sounds nervous. Maybe even scared. Paxton is her son, and they have an extremely strained relationship. He's seventeen. He's my cousin, and he and I grew up together. Even though there's a six-year age difference between us, we're close. He's my best friend. He goes to a year-round boarding school in Boston and he hates it, everything about it: the school, the spoiled kids he's surrounded by, the isolation. I don't blame him. It stifles him. It's changed him and stunted him socially and that breaks my heart. Basically, the school is an alternative parenting strategy. The school parents the kids so the parents don't have to be, you know, parents. Because, honestly, Jane can't parent at this point. And Paxton doesn't want her to. I hate being in the middle of them. I try to play peacemaker. I usually fail horribly.

Holding the phone to my ear, I don't know what to say. I

60

don't want to offer false hope and I know Paxton; I don't think he'll show for lunch, but I can't bring myself to say it, so I say, "Tell him I said hi. And to call me." I usually hear from him every day, but I don't want her to know that.

She sighs, and I can hear the doubt through the phone, I can practically feel it. She doesn't want to be doubtful. She wants to be optimistic. She dreams of optimism, like little girls dream of princesses and happily-ever-afters. But at heart, she's a reluctant fatalist. Disease drives her fate. It's the reason Paxton refuses to be around her. "I will," she says, finally. She's trying, and failing, to smile. I can hear it in the fluctuations in her voice.

In an attempt to cheer her up, I add, "Oh, and stop at Sweet Treats on the way home from Pasqual's and eat a slice of carrot cake cheesecake for me." Jane loves carrot cake cheesecake, and it always cheers her up. Me too. At least once a month we'd take a trip to Sweet Treats and drown any bad feelings in cheesecake. It's the cure for just about anything, at least for a little while.

Her voice brightens. "I will. I haven't gone since you've been away, you know. I think it's time."

I offer reassurance in a nod she can't see. "It's definitely time."

She changes the subject. "How's everything going with you?"

I shrug. "Same. Eight more weeks. I've got this." I do. I have to.

"You can do anything Scout. Anything you put your mind to." She's always encouraged me ... and only me. Almost like she's living vicariously, making up for all of the bad choices and the things she hates about herself. It makes me feel sorry for her. I've always felt that she's one of those people who never realized they have potential, or the power to create potential. Life merely happens *to her*, but she doesn't live it. She doesn't participate.

"Thanks, Jane. Well, you better go get ready for your lunch date." I don't want to say what comes next, because if he's a no-show she'll be crushed. "Text or call me later and let me know how Paxton is doing."

"Okay." There's already doubt and disappointment in her voice. I wish I could take it away for both of them.

A text comes in from Jane four hours later. *Paxton didn't show up.*

My heart sinks and I don't want to text back. I don't want to acknowledge the hurt she's feeling because then it's real. But I do text back with the only thing I can come up with that's genuine. *I'm sorry.*

She doesn't reply. What's she going to say anyway?

Saturday, April 29
(Scout)

I didn't hear from Paxton yesterday. I know he's hanging out with his friends since he's home for a long weekend. He doesn't get to go home often, so I know he's busy, but I have to text him to check in on him. *NYC this weekend?*

The response is almost immediate. *I go back to prison tomorrow night.*

Having fun? God, I hope he is.

Hanging out with Cisco today. That's a yes. Cisco is his one of his closest friends. They've known each other since they were five.

Good. Let me know when you get back to school tomorrow night. I like to know where he is and that he's okay.

Sure thing.

Thursday, May 4
(Scout)

I hate to give Gustov credit for anything, but if there's one thing endearing about him it's how much he loves his mom. He talks to her on the phone every day. I never realized until yesterday that that's who he calls every afternoon.

Every.

Afternoon.

I can't help eavesdropping now. What rock star calls their mom every day? It makes him more human.

Don't get me wrong, I still don't like him. He's just more like a real person, that's all.

Five more weeks and I'm done with this.

Five.

More.

Weeks.

Friday, May 5
(Gus)

When I arrive back on the bus after soundcheck, there's a stack of clean, folded laundry on my bunk. My sheets. And my clothes. All of them. Clean. Like, so clean I just want to bury my face in them and inhale for the next few hours because they smell like fucking sunshine. I haven't washed my clothes since we've been on this tour. And I only have a few outfits. They were ripe.

Impatient walks out of the bathroom and catches me smelling a pair of socks. That's when I put two and two together. "You washed my clothes, dude?"

She shrugs, but won't meet my eyes. She never makes eye contact. "It smelled like something died over there. It was time. Like, two weeks ago it was time."

As she's talking, I see one of her sticky notes lying on my bunk next to the clothes. It reads: *When your jeans can stand up on their own it's time to wash them. You're welcome.*

I nod and go back to smelling the socks. They smell *so damn good.* "I know it's not your job, but thanks." I'm taking a visual inventory of my stockpile and notice there are twice as many pairs of underwear and socks as I used to have. "Hey, either my socks and drawers were going at it like rabbits at the laundromat and multiplying, or someone bought me more." I turn and look at her questioningly.

She grabs her bag from her bunk and quickly heads for the door. "You can't keep wearing the same underwear day after day without washing them. It's disgusting," she says bluntly. When she does talk she gets right to the point, but that damn voice softens the blow. It's not just that it's soft and feminine, but her voice is enticing, and serene even. I can't put my finger on it, but I like listening to her.

She bought me socks and underwear?

She bought me socks and underwear.

"Who says I've been wearing any? I draw the line at manky skivvies. Commando's been where it's at for the past week."

A look of disgust flashes across her face and she shakes her head.

And I know I've crossed a line. "Sorry. TMI. But, thanks,

65

dude."

"It was nothing. Really. I had to wash my clothes anyway. And those are WalMart socks and undies, nothing fancy. I used the company credit card." Then she disappears out the door.

Maybe it was nothing to her. Maybe she did it because she couldn't stand the stench anymore. *She probably did it because she couldn't stand the stench anymore.* Whatever the reason, it was free of motive or the expectation of reciprocation. She was just being nice.

I fucking love nice.

Two points to Scout.

Wednesday, May 10
(Scout)

No show tonight. We're driving across Texas and even though I'm trapped on the bus with the band, it's a welcome change from our normal schedule. The guys are all doing their own thing—reading, listening to music, or on their laptops. Everyone's plugged into their own little world. The silence is welcome.

I've been texting with Paxton for the past hour. For some reason we started quoting movies—our favorites lines, most of them funny. It started with random movie trivia that turned into a bizarre conversation using only movie quotes. We do bizarre well. He's so smart and his recall is lightning-fast, which means he has me on my toes and thinking hard, digging deep for the next reply. It's fun. Before long he has to head off to a study session, so I start reading a new book I picked up at the truck stop this morning. It's a murder mystery called *The Cuckoo's Calling*, which isn't something I would usually read, but the writing is spectacular. Maybe I need to branch out into new genres more often.

Gustov climbs down out of his bunk and then returns a few minutes later and climbs back up. It's not enough of a distraction that I stop reading, but I'm aware of his movements.

The silence is broken by the tearing of plastic wrap, followed by what can only be a jar opening. Suddenly the scent of peanut butter hits me. Like a punch to the nose it hits me. I *love* peanut butter. And now that it's invading my senses, I'm ravenous. I would kill for a peanut butter sandwich.

Apparently I'm not the only one lured in by the smell of Gus's snack because Franco calls out, "Hey, pass me a few of those, dipshit."

My peripheral vision picks up motion, an exchange of food. Anything involving peanut butter sets my sense of smell to overdrive. I would pay for a spoonful.

As if he can read my mind, I see Gustov's big hand extended down at me from across the aisle. "Want one?"

There are two saltine crackers lying in the palm of his hand, a tiny cracker sandwich with peanut butter filling. I lean out of my bunk further to get a better look.

"You want one?" he offers again.

It's a mouthwatering sight. I don't know why I'm hesitating, but I'm hesitating. He's trying to be nice and all I can meet it with is suspicion. It's a trained reaction. I wish I could just meet nice with nice. So, I make an effort. "What is it?" I mean, I know what it is, but I've never seen anyone eat saltines and peanut butter together.

"It's only the tastiest snack known to man. You need one. Seriously. Take it."

I do and I back burner the suspicion for the moment. "Thanks."

I take a bite, and yeah, it's the tastiest snack known to man. Or woman. Before I finish it I already want another one, despite the crumbs I'm leaving in my bed.

"You can't stop at just one," he says. His hand reappears, and there are two little heavenly sandwiches in his palm this time.

I smile though he can't see my face, and take them. "Thanks."

"You're welcome. I've got a whole sleeve of crackers. Let me know when you're ready for another one. Oh yeah," he pauses, holding out a bottle of grape juice, "and I've got grape juice, too, if you need to wash 'em down. Nothing goes better with crackers and PB than grape juice."

I shake my head again, but I'm smiling. "What are you, five years old?"

Franco laughs from his bunk.

"Pretty much. At heart anyway." Gustov doesn't sound offended. There's wholehearted agreement in his voice.

My snarky comment just turned into a compliment with his admission. It softens me a little to him. "No thanks. I've got some water."

"Suit yourself." He hands me two more crackers.

I eat them. And as I chew, I think: this snack is like an olive branch he's just extended without even realizing it.

Saturday, May 13
(Scout)

I'm up early. We're in Tennessee. I've already gone for a run and showered, and I'm going to find a laundromat while everyone is still sleeping. As I'm stripping the sheets off my bunk and quietly putting them and my clothes into my duffle bag, I jump when someone taps me on the shoulder.

When I turn, Gustov is leaning out of his bunk. I see his lips moving, he must be whispering because I can't hear him. I hold up a finger to stop him before he finishes. "Hold on." I open up my bag and take out the case that holds my hearing aid. After inserting it in my left ear, I say, "Sorry, what?"

He stares at me for a minute, like he's been caught off guard. "So, you don't wear one in your right ear?" he asks.

It was a completely innocent question, but it brings heat to my cheeks. I point at my right ear. "This one doesn't work at all."

I assume he'll ask more questions or look shocked, but he doesn't miss a beat. "You going to wash clothes?" He's not whispering anymore even though everyone is sleeping.

I nod and return to my duffle bag.

"Mind if I come with you? I need to start making this cleanliness thing a weekly habit."

I shrug, because I know he's going to come no matter what I say. "I can take yours with me. It's no big deal. You don't need to come." The truth is that I don't really want him to come. I prefer to be by myself. And I'm a little embarrassed now that he knows about my hearing aid. And what if he gets recognized while we're out? I hate drawing attention to myself. Hate it. It makes me feel uncomfortable. Talking to him on this bus is one thing, but talking to him out in the real world is another.

He comes along anyway. The good news is that he's stone sober, which might be a first.

The laundromat isn't far, so we decide to walk. On the way, we duck inside a Dutch-themed bakery for some coffee, and Gustov strikes up a conversation with the friendly woman behind the counter. I envy how easy it is for him—talking to a stranger like they're old friends. I've never been able to do that. Gustov pays for both coffees and tips her ten dollars. She gives us each a flaky pastry she calls a "Dutch letter", and tells us to have a nice day.

After we step outside, Gustov's pastry is gone in three bites. He's wearing the wide eyes of a child when he swallows the last of it. "Holy shit, Dutch letters are the motherfucking real deal. We're stopping there on the way back to the bus and buying more. Like every last one Debbie has."

I noticed the woman's name tag, because I'm obsessive about taking in every last detail, but I didn't think it's something Gustov would have noticed. I'm surprised. And I have to agree with him about the Dutch letters. They're delicious. "Yeah, we should probably buy some for everyone else."

"Who said for everyone else? I'm going to sustain myself solely on these luscious little almond-filled pieces of heaven for the next few days." He winks so I know he's kidding. Sort of. I have no doubt he could put away a dozen of them.

Upon arrival at the laundromat, Gustov proceeds to empty the entire contents of his bag into one machine. It's filled to beyond capacity. I'm standing next to him, sorting my clothes and bedding on a folding table. I stop what I'm doing and look repeatedly from the machine to his face, and back to the machine questioningly.

He senses my evident dismay.

I look again from his face to the burdened machine, and back up at him. My eyes always stop on his beard, because I can't meet his eyes. Eye contact at close range is uncomfortable with most people. And I don't know how to explain it, but I don't want to look in eyes and see scrutiny. I don't want to see him staring at my scars. Most people talk to my scars, not to my eyes. I'm as used to it as I suppose a person can ever be. I don't want to *be* my scars to him ... or anyone.

He lifts his hands, palms upward, in a questioning manner. "What, dude?"

Shaking my head, I ask, "Have you ever done your own laundry?"

He bobs his head up and down as he answers. "Of course."

I doubt that. "Ever heard of sorting?" I don't know why this is

70

so irritating to me. It's probably because I'm overanalyzing everything and it's messing with my head. Why can't I just have a normal conversation?

"That takes too much damn time. It all gets clean either way," is his defense.

I begin pulling his clothes out of the machine. "Well, you're also going to kill this machine if you put this many clothes in." After they're all removed, I sort them into my piles. Gustov stands back, arms crossed, making no effort to stop me. I also note that he's smirking.

After our clothes are in three separate machines, I sit down and open my mystery novel while he runs back down to the bakery. The quietude is unexpected for a laundromat. Usually they're busy and dirty and loud. This one's not any of those things. Just as the clothes finish the rinse cycle, he returns with three boxes of pastries.

After we find three open dryers, Gustov pulls a small cardboard box out of his bag. "Wanna play a game?" he asks, as he slides a wooden box out of the packaging.

My curiosity is piqued. "You want to play a game?"

He shrugs. "Sure. We've got nothing but time." He glances at the dryer behind us. "Forty-seven minutes to be exact. More than enough time for a few rounds of Mancala."

"Mancala?"

"Yeah, Mancala," he says. He looks at me quizzically. "Please don't tell me you've never played Mancala. We need to remedy that ASAP if that's the case."

"Never heard of it."

He opens the wooden box, which turns out to be a folded game board hinged in the middle. He starts distributing flat marbles in equal numbers into circular indentions on both sides of the box. "I used to play this with friends all the time," he explains. "I saw it at the truck stop yesterday and had to buy it. It's been a few years and I'm jonesing for some Mancala."

Paxton and I played board games a lot when we were younger, but it's been years. My first instinct is to say yes, and before I can talk myself out of it, I'm agreeing. What the hell has gotten in to me?

He explains the rules, and we play. It's a fairly simple game of moving the marbles around the board and trying to capture more marbles than your opponent, but there's definitely some strategy involved. He beats me. So we play another round. He beats me again. And he taunts me this time when he does it. We play a final round, and this time victory is mine. I'm not shy about rubbing his nose in it, either. I feel like I'm playing with Paxton. And it's actually relaxing. I smile to myself, because even though I prefer to be alone, this whole morning has been kind of perfect in a weird, unexpected, unplanned way. I'm usually very organized, but this was spontaneous, and, well ... nice.

And I love Mancala. Who knew?

I also know this can't happen again. This was a moment of weakness. I can't slip into trust-mode with this guy. The last man I trusted with friendship broke me.

(Gus)

I had a great morning; completely, unexpectedly great. Hell, it felt almost *normal*. I didn't think that was allowed on the road. *Normal*. Hell, I didn't think that was allowed in my life at all anymore. And mystery solved on why Impatient doesn't answer me sometimes when I whisper to her late at night or early in the morning while everyone is sleeping. I always thought she was just ignoring me. I didn't know she was hard of hearing. Makes me feel a little less like the enemy. Don't get me wrong, she's still standoffish and quiet. Only now I think that may have more to do with her than me.

Saturday, May 20
(Gus)

Apparently I was wrong. Standoffish and quiet has everything to do with me.

I invited Impatient to go with me to the laundromat this morning, but I guess she did her laundry yesterday. Which is fine, but she's turned down every attempt I've made to be nice to her this week. She's avoiding me, like intentionally and obviously avoiding me. I don't know what I did, but I'm sure I did something. I thought we turned a corner last weekend on the whole friendship thing, but I guess I was wrong.

Scratch the part where I thought we could be friends.

We're back to sticky notes.

Fuck it.

I tried.

Whatever.

Wednesday, May 24
(Scout)

I'm back to keeping to myself. It's better this way. I feel more comfortable. I talk to Paxton every day; he's my lifeline to the real world outside of the weird, rock star world I'm trapped in at the moment. He asks a lot of questions about the band because he loves their music. I don't have many answers for him, because, well, I don't know their music and I'm definitely not discussing them personally — that's a line I won't cross.

And besides that, they're just people.

Paxton idolizes them.

I live with them ... and wish I didn't.

Two totally different views that I can't reconcile in my mind.

Friday, May 26
(Gus)

We've been on the road for just over a month now. Even though we're in a different city every night, repetition is king: sleep, eat, drink, call Ma, drink, eat, perform *while* drinking, sleep. Repeat. Once again alcohol is an amiable companion. Because people are just too hard for me right now.

It's monotonous, but I don't have to think too much at my current pace. It's routine and easy. And I've cut out women. There's never a shortage of propositions, but even sex isn't doing it for me like it used to. Seeing them so eager to please me makes me feel like a fraud. They want to be with Gustov. Not Gus. It's not that I act like two different people; *I'm just me*. But they don't know who that really is. I do. That's the difference. I'm done.

I'd rather just hang out on the bus. How fucking sad is that? It's the truth, though.

Four more weeks and I'm home.

Four weeks.

Fuck my life. Four more weeks.

And Impatient? She's another mental game that I can't shake. She doesn't like me. The past two weeks avoiding all actual verbal interaction is key for her again. It's like those few days when we talked and acted friendly never existed. Like they were some weird dream I conjured. I wish it never would've happened, because then I wouldn't miss it. I wish this didn't bother me so much, but it does. It's like I have people throwing themselves at me, wanting a piece of me, all day, every day. I love the fact that she doesn't do that. That also means she won't have anything to do with me. Shit, I'm drinking way too much these days to analyze like this.

She's back to using sticky notes for all of her reminders or instruction; it's her sole source of communication again. I don't know what happened between us, but I'm kinda pissed. Or maybe I'm lonely. Hell, I don't know. But I usually don't respond anymore. I just want to talk, not write notes. She still gets shit done despite my lack of participation or cooperation, though. It's nothing life or death, but she takes her job seriously. And as much as I resented the whole PA idea at first, it's been for the best. She's efficient and thorough, and if I have to admit it, even if she doesn't like me she's got my back work-wise. She's going out of her way to meet her obligations.

I'm beginning to resent being an obligation. Especially if that's all I am to her.

It's five-thirty and we just wrapped up soundcheck. The venue sells pizza, so I grab a few slices and a couple of beers and head back to the bus to eat while the guys go to a steakhouse down the street. Vegetarians and steak don't mix, so I'm sticking to three slices of veggie and three slices of cheese.

The bus is quiet when I climb on and take a seat at the table. Silence is rare when you share a bus with so many people; I don't take it for granted. I feel like it's the only time I can get out of my head and just relax. When I'm finished with the pizza, I reach in my pocket for my phone. It's not there. I try the other pocket. Not there either. The terror is fucking immediate. I feel that flash of panic when you realize you've lost something important. When it subsides, I decide to check my bunk. I hope I didn't lose it again. I've gone through four phones in as many months and it's always a pain in the ass to get it replaced.

I pull back the sheets and blanket, lift my pillow, check under my laptop, and shuffle through some paperwork Impatient left for me to sign. Nothing. "Shit. Where in the hell is it?" I'm talking out loud, as if the damn thing is going to come out from its hiding spot.

"It's charging."

I jump out of my fucking skin at the words, and turn. Impatient is sitting in her bunk across the aisle from mine.

Those are the first words she's spoken to me all week. She's sitting in her bunk reading a book and she's laughing at me. She's stifling it, but she's laughing nonetheless.

Her laughter immediately lightens my mood. "*Jesus fucking Christ*," I say. "You scared the hell out of me. I thought I was alone this whole time. You could be a fucking hired assassin, you know that?"

She's back to her book now. Any hint that this person has a sense of humor has vanished. Without looking at me, she says, "On the counter, by the toaster."

I walk to where she's instructed and, sure as shit, there sits my phone, plugged into the community charger. Exactly where I left it earlier.

I disconnect it and take it back to my bunk with me, pushing aside the mess I made during the mad hunt, and climb in. My eyes keep drifting back to her bunk as I scroll through missed texts and emails. From this high angle I can't see anything from the chest up but I can see the book resting in her lap and her long legs stretched out. Those damn legs. They're crossed at the ankle. I was right about her being a runner. She runs every day. It's the first thing she does when the bus stops.

I don't know why but I have to talk to her. I don't want to let this opportunity go. "How'd you know I was looking for my phone?"

She doesn't hesitate. "You always call your mom around this time of day."

I do. See, she pays attention. Like I said, nothing gets past her. "What are you reading?"

She stays tucked away in her bunk, but she answers, "It's a biography about an Afghani woman. She's leading the fight for equal rights for women in the Middle East." She always stays tucked away. Even if she's talking to someone face-to-face, she's tucked away. She angles herself away and avoids eye contact. At first, I thought it was part of her personality — the impatience and irritation. But it wasn't until I saw her, really saw her, and watched her around others that I realized she's hiding. Hiding the right side of her face. I'm no expert, but I'd guess that she's lived with her scars for a long time. She overcompensates for them like she's protecting them, protecting herself. Hiding is how she functions. I wish she wouldn't hide, but I'm in no position to judge. I've been hiding from myself for months.

"That sounds fun." I'm only joking, partially because I'm a little nervous, but it comes off insensitive and rude.

And that's exactly how she takes it. "There's this great big world out there where women are valued for more than their vaginas," she says flatly. She's a woman of few words, but when she says something she means it.

It takes my breath away. She's harsh. You'd think I'd be used to it by now. "Is that what you really think about me?"

"Don't act so shocked. It's your M.O. I watch it every night after the shows."

Not knowing how to respond, I try to joke around with her despite failing miserably at it only seconds ago. "Jealous?" I don't why I just said that. I've had a few beers tonight, but that's no excuse. I need to shut my damn mouth.

"Get over yourself, Gustov." She sounds pissed now, even her soft voice isn't tempering the anger. "Not if you were the last man on Earth." There's disgust in her voice. Then she circles back on the insult, leans out of her bunk, and glares up at me. "Are you really so self-absorbed that you can't fathom the fact that there are women out there who have no interest whatsoever in sleeping with you?"

I shrug, because I feel shitty. When did I turn into *that guy*? I'm not *that guy*.

She shakes her head, tosses her book to the foot of the bed, slips out of her bunk, and disappears out the door of the bus.

I stare blankly at her bunk. I want a do-over of the last five minutes. Instead, I call Ma because it always gets me out of this crazy world I'm living in and back to sanity. Under my breath, I repeat while I'm listening to the phone ring. "One more month and I'm home. One more month and I'm home."

"Hi, honey." Comfort, that's what her voice sounds like.

"Hey, Ma. What's my favorite person up to?"

"Just eating a late lunch here at the office with Mikayla."

We're on the east coast so she's three hours behind. "How's Mikayla doing?"

Ma sighs, it's a happy sigh with underlying sadness. "She sold her house. Closing is next month. Retirement is finally going to take her away from me." Mikayla's been Ma's assistant since the first day she opened her advertising firm twenty years ago. They're close friends and I know Ma feels like she'll be lost without her.

"Good for Mikayla. Sucks for you."

"Good for Mikayla is right. She deserves to enjoy retirement. I'm just being selfish."

"I know you knew this day was coming, not that it makes it any easier on you, but what are you gonna do? Mikayla's superhuman." She is. Ma's damn good at what she does. She's one helluva business woman. But Mikayla's always been her backup. Another set of eyes and ears that stayed on top of everything. They've worked together so long they can finish each other's sentences. I swear they speak telepathically half the time.

Ma laughs. "Mikayla *is* superhuman. And I don't know what I'm going to do. I don't even want to think about interviewing and hiring someone new. Mikayla's gritty attitude and ability to make things happen out of thin air is irreplaceable."

As soon as she says it my eyes dart to Impatient's empty bunk. Gritty attitude. Ability to make things happen. The wheels are turning in my head and before I know it, my mouth is getting ahead of me. "I might know someone."

"You might know someone?" I don't know why she sounds so surprised.

"Yeah, she's traveling with us. Her name's Scout, but I call her Impatient. She's my babysitter."

Ma scoffs at the babysitter tag, but I know she's relieved that someone's looking out for me besides Franco.

"I don't think she has a job when our tour ends. I overheard her talking to someone on the phone a few days ago." Impatient was talking to Jane (I still haven't figured out if Jane's a family member, or a friend) earlier this week and said she started sending out her resume. She sounded a little desperate.

Ma interrupts. "Gus, you shouldn't eavesdrop."

"Ma, she lives three feet from me on the bus. It's hard not to. Anyway, can I have her call or email you?"

"Sure. It wouldn't hurt to talk to her."

"Thanks. And do me a favor and don't tell her we know each other."

"Why not?"

"She hates me." It's as simple as that.

"I'm sure she doesn't hate you." Moms never believe stuff like this. That someone could dislike their child.

"Pretty sure she does," I confirm.

"How are you going to convince her to call me then, if this girl doesn't like you?"

"I'll have Franco talk to her."

"Okay." She sounds hesitant.

"Thanks Ma. I'll let you get back to lunch with Mikayla. Tell her I said 'hey' and give her a hug for me."

"Will do, sweetie. Good luck tonight." She says it before every show. Always has.

I answer the same way I always do. "Don't need luck; I've got Franco, Jamie, and Robbie."

"Love you."

"Love you too, Ma."

"Bye, honey."

"Bye."

When Franco returns from dinner, I rundown the situation and ask him to talk to Impatient in the morning. At first I don't think he's hearing anything I'm saying because he's just looking at me like I've finally lost it, but by the time I've finished, he's climbed onboard with the idea. If I know Franco, he'll treat this like a game. It's not that Franco's into deception, but he's definitely into a challenge. I think he wants to see how far this whole thing could go. And he's a good guy so he knows that if he wins, so does she.

Game on.

Saturday, May 27
(Gus)

It's early. The bus is eating up miles across upstate New York. I've been up for a while but I haven't heard anyone else stir yet, so I've been sitting in my bunk reading a book I downloaded on my laptop. I don't read very often for fun. My mind wanders too easily and I have trouble concentrating. It's hard work, if you want to know the truth. Bright Side used to read all the time. She'd read anything: books, newspapers, magazines. It's one of the reasons she was so damn smart.

As my mind's drifting to Bright Side, I hear a curtain pull back, and the shuffling feet of someone moving out into the aisle towards the bathroom. Every sound made by the movement is muffled and quiet, deliberately so. Although my curtain is pulled shut, I know it's Impatient. She moves around this bus like a ghost. For all her quiet attitude, unless you're interacting with her one-on-one, she disappears into the background, like she doesn't want to be noticed. Like she wants us all to pretend she's not here.

I hear Franco moving around now. His bunk is under mine, directly across from Impatient's. The swoosh of his curtain opening is accompanied by the creaky hinge on the bathroom door opening and shutting, which is followed by the sounds of a sleepy collision in the aisle.

"Shit. Sorry Scout. I didn't see you there. You okay?"

Her voice sounds gravelly like it does every morning for the first hour or so that she's awake. "I'm okay. And you didn't see me because your eyes are closed, Franco." I can almost hear a smile in her voice. Franco tends to bring that out in people. It's one of his gifts.

He laughs. "I try not to open them before ten in the morning. I've mastered getting out of my bunk, using the bathroom, and getting back into bed without opening my eyes. I just pretend I'm still sleeping."

"Please don't tell me that. We share the same bathroom." She's not smiling anymore, but it's not rude.

"I gotta take a leak, but I need to talk to you before you stow away in your bunk again. I promise I'll use the pisser with my eyes open this time."

81

"Okay."

After Franco finishes in the bathroom, I can hear him give a quick sell on the job prospect. I've still got my curtain shut, but I hear him hand her the slip of paper—the one with Ma's cell phone number and email address written on it. I didn't put her last name down because Hawthorne might set off an alarm.

She sounds stoked, and for the first time in a long time my heart feels lighter. Like I've somehow redeemed myself a tiny bit and maybe I can shed the asshole persona I've been hiding behind, or under, or inside of, for months now.

Saturday, June 3
(Scout)

I'm officially a degree-holding college graduate. Well, I'm not physically holding it, because I wasn't at the ceremony today. That's okay. I'm still proud either way. I've been smiling inside all day. Paxton and Jane both called to congratulate me. Their praise was like a physical hug I could feel through the phone. I usually don't need that sort of thing, but today I can't deny that it felt so good. They were here with me in spirit. For me. My celebration is complete.

Monday, June 5
(Gus)

This afternoon, I called Ma from a small coffee shop down the street, a block or so from the venue we play tonight. I wanted to phish for information about Impatient, without anyone on the bus overhearing. Ma was oddly tightlipped about the whole thing, which isn't like her at all. Usually she's open about everything with me. I don't know if it's because she feels like there's bad blood between Impatient and me and she's just being the overprotective mama bear, or if she's trying to keep this somewhat confidential because Scout and I have an existing working relationship and she doesn't want to jeopardize herself as a potential employer. All I could pry out of her was that Impatient called her this morning and emailed her resume.

That's it.

Nothing more.

Tuesday, June 6
(Gus)

I had an epiphany this morning.
I'm getting fat.
And soft.
Like my limbs and gut have been filled with cream cheese.
My lazy ass has probably gained twenty pounds this past month. I've always been active and staying in shape was never an issue before, it was the unintentional consequence of surfing almost every day. But it's impossible to be active when you're on tour. Okay, it's not impossible. Impatient runs every day, and from what I can tell she's in phenomenal shape. But being active requires effort. And these past few months, effort just doesn't hold my interest. I make an effort to survive my own self-destruction. Which is a little fucked up. Survive and self-destruct shouldn't coexist within the context of the same thought. But for me it's been the norm. The European tour was fueled by booze and drugs and not much food, which would probably explain why weight wasn't an issue then. This US tour is fueled by booze and junk food since apparently my appetite is back. Which is why I decided I need to make some changes and add some sort of exercise to my schedule.
I tried to jog this afternoon. Dismal failure. My smoker's lungs laughed at me about a quarter of a mile in. It was audible. I heard a peal of laughter emanate from within my chest followed by, "Gus, what the fuck do you think you're doing?" I'm pretty sure the vocalized taunting came from my lungs and legs working in concert, teaming up against me. The short-lived attempt segued into a long walk around the streets of Madison, Wisconsin. Don't get me wrong, Madison was cool, but this functioning like a doughy, middle-aged man shit isn't gonna fly. I've just been bitch slapped by poor choices and I don't like it. Guess who's getting back in shape? This fat ass, that's who.
Three more weeks and I'm home. I can surf again.
Every.
Damn.
Day.
For now, I'm sticking to long walks.

Saturday, June 10
(Scout)

I talked to Audrey again this morning. I'd be lying if I said I didn't have my heart set on this job. I want it more than I've ever wanted anything else in my life. It's a dream job. And not only is it a dream job, but it's a dream job across the country from home. I need that.

I also know better than to get my heart set on anything, so I try not to dwell on it. But Audrey's so personable and welcoming. I feel like I click with her. And I don't click with many people.

I also know Audrey is Gustov's mom. I did some research online after I talked to her the first time. When I saw her photo on the company website there was no denying that the last name wasn't a coincidence.

Which means Gustov had something to do with facilitating this opportunity for me. An anonymous favor. Which is incidentally my favorite kind. When someone initiates kindness anonymously, you know it comes from the most pure, kindhearted part of them because they'll probably never be singled out and thanked. It speaks to his character.

I still feel like I need to keep my distance from him. I don't really belong in his world. Not that he's rock star cliché like I first thought. He keeps to himself most of the time on the bus, but his lifestyle is still something I can't wrap my head around, even though I've been on this bus with him for the past several weeks. While people flock to him, people keep their distance from me. We're opposites. And if this job doesn't work out with Audrey, I know we'll never see each other again. What's the point in even trying to develop any sort of friendship at this point?

So, Gustov and I still don't talk, but, in addition to the sticky notes, I do find myself communicating with him in other ways. It's like subtle charades and he's good at it. His eyes are more expressive than anyone else I've ever seen. Just one look tells a story. And it's never benign. Every wink, squint, stare, widening, side-eye, scrunch, and eyebrow raise means something different and always gets a reaction out of me — an internal reaction that I usually hide, but that I also can't deny. It's a strange connection that I've never had with anyone else.

Tuesday, June 27
(Gus)

There's a sudden pain in my ribs. Both sides. Franco's punching me from the left side, and Jamie's poking me from the right.

"Wake up, ass hat," Franco says, practically shouting into my ear.

"We're on the ground, Gus." It's Jamie this time.

My eyes are sticky and crusted with sleep. And my nose, my entire head really, is stuffy and congested. My throat is sore, like I've been swallowing razor blades. I have a cold. Symptoms started last night before our last show of the tour, but after a few hours' sleep on this flight home, it feels as if the germs have waged an all-out assault on my immune system. Summer colds are bullshit. As I clear my throat and pry my eyes open, Franco punches me again. Hard.

I hold up my hand to ward off any further physical attack. "Stop. I'm up, dammit. I'm up." My voice sounds like sawdust, dry and dusty.

As we wait for those in the front rows to exit the plane, Jamie hops out in the aisle and pulls down our carry-ons. Robbie joins him from across the aisle.

When the semi-orderly evacuation finds our row, my body protests vehemently to standing and walking. Every joint in my body aches. Strike the foolish notion that this is a cold—it's definitely the flu. I trudge behind Franco, Robbie, and Jamie, following their taunts about how slow I am the entire way to baggage claim. I can't say it bothers me at all though. Over the past few weeks, things with the guys are back to normal. The tension and edge is gone.

After we find our bags at the baggage claim, we head outside to the taxi lanes. Franco, Robbie, and Jamie share a cab. Jamie and Robbie share a place in Carlsbad with a couple other guys, but they're staying at Franco's place in San Diego tonight. The three of them leave for Hawaii tomorrow. They're going on vacation for a week. Surfing for a week, no less. Me, I'm just happy to be heading back to Ma's. I don't need a vacation. I need home.

The cab ride takes about thirty minutes and though all I want to do is sleep, I can't get this nagging feeling out of my pressure-filled head. Impatient left Sunday afternoon from Dallas. I heard a muffled conversation between her and Hitler on the bus right before soundcheck. When we arrived back on the bus after dinner, she was gone. Her bunk was empty. She fucking vanished into thin air. It was like she'd never even been there at all. It was a shock I felt in my gut. I don't know if it was the fact that familiarity had been altered. I don't know if it was the fact that I knew I was on my own again, if only for two days. But what bothered me the most was that she didn't say goodbye, which is batshit crazy, because I know she didn't like me. We never talked outside of that morning at the laundromat in Tennessee. But we had established a routine of silent communication using sticky notes of all things, and the past three weeks we added hand gestures and facial cues. What started off impersonal turned into *intimately* impersonal. When you don't speak with someone out loud, you study their mannerisms and body language much more closely. You get to know them on a different level. Bright Side and I were that way. We could carry on an entire conversation without ever uttering a word.

By the time we pull in Ma's driveway and I pay, thoughts of Impatient have gone foggy and given way to exhaustion. I'm struggling to put one foot in front of the other to walk up the front porch steps, and all I can think about is sleeping the day away while Ma's at work.

My eyes are hazy and scratchy when I open them. The sun is setting outside my window. I blink a few times trying to clear my vision to take in the view. The sunset doesn't come into focus; instead it becomes a blur of fiery orange. I feel a sudden rush of grief. I blink, and realize that my eyes are filling with tears. Sunsets have always reminded me of Bright Side. She and her sister, Gracie, loved to watch the sunset. They did it every night. It was a planned event, and they called it "showtime." Seeing the sun drown itself out in the ocean tonight is bittersweet because it brings with it thoughts of her and the fact that I'll never watch a sunset with either one of them again. The pain builds in my chest until it erupts into sobs. I haven't cried like this for weeks. When I finally catch my breath, I'm covered in sweat. My body feels foreign, and my mind seems to float at a distance. It takes more effort than it should to heave my body out of bed and strip off my soaked T-shirt and sweats, and slip into a pair of board shorts from a pile of dirty clothes on the floor next to my bed. I don't want to make the journey to the kitchen, but I'm so thirsty and I need some aspirin. My head is throbbing.

I hear Ma's voice talking to someone as I round the corner into the kitchen. She stops mid-sentence when she sees me. "Gus, honey, what's wrong?" The back of her hand is to my forehead in a flash. "You have a fever."

"Flu," I confirm. "Better keep your distance, Ma. Hi, by the way. I missed you."

"Hi, Gus. Oh, I've missed you, too." She hugs me despite my warning and I'm grateful for it. I squeeze her and my muscles scream, but I ignore them. Arms still wrapped around Ma, I open my eyes and notice the person standing across the kitchen, cutting onions, mushrooms, and red peppers. Seeing her confirms that I've gone from feverish to delirious.

It's Impatient.

What the hell?

Her stance hints at her normal guarded defiance, but she also looks sheepish. Or scared. I can't tell which. Either emotion is all wrong on her. She nods her head. On the bus, that was *good morning*, or *hi*, or *good night*. I'm so fucking flustered right now, that I'm not sure it means what it used to.

I release Ma and look at her questioningly. She knows I'm looking for answers.

She clears her throat. "I guess I don't need to introduce the two of you. Gus, I hired Scout to be my new assistant." That was tentative, even for Ma. She's trying to gloss over this as no big deal.

But now that Impatient is standing in our kitchen, I realize that it's a big deal.

I shake my head and the percussive pounding between my ears amps up. Hours ago my mind had turned Impatient into some weird regret, and now that I'm standing in the same room with her again and can feel her tightly wound constitution, all I want to do is leave and go back to bed. I don't know if it's the fact that I feel like hell, but I hope she's not still here when I wake up because this house seems all wrong with Impatient inside. Maybe this is all just a fucking dream.

As I turn around, Ma's words stop me as I exit the kitchen. "It's taco Tuesday, Gus. Don't you want something to eat?"

"No thanks, Ma. I'm not hungry." I shuffle back to my room and fall asleep the instant I drop into bed.

Wednesday, June 28
(Gus)

It's closing in on noon when I finally wake up. I stretch involuntarily, and my body doesn't protest angrily anymore. Still, the glands in my neck feel swollen ten times their normal size. I swallow, and it feels like I'm trying to force a goddamn grapefruit through a drinking straw.

I cough and immediately feel a deep, uncontrollable craving rush through my body. Cigarettes. I grab the pack and my lighter off my nightstand and step outside onto the deck.

Every puff sates my need, while simultaneously agitating the beast that's taken my glands hostage.

I struggle through two cigarettes. Struggle is not an exaggeration—if anything, I'm being too kind. I feel like my lungs are preparing for mutiny.

After a long shower, I call Ma at work.

She answers on the second ring. "Good morning, honey. How are you feeling?"

"Morning Ma. Just peachy." My scratchy voice contradicts me. "Sorry about last night. I didn't mean to bail on you. I just needed to sleep this shit off."

"It's okay. Taco leftovers are in the refrigerator, if you're hungry."

"Sounds good. Thanks. I gotta run a few errands. You need anything while I'm out?" I'm making small talk, waiting for her to come clean about Impatient. Like maybe why she didn't tell me about her sooner. I don't understand why it had to be kept secret.

"That's sweet of you, but I don't need anything. Thanks." She knows we're dancing around the issue and sounds hesitant.

"Sure. Guess I'll see you when you get home."

"Should be home around five forty-five. And don't forget Mikayla's going away party at Delgado's is tonight. It starts at seven o'clock."

"Wouldn't miss it," I answer. Because I won't miss it. Sick or not, I'm going.

Ma walks in at five forty-five on the dot. She's always been ridiculously punctual. Never early, never late, always exactly on time. I'm always late. Obviously timeliness is not hereditary.

She leaves the front door open behind her and I'm afraid to ask why, when Impatient walks in. And holy shit. If last night was a surprise, tonight just blew that out of the water.

She's wearing a black dress. The simple fabric cascades over her body from the high neckline to the cuffs of the long, silky sleeves. It's modest, except that it falls a bit above mid-thigh ... and her legs look fantastic, especially paired with the heels she's wearing. I'm a sucker for heels. Her hair is curled slightly at the ends, which somehow softens her hard features, mollifying the stringent intensity that's housed inside. I'm used to Scout in shorts and an ill-fitting, long-sleeved T-shirt, her hair hanging straight. She's normally so ordinary. Not that ordinary is bad. Not at all. She's natural and there's something to be said for that. I prefer it. And right now she's still natural. No makeup, I'm glad she doesn't try to hide her scars with it. She doesn't need it. Her hazel eyes are an odd combination of green and gold, with not a hint of brown. They're striking and outlined by thick, long black lashes.

But her natural state is now wrapped in this dress. This tasteful and professional, but ... *damn* ... sexy dress. Despite the distracting new attire, I'm curious why she's Ma's new shadow. I understand that they're working together, but why was she here last night? Why is she here tonight?

"S'up, Ma?" Again, I'm looking for answers as I hug her.

She squeezes me tight before she answers, "Hi, Gus. How are you feeling?" Her hand is on my forehead checking for fever.

I cough. My sore throat has transformed into a nagging cough this afternoon. Lucky me. "I'm good, Ma."

She shakes her head. "You don't sound good."

I nod to give her the assurance she needs. "I'm good."

The dress walks past me without a word, only a curt nod, and again I'm confused as to what it even means. The nod. Here on my turf. Is it: *Hi, How's it going,* or *Fuck you?*

I turn and watch her walk down the hall. Where in the hell is she going? And then I say it out loud. "Where in the hell is she going?"

Ma starts looking through the mail on the end table. It's a distraction so she doesn't have to look at me when she tells me something I don't want to hear. "To her room."

That's when I lose my shit. "What?! Her room?!"

Ma continues her intense scrutiny of the pile of junk mail. There's nothing worthwhile in the pile of diversion—I know because I thumbed through it when I brought it in from the mailbox this afternoon. She's stalling.

So I repeat, "What do you mean by 'her room'?"

Ma sighs and straightens her shoulders to square off against me. "Scout is staying in the guest room until she can save up for a place of her own."

I shake my head and feel the anger building inside me. All my life, anger manifested slowly, if at all. These past nine months, it's been hair trigger quick, zero to fucking irate in two seconds flat. I hate it. And I know that what I'm feeling is irrational anger, but it's the principle of the situation that irks me. This isn't Ma's fault, but I can't hold it in. I point down the hall for emphasis and lower my voice as I say, "That is Bright Side's room."

Ma stares at me as her eyes turn shiny and her chin stiffens. She's never been one to hide her emotions, but she rarely cries. Sadness chases away my anger when I see the first tear fall to her cheek. She nods; she's agreeing with me, it *is* Bright Side's room. Always has been. Always will be.

I move toward her and hug her. She holds on like months of grief are catching up with her and spilling out as she cries into my shoulder. "She doesn't have anywhere else to go, Gus. She doesn't know anyone here. She's trying to make a fresh start."

I let her cry. And talk. And I keep my mouth shut and listen. I hate seeing Ma hurting. It just crushes me. She's always been so strong. "I miss Kate, too. You know that. No one will ever replace that girl in my heart. She was like a daughter to me, her and Gracie both, but Scout needs help. She's so smart and I see so much goodness in her, so much potential. She needs a place to stay for a while, but more than that she needs a support system, Gus, and I intend to give her both."

When she sniffles, I let her go. She smiles weakly and swipes at the mascara running beneath her eyes with her thumbs. "I'd better go freshen up so we can get to Mikayla's party."

I nod and kiss her on the forehead. "I'm ready whenever you are."

Ma disappears to her room and I decide I need a cigarette

before we leave since I don't smoke in Ma's car. I'm out on the driveway, holding the flowers I bought for Mikayla this afternoon, coughing my way through cigarette number two, when I hear the front door open and close behind me. That's my signal to snub it out in the ashtray in the garage.

"You want me to drive, Ma?" I always ask.

She always declines. She's always been staunchly independent. "I'll drive."

I'm relieved, because I plan on drinking my share tonight. I'm not going to get sloppy, but I'm going to sedate.

I look to Impatient. "You wanna ride shotgun?"

She shakes her head without meeting my eyes. Fine. I'm just trying to be nice. Whatever.

Ma smiles at me as I'm fastening my seatbelt and asks, "What was your number?"

I smile back because this woman knows me. She knows I was thinking it, so I answer, "Nine."

She raises an eyebrow. "Not five? First guess is always five. Nine is risky."

I agree. "Nine is risky. What can I say, I'm a rebel."

She laughs, and it warms my heart. "The number was eight. Your rebellious streak is rewarded tonight."

Bright Side and I used to fight over shotgun. Every time. It was a rivalry held over from our childhood. To settle it Ma used to think of a number between one and ten and whoever was closest got to ride up front in the passenger seat. I suspect Ma kept track in her mind and alternated evenly between rewarding each of us with a win.

Ma's eyes are on the road as she speaks, because she's always been a cautious driver. "The flowers are lovely. Lilies. Mikayla's favorite."

They are Mikayla's favorite. I always give her lilies for her birthday, because Mikayla's like family, my favorite pseudo-auntie. I hold up the bouquet wrapped in cellophane resting in my lap. "Only the best for Mikayla."

A smile breaks out on Ma's cheek. "She'll love them."

Ma reserved a private room at Mikayla's favorite seafood restaurant, Delgado's, for the retirement party. The room is expansive, with high ceilings and white linen tablecloths. There are twenty employees from the office and they all came, most with spouses or dates. It's a good turnout and I'm glad. Mikayla deserves a proper sendoff.

Mikayla predictably goes overboard when she sees me. "Oh my gosh, who's this handsome stranger?" She reaches up and pats my hair. It's grown out to hit my mid-back, but it's still shorter than my waist long she saw last. She pulls me in for a hug.

I laugh off the compliment, set the flowers down on the table behind me, and wrap the little woman up in a hug and lift her off the ground. "How's my favorite Mikayla?" I ask.

She giggles like she does every time I do this. It's one of my favorite things about Mikayla, she's sixty-five years old, but she giggles like a child. Her laughter is pure and free of the cynicism that plagues most adult's laughter. It's also a curious juxtaposition to her serious nature. She's so smart and driven career-wise, that's something that always made Ma and her click so well. They're cut from the same cloth. But when Mikayla laughs, she lets all of that go. I've always loved that.

When I set her down and reach behind me for the bouquet, she gushes over the flowers. "Oh Gus, they're just beautiful. Thank you, sweetie."

I nod and wink. "Anytime, Kay."

After we catch up for a few minutes I excuse myself to the bar to order a Jack on the rocks. Everyone else wants their time with Mikayla too, so I make myself scarce for the moment.

When I return to the dining room everyone is taking their seats for dinner. I slip into an empty chair at the end of the table next to Ted, the mailroom dude—my replacement when I left to go on tour last fall with Rook. He's a quiet guy, but super mellow, I think it's all the weed he smokes.

Dinner is excellent. Ma went all out. It's special-occasion fancy, with whole steamed lobster for the shellfish fiends and some kind of pasta dish that I call *heavenly-mind-blowing-noodle-fucking-fantasy* for me. And wine. Lots of wine.

Dinner segues into dessert, which segues into more wine, which segues into ... you guessed it ... more wine. Even though my cough still clutches at my throat, and is persistent as hell, I'm enjoying myself. A bottle or two of red will do that.

After a quick stop in the restroom to empty the bladder, I step outside for a cigarette. Ted's already outside smoking, too. He finishes up before I do and announces, "I gotta take a piss, bro," and walks away. I turn and take a final drag before tossing what's left out into the street. When I turn back I walk right into Impatient.

"Whoa, hey," I say. Then, "Sorry," because I knocked her off balance. Her high-heeled shoes don't help matters.

She nods quickly as she rights herself. "Audrey's looking for you. They're cutting the cake for Mikayla."

I rub my belly, because there's always room for cake. "Sweet." I could do with some cake. And besides that, I'm pleasantly buzzed.

A loud train whistle emits from my pocket. It's Franco's text alert. I slip out my cell and take a look as we walk back into the restaurant. The message reads, *Been here 5 minutes and already got laid!* Attached is a photo of Franco, Jamie, and Robbie standing at the entrance of a hotel wearing colorful leis around their necks. Looks like they made it to Hawaii.

I laugh and text back, *Enjoy it loser. It's the only action your sorry ass will get all week.*

After I hit send, I look up at Impatient who's looking at me questioningly. She doesn't want to be, but I can tell that she's curious.

I shrug, still smiling from Franco's text. "What?"

She shakes her head like she's going to blow me off, but then asks, "Franco?"

I nod. "How'd you know?"

"You're smiling. He's the only person that can get you to smile like that." She walks away, back into the restaurant, before I can question her. So I ponder it a second. She's right. That shithead is my link to any shred of happiness lately.

Saturday, July 1
(Gus)

I have that nagging voice in my head still, pleading with me to call Keller again. It's persistent, but has really amped up in both enthusiasm and bossiness this week. And this morning it's managed to bully every other thought out of my head.

It's early morning, so I grab my cigarettes, lighter, and phone, and head out to the deck. After I smoke a cigarette, I bring up his number on my cell. I was going to text, but my fingers are shaking so damn bad that I can't type, so I opt for a call instead. I'm dreading hearing his voice, because it's going to open up the Bright Side wound. Keller was her boyfriend. He sat there holding one of her hands, me holding the other, when she died. When cancer stole her from us. He's a good guy, but I can't separate him from Bright Side in my mind. I can't think about him independently. The damn guy loved her fiercely. Which is why I need to call him. He's the only person who can relate to my grief, my pain. On the other end, the phone rings. And rings. No answer. I almost hang up, but then I realize that my stomach is in knots and I don't want to go through this again later, so when I hear the prompt to leave a voicemail, I start talking. "Keller. Dude, it's Gus. Long time no talk." I pause and nausea roils inside. "Yeah ... so ... I was just calling to see how you and Miss Stella are doing? Give me a call sometime, so I know ... that everything's okay in Minnesota. You know ... that you guys are okay. Okay. Later."

I press the red circle on the touchscreen to end the call. I want to throw my phone over the deck railing, as far as I can, but I squeeze it in my palm instead, and then slam it face down on the wooden tabletop.

And then I light another cigarette. That phone call was a bad idea. My heart can't handle it.

When I finish up my smoke, I decide that breakfast is in order.

Impatient is in the kitchen. She's dressed in running shorts and a loose, long-sleeved T-shirt. Her face is flushed and I can see beads of sweat on her forehead. She's drinking a glass of water. I find myself wondering how scarred her arms are because I've

97

never seen her in anything other than long-sleeves. And it's fucking hot outside.

"Hey," I say. It's our standard greeting, if we decide not to substitute it for a non-verbal nod. It works. It's what we do. It's how we tolerate each other, I guess.

"Hey," she answers, equally disinterested.

I pull the carton of eggs out of the fridge, along with butter and milk. "How many miles?" I ask.

"Huh?" She turns toward me, looking surprised.

I point at her running shoes. "How many miles did you run this morning?"

She looks down at her feet like she needs a visual aid to process the question. "Oh. Eight."

I'm surprised. "You ran eight fucking miles this morning?" I've been running a little lately, but a couple of miles is a monumental task for me. And that's if I walk half of it.

"I'm registered for a marathon in a couple of weeks."

I begin to crack five eggs into a bowl, then pour in some milk. "Ever ran a marathon before?"

She shakes her head. "Nope. First time."

As I put the skillet on the stove I ask, "Want some eggs?"

She starts to shake her head. I wouldn't expect her to say yes, since she never accepts anything I offer her, but then she stops. "Do you have enough for both of us?"

I open the carton back up to show her the four remaining eggs.

"Sure. I guess. I haven't eaten anything since last night."

I cook our eggs. She continues to drink her water. We're eating in silence when my cell rings from inside my pocket. I slip it out and the first thing I notice, because I can't fucking help it, is the shattered screen. Must have happened when I slammed it down on the table. "Shit," I mutter. Then I notice the name of the person calling, and I freeze up. "Shit," I mutter again.

Impatient looks at me quizzically.

I want her to ask me if I'm okay. *Just fucking ask me*, because I need to tell someone I'm not. I'm not okay, not even close. I hit "ignore" and set the phone down on the table. Keller's name remains on my screen for a few more seconds before the call goes to voicemail and he disappears.

GUS

Ask me who it was! I want to yell at her. *Ask me why my heart can't take that conversation right now. Ask me why I can't get over her. Ask me why my best friend had to die. Or no, better yet, tell me why my best friend had to die. Tell me. Please. Explain it to me. I want to know. I need to know why I'm supposed to go through the rest of my life without being able to talk to her. Hug her. Hear her laugh. Watch the sunset with her. Watch her play her violin. Kiss her forehead. Tell her I love her. Hear her say it back. Why? Why?!*

Dragging my hands down my face, I try to rub away the hysteria that's building inside me. I push the chair back from the table and leave my plate of eggs half-eaten.

I go outside and I smoke a cigarette.

It doesn't help, but I do it anyway.

Sunday, July 2
(Gus)

There's a sticky note on my bedroom door when I open it.

Your new phone is on the kitchen counter.

I lost my phone several times while we were on tour and Impatient always managed to get it replaced for me. After the first time she helped, I put her name on my account so she could handle things without me even being involved.

I guess she's still handling things for me.

I don't know whether to be pissed or relieved.

I decide on a little bit of both.

Wednesday, July 5
(Gus)

My flu or cold, whatever the hell it was, has all but disappeared. Ma's been pumping me full of vitamin C in all its forms, the damn thing didn't have any choice but to flee and go pick on somebody else.

The guys are back from Hawaii. We all went surfing this morning and had lunch this afternoon. Tales of Oahu filled the first few hours, and then it shifted to music. Our music, specifically. The next album. The one, that under our contract, we're supposed to have recorded by the end of January. It's July. That's seven months away. Which wouldn't be such a stretch, if we had some new material. We don't. Which is kind of a pisser because it's all on me. I write our music. I write our lyrics. And I haven't written anything worth a shit since "Finish Me" last fall.

I can't bring myself to it. There's a block. I don't know if it's an unconscious choice that my mind's making or it's an unconscious choice that my heart's making. Either way, I'm fucked. Music has always been a part of me, an extension of my feelings, my life, my experiences. Ever since Bright Side died, every creative part of me has been stifled. Silenced. If she wasn't there writing with me, she was always the first person I shared a new song with. She had an ear for music like no one I've ever met. I loved her approval. Craved it. It made me want to write more, just so I could see her eyes light up when I played her something new. I'd give anything to see that gleam again, because without it, without her, I feel empty. My life lost purpose, and my creativity vanished completely.

How do I tell that to my bandmates? MFDM? The label? Our tour manager? *I'd love to help you out, you know, with your careers, your livelihood, but I'm a fucking barren wasteland. All tapped out.* That would go over like a turd in a fucking punchbowl. They're depending on me and I've got nothing for them. I feel like shit.

So, I skirt the issue. Again. "I'm working through a few songs, but I'm not ready to share any of it yet, dude. Give me a couple of weeks."

Yeah, in another month I'll still be in this sinking ship. It's going down fast. I feel sorry for the rest of them, because this sonofabitch doesn't even have life preservers.

Franco's over tonight. He had dinner with Ma, Impatient, and me. It was a nice change. I felt relaxed and calm. I actually laughed. Ma laughed. Even Impatient laughed, which is almost unheard of. I liked hearing it. But, that's Franco for you. He's likable. He's got charisma and no one's immune to its effects.

After the dishes are done, Franco heads out to the deck. "Come on, Scout. We're taking the debauchery outside so cock lobster can smoke."

"That's Mr. Cock Lobster to you," I taunt. It's so good to have him around, but away from anything music related. There's no pressure. Impatient pauses at the sliding door to the deck. I know she won't follow us out. She never comes out here just to hang out. There's always some excuse. It's okay; I wouldn't want to spend time with me either.

So when she steps out on to the deck, I'm surprised. She walks to the railing and leans over to take in the view. I know Franco and I aren't going to finish this evening sober, so I retrieve a bottle of whiskey from my room. When I return she's sitting across the table from Franco. She's sitting, as always, with her back favoring the left side of the chair, while her legs are crossed at the knee toward the right. This puts her in the perfect position to present us with the left half of her face, while keeping the scars hidden for the most part. It makes me wonder if this is habit or if she consciously makes an effort with everything she does.

After opening the bottle and taking a swig, I set it down in front of her.

She shakes her head minutely. It's a quiet refusal, but I can't tell if it's judgment or a gesture that isn't meant to offend. She's tricky sometimes. "I don't drink, Gustov."

I roll my eyes, grab the bottle, and tip back another gulp.

Then Franco takes the bottle from me and pours some into the water glass he carried out with him. I knew he'd be down for this. It's been a while since the two of us have had drinks together. We don't go out to clubs anymore, now that Rook's getting more popular. We always get recognized in places like that and that makes me a little uncomfortable. The whole concept of "fans" still weirds me out. I understand they're into the music. I get that. Hell,

I'm fanatical about certain music, too. But, that's the difference. I appreciate what they create. The people are just people. Not that they're not cool, at least some of them, but they're still just people. It's freaky when people shift into idolizing mode. When they forget you're a person and you turn into a name. You become your fame. You're not you anymore.

"Come on, it's not going to kill you to have a few drinks with friends."

She flashes her eyes at me and I can't help but feel like the "friends" label is pushing it. Are we? Friends?

I offer the bottle. "Bottoms up, sweetheart."

"I don't drink," she repeats. Then her eyes light up. "Wanna play Mancala?" She's almost smiling, like that was a dare.

"Hell yeah," I say, breaking into a huge smile. "Franco and I are always down for a little trash-talking game of Mancala." I don't know why that just made me so happy, but it did. It did.

Friday, July 14
(Gus)

I've been working this week in the mailroom at Ma's advertising firm. Ted's on vacation and Ma was going to hire a temp to cover, but I know this job inside and out—I did it for a couple of years. And it's not rocket science. So I volunteered to help out. Little does Ma know she's helping me out. I surf every morning, but I can't sit in that house anymore during the day by myself or I might lose it. I've been sitting home alone for a couple of weeks now. Solitude doesn't foster happiness, at least not for me. Not at this point in my life.

It's not that I really want to be around people either, but that I need to be busy. And I don't need to think about this job. I can just do it.

Which is better than my real job. Music. Too much thinking.

Monday, July 17
(Gus)

Ted never came back from vacation. I told Ma I'd help her out as long as she needs me, until she finds someone else. I'm kinda hoping it takes a month or two.

Friday, July 21
(Gus)

Ma hired someone for the mailroom. He starts on Monday.
Which means I go back to my real life on Monday.
I don't want to go back to my real life on Monday.

Sunday, July 23
(Gus)

It's the middle of the afternoon and I'm fucking restless. The water's too crowded to surf. There's nothing on TV. Ma's at a baby shower this afternoon. The deck is too quiet. I sat out there for the past couple of hours, drank, and smoked a pack of cigarettes. Now, I'm antsy. I can't sit still. I can't turn my goddamn mind off.

I don't want to be outside.

I don't want to be inside.

I'm at the point where I just ... *don't*. I know that doesn't make any fucking sense, but it's how I feel. *I don't.*

When I go back in my room for another pack of smokes I can hear Impatient's voice. I ignore it at first, but I realize that it sounds like she's in pain. I rush to her bedroom and her door's open, which is unusual. She's lying on top of the covers in a pair of running shorts and a long-sleeved T-shirt. And she's deep in sleep. Scary deep. Like if a meteorite fell from the sky and landed in the middle of the room it wouldn't wake her. My first inclination is to nudge her awake because I think she's in the middle of a nightmare, but the longer I stand and watch her, the more confusing the whole scene is. She keeps saying, "Michael," over and over again. Every time she says it, her face somehow morphs from pain to pleasure, from heart-wrenching sadness to ecstasy. Then she begins to moan. She's still in deep REM sleep and I know I'm in a fucked up state of mind and I've had more than my share to drink today, but ... *goddamn.* This just turned erotic as fuck. And now the moaning is mixed with, "Michael," again. Her voice is almost breathless now.

I should not be here. There's no doubt that she's mentally having some mind-blowing sex right now. I feel like a voyeur. Not only is my drunk mind getting turned on, but my drunk body is two steps ahead of it. I'm beyond aroused.

That's my cue to leave. But just as I step away from her doorway, across the hall, and back into mine, the depth and volume of her voice increases. Every negative emotion has left her and all that remains is the satisfying of pure need. Carnal need. There's room for nothing else, and it's somehow invaded me. *The need.*

I'm inside my room now. Door open. Eyes closed. Hand inside my shorts. Stroking.

Fucking stroking.

Holy shit.

This is fucked up.

I need to take a cold shower.

And forget this ever happened.

Monday, July 31
(Gus)

Ma and I had a long talk last night. She's concerned about me. My life. My health. My emotional state. My work. My future.

She made an appointment for me to have a physical with our family doctor. I'm in the waiting room now. I hate doctors' offices. They remind me of Bright Side. Bright Side at the end.

Dr. Donnelly was direct and to the point and covered all the basics: eat better, quit smoking, curb my drinking. I'm good otherwise. She likes that I'm surfing or running almost daily.

I didn't share any of the emotional shit.

I'll deal with that myself.

I'll heal myself.

Someday.

Sunday, August 6
(Gus)

Ma's out of town for the weekend. She drove up the coast to cut loose in San Francisco. It's good for Ma, she works hard and deserves the break. She always comes home a little lighter in the stress department when she's had a weekend away.

The house is quiet. I know I should be writing, but this block is still weighing on me. If you want to know the truth, it's bearing down full-force now. It's all I can think about—the fact that I can't think. Creatively, I'm at a standstill—completely mind-fucked. It was irritating at first. But, after a month, and with mounting pressure from everyone involved with the band—agents, managers, producers, the record label, etc. *fucking* etc.—it feels like a prison sentence. Music fills me with anxiety. It used to just fill me. I guess that's the difference money, contracts, and deadlines make. It's utter shit.

So I'm drinking.

A lot.

By Monday morning I'll wonder if Saturday and Sunday even happened, or if the entire time lapse was a hallucination—that's how much I intend to drink.

After a quick trip to the liquor store to buy Jack and cigarettes, I park myself in the lounge chair on the deck.

An hour later, I'm halfway through the first bottle and in need of a bathroom break. On my way back outside, I find Impatient in the living room.

She's wearing a scowl and it's aimed at the bull's-eye that seems to be me.

I'm in no mood for her shit today. We're usually civil, not friendly necessarily, but civil. But not today. I'm anxious and pissy, and unfortunately it looks like I'm about to take that out on her. "You know what your problem is?" I snarl. "You just need to get laid." Minus the alcohol I wouldn't say that to her, but my filter is suspended at the moment.

She physically sways like I slapped her. "What?"

I'm buzzing enough that this has just reached an entertaining level and I intend to continue. "*Fucked*," I say it slowly, enunciating the word and pointing at her. "You. You're wound way too tight.

You need to go get laid. The situation is dire, dude." And now I'm thinking about her dreaming a couple of weeks ago and exactly what she sounds like when she's getting physical.

She huffs. She's not amused, and I wouldn't expect her to be. Honestly, that's the reason I'm pushing this. "Not everything is about sex," she says.

I nod. It's been so long since I've slept with anyone, she may actually be on to something, but then I remember I've been pissed all day and I dive back into my aggression. "Only a fucking virgin would say something like that. Is that what's going on? No wonder you're so goddamn frigid." I don't know why I'm talking to her like this, but I am. And I can't stop. I hate it. After knowing her for a few months, I know she's more shy than anything else. Introversion is her coping mechanism. And after listening to that dream, I know there's no goddamn way she's a virgin.

Her face is blazing now. She's angry, like pick-up-the-lamp-and-throw-it-across-the-room angry. "Fuck you, Gustov. You don't know anything about me."

Shit. She's never cussed me out before. Now I'm looking at her bare legs and my thoughts are getting scrambled and I can't focus on anything else except the fact that we're arguing with each other about sex. My anger is morphing quickly. "Name the last time. I want to hear it." I want details too, because apparently I'm a sick bastard.

She's glaring. Those hazel eyes are boring a hole through my forehead.

I know I should just let it go, but this is the most we've talked in weeks and even though we're fighting, I don't want to stop. On some weird, irrational level, I need this. So, I push. "When?"

Her eyes drop, and so does her shield. It's only a few moments but there's regret or vulnerability, something I didn't expect. "New Year's Eve," she whispers. And then just as quickly, the shield goes back up and her eyes meet mine. She's staring and she's biting the inside of her cheek. Then her eyelids start blinking double time and they're getting glassy. The shield slips again. "He's an asshole."

"Boyfriend?" I question. My heart's beating a million miles a minute. I hate seeing anyone hurt and even though I was pushing her hard, now that she's crumbling I feel like hell. My emotions are on a fucking roller coaster, up one second, down the next. Alcohol doesn't help. I really need to stop drinking.

A single tear slips down her cheek and she quickly wipes it away with the back of her hand and fixes her angry eyes on me again. The laugh that escapes is contempt. "You're all the same, right? It *is* all about sex, like you said earlier. Maybe that's why you've never been in love."

That one simple sentence sets off a firestorm inside me. Bright Side's face flickers in front of me. Smiling. Light green eyes sparkling with mischief. She's been gone for months and I'm still fucking in love with her. It's my turn. I spit her own words back at her. "Fuck you. You don't know anything about me."

The attack doesn't faze her. She shakes her head. She's brushing me off again. "Oh, I know you. I watched you hook up with a different woman every night during the first half of the tour. That's not love."

I step toward her. I'm so close I can see the mossy green ring that wraps around each of her pupils. "Maybe I'm not looking for love." I eye her up and down. Damn, those long legs. They're distracting me again. And I'm suddenly ten shades of turned on.

She raises her chin defiantly and locks eyes with me. She rarely makes eye contact. "Obviously." It's sarcastic and scornful, but the emotion she's showing is real. She's let her guard down completely now. She's vulnerable, but strong at the same time. It's almost like when she's pushed, her strength rears its head.

"Obviously," I echo. My eyes have drifted to her mouth. Her lips are full and pursed into that pissy pout of hers.

She shifts her weight and the result is a determined challenge. She's not backing down from me. We're almost chest-to-chest and my fucking groin is aching. I don't know quite when this showdown transitioned from anger to lust. I suppose they're on the same spectrum — it all boils down to passion.

I glance back up to her eyes and they're zeroed in on my mouth, pupils dilated. Her breathing increases and her cheeks flush. I know this look. I've seen it a hundred times. I can feel the sexual tension radiating off of her body in waves.

Usually in this situation I'm thinking about sex, just sex; an act to satisfy a need. But looking at her right now, so open and vulnerable, all I want to do is kiss her.

I tip my head down until my forehead is resting against hers. She doesn't pull away, but tilts her face slightly to the right. She's trying to hide, even though our foreheads are still touching.

"Hey," I coax softly. My emotions have done a three-sixty from antagonistic, to sexual, to protective. It's the fucking roller coaster.

She flinches and turns her head even more making eye contact impossible.

With my forehead still resting against her left temple, I realize that I need to walk away before this gets carried away. If I kiss her I won't want to stop, and the look in her eyes a few seconds ago tells me she wouldn't stop me. "You were too good for him," I say. "And you should be looking for love, which is why I need to go back outside. You're too good for me, too." She is. She's smart and goal-oriented, she works hard, she takes care of herself, and she's beautiful. Most of all, she's fragile. I don't want to be just another ass who breaks her. I kiss her temple as tenderly as I can. It's an apology. "Sorry for everything I said earlier," I say quietly, and I turn to walk away, back to my bottle of Jack.

(Scout)

Holy.
Shit.
My heart is beating so hard and so fast I have some genuine concern that it may explode. I don't know where that came from. The argument. My admission. The attraction. It all came out of nowhere and even though Gustov's gone back outside, I'm still reeling. I can still feel the heat of his body against mine. I can still see the passion in his eyes. I can still feel the need tingling through me. The heat spreading. I've never experienced anything like that before. It was undeniable and irrational lust.

I need to go for a run and clear my head.

Friday, August 11
(Gus)

There's a sticky note on my door when I wake up. *Marathon is tomorrow. Audrey and I are leaving at 7:00AM if you want to come.*

That's an unexpected invitation. I know it must have taken a lot for her to write that note, especially after our encounter last weekend.

And if she's willing to invite me, I guess I'm willing to accept.

Besides, I need to get out of the house.

Saturday, August 12
(Scout)

I ran my first marathon today. I wasn't fast, but I feel a sense of accomplishment that I don't think I've ever felt before. I pushed myself preparing for it. Running started as a nothing more than a way to cope with everything this past spring. It was an escape, a distraction, a way to block out life. But it turned into a way to prove a point to myself that I was strong.

I am strong. Physically, I'm strong.

Mentally, well, that's another story.

But today during the race, every time I was struggling and I felt like I was ready to give up, Audrey and Gustov would pop up along the route and cheer me on. No one's ever cheered me on like that. So enthusiastically. Not for anything. It was the encouragement I needed for the mental part of this game to keep up with the physical game.

I don't know if I'll ever run another marathon. I feel like I've gained so much perspective today. I'll never stop running, but this goal has been conquered. Now I can continue running, for me. Just for me. Because it reminds me that I'm strong. In every way, I'm strong and getting stronger.

I thanked Audrey before heading to bed.

I tried to thank Gustov, but his bedroom door was shut. I know he was inside because I could hear music playing—the blues, something bone deep sad and emotional. I didn't want to knock, so I left a sticky note instead. *Thanks for coming today. I don't think I would've finished without you guys.* I feel like a barrier is slowly lifting between us. Even when our interaction isn't so positive, there's always something to gain as far as insight into how he ticks. There's a struggle deep within both of us, but after today, everything feels a little lighter. I saw him grin more today than I've ever seen. It's a small step, but it was real.

Saturday, August 19
(Gus)

The doorbell is ringing. It's been ringing for a couple of minutes. Jesus, can no one else in this house answer the door? I'm tired and I'm hungover. I don't want to get out of bed. I shoot a peek at the clock on my nightstand. Nine-fifty. Guess I should get up. The doorbell rings again, as if to second the motion.

After I put on some shorts, I head for the front door. The shades are drawn and the whole house is dark. Rubbing the sleep out of my eyes with the heel of my hand, I open the door. I'm met with blinding sunlight and it's way too damn bright for my current state. I squint my eyes and hold my hand up to shield my eyes from the glare that's taunting my receding state of drunkenness. I blink my eyes, adjusting to the brightness, and realize that whoever is standing before me hasn't said a word. I slowly draw my hand away from my face to reveal a man standing before me. I squint again to take him in. He's manicured and styled in that I'm-a-douchebag-rich-fuck kind of way: expensive suit, matching tie, shiny shoes, perfect hair, and glistening white teeth straight out of a toothpaste commercial. He still hasn't spoken a word, but his ego precedes him. He projects it out in front of him like a warning. Or an accolade. I'm tempted to shut the door in his face. Instead, I talk to him. "What can I do you for, *buddy*?" I ask, laying on the sarcasm. Truth be told, I couldn't care less who he is.

He clears his throat and the self-important voice that always accompanies a cocky douchebag answers. "I'm looking for Scout MacKenzie."

I eye him hard. I don't know who he is, but I'm not getting a good vibe from him. "What do you want with her?"

He smirks and if it's possible I dislike him even more for his bold, pretentious manner. "Scout and I are old friends. I was in town and wanted to say hi."

For two seconds I consider shutting the door on him again, but then I question him instead. "She know you're stopping by?"

He shakes his head and the smirk slips before it's replaced by a wolfish grin. "No. I thought I would surprise her."

I don't like this guy and for some reason I don't want him

116

looking for Impatient. I don't want her to *want him* looking for her. I need to go back to bed and start this day over. I sigh. "Hold on. I don't know if she's home. Lemme go check," I shut the door on him and finish my sentence. "*Dick.*"

Just then Impatient walks into the room. She's dressed for her morning run. I motion over my shoulder. "Door's for you."

Her eyebrows knit together. "For me?"

I nod and sidestep her so she can answer the door this time and I can remove myself from the situation. But I don't leave the room. I know I should give her privacy, but with the alarms this guy's already set off, I'm not leaving her alone with him. I stand out of sight, but within earshot.

When she opens the door she gasps. It's not fear. It's shock. "Michael?"

Fucking Michael. Ex-boyfriend-call-out-his-name-when-she's-on-the-verge-of-an-orgasm *fucking Michael.*

"Hi, angel." His salutation is smarmy and way too smooth, like it's been rehearsed. She isn't buying this, is she?

"Hi." She doesn't return his enthusiasm.

One point to Scout. Zero points to *fucking Michael.*

"How'd you find me?"

I instinctively take one step closer. I didn't like the sound of that at all.

"I talked to Jane. She gave me your new address. I needed to see you again. I've missed you, angel." He's laying it on thick. I can't see his face to know what kind of a show he's putting on for her, but I can hear the insincerity in his voice. He knows exactly what to say to her, but he's forgotten the part where he should actually mean it.

I can't see Impatient either, I'm behind the door, but I can feel the tug of war going on inside her. She's not scared, but she's apprehensive. "Michael." Her voice caresses his name hesitantly. Like she's said it, exactly like that, a thousand times before. "I think you need to leave." Her words say one thing while her voice says something else altogether.

I don't like hearing the need in her voice, the not-quite-forgotten love from deep within her.

"Aww, come on, angel. Let me take you out to breakfast. We need to talk. It's over with Melissa. We need to talk about us."

117

There's movement on the other side of the door. I get the sense that he's touching her and my fists ball up at my sides.

"Please go, Michael." It's a weak plea. I've never heard her sound so weak. I don't think she wants him to go.

I can't hold back. "You heard the woman, chief. It's time for you to leave." I step forward and open the door the rest of the way so I can stare him down. I've got three or four inches of height on the guy and he's got a good fifteen to twenty years on me. I usually don't try to intimidate, but I'm trying my damnedest right now.

He looks at Impatient and the look in his eyes is possessive ... and pissed. "Who's he?"

She sighs like she would rather be anywhere else but here. "Michael," she says again, with hesitant affection wrapped around his name, "this is Gustov Hawthorne. I work for his mother. She's been nice enough to let me live here for a few months until I can save up enough money to find a place of my own."

The smirk emerges again and I want to reach out and tear it off his goddamn face. When he looks at me, his air of authority returns, and with it I see her resolve start to fall away. She's putty in his hands. He knows how to fucking work her emotions like she's nothing but a marionette. He sees it, too, and I hate him for it. "Get your jacket, Scout. I'm taking you to breakfast," he commands.

I want her to say no and tell him to fuck off, but instead her shoulders sag and she obeys like a child. "Give me a minute. I'll be right back." She retreats to her bedroom and returns with a sweatshirt on over her long-sleeved T-shirt, running shorts and shoes still in place.

And then she disappears out the door with him. And something I can't explain happens inside me. My chest tightens and there's a lump in my throat. It's jealousy. And protectiveness. And desire. And crushing, fucking helplessness.

(Scout)

Inside my head, I'm screaming at myself. *What the hell, Scout! Don't be stupid. Don't set yourself back. You don't need him.*

But my body betrays me. It follows him to his rental car and climbs inside when he opens the door. It was that easy. Down the rabbit hole I go ... again.

When he climbs in behind the wheel his face is triumphant. He knows he won ... again.

Looks like I'm the fool. And fucked ... again.

We eat at a small burrito place just down the road from Audrey's. He makes small talk. Tells me how he's been traveling a lot. Tells me how many new accounts his firm has secured in the past several months. Tells me about the new boat he bought last month. None of it is important. He's just trying to impress me. It used to work. It's probably what lured me in three years ago. Back when I was a freshman at NYU — young and impressionable. We met at the coffee shop around the corner from my subway stop. He lived in Miami, but traveled to New York once a month on business. He was older and handsome and charming and he looked at me like I was the most beautiful thing he'd ever seen. No one had ever looked at me like that. And when I talked, he listened. He wanted to spend time with me. I fell in love with that. My first and only love. Looking back, I know that didn't last. I didn't see it though. I didn't see him looking at other woman when he was out with me. I didn't see his mind wandering when I talked. I didn't notice that our time together was more and more confined to sex, quick and hard, and for his pleasure, no longer mine. But I couldn't detach myself from him. He became my addiction. He still is apparently, because I'm sitting here with him, in his company, when I most definitely should be anywhere else. I feel dirty. I feel used. I feel lesser. But I can't leave. I hate that the most. I hate that I need to leave, but that I *can't*.

So, when we finish up and he confirms it's over with Melissa, and suggests we go back to his hotel, I nod. I go with him.

The lights remain off, as always, but the instant I hear the latch catch behind me, he's got me pinned up against the hotel room door with his body. His mouth is on mine, hot and demanding. I take it and my body starts heating up. I don't want my body to react to him, to his absence, but it does. He's the only man I've ever been with. The throbbing between my legs is building, which makes me feel weak. Like a failure. Like a traitor.

Like a bad person. But I can't help it. He's familiar.

He's already undoing his belt and unbuttoning his pants. And I'm unbuttoning his dress shirt. He always undresses first. When he's done he commands me to strip from the waist down. I do. Then he bends me over the arm of the sofa and takes me from behind. It's rough. The first six months we were together, we had mutually satisfying sex. The past couple of years, he fucks me. I don't like that part. But I'm used to it. His pounding body feels like it's punishing me. His hands dig into my hips so hard I know he'll leave me marked. My body slams into the sofa with each thrust. I can feel the beginnings of a bruise on each hip bone from the repeated impact. He's grunting like he always does, like an animal satisfying a primal need. I used to think it was sexy, but not anymore. I'm quiet, as always. He doesn't like it when I make any noise. Sometimes I think it's so he can pretend I'm not here. When I'm silent, I'm just a body being used to satisfy carnal depravation. I can feel his hot breath on my back through the material of my T-shirt. It brings stinging tears to my eyes. The grunts give way to his gravelly voice in my ear. "My cock's missed you, angel," he says. Then, "Shit. Shit. Shit. Shit," like he always says, between gritted teeth, when he finishes. And it always sounds like he's disdainfully congratulating himself on getting off. Complimenting his ego on a job well done.

I haven't had an orgasm during sex with him in well over a year.

When he pulls out, he plants a solitary, almost chaste kiss on the small of my back. It's my consolation, the romantic finishing touch, for accommodating him. Then he walks to the bathroom and I hear the shower turn on. He always showers immediately after sex, but I don't know if he washes away the guilt. I don't think so. I don't think he even feels guilt. I think he just wants to wash away ... me.

And I let him.

Until the next time.

I thought I was stronger. I thought I had changed. I thought I was better than this.

I guess not.

Michael just proved that.

When he comes back out from the bathroom he's dressed in his suit again, looking totally unaffected. He'll return to small talk as he escorts me out. He never takes me home. That's how it always works.

He extends his hand out, palm up. "Phone." He's telling me to give him my phone. Commanding.

I shouldn't, but I hand it to him. It's a new phone I got when I moved to San Diego. A new phone number. A number he didn't have. Until now.

He programs in his cell number and sends a text to himself. He smiles that wolfish smile as he opens the hotel room door and hands the phone back to me. His smile seems to say *you're welcome* and *good-bye*. It's narcissism at its best. Then he says, "I'll see you soon." And lastly, he shuts the door on me, dismissing me. He leaves me standing in the hallway. Hating myself.

I feel so weak. I am not strong.

But I also know I will not see him again.

I'm done.

This is over.

Sunday, August 20
(Scout)

After yesterday, I know I need to get my shit together. I need to start making changes to move my life forward in a more positive direction. And after talking to Audrey this morning, and hearing her encouragement and generous offer to help, I know where I need to start. Paxton.

I called my aunt and uncle first. I thought they would be more resistant to my idea, but they were surprisingly supportive and almost sounded relieved, which was bittersweet and made me feel both happy and sad: happy because I know what this will mean for Paxton, and sad because, once again, they are removing themselves from his upbringing, putting their parenting responsibilities on someone else. Luckily, it's a responsibility I'll gladly accept.

I call Paxton next.

"Hi, Scout." He sounds preoccupied.

"Hey, Paxton. What's goin' on?"

"Just playing my Xbox." That explains the preoccupation.

"You think you could turn it off for a couple of minutes and talk to me? It's kind of important."

I hear him fumbling around and his voice sounds on edge, nervous. "What's wrong?"

I smile, so he hears the reassurance in my voice. "Nothing's wrong. This is good news. I think."

"Okay." He doesn't sound convinced.

"I want you to move to San Diego. Next weekend. Finish your senior year out here."

Silence. I know it's stunned silence, but it still makes me nervous.

"Paxton?"

"Yeah," he says, sounding stunned. Stunned doesn't even touch what's going on.

"What do you think? You'd be living in the basement here at my boss's house. She's offered for both of us to stay as long as we need to. Until I can get a car and an apartment for us. She's so nice, you'll love her."

More silence. I know this is a lot to take in.

122

"Paxton?"

"Yeah," he says. He's thinking. I can hear his mind racing.

"What do you think?" I repeat.

"I can't believe it," he's talking to himself under his breath.

"Is that a yes?"

"For real, Scout?" The hope in his voice is almost heartbreaking.

"Yes."

He sniffs. If he's not crying, he's trying hard not to. "Yes, I wanna come, definitely." He pauses. "You sure this is for real?"

And now I'm smiling because I've never been able to give someone a gift like this, to change their life. It's the best feeling in the world. "It's real. So now I'm going to let you go and buy your airline ticket for next weekend. I'll email you the itinerary as soon as I have it. Start packing, okay?"

"Okay," he says. "Thank you. Really." His voice projects pure happiness. And I love hearing it.

"Have a great afternoon, Paxton. We'll talk soon."

"Thanks Scout. You too."

Sunday, August 27
(Scout)

Paxton's plane lands in fifteen minutes and we're stuck in traffic. We're going to be late. I hate being late. I have United's website open on my phone to the flight arrival screen and I've been refreshing it about every thirty seconds for the past half hour — as if with the plane this close, there's going to be some type of delay. Clearly, I'm obsessive.

I'm tapping out the beat to the song on the radio on my knee, not because I like the song, but because I can't sit still. Fidgeting is a nervous habit of mine, and I hate it. I wish I could generate calm at will. I've tried meditating, but I can't quiet my mind. It can be a beast sometimes.

Staring out the passenger window, chewing the inside of my cheek, I feel Gustov's hand on top of mine pressing it to my thigh. I turn to look at his hand. He's never touched me like this before and I can't deny that I'm feeling it everywhere, not just my hand. It sends currents shooting right through the heart of me. And just as quickly, his hand is gone.

"Relax. We'll get there. I promise." He always sounds so sure of himself, even when I know he's not.

"I just don't like being late," I explain, trying to justify my worry.

He huffs good-naturedly. "Probably should've asked someone else to drive you then. Tardy's my middle name, dude."

Looking over at him, I sigh. I know he's right. It's stupid that I get myself so worked up. He's completely relaxed, wearing that sleepy grin that I see more and more these days. "Sorry," I say.

"No worries, *Impatient.*"

Looking at him with narrowed eyes, I ask, "Did you just call me *Impatient?*"

He nods and fake coughs. "Yeah, it's kinda been my nickname for you. Like, ever since I first met you. I hate to tell you this," he says, lowering his voice slightly, "but you're fucking impatient." His eyes are wide when he says it, and he's smirking — but he's not being mean.

I huff ... and then take a deep breath ... and then I admit it. "I know I am." I widen my eyes back at him. "I'm *fucking* impatient."

124

"Admitting the problem is the first step to recovery. Maybe there's a twelve-step program?"

I smile. "Does it bother you? You obviously noticed it a long time ago. I had no idea that my impatience was worthy of a nickname."

He shakes his head. "At first maybe a little, but that's because my own life was so jacked. Not anymore though. Can't judge when you don't know what kind of shit someone else is dealing with. I've learned that the past few months. I have a feeling your heart is heavy, and when your heart is heavy, everything's harder. Dealing with life is harder. Believe me, I know. The negative is amplified, and sometimes that extinguishes the peace."

"Peace." I huff again. "I don't think we've met."

"You'll find it; someday you'll find it." He winks. "Trust me."

"I do," I whisper. I don't know if he even heard me. But I do. I don't know why, but I do. We're quiet for the rest of the ride.

When we pull up to the doors outside baggage claim, Paxton is standing there with a big smile on his face. I think he saw Gustov's truck before I spotted him. Gustov's truck is hard to miss: it's old, rusty, beat-up, and two different colors—the cab is one color and the bed is another. But I love it. I love it because I know he has enough money to buy just about any new car he could ever want. But what does he drive? He drives this POS that he's had for years. And I'm pretty sure if someone offered him a million dollars for it tomorrow, he'd turn it down. I. Love. That.

My chest is tightening with excitement and happiness as Paxton abandons his suitcases and starts running toward me. I hadn't realized how much I've missed being around him ... until now. He's my family. My one and only true friend.

I hug him and I feel like I'm home. I haven't felt like this in years. Paxton has always been home for me.

"Thank you, Scout," he says, his arms wrapped around me, his voice full of relief. He may be a teenage boy, but he's never been one to hold back his emotions with me.

I squeeze him harder. "You're welcome. I'm glad you're here." I release him and step back. He's beaming. He's taller than last time I saw him; we're eye to eye now. He shouldn't look this grown up. He should still be a kid, not a seventeen-year-old man.

Gustov's door creaks open and slams shut, drawing Paxton's

attention over my shoulder. Paxton is tracking him with undeniable awe in his eyes. Like I said, he's never been one to hold back his emotions around me.

"Paxton, I presume? Unless your cousin's just got a thing for hitchhikers, which is cool. Everyone needs a hobby." Gustov's standing next to me now.

Paxton lets out a nervous laugh. He stares at Gustov like he's a god. Paxton has always been painfully shy and guarded around strangers. He's not quick to trust. Not that I blame him; he wasn't raised in a home built on trust. Promises were always broken. I could adapt, because I was used to it and more mature. Paxton never quite adapted. He was young and vulnerable, and when his parents said they were going to do something, he expected them to follow through. Most of the time, they didn't. Paxton is the one person in the world I would never lie to, I guess because everyone else who's close to him already has.

"Paxton, this is Gustov Hawthorne. Gustov, this is Paxton."

Gustov extends his hand, which Paxton reluctantly takes. "It's just Gus, Pax. Welcome to SoCal, dude. How was your flight aboard the big bird?"

Paxton is still holding Gustov's hand, but he's not shaking it anymore. He's just staring up at him. I nudge his shoulder to rouse him out of his idol worship.

He starts and lets go, blinking rapidly. He's completely clammed up, so I prompt the question again. "How was the flight?"

He nods. "Good. It was good. Really good. Except for the turbulence over the Midwest, that was bad. But the rest was good. Really good," he rambles. He rarely rambles; it's a product of his nerves.

If Gustov notices, he hides it. "Well Pax, let's get these suitcases of yours into the back of the truck." Gustov grabs one and Paxton grabs the other. "This all you got?"

Paxton nods, but he looks ashamed for some reason. "Yeah."

Gustov pats him on the shoulder as he walks past to get inside the truck cab. "Living light. You're my kind of dude, Pax. We're gonna get along just fine."

With Gustov's words, relief flashes across Paxton's face. I know it's such a small thing, but I'm so grateful to him. His kindness just made Paxton's day. I smile. I feel like everything is going to be okay.

Tuesday, August 29
(Gus)

Pax starts school today. Impatient took him in yesterday and got him registered, but there was no point in her being late for work today. I'm around. Doing absolutely nothing. Besides, I like this kid. We hit it off yesterday. Sometimes you meet people and you know the meeting wasn't chance. That they need you or you need them, sometimes both. This kid needs someone. He needs friends. I have a feeling he's lacking in that department.

While I wait on Pax, I scarf down a few slices of the banana bread Impatient made last night. When he walks in the kitchen he looks nervous as hell, like puking-your-guts-out or passing-out nervous. I don't want to call him on it and make it worse, so I pretend not to notice. "What's the story, morning glory?" His eyes zero in on the banana bread in my hand. "You want some fuel?" I ask gesturing to the Ziploc bags on the counter behind me.

"Did Scout make that?"

I take another bite and talk through it. "Yeah. It's fucking fantastic."

He smiles, like the fact that I just dropped the f-bomb is the raddest thing he's ever heard. "My mom never cooks. Sometimes I think Scout learned just so I wouldn't starve."

That's a strange comment, because I get the feeling he actually meant it. Like literally. I don't know anything about Impatient's past, except Paxton's mom is her aunt Jane who she talks to on the phone sometimes. And I know about *fucking Michael*. That's it.

After Pax eats a few slices of bread I suggest we get on the road. "We better jet, dude. Your cousin will murder me and make shark bait of my remains if you're late for day one. She's kind of a stickler for punctuality."

As if on cue my phone chimes from my pocket. It's a text from Impatient. *Are you on the road yet?*

I hold up the phone so Pax can read the text. He squints a little too, and I make a mental note to ask Impatient if he wears contacts or glasses. He's clearly struggling to read the text. He looks up at me with confused eyes. "Who's *Impatient?*"

I laugh because I forgot that's how I set her up in my phone months ago. "Sorry, that's Scout."

He thinks for a minute, and then he smiles. "She is a little impatient sometimes."

"Sometimes?" I question. "Damn, you're generous."

He knows I'm kidding. Sort of. He laughs, too. His laugh is restrained, more like a chuckle. Like there's light bound up inside this kid that desperately wants to get out, but doesn't know how. It makes me feel a little bummed thinking about it. I used to take laughter for granted. I was surrounded by it for years. Then the laughter died with Bright Side. I feel like I've had to learn how to laugh all over again. I can relate. We both need to find our light.

As we approach the school, I give him a sidelong look. "Dude, you want me to drop you off in front of the school or down the street? I don't want to tarnish your rep with my shit wagon the first day of school." I love my truck but I know that doesn't hold true for everyone else. And I have a feeling that he's a kid with bigger issues going on. I don't want him to get picked on because some fuck nut sees him get out of my truck and decides to give him shit about it. I'm trying to play preemptive damage control.

He smiles. "Drop me off in front. I don't mind the *shit wagon*."

"Righteous." I hold out my hand in between us and he gives me a high five.

When I stop the truck, he looks over at me with wide eyes and a light sheen of sweat on his forehead. The expression screams panic. So, I give the Gus version of a pep talk. "Pax, you're cooler than the back side of a pillowcase, remember that. Now go give 'em hell, dude."

He smiles. "Thanks, Gus."

"Sure thing. See you at three-thirty. I'll try to park here. If I'm running late I'll text you. Fair warning, there's a ninety-nine percent chance I'll be running late, because I'm always late. It's who I am."

Guess who's fifteen minutes early to pick up Pax? This guy. I'm kinda proud of myself. I don't want to let this kid down, because if letting him down wasn't bad enough, it's also like letting Impatient down. And I don't want to do that either.

Pax walks out with his head down. I wonder if he walked around all day like that. Trying not to be noticed. Trying to blend in. When he looks up, he smiles. That small smile makes me grin.

"How was day one of the rest of your life?"

"Pretty good." That response was neutral and could go either way. I don't know him well enough yet to read him.

"You meet any chicks?"

He looks at me like I'm teasing him.

I raise my eyebrows. "What? That's a legit question. We're guys, girls rule us. It's a fact of life."

His mouth curves slightly as his cheeks redden.

"Aha. Already got your eye on a little filly. What's her name, dude?"

"Mason." His cheeks have amped the red level to a nine out of ten.

Laughing, I punch him on the shoulder. "I'm taking you to The Ice Shack for ice cream so you can tell me all about the lovely Mason."

I do.

And he does.

It's the happiest I've seen the kid yet.

Saturday, September 2
(Gus)

"Pax, I'm giving you fair warning," I say as I flip on the lights in the stairwell leading down to the basement. "If you sleep in the buff, cover up your snake because I'm coming down."

It's early. And it's Saturday. We should both be sleeping. I feel bad about waking him up, but it's the only appointment I could get on such short notice.

Pax shifts on the hide-a-bed sofa and throws his forearm over his eyes to guard against the assault of overhead light.

"Sorry, dude. Get your ass up. We've got places to go and people to see."

He doesn't move his arm, but speaks sleepily from beneath it. "What time is it, Gus?"

"It's six-fifteen. Like I already said, my deepest apologies, but we have to leave soon. Go scrub the stink off and meet me upstairs in twenty."

He peels back his arm, his eyes only slits. "Where are we going?"

"Top secret." It's not. We're going to the optometrist, but I'll let him in on that when he's fully awake.

We make the appointment with a few minutes to spare.

Pax is confused when we pull up and I get out. "Why are we here?"

"You ever had your eyes checked?"

He shakes his head.

"Well, there's a first time for everything. Vamanos, muchacho."

Pax fills out the forms and in minutes he's back with the doctor. I chat up the elderly woman sitting next to me while I wait. She's waiting on her husband who's in to have his cataracts checked out. She's probably in her eighties, super cool lady with stark white hair. By the time Pax comes out, I know how many kids, grandkids, and great grandkids she has—and I've seen photos of most of them. I also know she was born in Maine, but moved to San Diego forty years ago when her husband's job relocated them. She has a Pomeranian named Bitsy. And she

131

smells like baby powder. I like her. Pax is hanging his head as he trudges over to me.

"What's the verdict?"

"He said I need glasses."

Hell yes you do, I think. I've watched him squint for days now. "Sweet. Let's do this."

We sit down at a table with an adorable, peppy optician named Brandy. When she asks Pax if he wants glasses or contacts, he looks at me.

I shrug. "What do you want, Pax? This is all you."

He shrugs. "I don't like touching around my eyes. I don't think I could put contacts in, but I don't want to look like a dork in glasses, either."

I laugh. "Dork? You're a good-looking dude. You could totally pull off glasses." Glancing at Brandy, I add, "See, she's wearing glasses and rockin' the hell out of them." I add a wink for good measure. Brandy smiles and blushes at the compliment.

Pax stammers when he realizes he may have just insulted her. "Sorry, no disrespect. Yours look nice."

She smiles back sweetly. "Why don't you try a few frames on and see what you like?"

Pax spends the next thirty minutes trying on everything we throw at him. In the end, he picks a pair of black-rimmed frames. They look good with his dark hair and pale skin.

After Brandy instructs us to come back after two o'clock to pick up Pax's glasses, I pay for everything, and then we hit a few stores. The kid needs new clothes. He wore uniforms at his last school and doesn't have much outside of navy blue polos, white button-downs, and khakis. I don't know Pax, but I know he's not a polo and khaki kind of dude. He's indecisive when I tell him to pick out a few shirts and pairs of jeans. Either he doesn't really know what he likes, or he just doesn't want me to spend the money on him. I'm guessing both.

When he finally starts picking up items to look at, he always asks, "What do you think, Gus? Is this cool?"

The first few times I answer with, "I don't have to wear it. Do *you* like it?" I don't want him picking out clothes just because he thinks I like them. When I realize he looks a little overwhelmed, I also realize he's probably never done this before. I bet his mom always shopped for him. "Close your eyes."

"Why?" he challenges.

"Just do it, young Jedi."

He does.

"Now when I say open your eyes, I want you to go pick up the first thing that screams, *Hey, Pax, I'm fucking rad. You need me.* Okay?"

He smiles and nods. "Okay."

"Open your eyes."

He does and after a two second hesitation he walks to a T-shirt on a rack on the back wall that reads, *Epic is a state of mind.* It's a black tee with faded white ink.

"Nice choice. Not that I wanna steal your thunder, but I think I need that one, too."

He eagerly helps me find my size.

After that it doesn't take long before he's got several T-shirts, hoodies, and jeans and he's in the dressing room changing. I make sure he has an outfit for every day of the week so he only has to do laundry on the weekends.

After lunch we head to the skate shop to buy him some kicks. He's been wearing a pair of running shoes that are worn out and probably too small. And his only other pair are brown leather dress shoes that I'm sure were part of his school uniform, based on the fact that they looked like they belonged to a middle-aged man. He picks out some navy blue Half Cabs and wears them out, leaving the running shoes behind.

We pick up his new glasses on the way home. I don't say anything, but I watch him out of the corner of my eye the whole drive back to the house. The kid is looking around like he was blind and he's just been given the gift of sight. He's quiet, just taking it all in, looking at everything up close and far away. It makes me happy. "Pax, you're the shit in those specs. Just sayin'. Wait until Mason sees you."

He smiles shyly and his cheeks glow red hot, just like he does every time I bring up her name, and he looks away out the passenger window. I know he's still smiling. I can feel it.

When we get home he takes all of his new clothes downstairs and appears back upstairs only minutes later wearing new jeans and a Nirvana T-shirt.

"Come with me," I say and gesture for him to follow me to my room.

It's the first time he's been in in my room, and he's looking around wide-eyed. My room's pretty sparse, if you don't count the piles of dirty clothes on the floor. Only a bed, nightstand, and small dresser. I've got three guitars—two electric in their cases next to my closet door, and my old acoustic that always sits out propped up in the corner. "Yeah, sorry about the pig sty. I kinda needed to do laundry like two weeks ago."

I pull out a cardboard box filled with Rook T-shirts from my closet and plunk it on the floor. "I don't know if you've heard our music, but if you want a couple shirts, knock yourself out. If not, no sweat, dude."

His eyes light up. "Really?"

I nod. "Sure."

He kneels down in front of the box and starts digging through it. After he chooses two, he looks up at me. "Rook is my favorite band. Thanks for these."

That surprises me. "No shit?"

He nods enthusiastically. "Yeah, I've been listening to you guys since the album came out last fall."

"Wow. Thanks, dude." I know we get recognized on the street sometimes, but deep down it still shocks me when anyone knows about Rook.

"Actually," he says, "my dad's Jim Ridgely, your tour manager." He says it like an apology.

"Your dad is fucking Hitler?" I ask, immediately wishing I hadn't said that out loud.

He laughs and I'm relieved I didn't just insult him. I'm also turning this over in my head, figuring out how the pieces all fit together. If Hitler is Paxton's dad, that means he's also Impatient's uncle. It's no wonder she could deal with him better than everyone else. Not that their relationship seemed like family at all, but she's the only one who could deal with his shit and talk to him frankly without coming off like an ass. And now I know why he trusted her.

Pax pushes aside the fucking Hitler comment. "I actually can't believe I'm standing here in your room. Is this where you write?"

"Usually. Haven't really written anything in a while."

Now there's a look of confusion on his face. "What about your next album? There will be another album, right? Please tell me there's another album."

I nod, but I'm not into it. "There will be another album."

He smiles. He didn't hear the doubt in my voice. "Good. I need another album. Don't get me wrong, I could listen to the first one all day, every day, for the rest of my life, but ... " He looks up at me expectantly.

But.

That's my life.

But.

And all of the indecision and unknowns that it holds.

Sunday, September 10
(Gus)

Ma, Impatient, and Pax are out at a movie. Normally I'd go, but I went with Franco and saw the same film a few days ago. I should be doing something other than lying on the sofa mindlessly channel-surfing, but I'm too lazy to figure out what that something might be.

When there's a knock at the door, I'm cursing whoever it is because I don't want to get up. But after two rounds of knocking I can't ignore it anymore, and climb my lazy ass off the sofa. I'm already pissed at whoever it is before I open the door. Then it gets worse. It's *fucking Michael*. I've got zero patience for this sonofabitch.

Taking a deep breath, I release it slowly before I look at him and say, "She's not here."

He glares at the expensive watch on his wrist and looks irritated. "What time will she be back?"

"She'll be gone all afternoon." I shrug; it's fuck you.

He caught that. He raises his eyebrows in irritation and frustration. "You're sure about that?"

"Yup. Pretty sure." I'm done with this convo. I'm ready to get back to the sofa and my shit TV watching.

The dude actually starts tapping his toe while he's thinking. It's some kind of nervous, yet alpha, mannerism. I hate it.

I start to close the door on him but he reaches out and stops it with his hand. It's a bold move, considering we were more than done here.

"Tell her I stopped by," he says. It's a command, not a request.

I glance at his hand, still gripping the door. "Should I also tell her you forgot to take off your wedding ring, or should I leave that part out?"

He retracts his hand quickly and shoves it in the pocket of his dress pants. He was just pushed off the cliff into the valley of guilt, and it makes him squirm. It's not a regretful squirm; it's the squirm of a slippery fucker who's never accepted responsibility for any wrongdoing in his life. Judging by the look on his face, Impatient doesn't know.

I don't wait for him to say anything. "Get the fuck outta here."

GUS

And then I slam the door in his face.

Tuesday, September 19
(Scout)

It's been a long day. I just got home from work and I'm already looking forward to going to sleep in a few hours. I'm longing for it like the two of us haven't been together in days. Sleep's been messing with me the past few weeks. Anxiety is my nemesis. You name it, I worry about it. Working with Audrey is like a dream, but I still worry about it—my job performance, my ability to learn the business quickly and effectively, my interaction with clients. She always assures me that she's pleased with my work, but I have so much doubt and it's so deeply ingrained that it's hard for me to turn off the worry.

I worry about Audrey. It's not my job as her assistant to worry about her, but I do because I've become so fond of her on a personal level. She's my mentor and someone I aspire to be like. I admire her so much and I just want the best for her and somehow that translates into worry within me.

I worry about Paxton and how he's doing at school. I worry about Jane and her well-being and mental state. I worry about my past with Michael—and even though I've put that behind me, the worry still nags at me. I worry about Gustov, both him and our friendship. Sometimes I feel like I don't know how to do true friendship with anyone other than Paxton, but I know that I want to be his friend.

The hard part is that our friendship is slightly complicated by the attraction I sometimes feel toward him. It comes at the oddest times: when he's done something nice, or when he looks at me with a goofy look on his face, or when he says something unexpected. It just happens, and I don't know how to deal with that yet. It's new and foreign.

So I worry about anything and everything. Sometimes it's warranted. Sometimes it's not. I just worry. It's what I do. And it's exhausting.

It's not until I hear a meow that I open my eyes and navigate the hallway to my bedroom fully alert. It's a small, gray and white kitten. It's circling me, lovingly brushing up against my legs. When I squat down to pet it, it's purring. "Hey, there," I whisper. I can't help smiling until its tiny head tilts up toward me and then I gasp and pick it up. "Oh, you poor thing." The injuries aren't fresh, but they look like they healed with little or no human intervention. Its left eye is absent, the socket misshapen from trauma. Half of its left ear is missing. And its left front leg is grotesquely bowed out as if it was badly broken and never healed correctly.

The purring intensifies.

"You fucking little traitor." It's Gustov.

Startled, I freeze, still holding the kitten. "What?"

He points at the cat in my arms. "Spare Ribs."

Now I'm really confused. "Spare ribs?"

"Yeah, that's her name, Spare Ribs. I found her this morning down the street. She'd climbed into the Cominsky's trash can and was going to town on some—"

I interrupt him, smiling. "Spare ribs. I get it."

He nods.

Sometimes ... most of the time ... his originality entertains me. It's refreshing. Who names their cat Spare Ribs? "That's not very ladylike for a girl kitty," I say.

"Spare Ribs is a righteous name. And she's no lady, Impatient. Don't let her fool you, she's a hardcore hustler." He raises his arms to show me the claw marks up and down each forearm. "She fought valiantly. We're friends now." He looks at her in my arms again. "Sort of. I think she likes you better. Not gonna lie, I'm a little hurt, Spare Ribs. I offer you refuge and you fucking turncoat for the first chick who walks in. *Not cool.*"

I smile when he says Spare Ribs again, because it's just funny. "Have you taken her to the vet? This looks bad," I say, touching her damaged head.

"Took her this morning. Old injuries. She healed up fine. She's healthy as a horse; don't go feeling sorry for her. That's what she wants."

His words hit me: old injuries ... healed up fine ... healthy as a horse ... sorry for her ... that's what she wants. I swallow hard. *That's me.* I'm healed. I'm healthy. I don't want people to feel sorry for me though. I want them to ignore me. At least that's what I've always wanted up until I moved to San Diego. I don't know what I want anymore. And that's not a bad thing. Uncertainty is the beginning of change. Maybe it's time for change.

He puts his hand up to shield his mouth, as if the cat won't be able to hear him. "She's awesome, though. I just don't want it going to her head or she'll fucking own me more than she already does and I'll turn into a crazy cat lady. I may be about ninety-seven percent there already, and I've only known her for about eight hours. She's going to work me over. *Hard*. I just know it."

I'm pretty sure Gustov just earned about ten points in the nice department with all of this. Physically, he's this huge man. Who's also a rock star. Who lives with and adores his mom. Who befriended Paxton in an instant. *And* he's just rescued a hurt, stray kitten. He's definitely not the man I thought he was a few months ago. He's ... just ... good. And goddamn ... that's attractive.

Monday, September 25
(Gus)

Ma told me that, over the weekend, her mailroom guy lost his grandma. The funeral is in Seattle, which means he'll be gone for the rest of the week. I volunteered to help her out because, to be honest, I'd rather do anything than sit at home alone, just me and this motherfucking block. I can only stare at a blank piece of paper for so long. Or hold my guitar and hear radio silence. Or sit at the piano and let the keys taunt my lack of musical cooperation.

I *can't* write.

I don't *want* to write.

Everyone *needs* me to write.

I hate it.

So, I'll gladly work in the mailroom again.

"It's lunch time." Her voice rouses me out of my monotonous haze of sorting and stacking envelopes. Impatient is standing in the doorway of the mailroom.

I nod. "Yeah, thanks." I didn't bring anything from home this morning and I don't want to go to the deli around the corner. The last time I went in there, I got recognized ... and it was ugly. I felt claustrophobic and panicked. So, I'll settle for a few cigarettes out behind the building instead, even though my stomach is growling.

She holds up a bag. "There was a special at Antonio's. Buy two slices, get two free. Want half?"

I shrug. "Sure. You offering to feed me, dude?"

She laughs. "I'm offering to provide you food to eat. Feed your own damn self." Things have been so much easier between us lately. I can joke with her. She's not so uptight around me and we can actually laugh together.

We eat in silence sitting at a picnic table out back. When we're done, instead of leaving, she stays while I smoke a cigarette.

"I know what you're doing," she says flatly.

"Killing myself," I say, looking cynically at the cigarette in my hand.

"You're hiding," she says. "Why are you hiding here? Don't get me wrong, I love it here, working for Audrey. But you ... you shouldn't be here." It's straightforward Impatient.

"Why not?"

141

She sighs. "Gustov, you're stalling. You're wasting time. You're not living. You're not doing what you love."

"Which is?"

"Making music. You have this huge following; I saw them all at the shows," she pauses. "They love you." Her eyes are downcast, like the admission was hard for her.

I nod even though her eyes aren't on me. I'm accepting the compliment without verbal acknowledgment because that would kill this moment and make her embarrassed. She's so guarded, and I know that took a lot for her to say. "Yeah, well, writing music is a bit of a ... challenge ... right now."

Her eyes find mine again. "Challenge? What's that supposed to mean?"

I don't want to talk to her about this. I don't want to talk to anyone about this. "It's nothing."

She doesn't let it go. "It's not nothing. It's everything. It's *your* everything." Then she stands and leaves.

I'm left here pondering what in the hell just happened. She's right. I know she's right. I need to get my ass in gear.

But I can't.

Wednesday, October 11
(Gus)

"I think it's time for us to move out." Her voice is quiet. Unusually quiet even for her.

It's like a slap. A wake-up call. "What? Move out?"

She's mixing cookie batter in a big bowl on the kitchen counter. She bakes a lot. She doesn't eat much of it; I think she just does it to make everyone else happy. And it does make us happy because she's damn good at it. Though I think even if it tasted like shit I'd eat it, because it's her way of showing love. She has trouble letting love go freely, there's a block. It's not that she doesn't want to, because I feel it in the little things she does, but more that maybe she doesn't know how. She keeps her eyes on the bowl. "Paxton and I can't live here forever, Gustov. Audrey's been so kind to let us stay here this long."

"Ma loves having you here. Don't even worry about that." She does. Ma and I talk a lot and whenever she talks about them there's nothing but love in her voice. Ma's a giver and nothing makes her happier than helping people, especially when she becomes attached to them. She's a mom to everyone, selfless and so loving. She treats those she loves like family, because that's exactly what they are to her.

"I do. Besides, Paxton was an unexpected surprise for her. She didn't sign on to have him around too when she hired me and offered me a place to stay."

"Pax is fucking ace. He's a great kid."

She finally smiles and faces me. It's the first time she's looked at me all morning. "He is."

"It's Spare Ribs she can't stand," I add. I'm trying to make her laugh. Ma loves Spare Ribs. Too much. That goddamn cat has every human in this house wrapped around her cute little paw.

She ignores the joke and continues, "And Paxton idolizes you. I'm sure you've noticed, but he loves being around you. And I think it's good for him to have a positive male role model."

I laugh at that. "Bullshit. I'm nobody's role model."

She's not laughing with me. "Gustov, can I be honest for a minute?"

"By all means. And I appreciate honesty at all times, not just

143

this once, just so you know." She hides a lot, I know that. Not that she's a liar, she just holds back. Information, emotion ... she's private to the point that I wonder if it's suffocating her.

Her eyes drop back to her mixing bowl. She's scooping cookie dough out of the bowl and dropping it on the baking sheet. She's thinking about what I just said. Thinking about it a lot harder than I intended, but probably not as much as she truly needs to in order to believe it. After several seconds, she nods. "Point taken."

When she looks at me again I nod to acknowledge her.

She continues. "When I first met you, I thought you were an asshole."

I nod again. "You were probably right. Especially back then."

She shakes her head to dismiss my comment. "Stop. Let me finish." She takes a breath. "I was wrong. I was so wrapped in my own issues that I let it cloud my judgment. Every guy I saw, every guy I met, was automatically an asshole. It wasn't just you. But because you were the one I was forced to deal with for my job, that animosity was amplified. I have things in my past," she pauses like she's contemplating stopping right there, and then she sighs, "I made some bad choices. I did things I'm not proud of. For a long time I tried to blame that on other people. Now I'm trying to take responsibility." She pauses again, trying to compose herself. "Sorry, this isn't about me. What I'm trying to say is that I was wrong about you. You are a role model. You're kind. And you have this charisma that attracts people to you. You don't try, it just happens. Because it makes them happy to be around you. I know you're dealing with something right now, something dark, but in your heart of hearts, you're just ... happy. And good. I don't know how to do that. But, it's *who you are*. I admire that. And I want Paxton around that. I think that's who he is, too, but he's never been surrounded by it. I try my best with him, but I'm not like you and Audrey."

It makes me sad to hear her doubt herself; she's so much more than she gives herself credit for. I wonder if she's ever had anyone tell her so. "You don't see yourself, Impatient. You don't see the person the rest of us do."

She shakes her head in disbelief as she walks to the oven to put the cookies in. She's not just feeling sorry for herself; this is ingrained self-loathing.

When she shuts the oven door, I take ahold of her arm and gently turn her to face me. She closes her eyes when we're facing each other. "Look at me, please." She does. "Nobody's perfect. Believe me, I know that. But you sell yourself so fucking short. You're smart as hell. Ma loves working with you. And that's saying a lot because Ma needs someone who can keep up with her intellectually. The fact that you could step into Mikayla's shoes and not miss a beat, is nothing short of fucking miraculous. And you pay attention to everything going on around you. Even if you're not engaged in what's going on, you're still paying attention. And it's not nosy or intrusive, you're just hyper-aware, that alone shows you care. And don't even get me started on Pax. That kid loves you. He'd be lost without you. And I have a feeling that's how it's always been. And I know instinctively that you've never let him down. Have you let yourself down? Probably. But not him. Not ever. And that says a lot about the person you are. Hell, he's here with you now. I don't know the circumstances surrounding the family dynamic you've all got going on, but the fact that you're taking care of him because Jim doesn't? That speaks volumes."

"You know about Jim?" She sounds surprised, I guess because it's never been brought up.

I nod.

She's trying to hold back tears. "I just want Paxton to turn out better than I did."

Pulling her into a hug, I tell her, "You'll both be fine."

"Will we?"

"Abso-fucking-lutely. And you aren't going anywhere. Ma gets fierce when her nest is threatened. You don't want that. Believe me."

Thursday, October 19
(Gus)

My cell is ringing. I don't recognize the number, and the area code is unfamiliar. Usually I'd let it go to voicemail, but I'm bored. So I answer. "Hola."

"Hello?" It's a confused female on the other end of the line.

"Hello?" I question back. I have a feeling this is a wrong number, but I don't want to be rude and hang up on her.

"Gustov?" Same confused female.

"Yup."

"Gustov, this is Clare." Long pause. "How are you?" Unease doesn't even begin to describe what's buried in her voice.

Clare? It takes me a few seconds before my mind catches up. Clare from the European tour. "Oh hey, Clare. All's well here. How're you?" I haven't seen or heard from her since the tour. Not sure what this is about, but I'm curious.

"Good. Better." She sounds nervous and sighs. "I've had a lot going on since I last saw you. Been working on myself. Getting cleaned up."

She pauses again and I feel the need to interject because she's struggling, stumbling over her words. Even though I didn't particularly like Clare, I can't abandon her now when she's obviously trying to reach out to me. "Good for you."

I hear the exhalation of relief. "I'm so sorry, Gustov. Sorry for getting you wrapped up in my disaster of a life last spring."

"Not your fault, Clare. I made my own choices. I was in the middle of my own disaster."

"The reason I'm calling, well, is to see if maybe you'd like to have dinner tonight. I've been in San Diego visiting my aunt for a few days and I leave in the morning. I'd like to see you and apologize properly."

None of this sounds like the Clare I knew. She's speaking clearly, talking to me like a normal person. I can tell that she's being honest with me. She sounds vulnerable. She sounds ... nice. I'm a sucker for nice, and I also can't hold a grudge, so I answer, "Sounds good. You want me to pick you up?"

"No, I'll pick you up. That's part of the whole apology thing." She laughs, and I notice that it's not the high pitched, grating giggle I remember from before. It sounds more mellow, like a low, relaxed chuckle.

"Yes, ma'am." I give her my address and we agree on seven o'clock.

I'm tugging on my Catfish and the Bottlemen T-shirt when there's a knock on my bedroom door. "Gus, you in there?"

I open the door and Pax is standing in my doorway with a grin on his face that's half awe and half terror. I hold back a smile. "What's up, amigo?"

He motions with his thumb over his shoulder behind him and whispers, "There's a girl here for you."

I glance at the clock on my nightstand, six forty-five. "Huh, she's early."

The mixed look's still in place on Paxton's face, though awe's winning out now. "Do you have a date?"

I shake my head. "Nah, no date. Just a ... " for some reason I stumble on the word, because I don't really know what Clare is. "Just a friend. I haven't seen her in a while. Just getting some chow with her, that's all."

He shakes his head slowly. "She's hot, Gus. Like a fifteen on a ten-point scale."

I laugh because the kid never would've said anything like that a few weeks ago when he arrived here.

"She looks good, huh? Maybe I'd set you up with her if you weren't jailbait." I wink.

"I'm eighteen in a couple of weeks," he argues.

"Dude, you couldn't handle a cougar like that. You keep your eyes on the prize with Mason."

He smiles and his cheeks go crimson at the mention of his new high school crush.

I slip on my socks and Vans and walk out to the living room with Pax following closely behind. Clare's standing next to the sliding glass door looking out at the ocean view. I don't say anything for a minute, just letting her enjoy the scenery. Getting lost in calm and beauty is a gift.

If I didn't know this was the Clare from before, I wouldn't believe it now. Her ultra-thin frame is curvier, softer, and instead of being marketed for sex, it's tucked away discreetly inside a pair of jeans and a simple white T-shirt. Her dark hair shines in a simple cut that falls just short of her shoulders. I clear my throat to get her attention. "S'up Clare?"

She turns at my voice, and the face that greets me looks years younger and happier than the one I saw months ago. Her skin is clear, almost glowing. She looks fresh, like layers of everything bad and negative have been stripped away along with the heavy makeup and seductive clothing to reveal this new person hiding underneath. "Hi, Gustov."

"Gustov? Do people really call you that? I thought Scout was the only one who called you that." It's Pax. He's still a shadow behind me.

I laugh. "It is my name, Pax."

He's embarrassed. "I know. I guess I just thought everyone called you Gus."

I nod. "Most of them do. Or douche canoe, that nickname's popular, too. I'll answer to almost anything. Just ask Franco."

Clare smiles. "That's true. How is Franco?"

"He's good. He's building an old motorcycle now that we're home for a while. It's keeping him busy." He's obsessed with the bike and it's taking all of his time, which is good. I'm glad he's keeping busy with something he loves.

"Good for him." Clare looks around the room and smiles. "Your mom has a beautiful home. What a *magnificent* view." She glances back over her shoulder out the window.

"It's pretty amazing. We're lucky."

She nods her head.

"Pax, you wanna tag along and get some grub?"

He clams up and shakes his head. On the inside I can see him trying to play it cool, but on the outside he's giving off a different message. He looks like he's going to faint.

"Okay, soldier. Hold down the fort while I'm gone." As Clare and I decide where we're going to eat, Impatient walks through the living room from her bedroom toward the front door. She's dressed to run, which is strange because she always runs in the morning.

She doesn't say anything. Pax stops her at the door. "Scout, where're you going? I thought we were going to eat dinner? You made lasagna."

148

She looks back and her eyes pause on Clare and on me before they land on Paxton. "I'm not hungry. You go ahead, though." Her face is pale, her pink lips are closed in a frown, and there's pain in her eyes. Her voice sounds terribly sad. Sad like everything in her world is crashing down around her and she has no control over it. Sad like she desperately wants life to go one way, but instead it's going another. I know that kind of sad intimately. And when I blink she's disappeared out the door.

Clare and I end up going to a little Italian dive a couple of blocks from Ma's house. We walk since it's so close, and we make small talk until we're inside sitting at a tiny table for two. Then shit gets real.

"I'm sorry, Gustov. From the bottom of my heart. I was a mess. For a long, *long* time I was a mess." She smiles, but it's apologetic, like her words. I can tell that she's being sincere. Some things just can't be faked. "I actually just got out of a rehab facility a few weeks ago."

"How long were you there?" I ask. She needed it. I knew that before, but seeing her here now and seeing the transformation that's taken place, it's apparent the benefit is pretty goddamn miraculous.

"Six months. I checked myself in as soon as I got back to the states. Initially it was at the request of my employer, but before I even got there, I knew I needed it. I'd needed it for years, but I couldn't face it. I had been acting recklessly. Sometimes, punishing yourself is easier than facing down your demons, you know?"

I do. I nod. "I'm with you on that, sister."

She raises her eyebrows to acknowledge my admission. "I know you are, and I also want to say that I'm so sorry for your loss. I didn't know at the time what was going on with you, I just knew from the first moment I saw you that you were hurting. You were hurting like I was. I think that's why I was so drawn to you. I needed to feed on that agony. I needed my pain to commiserate with someone else's. I felt like I had a partner in grief, you know. Someone that got me, even though I knew you didn't like me."

I nod. I understand. Addicts don't choose tragedy. Tragedy chooses them. And addiction is the result. "Like I said, I'm with you. I don't blame you for anything that happened, Clare. Please don't think that. I accepted whatever you gave me. I could've turned it down. I should've turned it down. But I didn't." I take a deep breath. "We used each other. It filled a void we both had. I'm sorry for that. No one deserves to be used."

Her clear eyes are welling up with tears. "Thank you. Thank you for not hating me right now. I was so scared to call you this afternoon. I was so scared to face you. I'm still in follow-up therapy. I probably will be for a very long time. I've got some major issues I'm still working on. I've apologized to everyone in my life that my addiction hurt; you are the last person to whom I felt I owed an apology. So again, I'm sorry, Gustov."

I hand her my napkin, and smiling, she takes it, blotting her eyes. "Apology accepted," I say. "And right back at ya. I'm sorry, too. I knew you had something major you were contending with and I never tried to help you, because I was selfish and drowning in my own shit."

She dabs her eyes again and smiles. "I'm good now. I'm clean. Clean for six months. I haven't been clean since I was eighteen, if you can believe that. It feels good. I'm dealing with my eating disorder, too, which is harder than it sounds like it would be. I mean, I don't need coke to live, but I do need food. It's a daily struggle, but right now I'm winning. Today, I'm winning. I'm healthy and that's where I want to stay. I still can't give up the goddamn cigarettes though," she says, laughing. "But someday I will."

I huff in agreement. "They're evil. I can't give them up either." I think twice about asking, but then I give in to my gut. "So, what happened?"

"What do you mean?" She looks confused.

"What happened when you were eighteen?" I have a feeling that she brought me here for more than an apology. That maybe she has more she wants to talk about, more she wants to explain. And I'm a fantastic listener.

Her eyes drop to her plate in front of her. "I was raped."

That word makes me feel nauseous. Always has. The thought of someone forcing himself on another person without consent is sickening. I wait for her eyes to meet mine again before I speak. "It wasn't your fault. And I'm so sorry." God, am I ever.

The corner of her lips tip up slightly. "I know that now. For

150

years I blamed myself, but I know now that it wasn't my fault."

"It wasn't," I reassure. There's no situation where rape is the victim's fault. It's not possible. *Ever.*

She nods. "Back to you ... how are you doing? Any better? I don't want to ask if it's getting easier, because I can't imagine losing someone you love ever gets easier, but are you dealing with it better now?"

"She was my life. My best friend. She was everything, you know?" That's as honest as I can be and it makes me swallow back the lump in my throat that's suddenly appeared.

She nods. "Franco told me all about her. I asked him on the last day of the tour."

"Yeah. I don't know. I mean some days I'm just living, just doing what I need to do. Functioning. And other days it hits me and it hurts so bad, it's debilitating. I don't know if that makes any fucking sense? Some days I'm good and some days I'm not."

"Are you talking to someone about it?" She's prompting in a kind way and I know where this is going. She's going to suggest therapy.

I try to counter her with humor to divert. "I'm talking to you. That counts, doesn't it?" I smile, but she doesn't buy it.

"I'm glad you are, but I mean people in your life that you see more than every six months."

I glance over her shoulder at the poster of the Leaning Tower of Pisa behind her. "Talking about her hurts. I already hurt. I don't want to hurt more. So no, not really."

"At first it does hurt. *Like hell.* But what if eventually it didn't hurt anymore? What if someday it was healing? What if someday it made you happy to talk about her? To think about her? Wouldn't that be worth it?"

"To be honest with you, that sounds like some kind of far-fetched fucking dream. I'm not there."

She smiles. "But you could be. And you will be someday. Despite everything we went through, and as badly as we treated each other, I know your heart isn't made of stone. You're one of the good ones, Gustov."

I smile back. "I try, dude."

Her smile grows. "You are, *dude.*"

151

After we split a piece of tiramisu, we walk back to Ma's. We share a cigarette during the walk and both tell each other we need to quit. It's after nine o'clock when we approach her car in Ma's driveway. I invite her in, but she says she needs to get back to her aunt's and get some rest. Her flight leaves at six o'clock tomorrow morning.

She's looking at me with relief painted across her face again. "Thank you for agreeing to see me and for forgiving me. I think that was one of the last burdens I needed to release, that guilt I associated with you. I feel lighter and your kind heart did that. Thank you, Gustov."

I smile. "I'm glad you called. This was good. Thanks for forgiving me and my assbag ways, too."

She laughs.

"I'm proud of you, Clare. You're a different person. Keep up the good fight."

She nods. "I will. I have to." She winks. "My new, amazing life kind of depends on it."

I hold out my arms. "Come here."

She steps into my arms, and for a second something feels familiar. It's not sexual at all, but I remember her closeness. She squeezes, and I feel nothing but comfort and friendship. Her words reinforce what I'm feeling. "I'm here if you ever want to talk, Gustov. About anything. I've learned to be a good listener these past few months."

I pull back and smile. "Ditto, lady. Have a safe flight in the morning and stay in touch. I wanna know if you ever quit smoking. And if you do, let me in on the magic secret."

She laughs. "I think the secret is wanting to make the change and doing the work. I'm not there yet. You'll probably quit before I do."

"We should make a bet. Fifty bucks to whoever gives it up first."

"You're on. Good luck."

"Good luck."

I wait until she backs down the driveway and drives away before I go inside. My heart feels a little lighter than it did hours ago. There was no physical attraction to Clare, though she's more beautiful than she was when we hooked up months ago. Her energy was just good. Good to be around. I've blocked myself off from most people lately, and maybe she's right. Maybe I'm only making it worse.

(Scout)

I wake up when I hear the front door opening. I wait a minute to decide if it's Audrey or Gustov, since they've both been out. When I hear the footsteps on the hardwood, I know it's Gustov. I was sleeping on the sofa. I don't know why. I should've just gone to bed after I got out of the shower. But I couldn't. I'm mad at myself for being so affected by seeing him with someone else. She was pretty and it was obvious they've known each other for a while. She wasn't just someone he picked up. It's not jealousy I feel; at least I don't think it is. Hell, I don't know what it is, but I can't stop thinking about him and the fact that I'd never stand a chance with a guy like him.

His footsteps echo through the foyer. They're getting closer to the living room. I keep my eyes closed and pretend to be asleep when he stops just behind the sofa. He starts walking again then the steps vanish, quieted by the rug under the sofa. I can feel him near me. And then, a blanket is draped over me and I feel his lips press softly against my forehead. "Night, Impatient."

I want to open my eyes.
I want to pull him to me.
I just want.
But I don't.
He disappears to his room.
And I stay here alone.

Tuesday, October 24
(Scout)

I got a call from my uncle Jim this morning. He told me that Jane is in rehab.

The news was delivered quickly and efficiently ... because that's how he does everything. His voice sounded flat, emotionless ... because that's how he does everything.

He's not a bad guy, but he is detached. I know how to deal with him though, that's why he called me and not Paxton.

He wants me to tell Paxton.

I don't want to tell Paxton.

I want to keep this from Paxton. Paxton is happier these past few weeks being here than I've ever seen him. He deserves a little more happiness before he's plunged back into his parents' world.

So, I don't tell him. For now, anyway.

Saturday, October 28
(Gus)

I wish I could stay in bed all day and just sleep. I want to skip this day. I want to jump from Friday midnight, to midnight Sunday morning.

I hate reminders.

And today is the worst reminder of all.

It's five-thirty in the morning and I can't go back to sleep. Ma is awake; I hear the coffee pot brewing down the hall. She's always been an early riser, like Bright Side was.

I vocally kick myself in the ass. "Get up you big bastard. Let's face this day."

I search around on the floor for a pair of shorts. I should probably think about doing some laundry—it's reached a critical level. I find a pair of swim trucks and give them the sniff test. They smell bad but still look clean, so I slip them on.

Ma's in the kitchen when I get there. Her coffee mug is raised halfway to her mouth. She doesn't look surprised to see me up so early. Without hesitation she sets her mug on the counter and walks over to me. This is the part where we say good morning and make small talk. The part where we act like it's any other day.

Except that it's not any other day.

Ma wraps her arms around my waist, and I wrap mine around her shoulders and pull her in tight. We both hold on. She's tense, and she's trying not to cry. She always tenses up when she's trying to hold back emotion. It's hard for her because she's emotional by nature. It's not that she's a crier. She's not, but she wears her heart on her sleeve. She's easy to read because she shares her emotions with everyone she meets.

We stand there for a long time before I say anything. "Twenty-one. Can you believe it, Ma? Bright Side would've been twenty-one today."

Ma nods and repeats, "Twenty-one."

I don't know why, but I'm smiling thinking about her. For a moment I'm filled up with light. Bright Side's light. It truly was fucking infectious. "I bet she would've spent today on a wicked, drunken rager."

I feel Ma trembling with laughter against me, and hear her

155

chuckle quietly. It makes my heart happy to hear her laugh.

"I don't know about a rager, honey, but I'm certain she would have made the most of it. That's what Kate always did best. She always knew how to make the most of every day."

I'm still smiling. "She did. Guaranteed she would've done a twenty-first proud. *Rager*. I'm telling you, it would've been epic."

Ma laughs again. "Maybe you're right."

I release her and pour myself a cup of coffee and stir in a few scoops of sugar before turning back to Ma. "You going to the cemetery today?"

She smiles and nods. "I am. Do you want to come with me?"

I surprise myself when I answer without even thinking about it. "Wouldn't miss it."

After we both shower and dress, Ma drives us to the florist for two bouquets of yellow tulips. Then we stop at the convenience store for four Twix bars. By the time we park in the cemetery lot, Ma's hands are clenching the steering wheel so tight I swear she's going to leave an impression. I've been trying like hell the entire ride to not think about what we're doing. I thought that terror would overtake me. It's strange, because now that we're here, I feel calm. I feel like Bright Side is nearby. I haven't visited since the funeral, because I thought it would destroy me. I thought it would amp up my anger. I thought it would remind me that my life is shit without her. But, right now, in this moment, I feel more whole than I have in months. Leave it to Bright Side to haunt me from the grave—and instead of it being creepy, it's sunshine and rainbows and fucking unicorns.

"You okay, Ma?" I ask.

She nods. She can't talk. I pat her right hand, then step out of the car and gather the flowers, candy bars, and a blanket from Ma's trunk before walking around to open Ma's door. She's still holding onto the steering wheel for dear life. I shift everything I'm carrying to one arm and gently pry her fingers off the wheel. Taking her by the hand, I urge her out of the car and we walk hand-in-hand to Bright Side and Grace. When we reach their small, simple, matching headstones, I release Ma's hand and spread out the blanket. Ma sits down without ever taking her eyes off the headstones. She's not blinking and her eyes are full of fresh tears.

I don't know if Ma's visited Bright Side here, so I ask. "This your first time, Ma?" Bright Side passed in January. It's been nine months.

She shakes her head slowly and pries her eyes away to look at me. It's only then that she smiles. "I visit them every week. I don't stay long ... just stop long enough to make sure my girls are okay."

I have the best mom in the entire world. She loved them like she loves me. Fiercely and with her whole heart. "Well, looks like I really am the asshole then, first time and all."

She smiles at my joke.

I remove the cellophane from both bouquets and lay a bundle on the grass just in front of each headstone. It's warm today, they'll wilt quickly in the heat, but they're fresh and pretty now. Grace loved yellow tulips. And Bright Side loved whatever Grace loved, so I know they'll both be happy. Next I unwrap a Twix bar for each of them and set them next to the flowers in the grass. "Sorry, it's not frozen, Bright Side. I'm winging this visit today and I didn't have time to prep properly, dude. Deal with it," I taunt.

Ma laughs behind me. "She did like them frozen, didn't she? I'd forgotten that."

I shift back onto the blanket and hand Ma her Twix bar while I open mine. "Damn skippy, she did. She was picky as hell when it came to coffee and chocolate. Coffee had to be black and chocolate had to be frozen."

Ma laughs again. And then we eat in silence. The silence is nice.

After we finish our candy, we tell stories about Grace and Bright Side. They were family. We did everything together. There are a million stories to choose from.

The sun's getting high overhead when Ma and I decide it's time to leave. We've had the place to ourselves since we arrived. It's been peaceful and warm, and the sky is a bright ocean of blue. Ma kneels down and lovingly runs her hand over each headstone, her fingers passing over their names. The tenderness and adoration on her face and in her touch is lovely. There's no other way to describe it. It's a reminder of the beautiful things the human heart makes possible. She tells them both to be good. She tells them both she loves them. She tells them both she's hugging them. And then she tells them both good-bye. I have a feeling she does this every week when she visits. It's a ritual. A sincere, loving ritual.

I wait for Ma to walk to the car before I fold up the blanket and squat down in front of Gracie's headstone. I lean down and kiss it. I always used to kiss both of them on the forehead, so this feels symbolic. "Bye, Gracie. Take care of your sister for me, okay, dude? I love you." Then I turn to Bright Side's headstone. I kiss it, too. And I look at her name. Kate Sedgwick. That name holds so much power over me. The *best* kind of power: inspiring, encouraging, and respectable. It's a name that I've always associated with badass bravery. It's a name that always meant anything was possible. It's a name that was love and goodness and kindness. "Happy birthday, Bright Side. I hope you're in charge of showtime tonight. I'm expecting nothing short of fucking incredible on behalf of your big day, just so you know. No pressure, but you'd better step up and do epic." I pause, not because I feel weird talking to her, but because I don't want to leave. "I miss you, dude. I miss you *so much.*" I stroke her headstone one time and glance at Ma. She's waiting patiently next to the car. She'd wait for hours if that's what it took. "I love you, Bright Side. I'll never stop loving you. Peace out."

When we get home I call Franco. He answers on the second ring. "Cuntcake?" He sounds worried. And questioning. He knows what today is.

"Namaste, dipshidiot. Hey, I need a favor."

"Anything." He's already agreed. That's the great thing about true friends, they're there whenever and wherever you need them.

"I need to get in to see your brother today. Can you make that happen?"

"You want a tat?" He sounds surprised. He's covered in them from the waist up, while my body is a blank canvas. I always thought it would stay that way, but after this morning I know that's not possible.

"Yup."

"You going big? I'll need to let Julian know what kind of time he's looking at. He doesn't usually work Saturdays."

"Small. Two words," I answer. That's all he needs to know.

"I'm on it. Let me give him a call. I'll hit you up in a few minutes, man." He's so excited he hangs up without saying good-bye.

My cell rings less than five minutes later. We skip the usual derogatory name calling and get straight to business. "Well?"

"Pick you up in fifteen minutes. Julian will meet us at the shop."

"Sweet. I'll be waiting."

I head outside for a cigarette before Franco gets here. He won't let me smoke in his truck so I need to get this out of the way. His grin is joy, and excitement, and curiosity, and maybe even a little pride thrown in, when he pulls up to the house. He claps me on the shoulder when I climb in the cab. "I can't believe it. The candyass caves. Thought needles scared the shit out of you?"

I swallow and my stomach roils. I fucking hate needles. "Don't remind me." And then I catch an earful of what's playing on his stereo. "Now shut up so I can listen. This the new album?"

He turns it up. "Yeah. Sunset Sons is the shit, huh?"

"Fucking killer, dude. They can do no wrong." We continue listening while we drive. His brother's tattoo parlor is about twenty minutes away—just long enough to dwell on the situation and work my stomach into knots.

When we pull up to the storefront, my anxiety kicks into high gear. I'm light-headed when we step inside Julian's shop, but I swallow down the raging nausea, determined to make this happen.

Julian, a cool dude and mega-talented artist, greets us. He reaches out a hand to me, and when I take it, he pulls me in and pats me on the back twice for a bro hug. "How's it going, Gus? Long time no see." He's relaxed and in good spirits.

I'm not. I nod. "Good to see you, dude. Listen, I don't mean to be a dick, but can we just get on with this before I revisit breakfast and deposit it all over the floor?"

He and Franco both laugh as he takes a seat and grabs a pencil and paper. "What's it gonna be, big man?" Julian's always called me that. He's a good eight inches shorter than I am. And he's a skinny little fucker. Basically, he's just a smaller version of Franco and a little more baby faced, which makes him appear

159

younger, even though he's the older brother by a couple of years.

Pointing to the inside of my right forearm, I describe the vision I have.

I catch Franco's smile out of the corner of my eye before he punches me in the arm. "I knew it."

I continue. "I want to keep it simple, but kinda badass, you know? And just black, no color."

Julian nods. He's already drawing.

As I watch the letters come to life, I smile. He gets it. It's flowing script, but it's masculine and bold. "That's it, dude. That's it."

Franco's on my ass as I follow Julian to his room and I want to turn around and tell him to heel or punch him in the throat. He's doing it on purpose; I know he is. He's trying to push my buttons because he knows I'm nervous. Strike that. I'm fucking scared shitless.

My eyes pinch closed as Julian cleans and preps my forearm, only opening them after he's applied the stencil drawing. He asks me to take a look and give him the go-ahead before he makes it permanent.

It does look badass, but I only nod. If I open my mouth I'll heave.

When his gun buzzes to life, I close my eyes again.

"Want me to hold your hand?" Franco asks, his voice high-pitched and ridiculous.

"Fuck off, dude. I know you've always wanted a piece of this, but I'm off-limits at the moment."

He laughs and claps his hands in amusement. That's one of my favorite things about Franco, his sense of humor. He always knows when to use it. And it's always spot on. It's always just what I need.

Surprisingly, the tattooing feels more like an irritation than actual physical pain. If I can keep my brain shifted away from the fact that a needle is jabbing and piercing my skin in rapid succession, it's almost bearable. *Almost.*

"You doing okay?" Julian asks. "You need a break? We're about halfway there."

Keeping my eyes closed, I shake my head. "Just keep going. Stopping makes it worse."

"Well, this is something I never thought I'd see." It's a new voice that's joined our little soiree.

"What the fuck? I thought this was invite only." I challenge from behind closed lids.

Jamie answers, "Franco texted us. We had to come see this with our own eyes to believe it."

When I peek one eye open Jamie and Robbie are both standing in the doorway leaning their heads in since there's not room for another body in this cramped space. "Believe, motherfucker," I mutter.

I'm trying to focus on breathing steadily, but my need for a cigarette is nagging me to the point that it's a distraction I can't ignore. I need that calm. My body needs that calm. My mind needs that calm. That and the fact that the repetitive needle jabbing is no longer irritation and has transformed into pain now. "I need a fucking cigarette," I say, my voice strained. I'm not getting up out of this chair until we're done, but verbally acknowledging the craving seems to quiet it. Makes it bearable.

Julian laughs. "You're doing great, big man. Only a couple more minutes, then I'll go outside and have one with you."

"Deal," I say through gritted teeth.

When the hum of the gun quiets, I know he's done. I open my eyes and my throat seizes when I see her words on my arm.

Her words.

Do epic.

Damn, I loved that girl and everything she stood for.

"That's pretty damn epic, asswipe." It's Franco. And it's sincere.

They're all leaned in to take a closer look.

My skin is angry, raised, and red, but the tattoo is eight inches by two inches of beauty. "You're a goddamn Picasso, Julian. Thanks."

Julian grins. He and Franco have the same huge grin. He looks proud of himself. "Glad you like it, big man."

When I stand up, Jamie claims my vacated spot. "I'm next. Same tattoo." He looks resolved. He has a few tattoos on his back, but his arms are bare.

"Me too." Franco and Robbie chime in together.

I scan the small crowd, my confidants. "Really?"

161

They're all nodding. Solemnly. Our band. A band of brothers.

Jamie speaks up. "Remember, it was on Kate's list. Do epic. She was talking to Rook. We should all get it. And what better day than her birthday?"

I narrow my eyes at him. "You remembered today was her birthday?"

He nods. "Of course." Jamie is the most innocent of all of us. He's just ... good. Of course he remembered.

They're all nodding again. They all remembered. I look at Julian. "You have plans? Can you make this happen? I'll pay for all of them. Double, since it's your day off."

"Let's go have a cigarette and then we'll do this."

Julian makes it happen. We all walk out with matching tattoos. Though Franco's is smaller, on his wrist where his sleeve ends, because blank real estate was in short supply.

Outside on the sidewalk, I stop in my tracks. The sun is setting. It's like fire in the sky.

Bright.

Brilliant.

Orange.

The four guys stand with me in awed silence. They know how much Bright Side loved to watch the sunset.

My smile grows as the sun makes its final descent and plunges us into darkness. Bright Side was *definitely* in charge tonight.

"That's my girl."

Tuesday, October 31
(Scout)

Audrey and I are in her car, driving home from her office. She's been quiet the past few days. I'm not one to pry, but it's unlike her. There's a sadness in her eyes that's undeniable.

I don't like being around sadness, because it brings up all the feelings inside me that I try to push down. I'm great at suppressing emotion. I can force bad feelings down into my shoes and walk all over them until they're dust under my feet. It's the good feelings that seem elusive sometimes. I live in a world of middle ground. Stoic and unfeeling most of the time. It's easier that way.

When we get home from work, Gustov is waiting outside for Audrey. He's smoking, but as soon as she gets out of the car he stubs out his cigarette and pulls her into a hug. They don't say anything. They just hold on tight. That hug is pure comfort. It's love. I've never seen a parent and child with the kind of relationship they have. There's a level of mutual respect and admiration, loyalty and love that was uncomfortable to be around at first. It seemed contrived. Parents and their children don't have deeply rooted friendship. But these two do. The way they get each other, support each other, is beautiful. The closest relationships I have are with Aunt Jane and Paxton. I know Jane loves me in her own way and I love her, but it's not like this. And Paxton? We love each other like siblings, but a seventeen-year-old boy shouldn't be expected to carry me emotionally. I'd never begin to burden him with that. So, I go it alone most of the time.

Walking inside, I leave Audrey and Gustov alone to talk.

When I get to my room, I feel trapped. Like I'm lost. And every emotion I've been stomping on the past nine months starts rising. And rising. Until I'm crying and I have no idea why. I don't want to cry. And suddenly, Michael's face flashes in my mind. I don't want Michael to have this hold on me. I just want to be over him. But I can't. I gave him everything I was. Everything I am now is *less* than what it was before. There's a void. I'm incomplete. My mind is running a million miles a minute and my anxiety is skyrocketing. Maybe a shower will help calm me down. I always shower in the morning after my run, but I feel like I need to soak in misery for a while. I let the hot water pound against my skin. I picture it battering out the bad. Battering out the loss. Battering out the resentfulness and the bitterness. I stand there for a long time and I cry. I haven't cried in months. Being with Michael the other day brought back to the surface all of the ugliness. And all of the love. Damn Michael. I loved him and love was important back then. To me at least. In the beginning, sex was more than just an act. It was a commitment. It was a declaration of that love. But then the act turned into pure, unadulterated need and self-loathing. I used to tell myself I wasn't the bad guy. But now, reality's slipping in and I'm beginning to hate myself. To regret things I've done. The lines of sex and love and right and wrong have been blurred. I hate it.

"Shut the hell up." That was me talking to me. Out loud. I need to get out of this shower and get back to life.

After throwing on a pair of sweats and a T-shirt, I decide the best thing I can do to keep busy is to go make dinner so that Audrey doesn't have to.

When I get to the kitchen, Audrey and Gustov aren't there, which is strange because it's Tuesday and Audrey always makes veggie tacos on Tuesday. Gustov usually helps her if he's home. He's almost always home, unless he's surfing. He spends more and more time out in the water. Which is good. He looks better. He's lost weight and gained muscle. He's got some color. He looks like life is slowly being breathed back into him. I think being on the road kills him. He's a different person at home. I can see that difference now.

I hear the TV playing in the living room. Children's voices. Laughter—innocent and pure. Laughter so transparent that the happiness housed inside is undeniable. When I enter the room, Audrey and Gustov are sitting on the sofa. Gustov is stretched out along the length of the chaise on one end. His arms are bent at the elbows and his hands are resting behind his head. He looks peaceful and happy. I've never seen that look on him. He's smiling slightly, looking content. Audrey is sitting on the other end of the sofa. Her legs are pulled up under her to one side. She's still wearing her work clothes, which is unusual; she usually changes as soon as she gets home. She's smiling, too. The same contented smile that Gustov is wearing. It amazes me how much they look alike: same blond hair, same kind eyes, same tall, almost intimidating stature that somehow doesn't scare you because while confident, they're some of the warmest people I've ever met.

They don't know I'm in the room with them. The sound of a little girl's voice pulls my eyes to the TV screen. She's tiny with a head full of messy golden waves that fall down the center of her back. She's giggling like she doesn't know what sadness is. "Get him, Gracie!" she yells.

A boy, much bigger than the girl, runs into the scene. His light blond hair is long and pulled back in a ponytail and his skin is tanned from the sun. He's wearing a pair of swim trunks and holding three water balloons in his hands. He's running after the little girl. She's screaming and the sound is pure joy. She's trying to get away from him when he yells, "You can run, but you can't hide, Bright Side. Besides, Gracie's on my team." He looks off-screen. "Aren't you, Gracie?"

A voice comes from someone off-camera. Her answer giggles its way out. "I'm on Kate's team." And with that, a little girl walks on screen and pelts him right in the chest with a water balloon.

He looks stunned, but his answer is shocked laughter. "Gracie, I thought I was your favorite? What was that about?"

A sharp hoot of laughter comes from what I assume is the camera person, because it's louder than the others. "Way to go, Gracie! Get him!"

The boy turns to face the camera. "What the hell, Ma? Whose side are you on?" He's still laughing when he says it. Hearing him say that and seeing his face, I realize this is Gustov. He looks like he's thirteen or fourteen years old.

The camera person, who I now realize is Audrey, laughs again, but says, "Gus, language." She's scolding him, but she's *not* scolding him at the same time. It's obvious Gus has had his mom wrapped around his little finger his entire life.

The second little girl smiles up at him apologetically. "Sorry, Gus." Her voice is young and innocent. Then she looks at Audrey, into the camera, and her face lights up. It's the first time I've noticed she has Down syndrome. "It was fun though," she says mischievously.

Just then the other girl, the one with the wild hair, races back in and fires three water balloons. One hits him in the side of the head, and two smack him in the back. "Damn right, Gracie. It is fun." She shrieks when Gustov turns on her and chases her down the deck stairs to the beach sand below. This video must've been shot right here in back of their house. I recognize those stairs, that beach.

She's quick and out runs him for a while, but his long legs cover more ground than hers. When he catches her, he tackles her down to the sand. She's squirming beneath him and putting up an impressive fight. When he stands, she's in his arms. She's laughing, but she's pounding her fists against his chest. "Put me down, Gus! So help me God, if you don't put me down you're going to be sorry. I know where you live, I'll take you down in your sleep, dude."

He laughs. "I dare you, Bright Side. I. Dare. You," he says, before walking out in the water and dunking her under. He releases her quickly and struts out of the water like he's proud of himself.

She surfaces and sprints out behind him. He's not expecting it when she jumps on his back and takes him down to the sand. Though I'm trying to watch undetected, I laugh. I can't help myself. I want to cheer for her. Serves him right. I like this girl.

Audrey and Gustov both turn at my laughter. Audrey pauses the DVD player with a remote and smiles at me.

"I'm sorry," I apologize, suddenly feeling like I'm intruding on a very private moment.

"Nonsense," Audrey replies. She pats the sofa between them. "Come sit down."

I've watched TV with Audrey before, but never while Gustov is in the room. I shake my head. "I don't want to intrude."

Gustov tosses a throw pillow into the empty space between him and Audrey. "Too late, dude," he says. I would take offense, except the way he's just said it is teasing. He sounds like he did in the video. Or the way he does with Franco.

And for some unknown reason, I find myself taking a seat on the sofa and hugging the pillow to my chest. I'm nervous, but I also feel lighter. Maybe it's the fact that Audrey and Gustov are both smiling, that they're both happy watching these old home videos.

Audrey hits play again. The dark screen remains for a few

seconds.

The next image is the girl they called Gracie sitting at Audrey's dining room table in front of a platter of cupcakes. The frosting is pink. There's a candle in each cupcake. She looks older. I count the cupcakes and candles. Seventeen. It sounds like three or four people are singing "Happy Birthday" to her. She's singing along with them. When the song finishes, she claps her hands.

The blond girl walks up behind her, the one Gustov called Bright Side, although Gracie called her Kate. She's older too, and while she was cute before, she's stunning now. Her hair is still long and unruly, but it's one of the things that makes her beautiful. She looks free. She looks happy. She looks like nothing could ever hold her down. She puts her hands on Gracie's shoulders and bends over until her mouth is at Gracie's ear. "Make a wish, Gracie," she tells her.

Gracie pinches her eyes shut tight. Her lips are pursed. There's a lot of concentration and focus going into this wish.

When her face relaxes slightly, the girl called Kate asks, "Did you make a good one?"

"I made a good one. I wished that—"

A deep male voice cuts her off. "Don't tell your wish, Gracie. It won't come true if you tell us." I'd bet money that was Gustov.

Gracie pulls her lips in between her teeth, like she's physically restraining her secret wish, holding it inside so it doesn't force its way out.

"You ready to blow out the candles, Gracie?" It's Kate.

Gracie nods excitedly. She's bouncing in her chair.

Kate laughs. She has a great laugh. It comes from deep in her belly. It's genuine. "You've got this. One blow, and all the candles will be history. Okay?"

Gracie nods again. The look of concentration has taken over her face again. She's focused and her eyebrows pull in toward the center. She closes her eyes as Kate starts the count.

"On the count of three, Gracie. One. Two. Three!"

Gracie leans forward, eyes still closed, and blows on the candles. Two flicker out, but before she can open her eyes, Kate and another blond head that pops into the screen blow the rest of the candles out.

Gracie leans back and opens her eyes, astonished that all of the candles are extinguished. "I did it!" she cheers.

"You did it!" Kate and Gustov cheer together.

Gracie turns in her seat and looks at Kate with hope in her eyes. "I get my wish?" she asks.

Kate wraps her arms around Gracie's neck and hugs her. "Always. I'll make sure of it."

And just as I'm enjoying myself and getting sucked into the innocence, the screen goes dark again.

"Goddamn, Gracie loved birthdays, didn't she, Ma?" Gustov asks from beside me. He sounds like he's reminiscing.

Audrey nods. "She did. I don't know what she liked more: the cupcakes, or the candles, or the wishes."

The screen lights up again. It looks like a stage in an auditorium, maybe at a school or rec center.

A voice announces, "I'd like to introduce Kate Sedgwick."

Loud cheering and whistling comes from the audience.

Kate walks onto the stage holding a violin. She looks to be about eighteen, carrying the same grace and beauty as before. Her eyes are downcast, as if she's trying to ignore the crowd in front of her.

"That's my girl!" A guy's voice yells from the audience. It sounds like Gustov.

A smile creeps across her mouth as she looks up. She shakes her head, but she's smiling. Her smile seems to say, *Stop, you're embarrassing me* and *Thank you* at the same time.

She tucks the violin under her chin, and for the next ten minutes I can't take my eyes off the screen. I'm riveted. She's amazingly talented. I've gone to the symphony in New York. She's *that* kind of good.

When her violin falls silent, I can't help but say, "Wow." It's a whisper only for me, but I can't help myself.

Gustov looks at me, his eyes brimming with pride. "Damn right," he says.

Audrey sniffles beside me as the screen fades to black again. She pauses it. "She could tell a story with a song. That was beautiful. I need a tissue."

When Audrey returns and starts the video again, we watch Rook play a song down in the basement of this house, their faces bright with youth. Franco doesn't have as many tattoos. After some coaxing, albeit crude, Franco persuades Kate to sing with them. I'm stunned by her voice. Even though the sound quality of the video isn't great, her voice is massive, especially for such a small woman. She's as good as Gustov and I have to admit he has a great voice. They sing well together.

After the fade to black, a song starts playing. It's a single violin. And then a photo slideshow begins. It's three minutes of a heartbreaking song, which has to be Rook and Kate, accompanied by dozens of photos of Gustov, Gracie, Kate, and Audrey. The photos must span twenty years. The kids are toddlers in some but others look more recent. I don't know if it's the song fueling my emotional swings, but as I watch it I feel elated one second and sick to my stomach the next.

By the end, I feel spent. I don't know who Kate and Gracie are, but I have a very bad feeling. These girls were obviously as close as family their entire lives, and I haven't heard about or seen either of them in the months I've been around the Hawthornes.

Gustov pushes off the sofa. "Thanks for that, Ma. I'm going outside."

He needs a cigarette. Or he's escaping. Probably both, the way his voice just sounded. He doesn't hide his emotions. Even when he doesn't talk his mannerisms speak loud and clear.

I should let him go out alone. I know that. They've just let me in on something very private; I should take that gift graciously and keep my damn mouth shut. But I can't. I feel like this is the key to something; that this is the reason there are parts of Gustov that I don't get. Because watching the Gustov in those videos — he was so free and happy.

He's in one of the lounge chairs on the deck facing the water when I step outside. He doesn't look at me when I approach, he just lights his cigarette. His first pull is long and focused.

I feel like I need to ask, to make peace before I barge into his life completely. "Can I sit down?"

He doesn't take his eyes off the horizon, but his answer is gentle, "Sure. It's showtime." It's not what I was expecting, but I can't believe how relieved I am at the acceptance.

I take a seat in the chair next to him. "Showtime?" I ask.

Pointing to the water, cigarette held firmly between his fingers, he looks at me as if I should understand. After he takes in my puzzled look, he elaborates. "The sunset. It's showtime."

And the realization sinks in. "Oh," I answer lamely. I settle back into my chair and for the next ten minutes Gustov and I watch the water swallow the glowing orange orb. Piercing the darkness with words is startling given the solitude, so I speak quietly. "I don't think I've ever watched the sunset." Because I honestly don't think I have. I grew up in New York, surrounded by buildings and hustle and bustle. I was aware that the sun did set every day, but I never took the time to actually watch it happen. I feel a little cheated now, because this was breathtaking.

His eyes narrow infinitesimally. "Are you shitting me?"

I shake my head. "No. Never." The admission has we wondering how many other important things in life I've glossed over.

"How does a person grow to be twenty-something years old and never watch a sunset? Were you raised in a cave, or underground? It's one of the finer spectacles mother nature has to offer, and it happens every night." He widens his teasing eyes for effect. "*Every damn night.*"

I want to laugh, but I sigh instead and it still sounds like I'm amused because I can't hide it. "I know. I grew up in New York—"

He interrupts me with a smirk, "Ah, I was right, a cave. That also explains the accent."

I just stare at him.

He stares back.

And then we both laugh. It feels good, so I go with it.

"I love New York, but yeah, not a lot of opportunity for things like sunsets. Lots of tall buildings and not a lot of horizon."

He nods. "Do you miss it?"

"Sometimes. Usually not."

"Do you like it here? San Diego, I mean?" The way he's looking at me would be unnerving if he wasn't listening so intently. He wants to hear the answer. Most people I've dealt with in life talk but they don't listen. Even those closest to me. People have their own issues that keep them from devoting their full attention to me when we're together. That's fine. I understand. It's what I do, too. I listen with half my brain and focus on everything else that's going on with the other half. It's how I multi-task. How I take everything in. Gustov doesn't. He gives whatever he's doing his full attention.

I can't look away when I answer him. "I do. The people are different. No one's in a hurry. People talk a lot more. It's kind of hard to get used to, but I like it."

"That's because San Diego's the real deal." He winks at me before he lights another cigarette. After that first long drag, he looks at it thoughtfully. "How come you never complain about my smoking? I mean, you don't smoke and you take really good care of yourself. I know you probably don't like it."

I shrug. "It's not my place. I used to smoke. I know how hard it is to quit." It's as simple as that.

He's still looking at the cigarette in his hand, regarding it like it's a burden. "I need to quit." His voice lowers. "I know I do. But I can't. I've tried so many times." He looks at me like he needs me to console him or tell him it's okay.

"You'll figure it out. When the time's right it'll happen. You have to want it though. No one can do it for you."

He nods solemnly and silence settles between us.

I take that as my chance to ask, "Who are Gracie and Kate?"

He smiles again. It's small and loving. The same smile he wore inside. The same smile I wish he wore all the time now that I've seen it, because it transforms him. "My best friends," he answers.

It makes me smile. "Looks like you've known them your whole life."

He nods, but he's still smiling.

"Where are they?" I ask hesitantly, and that eerie feeling creeps back in.

His gaze drifts upward, toward the sky. "Heaven, I suppose. Gracie went first and I sure as hell know Bright Side would've beat down the goddamn door to get in if she knew her sister was inside. They're together, I have no doubt."

A chill runs through me. "I'm sorry."

He looks at me and though the smile is still in place the joy has drained from his eyes. "Yeah. It's fucked up. Today would've been Gracie's twenty-second birthday. Three days ago would've been Bright Side's twenty-first."

"They were so young," I say in disbelief.

He nods again. "Old souls. Young bodies. Gracie got sick and

171

died almost a year and a half ago. It took us all by surprise. And cancer stole Bright Side from us in January." The smile has faded completely, replaced with glistening eyes.

I don't know what to say, so I say again what I've already said. "I'm sorry."

He's still nodding, the repetitive gesture of someone lost in thought. "Yeah."

I want to hug him, which I never have the urge to do with anyone other than Paxton and Jane. I want to comfort him, but I feel removed from the situation, suddenly like an intruder. "I'm sorry," I echo. I hope he hears the comfort in my words. I'm not good at showing my feelings.

His eyes turn to me, still shiny with grief. "What's the story with Michael?"

I'm caught off guard. "What?"

"You know what I mean, what's your history?" He's talking quietly, but loud enough that I can hear him. He's not demanding information from me, he's just asking.

"Old boyfriend." I answer and that's where I leave it.

"Sorry, I don't mean to dredge up the past ... or the present," he adds. He's asking, without asking, if we're together.

I shake my head. "No. It's fine. I'm glad it's over ..." I trail off.

"But you still love him?" he asks softly. Goddamn, I wish he didn't read me so well.

I shrug. "I do, but I don't. It's complicated." I decide now's as good a time as any and ask, "What about the woman who you went out with a couple weeks ago? Girlfriend?"

He looks confused for a few seconds. "Clare? Hell no. Cool girl. Now. But, no. *Definitely* no."

I don't know why, but that lightens my heart.

He sighs and returns to our conversation, but he shifts it. I felt it. This is about pain now. "Love's a pisser."

I drop my head back against the cushion and roll it to look at him. He's staring at me again. His eyes are open, a gateway. He's honest, and he's kind, and most importantly he's not judging me. I nod in agreement. "Yeah, it sure as hell is." I don't know how I know, but I know his heart is broken, too. "Have you ever been in love?"

He hasn't blinked. "Once."

"How long did it last?"

Looking back up to the sky, he answers. "Twenty-one years ... and three days."

It hits me hard. Kate. He's talking about Kate. His Bright Side. No wonder he's walking around like a shell of a man. He lost the love of his life. Instead of fighting the urge, I don't hesitate this time. I slide my legs off the lounge chair and place them on the deck between our chairs and shift my weight from mine over onto his. I sit there on the edge of his seat against his hip and I just look at him. I guess I'm asking for permission. I don't usually do things like this. I don't usually offer comfort. He balls up my shirt just above my hip in his fist. His eyes are pleading now—begging for friendship, comfort, and consolation. He needs to let this out. I could analyze this. I could overthink it until I talk myself out of it. But I don't, instead I lean down slowly until my head's resting on his chest and slide my hands underneath his back until I'm squeezing him. Until I feel his warmth against me. And when his big arms wrap around me, I realize in this moment that I've never really been hugged. *This* is a hug. This is what human contact is supposed to feel like. It's supposed to feel ... *human*. Distilled until it's nothing but one human being transferring support to another human being in the form of touch that's unselfish and pure in intention. And I know he feels it, too, because his chest rises in a few stuttered breaths and he lets the tears go. I just hold him until his breathing evens out, at which point he pulls me up until my head is resting on the cushion next to his and the front of my body is molded to the side of his. Our arms are still wrapped around each other and I feel pressure from both sides, which tells me neither one of us wants to let go.

"Can we just lie here for a while? Like this?" he asks with a tremble in his voice. The vulnerability I hear makes my heart ache.

"Sure," I answer, because in all honesty, I don't want to let go either. This hug, him crying and opening up to me, the humanity in all of it is something I can feel in my heart. I feel alive and heavy with emotion, heavy like a tide that threatens to pull you under, but you somehow know it won't because your heart is buoyant enough to keep you afloat no matter what. It's blind faith ... hope, or at least as close to hope as anything I've ever felt. A faint, reluctant hope that I can feel in both of us. Buried deep.

Wednesday, November 1
(Gus)

"Can I ask you a question?" I'm a little nervous to initiate this conversation, because I know she'll get defensive. And I want her to open up to me like she did last night; I don't want to take a step backwards with her. I want her to trust me enough to give me her whole story. I'm learning to lay it all out there and I want her to do the same, because it feels so fucking good. I guess more than anything I want her to feel like she can be *Scout* around me, even if she's never been *Scout* around anyone else. She's so guarded. It must be fucking exhausting. I want to remove the burden. Everyone deserves to live free.

"You can always ask me a question. Doesn't mean I'm going to answer it."

Well, that was validation of my fear. Though I get the feeling self-preservation is such habit with her that she doesn't really think things through before she says stuff like that. "How'd you get your scars?" I'm not sugarcoating it, because I'm not really a sugarcoating kind of guy. And she's not a sugarcoating kind of girl. Besides, getting right to the point with her is the easiest way to communicate.

"That's rude," she says with little emotion, though there's mild shock in her eyes. This is a topic she avoids at all costs. A topic she doesn't know how to navigate openly.

"It's not rude. It's part of who you are, like your hazel eyes or your bad attitude," she shoots me a glare that's more embarrassed than it is angry. I meet it with a smile so she knows I'm kidding about the bad attitude, and then I continue, "Or the fact that you have stellar legs."

She shakes her head. It's a soft gesture, non-combative, but resolute, and returns her gaze to the TV.

I wait several seconds. "That's it?"

"Yup. That's it."

"We're not gonna discuss?"

"Nope." Eyes still fixed on a commercial I know she's not even watching. Nope sounds more maybe.

"Why?" I push.

"I don't ... discuss it." The pause tells me she's torn. Like she

174

wants to tell me, but she doesn't know how to have this conversation. So that's where it ends. She's done.

Damn, I'm almost scared she's going to get up and leave to avoid this further, so I shut up even though I have a million questions I want to ask. I'm always full of questions. But I really want to know how? And when? And why? And where? It's not morbid curiosity, and I'm not trying to make her uncomfortable. I'm asking because I want her to *be* comfortable. In her own skin. Literally and figuratively. I want her to just say, *Fuck it. I am who I am. Nobody's perfect.* Because nobody *is* perfect. Some people wear their scars on the outside. Others wear them on the inside. Same difference. Your character, your heart, your essence, that's what's important, because that's the real you. All the rest, our looks, the material stuff? It's just meaningless bullshit.

Saturday, November 4
(Scout)

My phone beeps while I'm out running early this morning. I glance down at the screen. It's a text from Michael that reads, *Pick you up at 11:30.*

My stomach immediately clenches and I have to stop running. I feel nauseous. I don't intend to pick up a relationship with him again. His last visit was a moment of weakness, mixed with the closure I needed. Instead of running again, I walk back to Audrey's. A slow walk. A sad walk. A shameful walk.

Once home, I strip off my sweaty clothes, the entire time telling myself, *I'm not going with him.*

In the shower, I continue telling myself, *I'm not going with him.*

Combing out my hair, *I'm not going with him.*

Applying lotion to my legs and arms, *I'm not going with him.*

Slipping on my dress, *I'm not going with him.*

Strapping on my sandals, *I'm not going with him.*

Grabbing my purse at eleven twenty-five, *I'm not going with him.*

Opening the front door at eleven twenty-seven, *I'm not going with him.*

Standing in the driveway at eleven-thirty watching his rental car pull up promptly as always, *I'm not going with him.*

Climbing into the passenger seat, *I'm not going with him.*

I'm going with him.

But only because I need to tell him it's over. And mean it. Again.

Because in my heart ... it's finally over. I've let him go.

And now I'm trying not to think about Gustov.

He skips lunch and heads straight to his hotel. The same hotel within walking distance from Audrey's house.

He also skips the usual update on his life's successes to impress me; they're forgotten in his haste. I can't help but notice the bulge in his dress pants. He's usually more controlled.

He parks in the hotel's back lot and as soon as the car's in park his hand finds mine and brings it to his groin. He closes his eyes and hisses when contact is made. "Shit, I've missed you, angel." He's missed my body, not me. He releases my hand and frantically works at the button and zipper until he's laid bare. No underwear today; he's not messing around. Closing his eyes, he lays his head back against the headrest. "You know what to do."

I look around shocked. I'm not doing this. And even if I were up for it, it wouldn't be here ... in broad daylight ... in a fucking parking lot.

After a moment's pause on my part, his eyes snap open. They're fully dilated with arousal and anger. "*Now*, Scout." He roughly grabs a handful of hair at the back of my head and forces my face down to his crotch. "Suck me off, angel. Give me what I need."

He's hurting me, and suddenly I'm forcing back tears. I refuse to open my mouth. "No," I say forcefully.

He jerks my head back to look him in the eye, and in the process I feel a patch of hair ripped from my scalp. I've never seen him look this crazed. He looks psychotic, eyes narrowed in anger and speaking through clenched teeth. "What did you just say to me?"

I'm scared, and my brain's warning mechanism is screaming at me. *Get away! Run!* Tears are forming in my eyes, I don't know if it's out of fear, anger, or pain, because I'm feeling equally intense amounts of all three. "Let go of me, Michael. We're done. That's why I came with you today, to tell you I *can't* and *won't* do this anymore."

He releases my hair, and before I can even process what's going on, he's outside the car running around to open my door. I beat him to it and try to make a break for it, but he's already there. He grips both wrists tightly. Too tight. It hurts. He knows how to inflict pain. In the past it's been done for his pleasure, but there were always boundaries. This is something else. He's *trying* to hurt me and it's working. He's twisting the skin back and forth against the bone. A pained sob tears from my throat.

His mouth is pressed up against my ear now; his breath hot and unwelcome. "You're mine, angel. *Only mine.* You're a good little whore, now come inside with me and stop making a scene. I'm going to fuck you senseless. We can do this the easy way, or the hard way, it's up to you."

177

My skin is crawling and I can't hold back the sobs. I feel bile rising in the back of my throat from his threats, and before I know it, I've vomited all over the asphalt and his shirt.

He releases me immediately and recoils, but not before his hand meets my face. That was a closed fist. The force and sting takes me to the ground and has me seeing stars. I'm still crying, the tears streaming steadily down my cheeks.

"Stop the act, Scout. Crying isn't attractive on you." It's a flippant insult meant to hurt my feelings and my heart. As his words sink in, I realize I'm scowling at him. He's usually arrogant and self-centered, but I've never seen this side of him. And I'm still scared, but now I'm more mad than anything.

The menace is still in his eyes and I know he's about to say something awful before the words leave his mouth. "The crying only draws attention to your face." He smiles and his face twists into an evil grin. "Remember when I told you that you were beautiful?"

I don't answer. I do remember. He's the only person who's ever told me that.

"*I. Lied.*" The evil smile spreads and it settles in his eyes. He's like a wild animal. "Why do you think we always fuck in the dark? Because I can't look at you and get off. You're easy. *Easy,*" he spits at me. "*And your pussy is so fucking sweet.*"

It's like another punch and my lips drop the scowl and part slightly. It's at that moment that I see this entire relationship for what it's always been. I'm prey. I've always been easy prey. An easy target. The damaged girl, inside and out. He must've seen it from the first time we met.

I scramble to my feet and I run. I run as fast as I can.

This time he doesn't chase me.

Halfway home my cell chimes in a text, *I'll see you in a few weeks.* Completely nonchalant, like what just happened wasn't completely psycho.

I don't respond.

I'll never respond.

He'll never treat me like that again.

No one's home when I get to Audrey's. It's just after noon. I've never been more thankful to be alone than I am right now. Inside my bathroom, I remove my dress. There's vomit on it, so I throw it in the trash can. My panties are next, I toss them in with the dress, wishing I could set fire to it all and watch them burn. Burn to ash, just like I wish I could do to the memory of him. To the memory of what just happened. This is the last time. Today was a twisted nightmare. I'm done.

I'm crying again. Or more likely, I never stopped. Standing in the shower under the scalding water, I let it burn my skin. The new pain takes my mind off the not-so-old pain. The physical pain that's still fresh. I hurt all over. He took no mercy on me.

The right side of my face is throbbing and tender.

My scalp burns where he pulled my hair.

My wrists are ringed in purpling bruises, a gift from his restraint. A telltale reminder of the size and strength of his hands. There's pain and tingling weakness.

I hurt.

I'm sobbing so hard that I'm nearly hysterical at this point.

I can't wash him off me.

I need to wash *him* off me.

I need to wash *me* off me.

I feel sickened by what happened. He's never gone that far before. Not even close.

But I can't help but feel responsible. I went with him, when I knew I shouldn't.

The blame keeps shifting from him to me. From me to him. I know it's all on him. *I fucking know that.* But my screwed up mind always turns everything back around on me. I'm always to blame for people treating me badly; it's how I've lived my life. People I love don't know how to love me back. They hurt me. That's how they love.

That's how they love.

When the water begins to run cold, I step out and just stand there dripping on the tile floor. I'm looking at myself in the mirror over the sink from afar. My right cheek is bruised, and my eyes are puffy and red. I tenderly touch my face. The bruises on my wrists look worse now that I see them next to my cheek, a vicious purple trio. As the wounds emerge, I gasp and take a few steps closer to the mirror. There's a fresh cut bleeding amongst the scarring and bruising on my right cheek. He punched me with his left hand.

His left fucking hand. "That lying bastard." He was wearing a wedding ring and I hadn't even noticed, because everything deteriorated so quickly into a nightmare. His. Wedding. Ring.

My shoulders rise in a sob, but nothing comes out. I'm cried out.

I skip clothes and walk into the bedroom and climb in under the sheet. I need to sleep.

For days I need to sleep.

Maybe I'll wake up and realize this was only a nightmare. And when I wake up I'll never talk to Michael again. Ever.

Sleep comes for me quickly, my mind taking pity on my body and shutting everything off.

(Gus)

It's around midnight when I get home. Franco and I went to Joe's Bar to watch a local band play. They were good. We stuck to a booth in a dark corner in the back and no one recognized us. The whole night was mint.

Ma's sitting in the living room reading. "Hi, honey, did you have a good time?"

"Hey, Ma. Yeah, I did." The answer surprises me. I did.

She smiles. "Good. Do you want something to eat? There are leftovers in the fridge. I'll heat them up if you're hungry."

I yawn. "No thanks, Ma." I pat my belly. "Had three grilled cheese and a basket of fries at Joe's earlier. Tank's full."

She laughs. I love to hear her laugh. I'm hearing it more and more lately.

I walk over and lean over the back of the sofa and kiss the top of her head. "I'm going to bed. Night Ma. Love you."

She reaches up and pats my cheek with her hand. "I'm going to shower and go to bed, too. I love you, Gus. Good night."

As I'm walking toward the hallway she calls out, "Gus, can you check on Scout before you go to bed? She hasn't come out of her room all night. I knocked on the door around seven o'clock to see if she wanted to eat with me, but she didn't answer."

"She's probably sleeping, Ma, it's midnight. I don't want to wake her."

"Just make sure she's not sick or something," she replies.

I shrug, but do as she asked. I knock softly on the door. I really don't want to wake her, so it's a half-hearted effort. I know she didn't hear it unless she's awake and has her hearing aid in. I've learned her limits where hearing is concerned. No movement inside and no answer. I turn the doorknob slowly and push my way in. I feel like I'm breaking and entering, burglar-style, in our own home. With the door open and the moonlight spilling in, for an instant I see Bright Side standing there in a tank top and panties, just the way she looked on her last night here before she went to Grant. When I blink, the apparition is gone. Damn, I only had one beer tonight. I shouldn't be seeing things.

When I glance at the bed, I see her lying there, Bright Side, hooked up to IVs and oxygen. Fighting to make the most of her last days. I didn't sleep during her last weeks with us. I stayed up all night looking at her, not wanting to miss out on even a minute with her. I watched her, just in case she needed anything. I held her hand, just so I could feel her, so I knew she was still real. Still my girl. Goddamn, I don't want to be in this room with her memory. It feels heavy, claustrophobic.

Every thought evaporates into the air like a wisp of smoke when I catch sight of something—something that doesn't look right. I open the door wider and the light from the hall floods in. Stepping closer to the bed, I stop when I get confirmation and my stomach twists. There's a bruise on Impatient's cheek that spreads to the edge of her eye, and a cut runs down the middle of her cheekbone. The scarring stands out bold against the purple background. I let my eyes drift over the rest of her and the sick feeling amplifies when I see a solid bruise three inches wide circling each wrist.

"What the fuck?" I wasn't supposed to say that out loud. I was thinking it in my head. Over and over and over, but it wasn't supposed to pass between my lips.

She stirs and I cringe, because I don't want to wake her. But at the same time I want to find out what happened. Find out what I can do to help. And find out who the motherfucker is so I can hunt him down and kill him.

"Gustov?" Her voice is hoarse. It's always hoarse when she wakes up, but even more so now, like her throat's been brutalized.

I kneel on the floor next to her, so we're on the same eye level.

I'm talking softly because I don't want to upset her, but loud enough that she'll hear me because I'm sure she doesn't have her hearing aid in. "What happened?"

Even in the dark, I see recognition flare in her eyes. She looks panicked. She's pulling the sheet up over her cheek and hiding her arms and hands underneath. I don't know if she's more self-conscious about the bruises or her scars. I've never seen her left arm bare before. The scars extend down from her shoulder almost to her wrist.

Spare Ribs was curled into her side, sleeping peacefully. She stands protectively and meows, probably sensing Impatient's stress. I shush the cat and pet her once before picking her up and setting her on the floor.

"Hey." I pull back the sheet so I can just see her eyes. They're shiny. "Hey," I repeat, it's quiet and coaxing. I need answers. I'm not sure I really *want* to hear them, but I *need* to help her. "What happened?"

She's staring at me now. The look on her face is determined. She doesn't want to talk. Slowly that fades and morphs into hurt and sadness as her forehead creases and the corners of her mouth turn down, tight with the effort of someone who's trying not to cry. And then the tears start, one or two before her strength crumbles and she's sobbing.

I don't know what else to do, so I sit on the edge of the bed next to her belly where the cat was tucked away. There's not much room. I start stroking her hair from the crown of her head down to her shoulder blades. Ma used to do this whenever I was upset as a kid, and it always worked. She's still crying, but I can feel her relaxing. When her eyes open, and the tears are no longer flowing, I don't know what to say to her so I run her soft hair through my fingers. Again. And again.

She sniffles and tries to smile at me. "You're not an asshole, Gustov."

I didn't expect that. I shrug. "Sometimes I am."

She shakes her head. "No, you're not. You're one of the good guys. Believe me."

I don't know where she's going with this, but I need to steer her in the direction of answers. "So, who is the asshole?" She knows what I'm asking, and my mind keeps going to fucking

Michael.

She shakes her head.

I touch her cheek gently and her instinct to hide her scar is paired with pain. I pull back my fingers quickly. "Sorry. You want some ice?"

She shrugs. "Doesn't matter."

"Pain matters. Swelling matters. Let's help both with some ice. And then we'll talk."

Ma's in the shower when I head back out to the kitchen. I can hear the water running. I don't want to worry her until I know what's going on with Impatient, so I decide to hold off until the morning to tell her anything because she'll sit up all night worrying if I only give her the few details I have now.

After a stop in the kitchen for a baggie of ice and a kitchen towel, I head back to Impatient. I'm almost there when I hear it. I'd say someone's knocking on the door, but the level of noise that's coming from the foyer would imply someone's pounding the shit out of the front door and skipping polite knocking.

The pounding is quickly fueling a fire that ends with me in a rage. By the time I reach the door I'm ready to pull the motherfucker off its hinges and go ripshit on whoever's on the other side. I swing it open, yelling, "*What the fuck?*"

And then I see him. Fucking Michael. My blood is boiling now.

He's standing there in his three-piece suit trying to look all composed and professional, except that he's practically vibrating and a vein at his temple is throbbing. I can smell the gin on him like he's been marinating in it instead of drinking it.

He hasn't answered me, so I try again. "Jesus Christ, was all the pounding really necessary, dickhead? We have a fucking doorbell."

"Where is she?" he growls.

I laugh, although that question is anything but funny to me. I know this guy put those bruises on her even if she won't admit it yet. He's bad news. Standing before me now, he's a head case on the verge of psychopathic. "As soon as you laid a fucking hand on her you lost the right to ask that question. I should beat your ass right here, right now, you sonofabitch. But I'm not gonna do that because, believe me, motherfucker, if I get started I won't stop until you're lying face down in the driveway, no longer breathing. *Leave.*"

He shakes his head and his body sways to right itself. He's drunk off his ass. "She's mine."

I shake my head and take a step over the threshold so I'm nose to nose with him. "What the fuck kind of creepy stalker talk is that? *Leave her the fuck alone.*"

"Are you fucking her?" The temple vein throbbing has amped up in intensity.

"None of your fucking business."

A short burst of disgust flares from his nostrils. "I knew it."

"Listen, I don't know what you think you know, jackass, but you need to leave Scout alone. If I find out you've contacted her in any way, shape, or form, I will find you, you piece of shit. *And I will annihilate you.* Are we clear?"

Before he can answer I've stepped back in the house and slammed the door in his face.

"Goddamn, I need a cigarette," I say to myself as I march through the living room toward the hallway. I need to get back to Impatient.

The bedside table lamp is turned on when I return. It's dim, but lights the room in a soft glow. She's dressed in a long-sleeved pajama top and shorts. The pillows are propped up against the headboard and she's leaning back on them. Her legs are pulled into her chest and her chin is resting on her knees. Her hair's messy and tangled and her eyes are puffy, like she's been crying for days.

"Here you go," I say, handing her the ice pack. My hands are still shaking with anger from the run-in with fucking Michael, and I'm trying to calm myself.

She takes it and presses it to her cheek, wincing against the pain.

I sit on the bed next to her. She seems relaxed, but not in a peaceful way. It's more like all of the energy has been drained out of her. "So. This is the part where I ask questions and if I'm lucky, you answer them."

She nods.

"When did you meet fucking Michael?"

"*Fucking* Michael?" she questions, though it also sounds like

184

agreement. One hundred percent agreement.

"Yeah, that's what I call him in my head. Seems especially fitting tonight." I'm trying to hold back my anger, but it's proving difficult.

She takes a deep breath and heaves it out, and just when I think she's going to keep quiet she says, "I met him a little over two years ago. I was at a coffee shop near my subway stop, killing some time. There was a storm outside. He came in, bought some coffee, and asked if he could sit with me because every other chair in the place was taken. Against my better judgment, I said yes. I thought he would just sit there and ignore me, because that's what people usually do. They don't want to stare at my scars, so they pretend I'm not there."

"But he didn't ignore you?"

She shakes her head sadly. "No. He talked to me. About normal stuff. It was small talk, I guess, but it didn't feel small to me. We talked for over an hour, and in that hour I never once felt ugly or broken." She's talking quietly, but her voice carries so much emotion. And it's the kind of emotion that could flip at any moment only you don't know which way it's going to go. Sad. Mad. Defeated. Vengeful.

"You're not ugly. Or broken."

Her eyes find mine, but there's no agreement in them and she continues without acknowledging my comment. "He asked for my phone number when I had to leave to catch my train." She shrugs. "And I gave it to him. He was handsome. And he was interesting. And he had on a nice suit. And he was charming. And I didn't think he'd actually call. No one had ever asked for my number before. I was sure he'd throw it in the trash on his way out the door."

She stops there, so I prompt her to continue. "But he did call?"

She nods and exhales a long, slow breath. "He did. He called a month later. He lived in Florida and traveled to New York for a few days every month for his business. He took me out to dinner that night." A faint smile crosses her lips, but instead of joyful, it looks disgusted. "I remember how nervous and happy I was."

"Did you sleep with him that night?" I don't know why I just asked that, but the thought of fucking Michael taking her virginity from her makes me sick.

She shakes her head. "We didn't have sex until his third visit. He took me to his hotel. Over the next few months his visits were a combination of dinner and sex. After that it was just sex."

"But, you loved him?"

When she nods this time, her expression darkens. "I did. And I was fool enough to think he loved me, too. He talked about us being together and getting married someday." She looks at me and the look on her face is heartbreaking. Fucking Michael played her for years. "He talked about it all the time, Gus. I was so fucking stupid that I believed him."

"You're not stupid, Impatient. You trusted him. He's a fucking bastard." Hearing her belittle herself because of this prick makes me want to throttle him.

She shakes her head and stares straight ahead out the window on the other side of the room. It's a blank stare. "And then I got pregnant." Her voice has lost all of the anger; the only thing pouring in now is sadness.

What? I try to let the shock pass quickly and I keep my mouth shut.

She's quiet, just staring out the window lost in it all, until her face drops and tears pool in her eyes. "It happened on New Year's Eve. I found out mid-February." She sniffs trying to hold back the tears, but they break free and start rolling silently down her cheeks.

I want to hug her but I'm scared she'll quit talking, so I take her hand in mine and squeeze so she knows I'm with her. That she's not alone.

When she starts talking again the emotions drain away, even though the tears are flowing. It's the face of shock and devastation, the kind of devastation that leaves you hollow. "I called him to tell him the news, because even though I was scared, I was happy, too." She shrugs. "I never thought I'd have kids. That anyone would want to have kids with me. So, to me the accidental pregnancy was miraculous. A gift." She pauses and sniffs again. "He didn't feel the same way. That's when he told me he was married. And my world fell apart." She wipes the tears from her face with her free hand. Defeat is creeping back in on her. Like she's living it all over again and it's so painful she's shutting

186

down. She shakes her head. "I didn't know .... All that time ... I didn't know." It's like she's pleading with me to believe her.

I nod to let her know I believe her.

"I think every bad feeling known to man hit me during that conversation. I felt sad. I felt betrayed. I felt angry. *So angry.* I felt like an idiot. And I felt I deserved every single one of those emotions, because most of all, I felt guilty. So *fucking* guilty. Because I'd been with someone's husband for two years and I had no idea. The guilt was unbearable. Marriage, relationships, should be honored ... and I'd been having sex with a married man. I felt dirty and used, but I also felt like it was my fault. Like I should've somehow known. I ran back through all of the conversations we'd had, and every time we'd met, looking for clues. And I didn't find any. The days that followed were lonely. I had no one to talk to about it."

"What about your aunt? Couldn't you talk to her?"

She shakes her head. "Not that I would've wanted to put my problems on her anyway, but February was brutal for my aunt. My whole family. Jane tried to commit suicide in early February. She was held under psychiatric evaluation for a couple of weeks after that." She loves and worries about her aunt, you can hear it in her voice.

Huh, that's why Hitler had to leave the tour. I feel bad for the dude now.

She continues. "Anyway, after a few days of drowning in the guilt, I realized that I was better off without him. I could raise a child on my own. I'd love the baby enough for both of us ... I already did." Her voice brightens when she mentions the baby and my stomach drops because I don't know how I know, but I know she lost the baby. She's staring at me now and the smile she's wearing is slowly torn apart by agony until it's nothing but grief. Her voice is only a whisper through the tears she's fighting. "I loved that baby so much. I would've been a good mom, Gustov."

I swallow back the lump in my throat before I agree. "You would've been a good mom." She would've been. She's one of the most focused, responsible, intensely passionate people I've ever met.

She attempts a smile at my confirmation, but rests her head on my shoulder instead. It's heavy, like her heart. She's letting herself lean on me now. "I miscarried on March twenty-ninth. That's the day I discovered what loss really felt like. Losing Michael was nothing compared to losing the baby. You know that saying, 'everything happens for a reason'?"

I nod. She can't see me, but she can feel me.

"I wonder if the person who said it had ever lost someone." It's not a question.

I find my voice and answer anyway. "Probably not. Loss fucking sucks."

"Yeah. It does. I still feel guilty. Like I did something wrong, you know. The doctor's said there was nothing I could've done differently, but I still feel like it's my fault, the miscarriage."

I squeeze her hand again. "Miscarriages happen a lot. It's not your fault. How did fucking Michael take the news?"

"I texted him the next day and told him because I thought he deserved to know. It was the first contact I'd had with him since our split. It was from a new phone number he didn't have. He called me back within minutes and left message after message telling me how sorry he was. That his wife found out about the affair and left him, which I doubted was true. He told me how much he loved me. How much he wanted to see me again. That went on for a week. I changed my number again and never heard from him until he showed up here a few weeks ago."

"And you went with him this time."

She sniffs again. "I did. I'm not proud about that. I think I just needed closure. To everything. I wanted to end it on *my terms* once and for all. That, and despite it all, a little piece of me still loved him."

"How'd that go? The closure?"

She squeezes my hand like she'd rather do that than talk. "Same as always. I got fucked and fucked over."

I'm seething now. "*That sonofabitch.*"

"No. It's my own fault. When I left his hotel room, I knew without a doubt in my mind it was over. That whatever old feelings I'd had for him, it wasn't love. It was more like habit, if that makes sense. It was something I'd done so many times that I'd associated it with love, when that's not what it was at all. It may have started out that way in the beginning, at least for me, but it morphed into something else entirely. So, when he came by earlier today, I met him only to tell him it was over. Because for me it finally was. Obviously ... he didn't take the news very well."

I drop her hand, because now I'm fucking raging. I need a physical release for this fury and I don't want to be anywhere near her when it happens, so I leap from the bed. My hands are clenched into fists and I want to hit something so fucking bad, preferably fucking Michael's face. "*Motherfucker.* He did that to you, didn't he?" I'm pointing to the bruises on her face.

She nods and the tears are in her eyes again.

I'm pacing the room. "What kind of sick sonofabitch hits a woman?" And then I turn back toward her. "You need to get a restraining order. He was just here looking for you."

She looks terrified. I hate that she looks terrified. "What? He was here?"

I nod. "When I went to get the ice, he was banging on the front door. Drunk off his ass, looking for you. I told him to leave you alone or I'd fuck him up. I should've beat his ass."

She doesn't say anything this time. Her eyes are as big as saucers.

And now I'm scanning her room. "Where's your phone?"

She looks to her nightstand first. That's where she always charges it. It's not there. "I think it's in my purse." She crawls off the bed and picks up her purse off the floor by the bathroom door and rifles through it. When she finds her phone she types in her passcode and she hands it to me.

She has thirty-two missed calls and fifty-three text messages. I start scrolling though the texts. They're all from him. I swear the dude is psycho. Over the past few hours he's ping-ponged back and forth between threatening her, to declaring his love, to telling her to fuck off, to groveling. Again. And again. Throw in the random dick pic, too. This guy is sick.

I open up the missed calls and recognize his number. All thirty-two calls. I nod to the phone. "Restraining order should've happened yesterday with this dude. He's certifiable. Put your shoes on. We're going to the police station. After we stop at the ER."

She shakes her head. "Police station, no ER."

She files a report for the physical abuse first. They record her statement and take photos. After that she fills out the necessary paperwork for a restraining order.

It's three-thirty in the morning by the time we get home.

He will never touch her again. I promise.

Sunday, November 5
(Scout)

When I open my bedroom door at noon there's a plate of peanut butter saltines and a glass of grape juice on the floor. The sticky note from Gustov on my door reads, *Let me know if you need anything.*

I pick up the food and set it on my nightstand before writing him a note. *Thanks. For everything.* I stick it to his closed bedroom door before I return to my bedroom, close the door, and eat the most thoughtful meal I've ever eaten.

Thursday, November 9
(Gus)

Impatient's been quiet all week. The bruises are fading, but her spirit is the thing I'm most worried about. She already had a lot on her emotional plate. What happened to her was trauma: physical, emotional, and psychological. I can't erase it. I wish I could, but I can't. So, I'll be here for her, even if she doesn't want me to. She's not pushing friendship away when she needs it most.

I leave a note on her bedroom door before I go to sleep. *Mancala. Pizza. Tonight. Be there or Spare Ribs and I will hunt you down and force you to play with us. That would take the fun out of it. So, how about we keep this easy and you just meet us in the living room at 7:00?*

Friday, November 10
(Scout)

Mancala and pizza was just what I needed. Gustov, Audrey, Paxton, and I all took turns playing in a Mancala cutthroat tournament. We stayed up late. I smiled for the first time all week. I didn't think about Michael. I didn't think about anything. I just had fun. It was the first time in my life I felt like I could just be me, surrounded by people who don't and won't judge me. People who don't see my scars, but who see everything else. It was freeing in a way I can't explain.

After I brush my teeth I leave a sticky note on Gustov's door. A taunt to make him smile; like he made me smile tonight. *You still suck at Mancala. Thanks for the pizza.*

Monday, November 13
(Gus)

More and more I find myself looking forward to waking up in the morning just so I can open my door and see if there's a little piece of her on the other side in the form of a sticky note. The first time she left a note for me on the bus I thought, *Well, this is fucking childish and irritating.* Looking back, hindsight is twenty-twenty. I was a train wreck; I wouldn't have wanted to deal with me either. I didn't want to deal with me, obviously; it's the reason I was drunk all the time.

I'm already grinning when I catch sight of the square-shaped yellow note on my door as it swings open.

The grin is short lived when I read her words. *Car accident = fire = burns = peoples' stares = embarrassment + anger + introversion + sadness*

Shit.

This is as real as she's ever been with me. I want to grab my keys and go to her. Find her at work and pull her away from everything she's doing and just hold her. I want to take away the pain that she's been through, both because of the accident and the insensitive assholes who've made her feel anything less than the perfect human being she is.

Instead, I grab my marker and sticky notes and I write a note of my own, like I always do. I don't know if she'll answer or if she'll shut me out, but I have to try. I keep it short because Impatient's all about the details in life, unless the details belong to her. The ones she doesn't share. *How old were you when it happened?*

**Tuesday, November 14
(Scout)**

11. My dad was drunk. That's why I lived with my aunt and uncle.

Wednesday, November 15
(Gus)

Was your hearing affected by the accident?

**Thursday, November 16
(Scout)**

That was part of the birth lottery. It's no big deal.

Friday, November 17
(Gus)

That one made me smile. I think the solemn tennis match is at an end for now, so I respond, *Kinda like my awesome sense of humor? I won the motherfucking birth lottery with that.*

**Saturday, November 18
(Scout)**

Keep telling yourself that.

(Gus)

And just like that, I know we're good. When a conversation ends in sarcasm with her, I know she's satisfied, at ease. And at ease is the only place I ever want her to be. Especially around me.

Sunday, November 19
(Gus)

"Ma, who's the old lady with the walker standing in our driveway in her nightgown, filching our newspaper?" I'm watching an old woman with silvery-lavender hair, in a pink and purple flowered housecoat, steal our daily news in slow motion outside our kitchen window.

Ma walks over and stands next to me, her smile wide. "Oh, that's Mrs. Randolph. Her daughter, Francine, moved in next door last month. Mrs. Randolph is visiting for a few weeks for Thanksgiving. She's feisty. You'll like her."

"Feisty? She's a goddamn thief. She just stole your newspaper. I think I'm in love with her." This Mrs. Randolph is a character, I can tell already.

Ma laughs. "You two will get along great. And she always brings it back after lunch and puts it right where she found it, so it's not really stealing. She's just borrowing it for the morning."

I'm outside smoking a cigarette when Mrs. Randolph comes creeping back over to return our newspaper. Her walker is loud and squeaky as it rolls over the concrete. I call out a greeting, "Hello, Mrs. Randolph."

She starts at my words and the newspaper slips from her grasp. She brings her hand to her chest and eyes me with irritation. "God lord, boy, don't go sneakin' up on me like that."

I could easily argue that I'm standing in my own driveway, not ten feet from her, and she's the sneaky one here, but I don't. Instead I approach her and introduce myself. "I'm Gus Hawthorne." I motion with my thumb over my shoulder. "I live here with my mom, Audrey."

She's eyeballing my cigarette and just when I think she's going to scold me about smoking, she says, "You got another cigarette?" She glances up at me and I notice that her eyes are cloudy. Cataracts I'm guessing. She squints at me. "What did you say your name was, boy?"

"Gus," I answer as I pull out the pack from my pocket and shake one out for her.

"I'm not so great with names anymore. You'll have to forgive me." She takes it and puts it to her lips with a shaky hand, and then looks at me and talks, the cigarette dangling from her lips. "Well, are you just gonna stand there, or are you gonna light it? I ain't got all day."

She makes me laugh and I retrieve my lighter and light it for her. The first pull is so weak I don't think the flame is going to catch, but it does. She blows the smoke out immediately. There isn't much, and I find myself wondering if any of it actually made it all the way down to her lungs at all. That was the weakest drag I've ever seen, but she continues just the same until she's finished. Satisfied, she drops it on the driveway next to her foot and steps on it to put it out.

I pull the pack out and point the open end toward her. "You want one for the road, Mrs. Randolph?"

She waves me off and turns her walker back toward her house. "Boy, those things'll kill you if you smoke more than one a day." She's not looking at me while she's talking; she's just creeping down the drive behind her walker. "'Sides, my daughter will be here soon and she'll kill me if she finds out I been sneakin' smokes again." She turns her head back to me and a devilish smile spreads across her full, wrinkled cheeks. "That's our secret, boy. She don't let me have no fun," she adds with a wink before turning to finish the journey home.

"Have a good one, Mrs. Randolph," I call after her.

She doesn't answer.

Thursday, November 23
(Gus)

Every day around noon, I grab my smokes and make my way to the driveway to meet Mrs. Randolph. She's incredibly timely. Exactly at noon she returns our newspaper. And every day I see her, just like today, she asks for a cigarette, and I give it to her. She barks at me to light it, and I do. It's a ritual that I've become pretty fond of. For all her bark, she's got no bite. I knew it from the first time I talked to her, but the more conversations we have, the more I get to see what a cool old chick she is. I ask her a lot of questions, and even though she acts put out to answer me, I know she secretly enjoys it because she stays longer every time.

I've learned that she's eighty-three years old (she ripped me a new asshole for asking her age, which of course took place immediately after she told me how old she is). She was married for fifty-two years to her high school sweetheart, whose name was Fritz. He had a decorated military past and retired from law enforcement. He died thirteen years ago. She doesn't say it, but I see it in her face when she talks about him that she misses him.

Today, she's talking about her daughter, Francine. Francine is a nurse. She works four days a week at a hospital in San Diego. Her shift is usually three in the morning until three in the afternoon. I've never asked her age, but I'm guessing she's in her late-fifties given what I can put together from Mrs. Randolph's other stories. Mrs. Randolph is proud of Francine, not that she admits it outright, but it peeks through in between the other comments.

"Francine working today?" I ask, knowing she is. It's Thursday; she always works on Thursdays.

"Yes. She's always workin'." She somehow doesn't sound happy about that fact.

"But she loves what she does." I met Francine a few days ago and talked to her about her job. She does love it. And I bet she's great at it, because she's so damn nice.

Mrs. Randolph huffs. "I'm glad she loves it, but that don't mean that she should let it kill her. There's no balance. She don't rest like she should. And she damn well don't have fun like she should. She used to take me to bingo every week when she lived

202

in Charlotte, but we ain't done that at all since I been here. I think she done forgot how to have fun."

The mention of bingo has me smiling. I bet this woman is fierce in a bingo hall. Bright Side, Gracie, and I used to go play bingo every once in a while, and the elderly women there were like wolves in sheep's clothing. Dressed in their Sunday best, their hair done up, looking sweet and innocent, they were nothing but sweet old ladies—until the first ball dropped and then they turned into sharks circling in bloodied water. They were rabid. Despite that, I smile at her. "I'll take you to play bingo."

She smiles. It's rare that she smiles and I love seeing it. "Would you, now?"

I nod. "Sure. I'm always down for a little bingo. I know a place. I'll check out the schedule and let you know."

She waves and turns her walker down the drive, smile still in place. "Okay, boy. I'm holdin' you to that."

"Have a good one, Mrs. Randolph." It's become part of our ritual for me to say it when she leaves.

And for her to say nothing in return.

I don't mind. Sometimes you have to listen to the things that people don't say.

Saturday, November 25
(Scout)

I return from my morning run to find Gustov and Paxton sitting on the sofa in front of a blaring TV in the living room. They're watching a soccer game. The commentators have heavy British accents. The whole scene is odd given the volume of the TV and the fact that I don't think either Paxton or Gustov are soccer fans. But the strangest thing is that there's an elderly woman sitting in an armchair that's been moved to a few feet in front of the TV. Her hair is an unnatural shade of pale lavender that shines in the sunlight coming through the window, making it look like it's slightly metallic. She's as absorbed in the game as I've ever seen anyone watching a sporting event. She alternates between a play-by-play of the action in a voice that mimics the British accent on TV, to cursing the players loudly in a gritty southern drawl, to whooping and cheering when something's apparently gone the way she wants it to. I know I'm tired after my run, but this woman is wearing me out just watching her. Still, even though I really need a shower, I walk up to the back of the sofa to get a better look. Paxton catches me out of the corner of his eye. "Morning, Scout," he says as if this is all perfectly normal.

"Morning."

Gustov turns around. Spare Ribs is curled up in his lap sleeping, although I don't know how, considering all the noise.

I nod my head toward the old woman, wordlessly asking what's up. Not that it's any of my business, I suppose, but I'm curious.

He smiles. "That's Mrs. Randolph. She's Francine's mom, from next door. She wanted to watch soccer, I mean 'football'," he says quietly, wrapping the word in air quotes when he says it. "Francine doesn't have cable. She's been jonesing for it. I guess Arsenal's her team. She loves some dude named Olivier. He scored a goal earlier and she went apeshit. She's fucking mint."

Paxton is nodding in agreement with a huge smile on his face. He's enamored with this woman.

When I look back in her direction she's still living in the game like she's in the stadium. She's wearing a Giroud jersey with the number twelve on the back, and she's leaned forward in her seat slightly.

"Sit down, Scout. You've gotta watch this with us. It only started fifteen minutes ago." Paxton is patting the sofa cushion next to him.

I don't normally watch sports, but this is about more than the game. This is a spectacle that I feel like I can't turn down. "I'm going to shower; I'll be back in ten minutes."

Ten minutes later I'm sitting in clean clothes, with wet hair, on the sofa next to Paxton. Spare Ribs woke as I walked in the room and stretched in Gustov's lap before walking over and curling up in mine.

Gustov shakes his head when the cat is comfortable. "I should've named her Benedict Arnold."

At halftime, Mrs. Randolph mutes the volume. "I can't listen to their nonsense. My boys are playin' good. They'll just say they're gonna blow it in the second half." She's talking to herself until she turns around. When her eyes meet mine, she squints. And then she stands and holds onto the back of her chair. Gustov immediately stands and offers his hand. She takes it and walks over until she's standing directly in front of me. She looks sharply at Gustov. "Where's your manners, boy? You gonna introduce me to this lovely young lady?"

My cheeks blush.

Gustov grins. "Mrs. Randolph, this is Scout MacKenzie. She's Paxton's cousin. She lives here with us." He's never said my name before. I *love* the way he says my name.

I offer my hand. "Hi, Mrs. Randolph. It's nice to meet you." Her hand is cool, but her grip is firm.

"I see you out runnin' every mornin'."

I nod. "I try."

"And I see you leave with Audrey every mornin'."

I nod again. "I work for Audrey. I'm her assistant. We carpool."

"Do you like it? Workin' for her." She's relentless with the questions.

Again I'm nodding. She's grilling me, but she's not overbearing and I find myself oddly wanting her approval. "I do. I love it. I just got my degree this spring; this is my first real job. I'm learning a lot."

She finally stops the questioning when she looks satisfied somehow with my answers. "That's the secret. You find what you love and you go for it. Life ain't about coasting. It's about pushin' the damn gas pedal all the way to the floor. Same goes for fun and love, no coasting. Pedal to the floor." She looks up at Gustov, still holding her left hand to steady her. "I'm ready to sit back down." He walks her back to her chair and helps her get seated. She looks up at him when she's comfortable and smiles. "You're a good boy."

He grins. "Thanks Mrs. R."

"And she's a good girl," she adds with a wink before unmuting the TV and giving her full attention to the booming game in front of her.

Sunday, November 26
(Gus)

"Ma. What're we doing for Thanksgiving? Same old?"

Ma's making a pumpkin pie. It's her pre-game warm up for the big show on Thursday. She does this every year. She bakes pumpkin pies starting the weekend before Thanksgiving and for about two weeks after. I eat it every day, morning, noon, and night. By the end of it, I've got the pumpkin shits and I can't even look at pie. That is, until the weekend before Thanksgiving rolls around again the next year and I'm standing here like a fucking pumpkin addict, going through withdrawal, shakes and everything, waiting for the first one to roll out of the oven so I can take half, put six scoops of whipped cream on it, and dig in. Yeah, I'm a glutton for pumpkin punishment.

"That was the plan. *Same old*," she says teasingly. "Is that okay? Did you want to try something new this year?" I can almost hear the hope in her voice. She wants me to suggest something different so she doesn't have to think about all the Thanksgivings of old with Bright Side and Gracie.

"I was thinking maybe we could invite Keller and Stella to come out and chill with us?"

She turns toward me. She likes the idea; I can see it in her eyes. "Have you talked to Keller, Gus?"

I shake my head. "Nah, I tried a few months back, but we never connected. You?"

"Well, I think that's a fabulous idea." She just avoided my question, which tells me yes, she has talked to him. Oh course she has, because Ma is a grade A human being.

"Awesome. I'll go give him a call."

When I finally get to my room to bring up his name on my phone, it takes me ten minutes to work up the courage to press "call." It's eight-thirty in Minnesota; I hope I don't wake up Stella if she's already in bed.

There's an answer after the third ring. I take a deep breath anticipating his voice and the rush of emotion that's sure to come with it.

Instead, a tiny, sweet, sleepy voice answers. "Hello?" It's his daughter, Stella.

"Well hello, Miss Stella." All the tension drains out of me.

"Who is this?" she asks, like she's screening his calls.

"This is Gus. Do you remember me, Stella?"

She yells, "Daddy, Gus is on the phone!" And then at normal volume, she says, "Daddy's in the bathroom. He's just goin' poop."

I laugh and it feels so damn good. "Ah, well, a man's gotta do that every once in a while. How are you doin' Stella?"

"Good. I go to pre-school, Gus. My teacher's name is Miss Cooper. She's nice, but she smells like apricot jelly. I don't like apricot jelly. My papa in Chicago likes it though. He puts it on toast."

This makes me laugh some more. I love little kids; every damn thing that comes out of their mouths is innocent and unfiltered. "How's your turtle?"

Her voice brightens. "Miss Higgins is good. She *loves* Minnesota." She pauses and I can hear Keller in the background talking to her. "Just a minute, Daddy. I'm not done talking to Gus." And then she's talking to me again. "Are you in California with your mommy, Gus?"

"I am. It's nice and sunny here. You should come out and visit, Stella."

She's talking to Keller now. "Gus says I should come out and visit him in California. Can I go? *Pleeeeeease.*"

I can faintly hear Keller now, trying to coax her. "Let me talk it over with Gus, baby girl, and I'll let you know. Can I have the phone please?"

"Just a minute, Daddy, I need to say bye." And then she's back to me. "Daddy needs to talk to you, Gus. Bye."

"Bye, Stella. Tell Miss Higgins hi."

"Okay."

Keller sounds a little tentative, but slightly amused, when he gets on the line. "Hey, Gus. Thanks for letting Stella entertain you for a few minutes."

"Yeah, she told me you were in the john building a log cabin."

He snorts out a laugh and it sounds relieved and embarrassed, like he's as happy as I am that this conversation is easy so far. "Please tell me my little girl *did not* use those exact words."

208

"Nah, she said you were in the bathroom goin' poop."

He sighs. "God, that's really not any better, is it?"

And just like that we're both relaxed. "She's awesome, Keller."

"Yeah, she is awesome. I have to admit I'm almost completely desensitized to any kind of embarrassment at this point. Little kids' honesty hardens you, man. There's nowhere to hide and it comes out at the most inopportune times."

I smile, because he sounds good. "You can't go wrong with straight-up honesty."

"So, what have you been up to, Gus? I think about you all the time and I have every intention to call, and then I have homework, or work, or Stella's ballet practice. Something always comes up. I'm sorry we haven't talked." He means it.

"No worries. I'm in the same good intention boat. That's kinda why I'm calling. Ma and I were just talking and wondered if you and Stella had plans for Thanksgiving this year? I thought maybe we could rekindle the bromance in San Diego." Last year I surprised Bright Side in Minnesota for Thanksgiving, with Keller's help. He called me and planned it all. I teased her that I was stealing her man away.

"The sacred bromance." He stops and laughs again remembering. "Damn, that's tempting. You're a good-looking guy." He hasn't lost his sense of humor. I'm glad. "But, I think Stella and I are just going to hang out here in Grant. My father might come up if he can get some time off."

I try again. "You should come out. If this is about money, I've got it covered."

"Gus, man, that's really nice of you to offer, but I can't accept that."

"Sure, you can. You just say, 'Yeah, Gus, we'd love to spend Thanksgiving with you and your mom. That sounds like a righteous fucking way to spend the holiday.' It's as easy as that. And then you tell me what time you can fly out and when you have to be home, and you let me take care of the rest." I don't know why, but I need him to give this to me. I need to see him and Stella to help me deal.

"Gus, it's too much. I just can't."

I sigh. "What if I told you you're gonna make Ma cry if she can't see Stella? Like, to the point of goddamn sobbing. I'm not kidding, she'll throw a full-on shit fit. It'll be ugly, dude. I'll be forced to record it and send the video to you. You'll probably feel guilty for the rest of your days. The brutal type of soul-searing guilt."

He's quiet. I can tell he's about to give in.

"C'mon dude. We really want to see you guys." It's as sincere as I can possibly be.

He sighs. "We're not going unless you let me pay you back someday."

I smile because I would never accept his money. "Sure, whatever you want."

He sighs again. "You're really sure you want to do this? It's going to be expensive."

"Don't have anything else to spend my money on, dude." I don't.

He's quiet and then he gives in. "Okay. We'd really like that. I could use a break for a few days." He sounds exhausted all of a sudden.

"Excellent. Text me times that work for your flights and I'll make it happen."

"Thanks, Gus."

No, thank you. "It'll be great to see you guys."

"Later, man."

"Later."

I don't know why, but I feel like a goddamn weight's been lifted off my shoulders.

Monday, November 27
(Gus)

It's cold out this morning, so I'm walking along the beach instead of surfing. The text alert comes from the phone in my pocket.

KELLER: *I just saw the email, thanks for the airline tickets. My father called this morning and said he got a few days off. Not to throw a wrench in the works, but do you think Audrey would mind if he came out to San Diego, too? I don't want to put you guys out.*

ME: *No prob. The more the merrier.*

KELLER: *Thanks Gus. See you Thursday!*

Tuesday, November 28
(Gus)

Bingo with Mrs. Randolph starts at ten-thirty this morning. She insisted I pick her up at nine-thirty. It's only a fifteen minute drive. She's dressed in a purple blouse and matching purple dress slacks. Her outfit highlights the lavender tint of her silver hair. She looks nice, and I know she put effort into her clothes and her coif this morning. She went ballistic when I showed up ten minutes late and said I've messed up everything and there won't be any good seats or cards left by the time we get there. We'll be fine, I assured her. It's a goddamn game of chance; there are no good cards. And as far as the seats go, there are monitors all over the room with the numbers on them so there really aren't any bad seats. Besides, I've been here before, and she hasn't.

When we arrive, I stop in front of the entrance and help her out of my truck. I think she's going to wait for me while I park, but when I return to the entrance she's nowhere to be found. I freak out momentarily and wonder how I'm going to tell Francine I've lost her mother, but then I realize she's probably already inside, buying her loot.

And that's exactly where I find her. She's at the cashier buying a stack of cards and two dobbers.

I pull a few twenties out of my pocket and try to pay, but she swats my hand away. "Put that money away, boy. This is my treat."

I laugh at the sting she left on the back of my hand and shove the bills back in my pocket.

After she pays, she surveys the room and points me in the direction of an empty table in the front corner.

I point to two empty seats at the table directly in front of us. "Why don't we just sit here?" I'm trying to save her the walk across the room.

She puts her hand up to shield her words. "Them people don't look like the friendly-type." Then she looks pointedly at the three women sitting across the table from the empty seats.

They don't look friendly. They look territorial and they're shooting daggers at me and Mrs. R. with their eyes. The vibe they're putting off is far from welcoming. So, I follow her to the front corner and when I make sure she's comfortable, I check my watch: five minutes past ten. "Hey, we've got some time before they start." I turn toward the snack bar to see what they're offering. "Looks like they've got quite a selection of delectable donuts and some damn tasty coffee. You want some?"

She's arranging her cards in front of her. It's meticulous, a science really. She doesn't look up when she answers. "Don't give me that delectable and tasty sales pitch. You don't know what you're talkin' about."

I laugh. "You're right. Looks like they've got a sad selection of day-old donuts and shitty coffee. You want some?"

She grins at that, but still doesn't look up at me. "I'll take a stale, chocolate donut and a shitty coffee. Two sugars."

I walk away laughing to myself. I love this lady.

We eat our donuts, which were, to our surprise, pretty damn delectable indeed, and drink our shitty, but sugar-filled coffee while we wait for the first game to begin.

When the first ball drops, I find out just how bad Mrs. Randolph's eyesight and short-term memory is. She can't read the monitors at all and she's squinting to read the cards in front of her, even with her reading glasses on. After watching her struggle with the first few calls, I start repeating the letter and number aloud after the caller says it. I say it quietly to myself, but loud enough that she can hear me. "B ten, B ten," I say repeatedly while scanning my cards and hers, as if I need the reminder while I search. I notice she does much better when I do this, so I keep it up for the remainder of the morning.

Mrs. Randolph walks out with four hundred-dollar bills. During the ride home, she's wearing a look of contentment and pride. I pull up in front of her house to drop her off, killing the engine and walking around to open the door for her and pull the walker from the bed of my truck. She tries to give me half. "Here, boy, you take this. You ain't got no steady job. Everybody needs a little spendin' money."

I shake my head. "No, I can't accept that. You won it. You keep it. And what makes you think I don't have a job?"

"You're almost always home. You don't go nowhere, unless it's out to the beach. You drive that old truck. And you just ain't got no fire. Nothin' drivin' you."

"I'm a musician. I'm in a band."

"Say what? Why didn't you mention that before?"

I shrug. "I haven't played in a while."

"Why not?"

"I don't know. I guess maybe you're right." I sigh. "Maybe the fire died."

She grabs my hand and holds tight. Her fingers are crooked with arthritis, but she's pretty damn strong. "Listen to me, boy. You only get one chance at this circus called life. Don't sit in the crowd watchin' it happen. You jump right in and be the ringleader. That's where you find your fire."

"What if your fire died with someone else?"

She shakes her head. "Nope. Here's the thing about life, boy. We meet a lot of people along this journey. Some of them are sonsabitches and some are special. When you find the special ones you don't take a moment for granted, because you never know when your time with them is gonna be up. I got over fifty years with my Fritz. Fifty wonderful years. When he died, I was lost for a few months. I lost my fire. But then I realized that life's short and I had a choice to make. I could keep bein' miserable, or I could go find joy and live again." She's squeezing even harder now. "If you only listen to one thing this crazy old lady tells you, I hope it's this: ain't nobody gonna stoke your fire but you, boy." She looks at me hard with her grey, cloudy eyes. "You go make life happen."

I nod.

She smiles and loosens her grip and releases my hands. "So, you any good?"

"At what?"

She huffs. "At music, boy."

"I'm all right."

"All right?" She gives me a scolding look. "Have some pride. Tell me you're good. I have a feeling you are. No need to be humble with me, we're old friends now."

I smile and nod and then I lay it on thick for her because even though she's got me thinking, I can't be serious. "I'm *fantastic*."

She rolls her eyes at my sarcasm and answers with a little of her own. "Who do you think you are, Elvis Presley? The good lord only done made one of those." She pulls the bingo parlor schedule from her purse and begins fanning herself with it. "That man certainly had himself some fire," she adds under her breath.

GUS

I laugh. "Have a good one, Mrs. Randolph."

Thursday, November 30
(Gus)

Ma is in the kitchen, wrapped in a bright red apron, up to her elbows in dead carcass cooking glory this morning. I've been a vegetarian since I was fifteen, and Bright Side and Gracie were, too, so Ma hasn't cooked a bird for Thanksgiving in years. I'm severely outnumbered by carnivores this year, judging by this gigantic turkey. Good thing she's making shitloads of green bean casserole and sweet potatoes to accompany that pumpkin pie. I'll be in food heaven all afternoon.

Ma and Impatient are both in the kitchen when I check in. "Need any help?"

Ma smiles. I haven't seen her this happy in a long time. She only busts out her apron when things get hardcore. "I don't think so, honey. Scout and I have everything under control. But, can you get some more whipped cream when you go to the airport." She looks pointedly at me. "Someone ate all of it."

I raise my eyebrows and shrug my shoulders, feigning innocence.

She smiles again. "I don't want Stella to have to eat her pie with no whipped cream."

"I'll buy extra." I look to Scout. "Wanna ride with me to the airport?" I don't really know why I'm offering because I know she needs to help Ma, but I can't help but feel protective of her after all the shit that went down last week. Plus, I like being around her.

She nods her head toward the front door. "When we're done with this, I'm gonna go for a run while I can. Thanks, though."

I nod. I understand, but disappointment tugs at me.

After a quick cigarette, I take Ma's car (because I can't get everyone in my truck) and head to the grocery store. Four cans of whipped cream and a Twix bar and I'm out the door and on the way to the airport. Keller and Stella's flight gets in about twenty minutes before his father's. I find the closest parking spot I can, which is like finding a needle in a haystack on a holiday weekend, and head to baggage claim. I'm early; it's a miracle. I take a seat and people watch. The airport is crowded and bustling with hurried people. Emotions range from extreme irritation to

216

complete, off-the-charts happiness on the faces before me. You can both see and feel which people are doing holiday travel out of obligation, and which ones are amped up on the prospect of what's to come. I like watching the happy ones. It feels almost therapeutic, like a reminder that this life is all about embracing the good and making the most out of the good moments, even if they're fleeting.

As I'm watching the masses, I catch the eye of a teenage boy. He's probably sixteen. He's standing by the baggage carousel with two adults—I'm guessing they're his parents. He's keeping a distance from them that says, *I'm not with these people*, but I have a feeling they're family. He has earbuds in his ears, and he's wearing a Rook T-shirt. For a moment, I debate my next move. I treasure being inconspicuous. On stage, I'm all about the crowd. Off stage, I'm just Gus. He's open-mouth staring now; I've just been recognized, so I wave him over. He looks behind him with wide eyes, as if I'm gesturing to someone else. When he looks back at me, I nod and smile and wave him over again. He says something to his mom quickly and points to me. Her eyes widen, too. This kid has his mom's eyes. She smiles and nods and I see her mouth form the word, "Go," and he walks quickly toward me, but not so quickly that he's lost his swagger. Teenage boys know how to work the image-thing, 24/7.

When he's standing in front of me, I hold out my hand to bump knuckles. "S'up? I like the shirt."

He glances down at the crow on his shirt like he doesn't know what to say and pops the earbuds out of his ears.

"What's your name, dude?"

"Josh." The swagger is fading and nerves are taking over. I was this kid not so long ago.

"What're you listening to, Josh?"

He smiles. He's trying to hold it back for the sake of appearance, but he's too nervous and excited. He's fidgeting with the earbuds in his hand. "Rook," he answers.

I smile again. "No shit?"

He shakes his head, but says quickly, "No shit. You guys kick ass."

"Thanks, dude. Traveling with your family today?"

"Yeah, going to see my gran in La Jolla for Thanksgiving." He

217

glances back over his shoulder and his mom and dad are standing at a distance waiting patiently with what looks to be all of their luggage.

"Well, have fun. I'd better let you get back to la familia; it looks like they're waiting." I stick my hand in my front pocket and pull out a handful of change. In amongst the coins are two guitar picks. Don't ask me why, but ever since I started playing I've always carried a few around with me. I hand one of the picks to him.

A smile appears on his face instantaneously. He looks like he's ten years old instead of sixteen. It's funny how joy unleashed makes a person seem younger. "Thanks, Gustov."

I pat him on the shoulder. "It's just Gus, dude. And you're welcome. Tell your gran I said hey."

He nods, still looking at the pick in his hand. When he looks up at me sheepishly, he says, "You think I could get a picture with you?"

"Absolutely." I hate having my photo taken, but I'll do anything to keep that smile on this kid's face.

He calls back over his shoulder while he pulls out his phone from his pocket, "Mom, can you take our picture?"

She practically runs over as if she's been waiting all her life for this moment, like there's nothing she wouldn't do for this boy. It reminds me of Ma. I know how lucky they are to have each other.

I extend my hand. "Hey, Josh's mom. I'm Gus."

She accepts my hand and shakes it vigorously. "Oh, I know who you are. Josh has posters of your band all over his room."

Josh protests, mortified. "*Mom.*"

She nods an apology to him and smiles at me. We pose for a couple of shots. I even ask them to take one with my own phone.

When they walk away, I feel good. Not because I've been recognized and praised—I certainly don't need the praise. I feel good because I just made that boy happy. I gave him a guitar pick and he looked at it like it was a goddamn gold bar in his hand. Bright Side always said our music made people feel something. I think I know exactly what she meant. Because right now, I *feel* it.

A text alert comes from the phone in my pocket a few

minutes later.

KELLER: *On the ground. Meet you at baggage 23C.*
GUS: *No hurry. I'm here.*

Ten minutes later, Stella is running at me full throttle and squealing my name. "Gus!"

I stand and scoop her up when she crashes into my legs. She's grown a lot since I saw her in January. "How's my favorite pint-size girly?"

She giggles. "Good. We just flew on an airplane. It was fun."

I nod. "You like flying?"

She answers absently. "Yeah," she says, draping her right arm around my shoulder and grabbing my ponytail. She runs it through her hand once, scalp to the end and then cranes her neck over my shoulder to take a look. "Your hair is *really* long, Gus." She says "really" like two separate words.

I laugh.

"It's *so* pretty."

I feel like one of her dolls, but I accept the compliment. "Well, thank you, Stella."

Keller finally approaches; he's out of breath as if he's been chasing her through the entire airport. He extends his hand to shake and in between deep breaths he says, "Hey, Gus. Sorry about the ambush. I've got a runner."

I laugh. "No worries. A Stella ambush is the best kind of ambush."

He laughs with me. He looks a little tired, but he looks good. His hair is longer than when I last saw him. There's a lot of it poking out from under his beanie. "I just need to grab our bag and Stella's booster seat."

"Take your time. I've got all day, dude."

I sit down with Stella in my lap and she proceeds to fill me in on Miss Higgins, her turtle, and life in Grant while we share the Twix bar I brought for her. She loves it in Grant, but I think she'd love it anywhere Keller is. She idolizes her dad. I know how she feels; I feel the same way about Ma.

Before long Keller returns with their belongings, and not long after that Keller's dad arrives. Stella goes apeshit upon sighting him. She's squealing excitedly and jumps off my lap, but before she can make a break for him Keller's got a handful of the back of her shirt. He's quick. He looks at me and mouths, "See, a runner," but he's smiling. She's giggling and waving her arms, trying unsuccessfully to get away.

After his dad hugs Stella, he hugs Keller, which puts me at ease. I remember Bright Side saying they had a pretty strained relationship.

I extend my hand by way of introduction. "Hey, Doc Banks. I'm Gus." I saw him at Bright Side's funeral, but I didn't stick around long enough to talk to anyone. This is our first encounter.

He shakes my hand, nods his head formally. "Of course. It's nice to meet you, Gus. I've heard a lot about you."

I nod and look to Keller. "Good or bad?" I ask. "What have you been telling him?"

Keller laughs and claps me on the back. "It's all good, man. It's all good."

The conversation on the ride home is dominated by the tiny redhead in her booster in the backseat. And we wouldn't have it any other way.

"Daddy, can we make a sandcastle again when we get to Gus's?"

"Tomorrow, baby girl. Today's Thanksgiving. Audrey's making lots of yummy food for all of us today. Maybe we can play a game inside after dinner, okay?"

"Okay." It's as easy as that.

I can't help but smile at how agreeable she is.

"Gus, you wanna have a play date with us tomorrow and make sandcastles on the beach?"

"Heck yeah, Stella."

At that, she cheers, "Yay!" And then she sings, "We're gonna have play date. We're gonna have a play date."

When we get home, Ma greets us all at the door with a hug, because that's what Ma does.

After all of the hugging, I gesture to Keller and Stella to follow me down the hall toward my bedroom. Impatient walks out of her room just as we approach. Keller looks startled when the bedroom door opens and someone walks out. I see him look inside the room, and I can't help but notice the sadness in his eyes. He's thinking about Bright Side. I live here, but Keller hasn't been here since Bright Side's last days. It has to be shocking to see the room where she died after all these months.

Stella breaks the silence for all of us. "Who are you?" she asks curiously.

Impatient looks down and a smile lights her eyes as she squats down in front of Stella. It's a smile that transforms her, patient and loving. Some people just love little kids. I'm one of them. So is she. "I'm Scout. What's your name?"

"I'm Stella." She tugs on Keller's pant leg. "This is my daddy. His name's Keller."

I have to laugh, because Stella's so goddamn cute. Impatient looks up at Keller but doesn't stand. "Hello, Keller."

"Hey ... Scout was it?" He's being polite, but he still looks a million miles away.

She nods.

I motion for Keller to follow me. "Why don't you put your stuff in here? You guys can crash in my room."

Keller shakes his head, but he's still in a fog. "I don't want to put you out. Stella and I can sleep on the sofa. We'll be fine for a few days."

Impatient stands and speaks up. "I just changed the sheets on the bed. Go ahead and take this room. I can sleep on the sofa."

Keller looks stricken, like he's just been presented with something unimaginable. I need to make this better ASAP. "That's okay," I say to Impatient. Then I grip Keller's shoulder until he looks at me, really looks at me. I nod my head toward my door. "Come on, you can sleep in my room. I changed the sheets on my bed, too. I'd hate for that to go to waste. It's like the first time all year I've done that."

He almost smiles.

I look at Impatient, trying to smooth this over. "Why don't you go grab Keller's dad and put him in your room?"

She nods. She looks a little confused, a little embarrassed, and a lot concerned. She knows what she's seeing isn't normal.

Stella reaches out and takes Impatient's hand. "I'll go with you. Let's go get Papa."

After Keller sets their suitcase on the floor next to my dresser, he turns to look at me and his expression is blank, like he's trying to wipe away the sadness, but he can't decide what emotion to replace it with. My heart aches for him. I know how hard it is to be here, in the presence of her ghost. I've dealt with it for months now. I'm learning to live with it. It takes time. And he hasn't had to contend with proximity. And proximity's just set him back months. I can see it happening. So I do the only thing can think to do. I hug him. And he hugs me back. It's half-hearted at first, but soon enough I can feel his muscles tighten around me. The squeezing isn't an embrace; it's a release of emotion, a release of grief. I pat him on the back. "Sorry about that, dude. Scout doesn't know what happened in that room. She didn't mean anything by it."

I feel him exhale, long and loud, before he releases me. He shakes his head to clear it. "No, I'm sorry, Gus. I thought I was ready to come here. That I'd be able to handle it." He pauses and looks at the floor before he meets my eyes again. I know how much he loved her. He's reliving all of it right now. He shakes his head again. "It's just hard." He searches my eyes for understanding.

I nod. "You don't have to explain, dude. I know. It is hard."

He smiles. "Thanks, man. Let's go. Katie would want us to make the most of today."

I laugh. "Bright Side fucking loved Thanksgiving. I hope you're prepared to eat double portions of pumpkin pie just for her."

He laughs and rubs his belly. "I think I can do that. I haven't eaten anything since last night."

The dinner table is full of food and people. Our Thanksgiving table is always a hodgepodge of misfits. And that's not an insult; it's just a fair assessment. Ma always invites people to join in on the festivities who don't have anywhere else to go. Her generosity is legendary. It's never the same faces from year to year, which is what makes it fun. You never know who you're going to sit next to, or what the conversation is going to be like. Today's table is twice as full as it normally is.

Keller and I take the two empty seats at the end of the table.

Ma's standing at the other end, smiling at all of us. "We're waiting on one more person, but he's just called to say his flight's been cancelled due to weather and he's not going to make it, so we'll go ahead and get started without him. I want to thank all of you for sharing your Thanksgiving with Gus and me. We are so blessed to have you here." She raises her glass. "To good food and good company." We all raise our glasses and echo her. She smiles. "Now eat up. Scout and I have been cooking all day, there's a lot to eat. Don't be shy."

We do. We eat and we talk. The volume in the room is high with several conversations going on at once, but it's comforting noise, rowdy with friendship and appreciation. As I look around the table, I'm struck by the odd pairings of people. Impatient's sitting next to Doc Banks. They're talking about New York. Pax, Keller, and Stella are talking to Mrs. Randolph and Francine about seagulls, and about how much Mrs. Randolph loves watching them fly over the ocean. Ma catches my eye and smiles, then winks at me. She raises her glass of wine to me. I raise mine in return.

"Happy Thanksgiving. I love you," I mouth the words.

She mouths the same back to me.

Looking around I think to myself that life isn't perfect. If it was, Bright Side and Gracie would be sitting here with us. But I know that's not possible. And for the first time, I realize that I finally know why Bright Side used to always say she didn't have any regrets. Because she lived in the moment. She didn't live in the past. She didn't give herself a chance to regret anything because she went out and made the most of what she had, even if it wasn't much. She never saw the negative, which so often pervaded her life. She looked for that one sliver of positivity and she blew it up until it was all she could see. Until it forced out everything bad. Right now, sitting here, I miss her. I'll always miss her. But I miss her in a different way today. In a way that makes me smile at the memory of her. I glance at my arm, at my new tattoo, and the words sink in. There's something epic that happens every day if you look hard enough for it. And every day is a chance to go out there and do epic. The key is putting forth the effort. She did. *Every fucking day she did.* We all should. Is it harder? Hell yeah. It's much easier to complain ... or self-destruct ... or do nothing at all. But where's the magic in that? It's like Mrs.

Randolph said, urging me to find my fire again. Mrs. R. and Bright Side would've been best friends, I'm sure of it.

As I look at everyone at this table I think, they all have their own shit, their own problems, just like me. But look how happy they all are, because they're living in the moment. It's fucking beautiful. This is what it's all about. Friends and family. And I have the best around.

Friday, December 1
(Gus)

Keller and I are sitting in lawn chairs on the beach watching Stella play in the sand with Impatient and Pax. The sun's bright overhead, but there's a light breeze that puts a chill in the air.

"How are you gonna get Stella clean, dude? She's wearing a good three buckets of sand. And that's just in her hair." We've been outside for the past three hours and she's having the time of her life. Keller and I just tapped out of the sandcastle making marathon to sit down and rest when Impatient and Pax came out to play with her.

He's shaking his head. "I have no idea. I guess we'll cross that bridge when it's time to go inside. Maybe I'll take her out in the water with her clothes on and hope it all washes away. Or I'll hold her upside down by the ankles and let gravity do the work." He's smiling by the time he's done talking, because he can't do anything else when it comes to Stella. She has him, and everyone else, under a spell.

"So, what's up with your family? Your parents got divorced, huh?"

He nods slowly like he's still trying to process what happened. "Yeah, it was a little crazy. My father filed for divorce and moved out of their place last year just before Christmas. I didn't find out until after Katie's funeral. With my mother being a lawyer," he pauses, "and, well, being my mother, the whole thing was pretty contentious. It dragged on for months." He lifts a brow and glances at me. "She's the type of person who always has to be right and get the last word, you know? So it was brutal for my father. He just wanted out. Just wanted to walk away, even if it was only with the clothes on his back. She wanted to fight, because that's what she does best."

"It was ugly, huh?" Dude, I feel bad for them. I've never understood how you could grow to hate someone you once loved. And to hate them to the point that you want to hurt them, break them.

"Ugly doesn't begin to describe it. He had a good lawyer though. She got the house, but he ended up with enough money to be comfortable."

225

"That sucks, dude. I'm sorry."

He shakes his head. "Don't be sorry. It was a blessing in disguise. My father always lived under the shadow of my mother. I never really had a relationship with him because of it. Since they've split, he's a different person. He's the father I always wanted and needed. It sucks that he had to go through it all, but in the end, it's the best thing he's ever done. He's finally happy. You have no idea what it's like to watch a middle-aged man come into his own. It's actually pretty damn inspiring."

"So where does he live now?"

"He rents a small studio apartment a few blocks from the hospital in Chicago. It's practical, simple. He can walk to work. He loves it."

"That's great. He's a good guy. I'm sorry I didn't meet him when he came out for Bright Side's funeral. I was a little ... out of it."

"No worries. We all were. Him coming to Katie's funeral was kind of a turning point for him. His life really started turning around that weekend. He and I grew closer. He met Audrey. Their friendship has really helped him survive the worst of this past year. You have a great mom, Gus."

"The best. You know, I never knew Ma was talking to your dad, that they were friends, until yesterday. I know I was gone most of the year on tour, but she never mentioned him. And watching the two of them yesterday, it was like they were BFFs. It was kinda cool."

"I know they talk on the phone a lot. They're good for each other."

"So, what else is going on? How are Bright Side's friends? You ever see the dudes that lived across the hall from her in the dorms? Clayton and the gimp? I can't remember his name."

He looks at me and laughs. "The gimp?"

And now I'm laughing with him. "Bright Side and I used to joke that he was into kinky sex, role-playing and bondage and shit."

And now he's laughing harder. "Oh my God, no. I think Pete's still a virgin and will be until after he's married. And then it will be strictly missionary, once a month. The guy is super reserved. Nothing wrong with that, but there's no way in hell he's into kink." He shakes his head and he's still smiling. "No. Way."

"You ever see him?" I ask.

"Yeah, I see him and his girlfriend every once in a while. They come in for coffee at Grounds every couple of weeks. He's a good guy. He took Katie's death pretty hard. He couldn't even say her name for months."

"And what about Clayton?" Clayton was an interesting dude. Quirky, just like Bright Side. I liked him.

"Clayton's good. He lives in L.A. with his boyfriend now. He's going to UCLA and waiting tables at some high-end restaurant in West Hollywood. I talk to him every couple weeks. He loves it there. I know he really struggled at Grant. I'm glad he found someplace he feels at home. Someplace he feels like he can finally be himself."

I know Bright Side always worried about him, so this is good to hear.

"Daddy, I found a sand dollar!" Stella yells, as she runs toward Keller.

He takes it from her with a smile on his face. "Awesome, baby girl. We'll take it home and put it in your room on your special shelf."

Her smile is the purest thing I've seen in a long time. "Okay, Daddy." And just as quickly, she's off to rejoin Pax and Impatient at the sandcastle.

"What about her roommate? Sugar, right? You ever hear anything about her?"

Keller nods. "Yup. Sugar." I think he's going to stop there, but then he continues. "You know she was always kind of a twat to Katie?"

"I know she had the name, reputation, and build of a stripper, but I didn't know she was a bitch. I knew she and Bright Side weren't pals, but—"

"She was a bitch," Keller interrupts. "But something happened between them that semester. I don't know what it was, but not long before Katie left to come back here last December they were getting along. I wouldn't say they were the best of friends exactly, but they talked. It was almost like Sugar finally realized she had access to this amazing person in her life and wanted guidance or something." He shakes his head, like he's still puzzled by it. "I don't know; it was bizarre. Good, but bizarre. And I guess Katie didn't tell her she was sick. She just told her she was moving back home to San Diego. Sugar came into Grounds in tears one morning about two weeks into spring semester when we'd all gone back to classes. She said she'd heard someone talking about her and wanted to know if it was true. When I confirmed, the girl sobbed. It was a full-blown ugly cry. That was rough."

"Do you ever see her around?" I ask.

"I see her around from time to time. She comes in for coffee with friends sometimes. I'm not friends with her, but you can see a visible change. She dresses differently, which is a good thing. There's a little more left to the imagination now. She doesn't look like a walking sex ad. Her hair is brown now instead of blond. I'm guessing it's her natural color. I don't know; she just seems like one of those people that kinda woke up. Sometimes it takes a big punch in the face to do that. I think she had a few back-to-back punches."

Bright Side would be smiling now, listening to this. "How about Duncan and Shelly? They good?"

"They're great. They both graduated last spring. Dunc got a really good government job. He works at the capital in Minneapolis, some kind of aide or assistant to someone important. I'm not sure what his title is, but he loves it. He wants to run for public office someday, so he's getting his feet wet and seeing how it all works. And Shel is still working at her mom's flower shop. She's pretty much taken it over and her mom is semi-retired now. And she also started teaching piano lessons. Most of her clients are kids. They're testing her patience, that's a good thing." He smiles. "Shel didn't have the easiest life growing up, you know. She was sexually abused for years. An uncle. It was sick and messed up. Dunc's helped her so much, but meeting Katie really changed her life. She's been in counseling for over a year now. She's in a good place. I'm proud of her. And they help me out with Stella a lot. I bartend on Friday nights and they take her and she spends the night with them. She loves it. And they love it. I'm lucky to have them."

I can't imagine what his life is like, trying to juggle school, work, and raising a daughter. "I don't know how you do it, dude.

You must be spent."

He laughs and his voice sounds tired, but happy, fulfilled. "I'm tired and I'm busy, that's for sure. But, honestly, I wouldn't want it any other way. Stella is my life. She's the reason I get up in the morning and do what I do. And my classes, even work ... it all helps me cope with losing Katie, you know? Especially the first few months she was gone. Any idle moment I had, I found myself drowning in despair." He pauses and runs his hand through his hair while he's thinking. "God, she would've hated that. She taught me so many things, but being brave enough to go out there and live life to the fullest, and to love with your whole heart—that's what she was all about. So, that's what I try to do every day to honor her memory. That, and be spontaneous every once in and a while." He smiles. "I don't know why, but it makes me feel a little more powerful when I do it."

I have to laugh at his honesty. "You're a rebel, dude," I say.

He laughs with me. "I know. I'm a badass."

"That you are, my friend. That you are." He is—a badass dad and a badass friend.

Sunday, December 3
(Gus)

I hear a timid knock at my bedroom door. It's the knock of a person who didn't want to knock in the first place, or doesn't want the person inside to answer.

It's nine o'clock in the morning. I'm awake, but I'm still in bed. "Come in!" I yell.

The door pushes open slowly, and Pax's head pokes through. "Hey, Gus. Good morning."

"Buenos dias. What's up?" I wave him in because he's still standing outside with only his head peeking through the opening.

He pushes the door open, but asks, "Can I talk to you for a minute?" before he steps in.

"Of course."

He wastes no time shutting the door behind him and sits on the corner of my bed. He looks nervous. I haven't seen him like this in weeks.

"Dude. Spill. What's goin' on?" His nerves are making me nervous.

His eyes are cast away from me and his cheeks are reddening at an alarming rate. "I have a date with Mason," he blurts. Then he releases a long breath. He's trying to calm himself down, and I kinda fear he may start hyperventilating.

I clap my hands to cheer him on. "Well done, dude. *Well. Done.*"

He finally looks at me and smiles, but his eyes are panicky. "We've been talking a lot at school lately, and I asked her for her number on Friday. I called her last night. I asked her if she wanted to go out with me today, and she said yes."

I'm smiling now. "Right on. So, what's the problem?" There's definitely an issue or he wouldn't be in here.

He takes a deep breath and the panic returns to his eyes. "What am I supposed to do now? I've never been out with a girl."

"Seriously?" I knew he didn't have a lot of experience with girls but he's almost eighteen years old, I figured he'd been around the block a time or two.

"Yeah. Never," he confirms.

"Well dude, I've never really been a dating type of guy, but

230

why don't you take her out to lunch, or the movies, or the beach. There are tons of options."

"We have to do something we can walk to. Her car is in the shop I guess and well, I don't have one, so —"

I interrupt him. "So take my truck. I don't need to go anywhere today."

His eyes widen. "Really? You'd let me take the shit wagon?"

"Sure. You have a license, right?"

He nods quickly, mouth still gaping.

"She's yours. Be good to her, though. She's not much, but I love her."

He's still nodding, he hasn't stopped. "I will. I have to pick up Mason at noon. I'll be home by five."

"No hurry. I plan on getting out in the water this afternoon, so I won't need it. Take your time."

I climb out of bed, and sift through the pockets of the jeans I wore last night. Pulling out my keys, I toss them to Pax.

He attempts a smile when he catches them, but it's still strained. "Thanks Gus."

"No worries." And then something else crosses my mind and I start digging through my nightstand drawer. I toss him a handful of foil packets.

He catches them, but when he realizes what he's holding, he drops them to the floor. Then he scrambles to pick them up again. It's clear he's baffled and embarrassed.

I laugh, trying to calm his nerves. "Put a raincoat on it every time, dude."

He shakes his head, staring at the condoms in his hand. "I don't need these."

I'm smiling again because the kid's innocence kills me. He's never been on a date and clearly he's a virgin. It's like spotting a golden unicorn. "You don't know that, dude. Maybe not today —"

It's his turn to interrupt. "*Definitely* not today." I swear I almost see him shudder in fear.

I nod and try to stifle a laugh. "Okay. Not today, but sex is in your future at some point. You're human, for Christ's sake. Take them. Keep them. Use them when you're ready. Come back for more if you're scared to buy them. I won't pry, but I will supply."

His eyes are big as saucers, but he stuffs them in his pocket.

"Okay. Thanks again, Gus."

He's walking to the door when I stop him. "Pax?"

He turns with his hand on the doorknob. "Yeah."

"You've got this. Just be yourself. You're awesome."

He smiles and for the first time in the last few minutes, it's genuine. "Thanks."

When the door shuts, I have to laugh. The last five minutes were like an awkward PSA. I love that damn kid.

Monday, December 4
(Gus)

I'm sitting at Ma's piano now, because I picked up my guitar for the first time in weeks this morning and it felt like a burden in my hands. It felt like rejection. Like it didn't want me there. So I set it back down in the corner of my bedroom and went down to the basement.

I haven't sat on this piano bench for over a year. I rarely write music with the piano. I almost always write songs using my guitar, but sometimes inspiration strikes and I come up with a melody while I'm messing around on it. Let's hope this works. I need luck. I need music. I feel empty without it.

The ivory keys are cold. Neglected. Ma doesn't play much anymore either.

I move my fingers over the keys, gliding through a few scales. I let my mind wander and play the first thing that comes to mind. My fingers move in a familiar pattern and I begin playing a classical piece. Mozart. I learned several piano concertos when I was growing up and taking lessons. Ma insisted. She's good; piano is definitely her instrument.

One song flows into the next, pouring from my memory. It feels good to play. I feel affirmed as my fingers remember the keys, the intervals, and the sounds of the piano. There's acceptance in it. The house is quiet and calm, and the music fills the room. It fills the empty space like a spirit, another being. And suddenly I don't feel so alone.

Alone. I think that's what bothers me most about losing Bright Side. With her I was never alone. Even when she lived hundreds of miles away, I was never alone. I could feel her. She filled me. Like the music is filling the room right now.

The song I'm playing now was one of her favorites. Debussy. She used to always say Debussy was sexy. I used to laugh at her, but she was right. She'd ask me to play this song over and over again. She loved it.

So, I'm playing it for her now. "I hope you're listening, Bright Side," I say out loud. I know she's around. I know that sounds weird, but sometimes I just know she's nearby. It's like a fleeting glimpse of comfort ... and then I blink and it's gone.

233

I miss her so much.

As I reach the final decrescendo, I see something move out of the corner of my eye. I swivel on the bench and see that Impatient is standing on the last stair, watching me.

"Hey," I say, a bit startled. "How long have you been peeping on me?"

She shrugs and a small smile appears. I love that smile, probably because I so rarely get to see it. "A while." In those two words, soft and simple, is the fleeting comfort I mentioned early. I'm not alone.

I nod. "You like Debussy?"

She nods. "If that's who that was, yes. It was beautiful. I didn't know you played."

"Ma made me learn when I was a kid. Speaking of Ma, shouldn't you be at work?"

She shakes her head, as if to clear away the moment. "Yeah. Audrey needed a file she left on her desk here. I came back to get it, and I also made some egg salad. I came down to see if you want a sandwich. There's plenty." She's always trying to feed me.

"Sure. I'll be up in a minute. Thanks."

She smiles again. I've noticed more and more that doing something for someone else makes her happy. Even if it's making a sandwich for lunch. So, I never turn her down when she offers something. Even if I'm not hungry. I like making her smile.

I play another song before I go upstairs, because the comfort is still clinging to me.

And I'm clinging back like hell.

As I'm playing, a few notes stand out. The way they fit together strikes me in a way I hadn't heard before. I stop the song and play the notes again. Then I transpose it to a lower key. The combination flits across my mind. There and then gone.

I start the song again, and when I get to those notes, I stop. The new melody springs back into my mind, and I play those keys again.

Followed by a few more.

I find the bass notes in my left hand, and the sound becomes fuller. I play it again.

And suddenly I can hear it in my mind. I can visualize the strings and frets of my guitar, and I hum the sound to myself. This is no simple chorus. This is a hook. And it actually sounds pretty damn good.

And now I'm smiling. I'm smiling while that hook repeats on a loop in my mind, a tiny ember flickering to life.

I guess sometimes all you need is a little inspiration. And sometimes inspiration is a smile from the right person at the right time.

Tuesday, December 5
(Gus)

It's time.

After seeing Keller and Stella last week, I know it's time.

After experiencing my first glimpse of musical inspiration in months, I know it's time.

All day, I've been staring at the disc Bright Side left for me. It's been sitting in my room for months now. It's dusty. I haven't touched it.

Until now.

Now I'm inserting it in my laptop.

I hold my breath and hit play. And suddenly I hear her voice, just like I knew I would.

"Hey, bestie." She pauses. She hasn't called me that in years, and she's giving me time to absorb that. Then she laughs, and the sound of it hits me full-force, right in the heart. Jesus, I've missed that laugh. She's laughing because she knows I hated it when she called me "bestie" when we were younger. I always told her only girls call each other that. Today, I can't deny how much I love hearing it.

She continues. "I know you're listening to this months after I'm gone. Who knows, maybe it's next year already." She knows me. She knew I'd put this off as long as I could. "And I know these past months have been shit. How do I know? Because, I can't even imagine our roles being reversed. I can't imagine losing you. I don't know what I would do without you, Gus. You've been the one person I've clung to my entire life. You're my life preserver. Whenever I thought life was just too damn hard or that it couldn't possibly get any worse, all I had to do was think about you or talk to you and that made everything better. For twenty years. *You.* Your laid-back attitude. Your wicked fucking sense of humor. Your caring nature. Your love. It saved me. Every. Single. Time. It reminded me of the goodness in the world. You, me, and Gracie. We took on the world together. We were a team. The best.

"I know that God put certain people in my path in life to teach me something. Not only did you teach me how to swim, and how to surf, and how to play guitar, and how to drive, and how to swear," she pauses and that beautiful giggle comes through the speakers again, "but you showed me what unconditional love feels like. I knew, without a doubt, my entire life, that whenever and wherever I needed you, you'd be there for me. Whether it was to help me work through a song I was writing and struggling with. Or to watch the sunset with me. Or to love Gracie as much as I did. Or just to talk. Or to hug me because I just needed a hug. Or to hold my hand while I had blood drawn or IVs inserted, even though you hate needles. You always knew how to make me feel better, even if you didn't know you were doing it. There's always been a connection between us. I knew what you were going to say before you said it, because I knew what you were thinking. I could see it in your eyes. I could see it in your expressions. I could hear it even when you didn't vocalize it. And I know it was the same for you. You could finish my sentences ... and they were always *way* fucking funnier when you did, dude. I'll miss the way you answered the phone when I called. I'll miss your lazy, beautiful smile. I'll miss being called Bright Side. I loved it when you called me that. It made me feel like I could do anything. Get through anything. It was a badge of honor I wore proudly. Because it meant that I was special to you. And that meant the world to me. Please know that as friends go, you hold the prize, dude. You've mastered friendship. You're a goddamn friendship Jedi. I could live a thousand years and never have a better friend than you.

"I love you to the fucking depths of my soul and back again. You're part of me. Probably the better half. I know your mom always joked about us being long lost twins, but I don't think that's accurate. I mean, we don't even look alike. I'm way better looking than you are." She's trying to joke, but I can hear her voice getting thicker, heavier. "Whatever," she whispers. "What I'm trying to say is that I don't even think blood relatives have the kind of bond that you and I have. It was a gift. *You* were a gift. A gift that made my life worthwhile. A gift that made life fun. A gift that filled me with music. A gift that filled me with love. A gift that inspired me to live on the bright side.

"Gus, I know you. I know you're dealing with me being gone, that you're accepting it, or you wouldn't be listening to this right now. I know you're trying to figure out where you go from here. I want you to keep writing and performing. *Please.* I'm begging you. Aside from being on Earth just to be a stellar fucking human

237

being, you're also here to share your unfathomable talent with the rest of us mere mortals. If you need a kick in the ass, open up my laptop and start poking around. There's a folder titled 'Gus's much-fucking-needed inspiration.' That's right, I know you're probably struggling with writing. I know you shut down when you're stressed and I would imagine my departure has brought on some mammoth goddamn stress. Please let the stress and the sadness and the anger go. It's time to do epic again, dude."

I glance at the tattoo on my right arm and smile. She continues. "Listen to 'Gus's much-fucking-needed inspiration' and let it inspire you. There are a few songs I wrote that you've never heard. There are a few choruses that I never wrote the rest of the song around. There are guitar riffs and violin arrangements. There are words or phrases that for some reason stuck with me. I tried to pick out the best of the best and put it all in one place for you. If you only listen to the audio files once, that's fine, but please listen to them in their entirety. I know you; don't skip out early because it's hard. Just be brave, put your big boy pants on, and do it. Something you hear is going to click with you and you're gonna run with it. And it's going to turn into a kickass Rook song." She's right, it's time. It's time.

"Two more things. I know if you aren't already smoking that you want a cigarette right now, so I'm gonna say it. You should quit. I tried not to be bossy or nag the hell out of you, but you really need to. ASAP. I like you alive and healthy. I'm not going to say this because I'm trying to put a guilt trip on you. I'm going to say this because it's the truth and I only want what's best for you." She pulls in a deep breath, which only helps reinforce the message she's trying to convey. She was on oxygen when she recorded this and I can hear the labored breath. "Cancer fucking sucks, Gus. You don't want this, dude. I don't want this for you. *Please quit.*" She pauses again. I need the pause. Her words hit me right in the gut. They take my breath away. She's not trying to be mean. She's not trying to throw guilt rocks. She's just trying to get it through my thick fucking skull that smoking is killing me. This is first time in my adult life that I've felt like I *want* to quit smoking, not that I *need* to. There's a difference. That difference is the motivation that makes things happen in life. I reach in my pocket and pull out the pack I always carry with me and I drop it in my trash can. A flash of panic hits me before I hear it hit the bottom. As soon as I hear Bright Side's voice again, the panic fades.

"Last thing, but equally important," she says with renewed determination. "I hope you find someone to give your heart to. If our friendship is any indication of your capacity to love, the woman you end up with will not know what hit her when you fall in love with her. I hope you find her soon so that you have an entire lifetime to love her and she has an entire lifetime to experience all of the greatness that is Gus Hawthorne. Besides, the world needs Hawthorne babies. Lots of them. Kids love you, Gus. And you'd totally show up all the other dads when you go to Gus Junior's third grade career day. Just imagine: after little Johnny's dad introduces himself as a stuffy-ass stock trader, you can introduce yourself as the Rock God of Rook. How badass would that be? I'll be watching, because I totally want to see that play out."

There's a pause again. She's trying to figure out how to wrap this up. I hear her sniffle and I know now that she's trying to hold back tears. "I know this is the part where I'm supposed to say good-bye, but we agreed not to say good-bye anymore. And the truth is, I don't want to leave you. So, I'm going to tell you instead that I'll always be with you. I've already talked to God about signing on as your guardian angel." I don't doubt that she actually had that conversation *out loud*. She always talked to God like an actual person who was going to talk back. It always made me laugh, but I also liked the unabashed faith she had that it might actually make a difference. "I think he's cool with it, so, you know, I'll be around. I'll be watching and listening. Except when you're having sex, been there, done that; I know what you look like naked, dude." I hear her teasing smile winning the battle against the impending tears. "I'll leave you be and give you some privacy for the love sessions." I laugh out loud at that. Only Bright Side would talk about God, guardian angels, and sex in the same string of thoughts. "I guess I just want to say thank you, dude. For everything and more. I love you, Gus. Always."

My chest feels tight, but I'm not crying. I thought listening to this would crush me, destroy me, set me back months. Instead, I feel calm. I feel peaceful. I've just been given something I never knew I could have. I just got five minutes with my best friend again. I got five minutes to hear her familiar voice and her beautiful laughter. I got five minutes to hear her encourage me to be better. To do epic.

I don't waste anytime opening up her laptop.

And picking up my guitar.

And you know that feeling when you just know something fucking amazing is about to go down?

Yup, that's exactly how I feel right now.

Wednesday, December 6
(Scout)

Gustov has been playing his acoustic guitar a lot this week. He always leaves his bedroom door shut, but since my room is right across the hall, the sound seeps in. Even with my door closed and my hearing aid removed, I hear him faintly. I'm not complaining—it's the best imaginable way to fall asleep. My fondest memories of my dad are the times he would play his guitar and sing me to sleep when I was little. I haven't thought about that for many years, but this week it seems like everything's come to the surface.

It's ten-thirty and I'm lying in bed. I should be sleeping because I'm helping Audrey with a big presentation at work tomorrow morning. Instead, I'm listening. Gustov didn't come out of his room tonight for dinner. I haven't seen him at all today and I feel a little off because of it, like I can't end my day without seeing his face.

And then I hear something that makes me strip back the covers and put my feet to floor. Before I know it, I've inserted my hearing aid and I'm standing in my pajamas in the hallway in front of his door.

Just standing.

And listening.

He's singing. His voice is barely audible. More humming than words. But he's *singing*.

I sit down next to his door with my back against the wall and I listen.

The humming continues and meshes with the guitar. He strums over and over, each time changing something, fine tuning. Pretty soon the humming gives way to words. A verse at a time, but I swear it's like listening to the creation of magic. Pure magic.

His voice has invaded me. I'm not just hearing it. I'm taking it in through all five senses.

It's intimate in a way I can't even begin to explain.

It's not the tactile sensation normally associated with intimacy; it's cerebral. All in my mind. It's steeping and brewing within me.

It all morphs and evolves into an entire song within a matter of hours. And when the music finally descends into silence, I feel so lucky that I was here to witness this, to experience it, to share it with him. Even if he had no idea.

I glance through my door at the clock on my nightstand, and the glaring red numbers tell me it's almost three in the morning. I need to go to bed, but I don't want to let this moment go. I want to curl up right here on the floor next to his door just so I can be close to him. So I close my eyes and I give myself another few seconds to linger in the dissipating magic before I stand.

Before I walk back to my bedroom, I walk to the kitchen. There's something I need to do.

I return to Gustov's door and set a sticky note on the floor, along with a plate and glass. I knock and then take the three steps required to put me behind my bedroom door.

I hear his door open just after mine closes.

(Gus)

I open my door to find a plate filled with saltines slathered in peanut butter and a glass of grape juice on the floor in the hallway. My stomach growls in demanding appreciation at the sight of them. I haven't eaten since lunch. When I pick up the plate, there's a sticky note stuck to the hardwood floor underneath it. It makes me smile. *Eat this. You didn't have dinner. And thank you. That song filled my soul tonight.*

She was here, listening, the whole time. I want to knock on her door. I want to hug her. I want to thank her for sharing the past few hours with me.

I don't know how to explain it, but the way the song came together, I knew I wasn't alone. I haven't written like that since Bright Side was around. I always feel her in my heart these days, because that's where she lives. I walk around with her inside me every day. And it doesn't hurt anymore. But the presence I felt tonight wasn't internal. It was physical. Tangible. Like someone was in the room with me, *feeding* me. Little did I know, she was just on the other side of the door.

Filling *my* soul.

Friday, December 8
(Gus)

I've been writing nonstop this week. Going through Bright Side's stash on her laptop has started my creative juices flowing again. I've even used a few of her melodies and choruses as a springboard to get me started. Other songs have grown out of the feelings she conveyed in lyrics she'd written. Not the words themselves necessarily, but the emotion behind the words. Those are my favorites. I'm also drawing inspiration from the sticky notes Impatient's been leaving on my door—I find them every morning. Most mornings, she's already left for work or gone for a run by the time I open my door. It's never more than a couple of words but it lets me know she's been listening. That I'm not alone. That she digs what I'm doing. Or that sometimes she doesn't. I should probably just invite her in at night when I'm working, but half of me is scared it will stunt my mojo. The other half is scared I'll choke altogether in her presence, because she's one of the only people I find myself looking to for approval, probably because it's so damn hard to earn it. She doesn't fling compliments freely in the direction of everyone around her; she picks and chooses, and when she says something, she means it. There's no bullshit with her. For now, I like knowing she's just on the other side of the door, listening. Her presence is a palpable force in the room, driving me to dig deeper. To do better. To do epic. I haven't felt that in such a long time. So for now, I've got two of my favorite girls pushing me, bullying me, cheering me on in their own physically non-existent, but emotionally so-fucking-present way. It's eerie, but it works. It more than works. It's fueling me.

Music is a visceral experience if you're doing it right.

I'm doing it so fucking right this week.

Impatient's note this morning reads, *Song 2. Chorus. Perfect now.*

I grab a pad of sticky notes and a Sharpie from my nightstand, because that's where I keep them now, and write back a reply. *Thanks. It's getting there.*

243

Saturday, December 9
(Scout)

It's early. The sun's coming up. I'm headed out to run. When I open my bedroom door, Gustov's door is open, too. I peer through the doorway, but he's not inside.

Then I walk into the living room and I find out why. He's outside, pacing the deck. I see him through the sliding glass door. Back and forth. Back and forth. And his lips are moving. He's talking to himself and he looks tense, distraught. As I approach, I can hear his words through the glass door.

"You don't need one. You don't want one. You don't need one. You don't want one." That's what he's muttering to himself.

Confused, I open the door. "Gustov? Everything all right?"

He's startled out of his internal conversation. He raises his head to look at me, but doesn't say anything. He's fidgety. He's never fidgety. He's always laid-back and fairly calm these days.

"What's wrong?"

He stops pacing and puts his hands on his hips. He inhales deeply once and then drops his chin. "I quit smoking a few days ago."

"That's great," I offer.

His eyes flash to mine and he looks a little irritated and a little helpless. "It is *so not* fucking great. I want a cigarette so bad. *So* fucking bad." And he's pacing again.

"Maybe you just need some oral stimulation." And as soon as the words are out of my mouth I know how bad it sounded. Really bad.

The pacing has stopped and he's smirking at me now. "Jesus. Did you just say what I think you just said? When did we segue this conversation to BJs?"

Well, at least I took his mind off his withdrawal. My cheeks are burning. "Gum. Toothpicks. *That* kind of oral stimulation. Like a substitute. When I quit smoking, I chewed a lot of gum. I know it sounds stupid, but it helped. I've got some in my purse. I'll go get you a piece."

When I return, he takes the piece of gum, unwraps it, and pops it into his mouth. "Thanks. Though unless this is jam-packed with an intense fucking amount of nicotine, I don't think it's

244

gonna do shit for me."

I raise my eyebrows. "Suck it up, buttercup."

He shakes his head, but he's smiling. "That's how it is?"

I nod and start down the stairs toward the beach. "That's *exactly* how it is. If I can do it, you can do it."

"I can't do it!" he calls after me.

"Yes you can!" I yell back.

(Gus)

I calmed down a bit after Impatient left and my cravings subsided. I don't think it was the gum, but I was able to go back to bed with Spare Ribs and sleep for a few hours.

When I open my bedroom door around noon there are a couple dozen packs of gum on the floor—every brand and flavor imaginable. And there's sticky note stuck to one of them. *Suck it up.* :)

That damn smiley face is sneering at me.

"Suck it up," I repeat. And then I put the sticky note on my bathroom mirror so I have the reminder.

Wednesday, December 13
(Gus)

"Hey, asswipe, what's shakin'?"

"Come over. I've got sixteen solid songs."

There's a long pause on the other end and then, "Seriously?"

I'm nodding my head dramatically even though he can't see me. "Seriously."

Another long pause. "I'll be over in ten."

Ten minutes later, I'm standing in the driveway wishing I was smoking a cigarette, but most importantly *not* smoking a cigarette because I'm fucking determined to kick this shit and it's already been a week, when Franco pulls up to our house. He gets out of his truck and his grin is huge, even by Franco standards. His headphones are hanging around his neck, a pair of drumsticks are tucked into his back pocket, and he's carrying a case of Modelo.

I point to the beer. "I see you brought lunch."

"I like to call it inspiration," he says. He actually is pretty damn creative when he drinks, but I don't say anything.

He knows the refinement and fine-tuning that needs to happen now is up to me and him. It used to be Bright Side I relied on. He knows those are big shoes to fill, but Franco hears music with his heart. He gets amped up about it. I need him this time.

We stop in the kitchen on the way through to my room. Franco grabs the Tupperware container of Impatient's homemade cookies from the counter and two oranges from the fruit bowl and places it all on top of the box of beer and starts walking.

I'm staring at the mixtures of tastes he's clutching.

"What, man?" he questions.

"That's fucking disgusting. You're seriously going to eat oranges and cookies while you're drinking beer?"

He doesn't miss a beat. "Yeah."

I shake my head. "Dude, that's a bad combo. That's like toothpaste and OJ."

"No way. Scout's cookies go with everything."

"Sure you don't want a glass of milk? I'm a dunker," I say as I open up the cabinet and pull out a glass.

He laughs. "You're such a fucking rock star." That was sarcasm at its best, but after he watches me pour a tall glass of the cold stuff, he clears his throat. "Pour me one, too."

It's my turn to laugh. "You're such a fucking rock star," I mock. Then I pull open the drawer next to the fridge, looking for a straw. "You want a bendy straw, dude?"

His face lights up at the sight of the blue and white plastic straw. And then it fades quickly as he reins it in, because that was a lot of damn excitement for a grown man to exhibit over a straw. He clears his throat again. "Yeah. Sure. I mean, only if you're gonna have one."

I stick one in each glass and flex the tips. "Yup. Bendy straws are the shit, dude."

He immediately takes a drink through it when I hand him the glass. And then he smiles that shit-eating grin of his. "Bendy straws are the shit. Now let's go do rock star stuff."

After milk and cookies we get down to business for the next eighteen hours. The sun sets and rises again before we quit. The beer is gone. The songs are better than they were before. And Franco is stoked.

I love it when Franco's stoked.

He's always straightforward with me, so his excitement is also approval. It means that we're onto something here.

I'm so relieved. I've been living under this shroud of my own disappointment and doubt and disregard for almost a year now. I know we're not home free, since we still need to play this for the rest of the band and for MFDM, but I don't feel like a burden anymore. I feel like Gus again.

When Franco leaves, I'm home alone. I grab my Sharpie and pad of sticky notes and I write a note and stick it to Impatient's door before I go to sleep. It reads, *Songs are done. I couldn't have done it without you. Thank you.*

Thursday, December 14
(Gus)

There are two sticky notes on my door when I open it. It's a long message and it makes me smile. *I didn't do anything. I listened. That's it. You, on the other hand, made me feel. Feel more than I probably ever have. I felt happiness, sadness, fear, and anger, but most of all I felt hope. I've never been so honored to eavesdrop.*

I don't need praise. Never have. I've always been more about just giving it my all, doing my best, and pushing myself creatively.

But her note? I'd play for her every day to hear that over and over again—to make her feel hope.

Saturday, December 16
(Gus)

I knock loudly, push her bedroom door open an inch, and shout through the crack. "Cock-a-doodle-do! Rise and shine, Impatient!"

"What?" is her sleep-scratchy response. "No roosters allowed. Go away."

I push the door open further and peek in, making sure she's covered up so I don't embarrass her. "Not gonna happen. Someone's buying a car today. And her name is Scout MacKenzie." I inhale sharply, a fake gasp. "What a coincidence, *that's you.*"

She opens her eyes and looks at the alarm clock on her nightstand. "At seven-thirty in the morning?"

I nod and smile. "Yup. Don't sass me, dude. Get your ass in the shower. You're skipping your run this morning. I found you a car in Carlsbad. We need to get on the road soon. Franco's picking us up and giving us a lift. I'm going to wake up Pax."

The truth is I didn't really sleep last night because I was too excited about this. I'm forcing them to join in on my mission.

"I hate you," she growls. I'm not gonna even lie, it sounded pretty hot, especially since she was smiling when she said it.

"I know. Hustle, lazy ass." I step out of the room and immediately close the door, because I know she won't get out from under the covers with me watching. And I don't want to hear her smartass reply. Okay, who am I kidding, I *totally* want to hear her smartass reply, so I crack the door again just in time to hear her say, "Compliments will get you nowhere, *lazier* ass." And then I shut the door again quickly before the name calling continues.

With Impatient and Pax roused, we get on the road. Franco came by and is dropping us off at the car dealership on his way to Jamie and Robbie's place this morning. Impatient, Pax, and Franco all seem a little sleepy and there's not much in the way of convo during the ride, which is fine. We listen to a new album I downloaded last night instead. Royal Blood. They're wicked good. Heavy bass and drums, the perfect soundtrack for the start of a gorgeous day. I'm into it.

Impatient and Pax have their driver's licenses, but have never owned cars before. Pax didn't need one at the boarding school he attended in Boston, and Impatient always lived in the city where public transit was the way to go. Here in Southern California a car is a little more of a necessity. Impatient's been saving for one. She only wants to spend eight grand. She's been researching models and scouring the internet for weeks. I think she's just scared to pull the trigger, because she's intimidated by the process. Yesterday while they were at work and school I drove up to the Carlsbad Honda dealership and checked out a few. Let's just say some money's already traded hands. She doesn't know that. I hope my cockamamie plan goes off without a hitch or we're walking home.

The sales guy, Donovan, is a pretty chill dude for a car salesman. I thought they'd all just be douches, but we hit it off pretty well. He's waiting for us when we all walk in.

After introductions are out of the way, Donovan leads us to the lot, toward the car I asked them to set aside. Impatient drives the car. She loves it. I can tell. She's not the type to get giddy, but she smiled during the entire fifteen-minute test drive. That's huge. She tells Donovan that she likes it, and that she'd like to discuss the price. As we walk back to the sales office, Donovan looks to me and I nod. We worked through this scenario yesterday. Cramming the four of us into his tiny office, he turns to her. "Well Scout, for that model, we're looking at nine thousand."

She looks puzzled, but ponders this a minute before politely asking, "Can you excuse us for a moment, please?"

After he leaves the tiny sales office, her eyes squint. This doesn't make sense to her. "Something must be wrong with it." Of course she's skeptical. "That car should be at least fifteen thousand based on what I've seen cars listed for on the internet."

I shrug and point to the sales banners hanging throughout the showroom around us. "They're having a sale. I guess this is just your lucky day. Besides, he said it's a certified used car and comes with a two-year warranty. They've already checked it out. I'd say you're golden, if you want it."

She takes a deep breath and looks from me to Pax, and back to me. She wants it. Bad. She's chewing on her bottom lip thinking it through. "I don't really know how to do this. I only have eight and that needs to include fees and taxes. I'm not sure how to start negotiations."

I shrug again. "Don't know what to tell you. I bought my truck off a dude at the beach for two g's cash and some surfing lessons when I was sixteen. Not your standard car transaction. But I'd suspect that if you just cut to the chase and tell Donovan what you want and stick to it, he'll either tell you yea or nay. Either you go home with the car or you don't."

She nods. She's not blinking. She's thinking. Hard. "I really want it."

I smile because it's so cute the way she said it. Cute, but super confident. That rarely happens. "I know you do."

She nods her head and puts on her game face again. "Let's do this." She waves her hand and motions for Donovan through the glass window.

She makes her offer like a boss.

He leaves to consult his manager, but I suspect he just ran to the can. He returns with a paper in hand with some figures scribbled on it. It looks familiar; I went through this same drill yesterday with him.

They accepted her offer.

She's over the fucking moon happy.

We all move to the finance office, again, just like I did yesterday. And she signs her paperwork.

When we're done, they hand her the keys and she clutches them like they're sacred and stares at them the entire walk out to the parking lot. When we reach the back of the car she looks up at me and smiles. I would give anything to freeze time and take in this expression for hours. It's so many good things all rolled up into one: it's confidence, satisfaction, pride, and complete, unbridled joy. And it's not just about the material possession; it's about the process and the accomplishment. She opens her mouth to say something, but then she hugs me instead. She's squeezing the shit out of me and hangs on for probably ten seconds. It's thank you. A million and one thank yous.

She has no idea this car really did cost fifteen thousand dollars. Or that I paid for half of it yesterday.

And she never will.

I made a lot of money off the first album and I still have most of it. I don't spend a lot. I don't need a lot. I'm stoked to share it with people I care about.

She's so proud and happy with herself right now. She rocked the hell out of the negotiations, even if they were rigged. She didn't seem self-conscious at all when she was focused on her task. I think her appearance is always on her mind. Sometimes at the forefront. Sometimes in the back. This morning, it was absent. She wasn't hiding. And it was awesome.

Pax calls out, "Shotgun!"

I reach into my pocket, pull out a key, and toss it to Pax.

He catches it and looks questioningly at it.

"I call shotgun, but you're driving, dude," I counter.

Scout shakes her head. "You've never ridden with him, Gustov. He is *not* driving my car."

I smile and taunt her. "You're such a pussy when it comes to driving. Seriously, he can't be that bad?"

She's not offended, but she's gone from shaking her head to nodding. "He's that bad."

Pax is pointing to himself. "Standing right here. And I can hear you." It's a reminder, that while she's not offended, he is.

"Well, dude, try not to kill me then. Or wreck your new-to-you car."

His eyes bulge like a cartoon character. "What?" It's loud, which is so unlike him. The people across the lot are gawking at us now.

I smile and point to the car parked next to Impatient's. It's fifteen years old and has a shit ton of miles on it, but it's a clean beater and runs great. It's also Pax's now. I bought it yesterday. "It's yours. We'll call it an early birthday present." His birthday is tomorrow.

He's stunned.

Impatient is stunned.

This is priceless.

I love doing nice things for people. Not that it has to be a grand gesture, because let's face it, a car is a little over-the-top. Just something nice. It's grounding. It reminds me that we're all in this game called life together. It's also circular ... you give it ... you get it.

I gave it.

And looking at them, standing here so gracious, and so happy, I'm getting it back tenfold.

And now it's Pax's turn to hug me.

And then it's Impatient's turn to hug us both.

We're standing here, in a group hug, practically singing fucking "Kumbayah."

The people across the lot are still ogling.

I buckle in next to Pax and ride home with him.

Scout was totally right. Pax could use some lessons in signaling, merging, stopping, and even just keeping the car in his own lane. I'm not a religious man, but I may have recited the Lord's prayer two or twenty times during the ride.

When Pax walks ahead of us into the house, I pause with Impatient outside. "You're right. He's fucking horrible. The dude has no fucking depth perception. He tails the car ahead of him like he's being towed. The passenger side imaginary brake pedal is for real. I wore it the fuck out."

She smirks. "Told you." And holds out her fist.

I bump knuckles. "I need some fucking gum. My nerves are shot."

Wednesday, December 20
(Scout)

"They didn't even call, Scout. It's my birthday and they couldn't even make a goddamn phone call." There's disappointment in his voice, like he's floating alone in a sea of letdown.

I nod and battle with myself, wondering if this is the time to tell him about his mom.

He beats me to it and starts talking again before I do. "I shouldn't be surprised, really. I'm sure mom's drunk and dad's busy."

It's then that I make the decision. "Paxton, Jane's in rehab."

He's sitting on the corner of my bed with his back mostly to me, but turns to face me. The movement is slow like he's trying to decide if he heard me correctly or not. His eyebrows are tight with confusion, but his eyes look hopeful—an expression that contradicts itself, like he's been handed the gift he's always wanted but if he opens it a grenade might go off. "Rehab?"

"Uh-huh. She checked herself in about two months ago. From what I understand she can't have contact with anyone outside the facility until she completes the program. She'll be there another two to three weeks." I'm holding my breath the entire time I'm telling him, because I don't want him to be let down if she doesn't complete it. My dad's a career alcoholic; I know what it's like to be in Paxton's shoes. I knew never to let my heart hope.

His eyes drop. He's thinking about it, but when his eyes rise and meet mine again the momentary hope is gone and he shakes his head doubtfully. "She's not strong enough. She'll never do it."

My heart clenches like a dishcloth being wrung out inside my chest. "Sometimes it isn't a matter of being strong enough, Paxton. Alcoholism is a disease."

"Don't. Just don't, Scout. I know you've lived with it, too, but she chooses to wake up every day and drink. She chooses it over me. Every fucking day of my life." He takes a deep breath and it's as if the happiness of the past few weeks is deflating before my eyes.

I know how he feels. My dad's alcoholism is the reason I haven't lived with him since I was eleven. It's the reason uncle Jim

254

thought it would be better if I lived with him and Jane. Here's the thing about alcoholism. It's destructive on many levels and to many degrees. While Jane uses it to dampen her feelings, the depression, the inadequacy; my dad was a partier. He used it to turn himself into the person he wanted be. The person he thought other people wanted him to be. The problem was he forgot who he was when he was sober and embraced the drunk version instead. And when that happened I never saw my real dad again. He was absent. The drunk dad pursued people and a lifestyle and forgot to be a parent. It's not that he's forgotten about me altogether. I still talk to him about once a year. Does he love me? Sure. Is he good at showing it? Not at all. That's life. I've accepted it.

Paxton hasn't. I'm not saying he should. He's only eighteen. And Jane's depression immobilizes her. Couple that with the alcohol, and it breeds resentment in Paxton.

His eyes are filling up with tears. I hate this part. It kills me when he cries. I've seen it too many times. He has the gentlest heart and watching it get crushed repeatedly is almost too much.

"Come here," I say gently.

I'm sitting on my bed with my back against the headboard. He crawls up the bed toward me and is sobbing by the time he wraps his arms around me. I hold him and I let him cry, just like every time before, and I pray to God that Jane helps herself so that I don't have to watch this sweet boy cry anymore.

When his breathing resumes to a natural cadence and he's just resting his cheek on my shoulder, I ask, "Did you have a good birthday, Paxton? I mean before all of this." I know he did.

He nods against my shoulder.

"What was the best part?" He needs to focus on something positive.

He sniffs a couple of times to clear his nose. "I don't know. The cupcakes were *really* good." He lifts his head slightly so that he's looking at me, and he quickly apologizes, "No offense, Scout, you make really good cakes."

I laugh. "None taken. I agree; Audrey's cupcakes are way better than my cake."

He smiles and rests his head back on my shoulder. "I think what I liked most was just hanging out with you and Gus and

Audrey. It felt like a real family, you know? I know eighteen-year-old guys shouldn't get so excited over a barbeque, watching their favorite movie, and eating cupcakes ... but I did. Everyone just wanted to make me happy today."

"Of course we want to see you happy, Paxton."

"I know you always do, but they don't have to. They just do it. And not just on my birthday. They do it every day. Every day they're nice, Scout. I like it here. Why couldn't you have found Audrey and Gus ten years ago?"

I laugh. "Because I was fourteen, I wasn't really in the market for a job then."

He laughs, too. "I guess so." It's quiet for several moments before he says, "I'm glad things didn't work out between you and the jerk."

"Why do you say that?" I know he never liked Michael. He always called him *the jerk* and that was after meeting him once.

"Because there's someone out there who's perfect for you. You just haven't realized it yet."

"You think someday I'll meet *the one?*" I ask, smiling.

"I think you've already met him." He's talking about Gustov. I know he is.

I don't answer.

Friday, December 22
(Gus)

"Is this *the Joe*, proprietor of the infamous Joe's Bar?"

"Hey, man, is this Gustov *the globe-trotting rock legend* Hawthorne?"

"Nah, this is just Gus. I am shopping the hell out of some groceries at the moment though. That's as legendary as it gets in my world these days." I'm in the middle of the grocery store pushing my cart down the cereal aisle and trying to decide between Fruity Peebles and Captain Crunch.

He laughs. "I won't keep you long. I know Rook is big shit now and you've outgrown my bar, but the band that was supposed to play New Year's Eve just backed out on me. I was wondering if you guys would like to slum it and play a set? Should I be talking to your management or something? Like I said, I know you're big time now and you can tell me to go fuck myself, but I miss having you guys in here."

Anxiety initially grips me, but without thinking I'm asking, "So, next week?"

"Yeah, I know it's short notice. Sorry, brother."

And then I'm confirming, "We'll be there." Where the hell did that come from? Playing in my bedroom is one thing. I don't know if I'm ready for the crowds again.

"Really?" He sounds shocked.

"Let me call the guys, but yeah, I think we can make it happen. I'll call you back."

"Right on. Call me."

"Will do. Gimme five."

I send out a text to Franco, Robbie, and Jamie. They all respond immediately, which means that they're hyped. And now, so am I.

I call Joe back. "We're on, dude. What time do you want us there?"

"You can go on at eleven o'clock."

"Sounds like a plan. See you Saturday." And just like that, excitement takes over. I hope it's the real deal.

257

Saturday, December 23
(Gus)

My phone rings in my pocket. When I see the name on the screen, I smile.

"Well, if it isn't the stud from the frozen north."

Keller laughs on the other end before he says anything. "Nah man, not the stud. How about the dad? And greetings from cold and snowy Grant, Minnesota."

I never think much about the weather here because it's always fairly consistent year round, but I've always been fascinated by the extreme changes most of the rest of the country experiences. Not that I'd ever want to live through it, but it's fascinating. "Cold up there, huh?"

"Yeah, it's a little chilly today. I don't think we're going to break zero for a high. It got down to twenty below last night."

"You may as well just live in the Arctic Circle, dude."

"The only downer about it getting this cold is that Stella can't go outside and play. She's a snowman building machine lately. She pretends she's an ice princess from one of her movies. She'll sing the entire soundtrack before she's done."

"Ah, Miss Stella's a singer. She's a natural performer." She is. She's got more personality and charisma than most adults I've met.

"She says she wants to sing like Katie. That's fine by me, but I swear I need to buy her another movie, because I hear those songs in my dreams. They haunt me. I can't get away from them." He chuckles, and I smile. He'd probably listen to those songs every day for the rest of his life if it made his little girl happy. That's one of the things I like most about Keller; he always puts others ahead of himself.

"What else is Stella up to?"

"Just getting ready for Christmas. Stella's really into construction paper, glitter, and glue at the moment, so every available flat surface in our apartment is adorned with sparkly paper reindeer, bells, mistletoe, trees, ornaments, etcetera, etcetera. Stella swore she didn't, but it's very suspicious that even Miss Higgins is sporting a glittery shell this holiday season. Stella's blaming the new bling on Santa's elves who apparently visit at night while we're sleeping. And I'm choosing to believe her story because she wants so badly for it to be true."

Now I'm laughing. "Stella bedazzled her turtle?"

"She did. There's probably some kind of animal rights violation involved there, so don't tell anyone."

"My lips are sealed. I don't want Stella spending Christmas in the gray rock motel wearing an orange jumpsuit. So, are you going to Chicago for Christmas?"

"No. My father's actually coming here tomorrow and spending a few days with us. We're all going to Shel's parents' house on Christmas day. Dunc's finally going to propose to her. He's had it planned for months now. I can't wait to see the look on her face." He sounds happy.

"That's great, dude. They're good people."

"They are," he says sincerely. That's another thing I really like about Keller. He genuinely wants the best for others. "How about you? What are you doing for Christmas?"

"We'll hang out here at the hacienda with Pax and Scout. Introduce them to early morning cinnamon rolls on the beach."

"You know, Stella asked if I would make cinnamon rolls on Christmas morning. She remembers Katie making them for us last year."

"You gonna do it?"

"Of course. I'm no baker though. I bought a tube of them at the grocery store last night. They're the pre-made kind you just throw in a pan and bake. They won't taste like homemade, but they'll taste a helluva lot better than my attempt at homemade."

"You're a great dad, dude."

"I try, man. Well, Stella's ballet lesson is just about done. I'd better let you go. I just wanted to call and wish you a Merry Christmas. Tell Audrey, too, if you don't mind."

"Will do. And Merry Christmas to you and your little ice princess."

"Thanks. Bye, Gus."

"Later, Keller."

And just like that, my Christmas is made. That one unexpected conversation helped reinforce what I already knew; that life is all about people.

259

And before I do anything else I log onto Amazon and I buy Stella every Disney movie that Gracie used to watch and loved to sing along to. I don't know how many are in the cart by the time I checkout, but there are at least ten. I also throw in a few more current Disney movie soundtracks on CD and a little purple CD player for Keller. And I pay the extra shipping fee to get them to Grant by tomorrow.

Sunday, December 24
(Scout)

Audrey mentioned yesterday that she had company traveling in today from out of town, so I'm not surprised to see a cab in the driveway of her house as I'm returning from my morning run.

The driver is pulling a suitcase out of the trunk as a tall, distinguished looking middle-aged man pulls a few bills from his pocket. They say their pleasantries and the visitor starts walking toward the front door with his suitcase rolling behind him.

When he reaches the front door and raises his hand to knock, I call to him. "No need to knock. You must be Audrey's friend." I'm sweaty and out of breath, so I keep my distance.

He turns at my words and addresses me quite formally. "I am indeed, miss." He has an accent that sounds foreign, maybe Eastern European.

I approach him and extend my hand, and he reaches out with his. Slender, extremely long fingers wrap around mine and shake firmly. It's the act of someone who does this frequently, professional, yet friendly. His warmth eases my nerves. I'm always nervous when I meet someone new. I clear my throat. "Hi. My name's Scout MacKenzie. I'm Audrey's assistant."

His resting face brightens into a smile and wrinkles form at the corners of his eyes. "Ah, Scout, of course. I've heard so much about you." My nerves must show, because he adds quickly, "All good, my dear. All good."

I can't help but smile at his words, I don't know if it's his accent or if he's just so charming that the compliment is working double time on me. "Well, come in ... "

He fills in the blank for me when I pause at his name. "Gustov."

Gustov? That is not a common name. Is this a coincidence?

He chuckles at my confusion. "I'm Gus's father."

All of a sudden the names, and people attached to those names, flip in my mind — this is Gustov and Gus is Gus. I nod, "It's nice to meet you, Gustov," while at the same time taking in everything about him. I always thought Gustov — I mean, Gus — resembled Audrey. They're both tall, with the same blond hair, same nose and lips, and same commanding presence tempered by

261

a kindness that's unmatched. But looking at this Gustov, I see Gus's same intense dark brown eyes, same bone structure in his face, same tall, broad frame, and same warmth. An uncanny ability to put anyone at ease.

When I open the door, he follows me inside. I wait while he removes his tweed blazer and drapes it over his suitcase that he's parked up against the wall. Just as I'm about to tell him I'm going to go find Audrey, she walks around the corner.

"Gustov!" she exclaims. "It's so good to see you." She's beaming.

"My Audrey. Come here." He's wearing a smile that exudes such warmth, such affection, that it must be reserved only for those closest to him. Those he cherishes.

And when they hug, it hits me: if this is Gus's father, this must be Audrey's ex—boyfriend or husband, I don't know. This officially just got weird. Until it only gets weirder when Gus walks in the room and says, "The sperm donor returns. How goes it, maestro? How was the journey from bean town?" And now he's smiling, too.

Three people.

Family.

All trading hugs and smiles.

I feel like I should leave the room because I know I'm staring. My family is certainly anything but traditional, and has plenty of skeletons in the closet, but Audrey and Gus seem so normal. Exceptionally perfect, despite the lack of a father in the picture. I've just always thought of them as not needing another man in the house, like they were so complete together, just the two of them, that Gus must've been the product of an immaculate conception.

As I start to remove myself from the embarrassing-only-to-me situation, Gus stops me. "Wanna grab some breakfast with us? Pax is coming, too."

"Um, I need to shower."

"I'm glad I didn't have to be the one to point that out." He winks.

"Gus," Gustov scolds, but he's smiling and shaking his head.

Gus turns to him. "I'm just keepin' it real, dude. She's a wicked runner. Fierce output of energy produces fierce production

262

from the sweat glands." He turns to me. "How many miles did you run this morning, Impatient?"

"Twelve," I answer and I feel heat rushing to my face under all of the attention.

Gus is facing me, with his back to Gustov and Audrey. His eyebrows rise and then he grins and mouths, "Hell yeah," to me, showing his shock and approval all at once. Then he says, "See? She ran a goddamn half-marathon this morning. That shit would make anyone stinky."

I can't help but smile and accept the invitation. "Sure. I'll go to breakfast. Give me twenty minutes."

At the café over eggs and coffee, I learn the whole story. Gustov really was a sperm donor. Literally. Gustov moved to San Diego with his family from Ukraine when he was thirteen. He and Audrey attended the same music academy and quickly became friends. Their love of music was at the heart of it at first, Audrey played the piano and Gustov played the violin, but other interests are what solidified their friendship. When they graduated, Audrey went to San Diego State and got her marketing degree, leaving music behind. Gustov ended up at Julliard and went on to have a successful career playing with the Boston Philharmonic and more recently as a conductor. They remained the best of friends throughout their adult lives. When Audrey decided she wanted a child, Gustov was the person she turned to. Audrey is the type of woman who knows what she wants and didn't let the fact that she was single and career-minded get in her way. She and Gustov discussed it during one of his visits to San Diego, and he signed on without reservation to give his best friend the one thing she wanted most in life—a child. Before he left town, the arrangements had been made for him to return to make his "donation" and for the process to begin. It was all very clinical, in vitro fertilization.

Listening to the story and watching them tell it so matter-of-factly, with all of the humor that Gus interjects, is so strange. It's an unconventional story. Told by unconventional people.

And that's when it hits me. Maybe unconventional is okay. Maybe family doesn't have to be perfect to exist. Theirs certainly doesn't. And it works. It more than works. They only see each other once or twice a year. Audrey raised Gus on her own and has always been the single parent because that's how she wanted it, but that doesn't stop Gustov from loving Gus with his whole heart or from Gus loving him in return. It just works.

I've always felt defined by unconventional. Don't get me wrong, I was always grateful to my aunt and uncle who raised me, but I always felt different, like an oddball. Because I didn't have a mom and dad. Or even just a mom *or* a dad. And before that, when I was with my dad, I was so young that I barely remember having a sense of normalcy. Because it was never normal, really.

Spending time with these people today is like free therapy. It lends perspective, and though I've probably been presented with my fair share of perspective throughout the years, I've never had this type of epiphany. My family doesn't have to define me. I have a mom. I have a dad. I have an aunt and uncle. I've accepted them for who they are, and I don't resent their flaws. We all have flaws. I've just never been able to accept who we are *together*, as a family. Their parental role never felt *right*. I always wanted to fit into a neat, tidy description of the perfect family. But maybe there's no such thing.

I guess the biggest epiphany of all is that, sitting here, I realize how much I love my family, all of them. And even if they don't love me back the same way, or to the same degree, maybe that's not what's important. Maybe it's about *my* heart. Maybe it's about me feeling fulfilled and accepting that love is never perfect, and that, if it allows you to feel at peace, it's okay if it is a little one-sided. Maybe it's about opening up your definition of family to include friends, too. Because friends are the family you choose.

Monday, December 25
(Gus)

I'm up early. It's Christmas. I've always loved Christmas, though last year I pretty much skipped it because life was shit and I didn't feel like celebrating. Bright Side was dying. I'd just come home after a long tour. My mind was fatigued. My body was half-dead from the abuse I was putting it through on a daily basis. It was fucked up.

But today? Today is different. Today we celebrate. Gustov hasn't been with us for years during the holidays.

It's habit to go outside right after I wake up. Even though I don't have that morning cigarette, I still go through the motions and I chew gum instead. When I slide open the door, Gustov is sitting out on the deck in one of the lounge chairs, drinking a cup of coffee.

"Morning, maestro."

He turns toward me and smiles. I've always loved it when he smiles at me like that. That smile always made me feel like he was proud of me, proud that I was part of his life. Validation of so many things that I doubt about myself. "Gus. Good morning. And Merry Christmas."

"Merry Christmas." I nod to his coffee. "I see you already brewed some java."

He raises the cup and a roguish smile emerges. "I sure did. It's good. You should have a cup with me."

He always brings his own coffee with him when he visits. It's European, Turkish I think, and strong. Like so strong, I have to cut it with half a mug of milk and add a shit ton of sugar. I don't even like milk in my coffee, but it's the only way to make his coffee tolerable. "I'll pass, dude. I don't know how that shit doesn't eat out the inside of your plumbing."

He laughs at that, and then he falls quiet for a few minutes as we watch the sun rise. "Kate was the only one who liked my coffee."

That makes me smile. He's right. She was. "Liked? She loved it. You, my friend, were a bad influence on Bright Side."

He looks offended. "How so?"

"You introduced her to her two vices: coffee and the violin."

265

They're two things I'll forever associate with her.

He smiles and nods thoughtfully. "I shall gladly take the blame for both of those." It's the smile he always reserved for Bright Side and Grace. Even though he wasn't around a lot while I was growing up, he always took the time when he visited to spend time with Kate and Gracie, to make them feel special. Their dad was never around, and Gustov had a soft spot for them both. "It's strange being here without them, isn't it?"

I nod. "It is."

He looks at me and I know what he's about to say is something I need to hear. He's always been this wise, old soul, I think that's why Bright Side liked him so much. "We all have our own journey. The older I get the more I'd like to believe that I'm here to set an example for a younger generation ... like you. But what Kate and Grace," he looks pointedly at me to make sure he has my attention, "and you, my boy, have taught me over the years is that I am the student, not the teacher. The three of you young people are the most sincere, passionate human beings I've ever met. The care you put into your friendships is unsurpassed." His face softens as he smiles at me again. "You are *so* like your mother."

I smile. It's all I can do; because that's one of the nicest things anyone's ever said to me.

He nods and smiles to acknowledge my silent acceptance of his compliment. "Where is Kate's violin?"

"It's in my room. She left it to me." I pause, then say, "You should really take it. You gave it to her."

He smiles and shakes his head. "I may have given it to her and encouraged her to play, but it belongs with you."

I've been thinking about this for a long time. "I want to have it mounted in a glass case to display on the wall. What do you think?"

He nods. "I think that would be a fitting memorial to a very talented and dear girl."

Instead of feeling sad, I feel resolved. "Will you play it one more time? Today? I think Bright Side would like to see you play it one more time before it's retired."

He looks up to the sky and his Bright Side smile returns. "I would be honored."

Silence settles in for a few minutes before he says, "I haven't seen you smoke since I've been here. Am I too hopeful to assume you've quit?"

"I quit. I'm sucking it up. Oh, but I'm addicted to gum now." I point to my mouth to illustrate my point. "Traded one filthy habit for another."

"Good. And one more thing, Gus. I know we haven't talked much about your career, but I keep an eye on you. Through Audrey, of course, but I also follow your tour schedules, your album rankings, reviews, and interviews online. I have a feeling you haven't peaked yet, not with your incredible potential. With that comes success and failure, depending on how you foster, nurture, and embrace that potential. I think you're at a point in your life now to do all of those things in a way that fulfills you. And I wish you all the success you can handle before it breaks you. Everyone has a limit and some break far more quickly than others, destroyed by fame and money," his face looks intense for a moment, before he looks back at me, smiling gently. "I know neither of those appeals to you and I hope for your sanity's sake, they never do."

"Who just said they weren't wise?" I tease, but his words linger in my ears. They reinforce a lot of my hopes and fears. He's right. He's always right.

Ma makes two pans of her famous cinnamon rolls. We're all sitting on the beach wrapped up in blankets, because it's chilly out by the water. Pax and I destroy one pan between the two of us like a couple of greedy savages. And everyone else shares the other pan like civilized people.

A text comes in from Keller while we're eating. When I open it, it's a video of Stella and him singing, the little purple CD player sitting on the table next to them. Stella's really belting it out. I turn up the volume and we all watch. Every one of us is smiling because what's going on in this video is pure joy and love, and that's what this day should be all about. When they're done singing they both wish me a Merry Christmas and thank me for the gifts. I didn't send the gifts for a thank you like this, but I know I will never erase this message.

When we return to the house, I go straight for the tree and

hand out my gifts to everyone. Gift giving, not gift getting, is my favorite part of the holidays. I got Pax some nice headphones, Impatient a first edition of her favorite book, and Gustov a bottle of his favorite wine. I'm most excited about Ma's present, so I save it for last. Bright Side and Grace used to always spend Christmas morning with us, because their mom was a slacker on the whole parental obligation front, and we used to exchange one homemade gift. Bright Side and Grace never had any money, but they always managed to make something heartfelt and meaningful, so Ma and I tried to do the same. This year I'm giving her music: it's a few verses of lyrics that Bright Side wrote, God only knows when, accompanied by a couple dozen measures of piano music I wrote last week to go along with it. I hand wrote it all out on thick vellum and had it matted and framed. I tell Ma before she opens it that it's from Bright Side and me, and the happy tears are already flowing before it's unwrapped.

Day made.

The only thing that makes the day better is listening to the maestro play Bright Side's violin. We're all sitting in the living room after dinner when I bring it out and present it to him. Ma, Impatient, Pax, and I sit on the sofa and Gustov takes a chair off to the side. He always sits on the very edge of his seat when he plays, like he's poised to leap up off of it at any moment. He sits like he's spring-loaded, and only the music keeps him confined to a sitting position. He quickly tunes the instrument and rosins the bow. And then he plays. They each had their own style, he and Bright Side. Finesse was a common link, and grace, but their emotions came through differently. Bright Side played with her entire body; it was a reaction to the music. If you had put earplugs in and just watched her play, I swear you would've still heard the song. And you definitely would've felt it. The maestro is all energy when he plays, vigor more than emotion. It's like winding up a top and letting it go. Him playing her instrument is a fitting, beautiful way to seal the day. It's like the coda in the song of her life. I finally feel like that part of Bright Side can rest. I'll hear her forever playing in my mind, and that's enough for me.

Tuesday, December 26
(Scout)

I'm packing my lunch for work when Gus walks in the kitchen. Paxton is still sleeping and Audrey took Gustov to the airport early this morning to catch his flight home.

"There's some banana bread left if you want some."

He stops and thinks for a minute, he looks tired, and then he nods like he's made up his mind. "I want some."

He's always hungry. I can't do much for him, but I do like feeding him. It's something I can do every day. It's a guaranteed connection. I like doing nice things for him, because he's always so nice to me.

"I like Gustov."

He pulls three slices of bread out of the Ziploc bag and takes a bite out of one before he answers, "The maestro is a good dude."

I'm full of questions and this might not be the right time to ask, but I'm going to try. "Do you wish you saw him more often?"

"Mmm ... I don't know, it's hard to say. I mean, it's always just been the way it is, you know? He lives his life on the East Coast and we live ours here. We talk. I know he's always there if I need him and when we see him it's always a big deal. I kinda like that."

"It sounds like he and Audrey have always been best friends."

He smiles. "Always."

"And they love each other, that's pretty clear. I wonder why they never dated?" It's none of my business, but it seems odd given they have so much in common.

Gus is on his second slice of bread and he's talking with his mouth full. "Oh, they did date. They went out a few times when they were in high school, I guess. It didn't work."

"Why not?"

Gus shrugs like the answer is obvious. "Gustov is gay. That kinda put a damper on the evolution of anything romantic."

"Gustov is gay?" I don't know why I'm surprised. It doesn't matter. It's just another twist in their family story.

Gus nods. "Yup. Ma was the first person he came out to. She helped him a lot, from the stories I've heard. I think going through that together is the reason they're so solid all these years later.

269

They always had each other's backs after that." He takes the last bite of bread and goes for the milk in the refrigerator. That's where the story ends.

This family's uniqueness and compassion surprises me at every turn.

Wednesday, December 27
(Gus)

We ran through our New Year's Eve set this afternoon at Franco's place. The first few songs sounded like shit. It was like my guitar was fighting with me. My voice was fighting with me. I felt like my nerves were strangling me at every chord. I think I chewed through an entire pack of gum. Writing is different than performing, that's for damn sure. But after a few times, once I relaxed and let the music just take me away, everything fell into place. We'll do this again tomorrow and the day after. We'll be ready.

Sunday, December 31
(Scout)

I'm nervous. Paxton and I are riding with Gus to Rook's show at a local bar. I purposely never watched Rook play while I was on tour with them. I always told myself I did it to stay disconnected from the hype. I hated the hype. I only had to deal with Gus on a business level. The performer side of him seemed too personal, too artificial, too unpredictable, and I didn't want any part of it. I didn't want to see him in that light, because I thought it would make me dislike him even more. Now I fear it may have the opposite effect. Time and familiarity has completely transformed my opinion of him. And after listening to him write and play at home these past few weeks, I'm more attracted to him than ever. And I'm fighting it, which is difficult because every day I notice something else about him, about his personality, that draws me closer. So, I'm nervous.

"What song are you going to close with tonight, Gus?" Paxton asks eagerly. "I hope it's 'Killing the Sun'."

Gus nods. "That's usually how it goes down, Pax." He seems nervous, too. Not himself.

He pulls into a dirt lot that's packed with cars and parks behind the bar in a spot clearly marked 'No Parking'.

Paxton jumps out as soon as the truck is in park and starts pulling Gus's guitar cases and amps out of the bed. And I take this moment of privacy to talk to him. "Hey?"

He's distractedly searching his pockets. He's not listening.

"Hey? Over here." I wave my hand to get his attention.

He glances at me. "Yeah?"

"Are you okay?"

"I need a fucking cigarette." He really wants one. It's the reason he was absently checking his pockets for the pack of cigarettes he used to carry. Old habit.

"No, you don't," I remind him.

"I need a fucking piece of gum."

I dig a piece out of my purse and hand it to him. "Suck it up."

He's motioning with his fingers like he wants more. "Gimme three."

I hand him two more and he takes them immediately,

unwraps them, and pops them into his mouth. He talks while he's chewing. "I don't know, Impatient. I thought I wanted this, but now that I'm here I don't know if I do."

"Paxton's really excited to watch you guys play." It's the only encouragement I feel like I can offer that will make a difference. And it works.

He smiles, a genuine grin. "He is pretty stoked."

I nod again and smile. "This is probably the best night of his entire life. And I'm not just saying that."

He nods again. "What about you?"

"I'm pretty excited, too."

"You don't have to lie to me." He doesn't sound hurt, he's just being honest.

I push on, even though it's hard for me. "I'm not." And suddenly, I feel a surge of energy. This is about him finding himself again, and I need to help him believe he can do it. "I want to watch you play your guitar. I want to listen to you sing. This is my first Rook show. I want to be impressed. Show me what you've got, rock star."

He smiles. "That sounds like a challenge." He winks. "I like a good challenge."

"You do?"

The smile remains, but it's transforming into something far more sexy. "Hell. Yes."

I surprise myself when I add, "So do I."

He echoes, "You do?"

I nod. My entire life has been a challenge. But this? This is a different type of challenge, one that I'm beginning to accept, despite my fears.

He stares at me for several seconds, and when his eyes drop to my lips, all I want is for him to kiss me. That's all I want.

But then he turns away and drops his feet to the ground outside the truck. I think he's going to walk away and leave this conversation unfinished, but he turns back to me and says, "You might be sorry you said that, Impatient, because, like I said, I fucking *love* a challenge." With that he shuts the door and walks to the back of the truck to meet Paxton. And he leaves me sitting here feeling feverish in such a good way. I might be in trouble.

The bar is small inside. Gus said it will hold two hundred,

but I don't know how. By the look of the place, nothing's ever been fixed or updated, from the dark wood walls, to the torn vinyl booths around the perimeter of the room, to the worn, uneven, wide-planked wood floors. It smells like a brewery. I can't imagine how much beer has spilled on and soaked into the floors over the years. This place is a real dive, and it's amazing to think that Gus and Rook got their start here, when they've played some of the most well-known venues in Europe and the States.

Paxton is in his glory, helping the band bring in their equipment and set it all up. He's wearing one of the Rook T-shirts Gus gave him, and I know for a fact I've never seen him happier than he is tonight. I wish he could live this for more than a couple of hours.

I hear voices near the entrance, and I can see the bouncers turning away mobs of people at the door. Everyone wants in to see Rook play. Paxton and I were going to watch from backstage, but Paxton wants to be out in the crowd. So after the stage is set, we find a spot amongst the masses of people already gathering in the audience. Being in the middle of all these people makes me uncomfortable, but I'll do anything to keep that smile on Paxton's face.

When Rook takes the stage, the place erupts. I've never heard anything like it. If adoration has a sonic equivalent, that was just it. It's love. Mad love for this band. And it makes me smile. Paxton is jumping up and down, yelling, and clapping. Yup, I've never seen him happier, not that life always calls for this kind of excitement, but this is what I want for Paxton every minute of every day.

Gus clears his throat as he approaches the microphone and he smiles, but something is off. His eyes are searching the crowd and the intensity in them doesn't match his smile. "Hello San Diego!" he calls out. "It's good to be back at Joe's!" His eyes are still searching. "We're gonna play a few songs for you tonight. But, before we get started I need you to bear with me a minute."

A woman near the front takes her shirt off and swings it like a lasso over her head. Franco is laughing from behind his drum kit and points a drumstick at the woman in only her bra and says, "Not that kind of bare, but I love your enthusiasm, chica."

The crowd laughs, but Gus still looks intent. He's not seeing or hearing what's going on around him. His eyes are still methodically scanning as he calls out, "Pax, where are you?"

Paxton starts waving his hands over his head. Usually he'd be embarrassed by this kind of attention, but I think the excitement has outshined any hint of shyness.

When Gus spots the waving hands his eyes lock with mine and he points at us before crooking the same finger, calling us to him. "I want everyone to give the stud in the Rook shirt and the pretty girl with him some room and let them move up front."

Paxton grabs my hand and starts pulling me through the crowd. I'm bumping shoulders with everyone we pass and everyone's staring at me, which is usually a nightmare. And though I still feel a little self-conscious, I can't stop smiling while a blush heats my face ... because Gus just called me *pretty*. He called me pretty to a room full of people. I know this shouldn't be a big deal. Beauty is on the inside, blah, blah, blah. I know that. I preach it. It's my mantra. I've repeated it to myself for years. Repeating and believing are two different things. And when you grow up *not* feeling pretty, then when something like this happens ... it's huge.

When we stop directly in front of him, up against the stage, I finally look up. He's staring down at me and his smile has transformed. It's real. It's the smile he wears after he's surfed, or played with Spare Ribs, or watched the sunset, or hugged Audrey. It's bone-deep contentment. It's my favorite version of Gus. I smile back to let him know I'm with him and that I'm proud of him. And then I say, "Thank you. Show me what you've got."

His smile grows and he winks. "Challenge accepted, Impatient," he says into the microphone.

He strums his guitar twice, glances back at Franco, and nods. And just like that it begins. For the next hour I watch Gus own that stage. Challenge accepted indeed. From my place up close to the stage, I'm in awe. I can feel the bass and the drums thumping inside my body, and I'm close enough to reach out and touch Gus, if I wanted. I can feel the heat of the stage lights, and the sound of the music seems to pour over me. My eyes roam over every square inch of him, taking it all in. This whole experience is sensory overload.

I watch his feet move from one side of the stage to the other while he's playing his guitar, before they come to rest in front of me at his microphone stand while he's singing. And when he sings his words seem to seep in through every pore and fill me completely. I don't hear them; I *feel* them. I feel every word, every syllable. His voice, his delivery, it grabs ahold of me. The emotion in his voice makes my heart feel like it's going to burst. He is so passionate. And *holy shit* is it sexy.

As the performance goes on, I find myself shamelessly checking out his ass in those jeans every time he walks away from us. I can't believe I've been living across the hall from that ass for months now and I've never noticed how spectacular it is. And the way his chest perfectly fills out the T-shirt he's wearing, his biceps tugging and stretching the sleeves, seems totally new. I watch his taut forearms tighten and flex with constant use.

And his hands. *His hands.* Watching his fingers manipulate that guitar, bending it to his will, he manages to make it scream ... or sing. I know music is visceral, but my imagination is running wild watching those hands. How they would feel on me. What they could do to me. Jesus, suddenly I feel like I'm going to lose my mind. I thought there was attraction before, but now I'm blatantly staring at the bulge in his jeans and full-on fantasizing. All I feel is need. So. Much. Need. The kind of need that's demanding relief.

And every time my eyes meet his face again, it's as if they're being pulled there. I realize that he's staring at me, and the look in his eyes is sinful and playful and so, so naughty. It's fueling the crowd.

And it's fueling me.

I don't know how long they've been playing. It could be tomorrow already for all I know, and believe me I'd stand here all night long and watch him, but when he pulls his guitar strap over his head and separates himself from it, his shirt is drenched with sweat. He pulls the shirt over his head, and the women in the crowd whistle and scream as he huddles up the rest of the band at Franco's drum kit. The cheering of the crowd continues as they talk, and though we can't hear what they're saying, the look on all of their faces has turned serious. When they break apart, Gus walks over to the edge of the stage, grabs a stool and his acoustic guitar, and returns to the mic. After he adjusts the stand, he takes a seat and strums his guitar a few times before he speaks. While he speaks, he absently tunes the guitar. "So, we recorded this song a long time ago, but we've never played it live." He shrugs while he says it. It sounds like an admission and an apology all at once. "Hell, we haven't even played it as a band in a very long time, so we're gonna do our best to not fuck it up, but don't throw shit at us if we do. Deal?" The crowd yells their agreement. His eyes drift from the neck of his guitar, when he's satisfied with the tuning, to me and he smiles nervously. He's looking for support.

"Show me what you've got!" I shout, and smile.

He nods and his smile warms as he speaks into the mic. "This song is called 'Finish Me'." He tips his head back until he's staring at the ceiling and takes a deep breath and then he says something no one can hear. Then his chin drops and he starts strumming his guitar. It's just him now, and the sound is breathtaking. It's slow, passionate, and almost eerie. By the time the rest of the band joins in, I'm lost in it. And when he sings, I'm drowning. Drowning in the depths of the emotion pouring out of him. It's raw and it's pain and it's love, pure and fearless. He's drawn me in. I'm on the inside, the inside of this storm of emotions. I grab Paxton's arm and hold on with both hands as if I'm going to get pulled away in the tidal wave washing over me. And when it's only Gus strumming his guitar again and it eventually dies out, it hits me. His grief hits me. He wrote this song about Kate, that's why they haven't played this song.

He *couldn't* play this song.

But he just *did*.

And it was the most beautiful, angry, powerful thing I've ever heard.

But his eyes, his eyes are shining. There's relief in them. And pride. And love. So much love that I can't keep from smiling at him.

He smiles back at me, and when he does I know he's going to be okay. This was a step he needed to take. And he didn't just take the step ... he crushed it. He played *the hell* out of it.

And the best part is ... he knows it.

The crowd swells into massive applause, cheering their enthusiasm and filling the place with noise. Gus smiles, wipes his brow, and clears the stool from the stage. He exchanges guitars, and takes his place behind his mic stand again, adjusting the height. He looks lighter than I've ever seen him. He's standing taller. He looks out at the crowd and his eyes scan the entire room. As he does, a smile blooms on his face, and his eyes fill with light. Biting his bottom lip, as if to contain an even bigger grin, his eyes drift upward as he says, "That was for you, Bright Side. I hope you were watching, you little shit." The rest of the band claps and laughs with him. He turns and looks at Franco and I see his shoulders rise and fall in a deep, cleansing breath. The cheers have quieted down, and I hear him say, "Fuck, that felt good," before turning back and addressing the crowd. "We've got one last song for you tonight. And I'm gonna need all of you," he gestures to the audience with both hands, "And I mean, every last one of you, to sing with me. Let's fucking kill the sun, shall we?"

The final song causes the crowd to erupt into chaos, and I'm loving every second of it. I don't know the words to the song, but judging by the deafening volume, I'm the only one. Everyone in the room is singing. For that three minutes, I feel like I'm part of something huge. And for the first time, Gus's tattoo makes sense. Because this ... everything I see ... everything I hear ... everything I feel ... *it's epic.*

Gus.

Rook.

They *do epic.*

The show wraps up just as the clock strikes midnight and Gus calls out, "Thanks for coming out tonight. You're the best fucking crowd we've played for in ages. Now go celebrate, you badasses. Happy New Year!"

Paxton and I grab a couple of Cokes while Gus and the guys talk to their fans after the show. They sign autographs and take photos for about an hour, after which we help them break down their equipment and load it in their vehicles.

The ride home is filled with one-sided chatter. Paxton talks the entire drive. I've never seen him like this, so animated, and energized.

When we get home, the house is unusually quiet. Audrey is in Chicago celebrating New Year's Eve with Dr. Banks. Paxton hugs Gus and thanks him again for the fifth or sixth time and retreats to the basement to go to sleep. It's two o'clock in the morning. I should be tired, but my body and mind won't quiet down. If it wasn't so late I'd probably go for a run to burn it off, but instead I offer to make Gus something to eat. He wants grilled cheese. So I make four sandwiches and pour two glasses of milk while he takes a shower. He returns wearing only a pair of shorts and we sit on the stools at the island in the kitchen to eat. My ear is ringing dimly in the silence. It would probably be annoying if it wasn't a reminder of what I just experienced. The memories are all running through my mind: the sounds, the visuals, the feelings.

The silence seems to offer respite from the rowdy evening to Gus. So I give him time to reflect, or not to think at all if that's what he needs, while we eat. But as we're finishing up our sandwiches, I break our peaceful quiet time. "Thank you."

He looks at me, talking through chewing his last bite. "For what?"

"For making Paxton's year."

He's not good at taking compliments. He looks down at his plate, but a bashful smile breaks out. "He did have fun, didn't he?"

"I'm telling you, this was the best night of his entire life. Ask him in the morning, he'll tell you." It makes me smile just thinking about it.

Gus glances at me and his expression is apprehensive. "What about you? Did I meet the challenge?"

I lick my lips. "And then some." I'm nervous all of a sudden. He's sitting on my right side. I never let people sit on my right side, with a full view of my scars. I turn fully on my barstool to face him.

Before I speak, he places a hand on each knee and spins me back to my prior position facing forward.

"Why did you do that?" I ask.

"Because I never get to see this side of you." He gently touches my cheek, my scar, and a finger traces it.

Though I fight the flinch, my eyes instinctively squeeze shut and tears prick the backs of my eyelids. My chin drops and I pull my lips between my teeth and bite down trying to ward off the emotion that I know is coming. When I no longer feel his touch, I take a deep breath and open my eyes.

He's staring at me and there's no judgment, or disgust, or pity in his eyes. "I showed you a different side of me tonight. It's

KIM HOLDEN

your turn." His voice is quiet and gentle. Gentler than I ever would've imagined he could be.

I give him a disingenuous half smile. "Our other sides are very different."

He glances down thinking for a moment before he reaches out and grips my knees and turns them toward him again so I'm facing him. When he scoots to the edge of his stool he doesn't let go of my knees. His legs are spread. A knee touching each of mine to the outside. I'm looking down at his hands on me and our tangle of legs pressing against one another, when he says my name to direct my eyes back to his, "Scout."

Scout. When he says my name it sounds like a promise. And my entire body reacts to it, both physically and emotionally. He's searching my face, and out of habit I look away again.

"Look at me," he says.

I do, though I have to fight the urge with everything I have to not look away.

"I've been hiding from performing for a long time now. Hiding from that other side of me."

I shake my head to reject his misgivings, because he was born to perform.

"What?" he asks.

I'm still shaking my head adamantly. "You shouldn't hide. What I saw tonight ... " I sigh because now I'm getting emotional thinking about it and I know he doubts himself way too much, so I need to say what I can to convince him otherwise. "You, up on that stage. God ... *it was incredible.* Your voice, your music ... just your *presence* ... was amazing. You asked if you met the challenge earlier ... but *damn* ... " I hesitate. " ... *You blew me away.*"

He's still staring at me, with no hint of a smile. As he leans forward slightly, the pressure on my knees increases and with it I feel the air around us charge. His eyes drop to my mouth before finding my eyes again. "Maybe you see my other side differently than I do. What you just described ... " He shakes his head. "That can't be me."

I cock my head in disbelief. "Why not?"

"Because I'm always doubting my talent. I'm always questioning whether I'm good enough. Hell, for over a year I couldn't even write a new album."

280

I want to shake him, but I tighten my hands into fists instead. *"How can you even say that?* You're the most talented person I've ever met. And you *did* just write a new album."

He takes my fists in each of his hands and gently pries open my fingers. "So, basically what you're saying is I should tell all the doubt to fuck off, because I'm better than I think I am? That *you* see me differently than *I* see me?"

I lock eyes with him and I nod. "Yes. That's exactly what I'm saying."

He squeezes my hands and raises his eyebrows to emphasize his point before he even says the words. "That's exactly what I'm saying, too."

While I'm thinking about what he's just said, replaying the words in my mind, he places a hand behind each calf and lifts my legs until my feet are even with my seat. Then pulls his legs together until his knees touch and rests my feet on top of them. "You don't see the woman I see." His hands part my legs and he lowers them until each of my knees touches the outside of his. I'm trying to listen, but my focus is shifting from the things his lips are saying, to the things his hands are saying. The story is unfolding in his touch. His hands find my knees again, but this time they slide slowly up my thighs. Mid-thigh they roll to the outside toward my hips. At my hips, he doesn't stop until his hands are cupping me from behind and he slides me forward until I'm sitting on his lap, straddling him.

And now my heart is racing and I've never been more aware of touch and how it can set all five senses in motion than I am at this moment. I want to take in everything about him, everything about us, but I'm not sure what to focus on first. So I keep my eyes downcast and I put all of my attention on the feel of his hands moving up and down my back ... up and down ... in a slow and soothing massage. The repetitive motion coaxes my eyelids closed. And as soon as I'm plunged into darkness it awakens a need inside me. I need to touch him more than I've ever needed anything in my life, so I place my hands on his sides near his ribcage. He doesn't have a shirt on and he's still warm from his shower. My eyes remain closed but I feel him lean in until our chests are brushing and his mouth is at my ear. And the conversation, a compelling combination of words and touch, continues. "I couldn't have played without you there tonight. I panicked when I got on stage and I couldn't find you in the crowd, that's why I asked you and Pax to move up front. I feel different when you're around. I feel better, like maybe I can deal with all the shit. I don't know what it is about you, but you make me want to be Gus again. Both sides. I had so much fun tonight. I haven't played like that in over a year."

Hearing that, hearing the healing and hope in his voice, sends my heart soaring. "You have no idea how happy that makes me," I say into his shoulder.

He's still at my ear. "Thank you. It was you." His hands make their way up my back again, continuing until they're on either side of my neck and his thumbs are resting under my chin. He urges my head to turn to the left with his thumbs, fully exposing my scars, and says, "I meant what I said earlier." A soft kiss falls on my marked cheek and my eyes tighten shut. "Pretty girl. You're beautiful." Another kiss paints another scar. "Every," another kiss, "thing," another kiss, "about," another kiss, "you," this kiss falls lower on my neck, "is fucking perfect."

I'm getting dizzy with him touching me like this so I open my eyes and turn my head to face him.

(Gus)

When she opens her eyes, they're dark and shining. She's looking at me like she did earlier tonight while I was on stage. The look is undiluted sexual need, pure and radiant. But there's also something else. She's trusting me with the most vulnerable part of her, and she's not backing away from it. That courage? It's incredibly sexy.

I can't go another second without her mouth on mine and take her face in my hands at the same time she reaches for mine. The moment my lips touch hers, I want to be inside. And my teeth lead the journey of exploration; tugging at her bottom lip I trace it with the tip of my tongue. The act prompts her fingers to snap apart and rake through my hair until her palms are covering my ears, blocking out the silence in the room and all I can hear is my own heartbeat thundering in my chest. It mirrors the desperation I feel.

Releasing her lip I plunge inside, she's ready for me. Our tongues brush gently at first, but it's only seconds before the need amps up to an all-out war inside her mouth. The most beautiful fucking duel I've ever tasted.

She pulls away gently. "Gus?" Her voice is breathy, air more than sound.

It's the first time she's ever called me Gus. And goddamn, it feels like acceptance and approval; she finally let me in. "Call me Gus again."

"Gus." It's the same whisper.

We kiss, and the tangle resumes momentarily before I answer. "Yeah?"

Her hips announce their intention at the same time she grasps my hair in her hands at the base of my neck. "I need you —" It sounds like an admission more than a demand.

I cut her off with another kiss, because, Jesus Christ, her voice —that breathy, faint confession. It's all driving me wild. And forget about her hands in my hair. That always does it for me.

Her hips roll again and I meet them, pressing my erection into her. Her whole body tenses and the grip on my hair intensifies. I groan, because, shit, *this feels so fucking good*. I need to get us out of here before we end up fucking on top of the kitchen island, because that's what's going to happen in about two minutes if I don't move us to my room. With her arms still around my neck, I stand and she wraps her legs around me. It's a good thing I know my way around this house in the dark because I'm not parting my mouth from hers so I can watch where I'm walking. I'll rely on my memory and instinct to get us there because the rest of me is too goddamn busy.

I set her down when we reach our destination. Two steps inside and the door's shut behind me and my shorts are on the floor.

She's fighting the button on her jeans when her eyes lift and she sees me standing in front of her naked. Air escapes her lungs in gasp of shock ... and want. *So. Much. Want.*

I step toward her and remove her hands from her jeans and take over for her. She lets me, so I shimmy her jeans and panties down her long legs. When I reach for the hem of her shirt, I look at her questioningly. She never bares the scars I know are

283

underneath and I know this moment could go either way. And I'm fine with that. I only want her to give me what she's comfortable giving me. So when she nods and raises her arms allowing me to slip her shirt up and off, I'm cheering inside. Cheering on her courage. The scarring is limited to her right side and her arm. It's not shocking. It's what I expected. And it's just her. And everything about her is beautiful. Her eyes are downcast again. Lifting her chin, I point to my eyes. "Eyes right here." Our eyes meet.

And in her eyes I see unease threatening her confidence. "No one's ever seen me like this."

"Lucky me. Because. You. Are. Beautiful." And now I'm feeling a little triumphant because obviously even fucking Michael wasn't given this gift. "Thank you."

Now she's smiling with relief and the confidence is returning. "Thank you." And then the smile twists into desire again.

My eyes drop to her body. She's standing before me in just a white cotton bra. Goddamn, I thought I was aching before, but that's ratcheted my desire to all-out pain. I reach behind her and unclasp her bra and before it's slipped down her arms, I've got her breasts in my hands. My thumbs sweep softly across her nipples and they harden at my touch. It's an immediate reaction that never fails to excite me.

Her breathing has increased again and each breath is full of urgency, as if she's trying to suppress any vocal reaction to the pleasure she's experiencing.

I run my eyes up and down her body one more time—it's visual foreplay. Her body is gorgeous. And then I look her in the eyes. "You okay?" She's so quiet, which is in stark contrast to everything else her body is saying.

She nods.

"I can't seem to do much right lately, but I swear to God, Scout, that I will make you feel so ... damn ... good. Just say the word."

Her eyes are pleading now, and her hands are anxiously stroking the small of my back. It's a restrained gesture that hints at the promise of uninhibited abandon. "*Please.*"

I don't waste any time wrapping my arms around her and pulling her against me. Damn, her skin. She's *all* skin. Beautiful, warm, sensitive, nerve-filled skin. I feel her. I haven't felt anyone for months and months. Women were just bodies to satisfy my need. But with Scout, I *feel* her. I feel everything about her.

I walk her toward the bed until the backs of her knees make contact and I lay her down. We inch our way up to my pillows. She's on her back and I'm on top of her. My body hasn't left hers. It doesn't want to. Every time she lifts her hips to scoot up the bed I meet the rise with pressure from my own and we move fluidly as one, like waves. A tide that rises and becomes more forceful, more demanding. And each crest coaxes an appreciative and pleasure-filled groan out of me, coupled with subdued silence from her.

"You don't have to be quiet, pretty girl. Feel this with me."

That's all the persuasion she needed. "Mmm." The moan is relief and ecstasy, accompanied by an exhalation that's one of the sexiest sounds I've ever heard a woman make. Like she's lost all control. It's the abandon I knew was penned up inside.

Her head's resting on my pillow now. I'm grinding my hips against her, with her, and she's holding me tighter and tighter to her body, like she's afraid I'll disappear if she lets go.

We're just looking into each other's eyes when that goddamn sexy moan comes again.

"Talk to me Scout. Tell me what you need." I want to hear it all.

She pants out, "Now. I need you now, Gus. I can't wait."

Neither can I. I kiss her and then roll off of her and reach into the drawer of my nightstand for a condom. I've got it ripped open and rolled on in record time.

She doesn't make any attempt to take the lead or to reposition herself, so I nestled between her legs on my knees. Holy shit, I haven't been this fucking turned on in so long. I forgot what this felt like. I want to go slow. I want to lick every inch of her body. I want to touch her and tease her. I want this to *last*. But, she's ready, and I'd be lying if I said I wasn't right there with her. I'm so fucking ready.

I'm raised up on my knees before her. Looking at her. She's beautiful. Her dark hair is fanned out around her head. Her eyes are bright and fixed on mine. Her chest is rising and falling with each pull of breath, nipples swollen and hard.

I lower down so my ass is resting on my heels and splay my

fingers under her, my thumbs against her hip bones. Grasping her firmly, I slowly slide her up my thighs. Goddamn, her skin again. On me. I'm going to explode.

Her legs are bent at the knee on either side of me, her perfect ass resting on my thighs. I position myself at her entrance and have to admit that I can't help but stare at us ... touching. At the most intimate, private parts of us about to meet, about to become one. All I want to do is watch *me* be welcomed and swallowed up by *her*.

My hands pull her into me at the same time my hips push me into her. It's slow and exaggerated and she gasps when I fill her, a rush of air and uninhibited satisfaction. Her need being sated.

I feel her legs tense and her body meets my every move. Her eyes are closed and her face looks slack with pleasure and pursed with concentration. This is not the Scout I've known for the past few months. This is Scout from the dream I overheard months ago. This is Scout letting go and giving in to everything her body's craving. Giving in to everything it's getting from me. Giving in to everything it's giving to me. She's so fucking into this. And so am I.

So.

Am.

I.

Fuck.

My eyes drop back to our connection. Me gliding out of her and gliding back in. Over and over. Everything's building. I can feel it in her, too.

I switch positions without breaking our connection, so that I'm lying on top of her. Skin, all of it, touching again. Her arms and legs are wrapped around me. My mouth on hers. The movement of her hips is turning my world upside down in the best way possible. She's so fucking tight, and she's pulsing around me.

"That's it sweetheart, let it go," I pant.

She does. *God, does she ever.* It's moans, and unintelligible sexy sounds, and words distorted by release.

That's it. I'm done for. It's coming. Coming. Coming. "Oh, fuck. *Fuck*," I call out.

She's still writhing around me and the last thing I hear come

from her mouth is, "Kiss me, Gus."
    I do.
    Again.
    And again.

Monday, January 1
(Gus)

I know before I open my eyes that she's not in bed with me anymore. She fell asleep with her arm around me, her head lying on my pillow, her long legs tangled with mine. I couldn't sleep. Or more accurately *didn't* sleep but only for a few hours this morning.

I lay there with her.

And with myself.

And I was at peace.

It's been so damn long since I was at peace, that I didn't want to give it up to sleep for fear it wouldn't be there when I woke up.

I was right.

It's not here.

She's not here.

And I know she's not far away. She's probably just out for a run, or maybe she's eating breakfast. But she's not here. Her nearness brings me peace.

And now that I've felt it, I crave it. Like my fucking cigarettes, I crave it.

I'm roused from thought by the sound of my phone buzzing on my nightstand. "Jesus Christ, who's calling at the crack of –" I was going to say dawn, but when I look at my clock it reads almost twelve o'clock, so I chill out and finish with, "–noon?" It's MFDM. I clear my throat and answer, "Happy New Year, kemosabe."

"Happy New Year to you, Gustov."

"What's going on in your world this morning?" I ask while crawling out of bed and searching for some underwear, or at the very least some shorts.

"Word on the street is you played a local bar last night?"

"Damn, news travels fast. Word is correct."

"*Good* news travels fast. I also hear you've got some songs ready."

I pick up my shorts from where I shed them last night and slip them on. "Shit, that's a lot of intel. Who're you paying to watch me these days?"

He knows I'm kidding. MFDM and I get along well, and have

since the first day we met. "No one. I talked to Franco this morning."

"Ah. Good call, going straight to the source."

"That's how I roll," he answers. He's a fairly serious guy, so when he tries to sound hip it always cracks me up and just ends up being funny instead. Which is probably better. I do funny pretty well.

I'm laughing. "Right? Cut to chase, dude. Where's this conversation headed?"

"Studio in L.A. tomorrow morning. It's booked for the month. So is an apartment, same complex as last time. I need you guys there by ten o'clock."

My stomach clenches and I literally see the remnants of last night's peace fly out the goddamn window. Recording the last album was stressful. I don't want stressful right now, not when I'd finally released it. But I say what I need to say. "We'll be there. And dude?"

"Yeah, Gustov?"

"New year and all, can you just call me Gus? I need to do this album and tour as Gus, not Gustov."

"Sure, Gus." When he says it, there's something in his voice I can't put my finger on. It sounds like approval. Like when you're little and you do something that tickles the shit out of your parent and they tell you *good job*. That's what it sounds like.

I make calls to Franco, Jamie, and Robbie. They're hyped. They're ready.

I wish I was. I mean, I am, but at the same time I'm not.

I don't know what else to do with myself, so I pull my duffle bag out of my closet and I start throwing clothes in. Each movement feels robotic. I'm getting used to packing up my life. But right now the only thing I'm thinking about taking with me, is the one thing I can't.

Her.

(Scout)

I got out of bed early this morning and went for a long run. The adrenaline from last night carried over and had me pushing my normal pace and distance. I felt different this morning. I felt

289

accepted. Confident. I ran in a short-sleeved T-shirt. I haven't bared my arms since before the accident. And I didn't care when people looked at me, because I knew that the one person who matters thinks I'm beautiful.

I ate and I've showered. And I'm standing at his bedroom door in shorts and a short-sleeved Rook T-shirt I stole from Paxton. Just as I'm about to knock, my stomach knots. And I start doubting myself again. What do I say? How do I act? Everything's different now.

But I take a deep breath and I knock anyway, because if last night taught me anything, it's that inaction is never rewarded. Results are the consequence of being an active participant in life. Because I've never felt more alive than I did last night.

When he answers, he looks tired. His hair is pulled back in a ponytail and the shorts he's wearing are riding low on his hips. God, he's so beautiful. His mouth spreads into a small smile, but it doesn't look happy like it did only hours ago. "Hi," I whisper.

He reaches for my hand and laces his fingers through mine. "Hi," he whispers back. I see his lips move more than I hear him. His grip on my fingers is gentle and he's rubbing his thumb across the back of my hand. "Nice shirt." With that he does smile slightly. A real smile.

I smile, too. "Yeah, I saw them play live once. They're all right." I wink to let him know I'm teasing and his smile widens. "You want something to eat?" I ask. "I can make you some eggs."

He shakes his head and pulls me into a hug. He's squeezing me so tight. Something is wrong. Because I don't hear well, I've always paid closer attention to the other ways in which people communicate. And this hug? It's full of dread.

"What's wrong?" I ask, not sure I want to hear the answer. My heart is breaking at the possibilities, none of which involve me. I can handle getting hurt; I've done it my whole life. He doesn't need any more.

He turns us until I'm looking at a bag on his bed packed with clothes. I know that bag. It's the bag he had on the tour bus. It's the bag he travels with. The one he takes with him when he's not home.

Not.

Home.

"You're leaving." It wasn't a question. I feel like I'm stating the obvious.

He's still hugging me tight.

"Another tour?" It can't be another tour.

"Going to L.A. for a month to record the new album."

And now my heart's racing in good way. This is what he needs. Their fans *need* to hear the new Rook songs. "That's great."

He huffs at the excitement in my voice and it verges on amused. "What? You make me your sex slave for a night and now you're ready for me to exit?"

I laugh, because I'm so relieved that he's broken the ice on last night's events. "No, that's not what I was getting at at all. I just mean I'm excited that you're recording your new songs. They shouldn't be confined to this house, to this room. The world needs to hear them." He doesn't look excited like he should. "What's wrong?"

He shrugs. "I'm stoked about the music. I just don't want to leave again." Just then the cat walks through the door meowing. "Besides, who's gonna feed Spare Ribs?"

"You go create magic and I'll feed Spare Ribs."

"Thanks. Which reminds me, I need to go to the store and stock up on her food. She eats morning and night and only a half a can at each feeding. She doesn't know her limits. Put any more than that out and her inner hobo comes out from her time on the street and she gorges and chucks it. And she only likes that stinky ass seafood medley."

I nod. "I know." It is stinky. Every morning and night, when I watch Gus feed her, he pulls the collar of his T-shirt up over his nose before he opens the can. And if he's shirtless, he's screwed— he gags every time.

"Oh, and she gets irate if you don't clean her shit house every day. She'll track you down and berate and belittle you like the servant you are with her bossy-ass, cursing meows."

I'm holding in a smile because he's so serious about this cat. "She rules you, you know." I tease.

He smiles. "Hell yes, she does. She's Napoleonic, like a tiny, little dictator. I love that damn cat."

He truly does.

We spend the afternoon stocking up on cat and human essentials, followed by pizza with Audrey and Paxton. By the time we return home, it's nine o'clock. Audrey and Paxton disappear to their rooms and we're left standing in the living room.

Gus is standing a few feet from me and he's just looking at me. He doesn't look sad anymore, he looks determined. I love his newfound determination. "You look tired," he says.

I am tired. "I'm not tired."

He smiles at the lie and follows it with one of his own. "Me neither." When he gets really tired dark circles form under his eyes. They give him away. He extends his hand toward me — it's an invitation.

I take it and follow him down the hall in the dark. I swear I would follow him anywhere. When we step inside his room, he lets go of my hand and shuts the door behind me. There's no moon out tonight and the room is so dark I can't see him. And it's so quiet, all I can hear is my own breathing.

When his fingertips brush against my wrists my first inclination is to reach out for him but I stand still and wait. They glide lightly up the length of each arm simultaneously, disappear under my sleeves, and then skim back down to my hands. He's standing behind me. I can't feel his body but the heat coming off him is palpable.

"I like you, Scout. I *really* like you." He laces his fingers through mine. "I don't know what that means, but I feel like I can't leave in the morning without saying it. And I don't want to fall asleep alone. Stay with me?" His voice, everything about his voice, finds its way inside me and once inside, it smolders.

"There's no place I'd rather be than here with you tonight." I mean it. God, do I mean it.

"Thank you." He presses his lips to the back of my head. It's a kiss that's loving and sweet, but there's depth that's nothing short of reverent. He lives life with his heart fully exposed. From the inside out. His life isn't about what's going on outside, the Gus the rest of us see and perceive. He doesn't live life, he feels it. I've seen it. I've seen grief strangle him. And I've seen happiness make him glow with a brightness so intense it's almost blinding. That's what makes him so special. It's not his talent or his looks. It's how much he *feels.*

After we strip down to our underwear, he sets the alarm on his phone and I remove my hearing aid, and we crawl into his bed. He wraps his arms around me and pulls me into him, the back of me against the front of him. His skin is warm and there's so much of it exposed. Touching him like this should be scary for me, because we're just *touching*. It's not sexual, it's intimate and human. All of the focus is on contact. He can feel my scars. All of them. And his touch, the way he's holding me so completely, makes my heart overflow. I exhale a long breath. I've been tense, guarded ... forever. But lying here with him is like slowly letting the breath escape that I've been holding for over a decade. I can feel it pass through my muscles and bones, and I feel pliable in his arms, like I'm finally *me*. The person I've been searching for. The person I knew was deep inside, but who was distorted but the protective shell I wore on the outside. I'm smiling through tears that are trickling down my cheeks and onto the pillow.

"I just want to hold you tonight. It's not that I don't want to tear your bra and panties off and dominate you with my manhood until you're screaming my name ... *because I do*." He presses his erection into my backside to illustrate his point. "*Goddammit, I do.* But I just want tonight to be about us and this insane, unstoppable need I have to be near you. Around you. To be your friend. To make you smile. To make you laugh. To make you happy. To protect you. I want to learn everything about you, Scout. Your past. Your present. Your future. But there's time for that tomorrow and the day after that. Tonight I just want to fall asleep with you. And tomorrow morning I want to wake up with you. I'm working on the whole living in the moment thing, and now ... this moment, that's all I want."

There are so many things I want to say to him, but I'm so overcome by everything that's just transpired that I know it would come out all wrong. I couldn't do it justice. So, instead, I take his hand that's resting on my hip and bring his palm to my mouth and I kiss it. And I tell him, "Me too, Gus." And I don't let go of his hand; I hold it against my chest over my heart.

And we fall asleep. And it's sleep like I've never known, deep and restful and healing.

Saturday, January 6
(Scout)

"I don't need a fucking cigarette. Tell me I don't need a fucking cigarette." This is what I hear when I answer the phone. He sounds stressed.

"You don't need a fucking cigarette."

"I do." It sounds distorted a bit, like his mouth is full.

"You don't. How many pieces of gum are you chewing?"

"Five," he answers.

"Good man. Suck it up."

He takes a few deep breaths. "Thanks Scout. I gotta get back in the studio. I told them I needed a piss break, but I really just needed to be talked off the ledge. I'll call you back later tonight."

"You don't," I repeat. "You've got this." It's adamant.

"I know. Adios."

"Bye."

Thursday, January 18
(Gus)

I call Scout every day. She grounds me to reality, because what we're doing in the studio seems so unreal. I don't mean that in a bad way. I'm looking at this album differently than I did the first one. With the first album, we didn't have a fucking clue what we were doing. Don't get me wrong, I wasn't a pushover, but we entrusted the project to MFDM and let him drive it. I'm driving this time. I'm still leaning on him for his expertise, but the vision's all mine.

She answers on the third ring, "Hi, Gus." My heart stutters every time I hear her first words when I call. She's smiling, I can hear it. It's not a smile born out of excitement, it's a smile born out of contentment. It's my favorite smile on her.

"What's happening at chez Hawthorne this evening?" It's ten o'clock, so she's probably getting ready for bed.

"I baked some peanut butter cookies."

My mouth's watering. "Mmm ... I love me some peanut butter cookies."

"I know. They're for you. I'll get them to you soon."

"You should hand deliver them. I'd like to taste you both. My appetite's *huge* and it feels like weeks since it's been ... *satisfied.*" She's always a little shy when I make any kind of sexual reference when we talk on the phone. It's cute, that's partially why I do it. The other half of me is hoping she'll open up to it eventually.

The line's quiet.

"Scout, you there?"

"Yeah, I'm here. I was trying to decide if I should deal with the cookies or go in my room and pleasure myself."

What the fuck did she just say? "Can you repeat that again ... *please?*"

"You heard me." She's still smiling.

Loud and clear. "Maybe I did, maybe I didn't. I need to hear it again to be sure."

"I said, I was contemplating going into my room, taking off my panties, and touching myself."

Holy shit. I'm hard now. So fucking hard. "Jesus Christ, tell me more."

"I'm thinking about you. Thinking about us. How good you felt inside me. And it makes me hot. Sometimes I need a release. Like now."

"Fuck me," I say under my breath. I'm shutting the door on my bedroom now and unzipping my own shorts. "Please tell me you're in your room? Please tell me you're lying on your bed?" I fucking need this visual, because things are about to go down.

"Is that where you want me to be?"

"Yes. Hell yes." I've shed my shorts and underwear and I'm lying on my bed now. Dick in hand.

"Where are you?" She's breathing harder now. It's subtle, but I hear it.

"I'm lying on my bed."

"Are you touching yourself?" Goddamn, she doesn't even sound timid.

I sigh, because, yes, I'm doing a lot more than touching.

"Gus, I want you to feel how wet I am."

"Scout, you're fucking killing me here." Who knew this girl had such a naughty side?

"I'm ready for you."

"What do you want me to do you?" I'm into this little fantasy one hundred and ten percent.

I hear the doorbell ring, but there's no fucking way I'm pulling myself away from this. I'm the only one here and whoever's at the door is just going to have to fuck off for now. Phone sex trumps visitors.

"You didn't answer me, Scout. I need instruction."

The doorbell rings again.

I'm hanging on her answer while I'm focused on the ecstasy that's taking place firmly in my hand. I'm about to blow my load at any moment and I don't even care about the mess I'll have to clean up because I'm not putting this phone down to reach for my underwear on the floor.

The doorbell rings again.

I yell, "Jesus fucking Christ! I'm about to cum here; go away!"

"Are you talking to me?" she asks, though she doesn't sound offended, she still sounds horny as hell.

"You? *God no.* There's someone ringing the doorbell and they won't go away. I guess they don't realize I'm in the middle of jerking off to a sexy woman on the phone right now."

"Answer the door, Gus." That sounded forceful.

No fucking way. "Fuck no. Keep talking."

"Listen to me. I've been driving for two and half hours. I've been thinking about you *all day*. I've been thinking about sex with you *all day*. I'm so horny I can't process a coherent thought outside of what I want you to do to me. I'm wearing a dress and I already took my panties off in the car and put them in my purse. Please let me in before I masturbate on your doorstep."

I pause, but only for a second, before I end the call, leap out of bed, and streak to the front door naked. After fumbling with the locks, because my hands aren't getting the messages my brain's sending them because it's too focused on sex, I fling the door open. And sonofabitch, there she is. She's standing on my doorstep in a sleeveless, little black dress with her purse in one hand and a giant Ziploc bag of peanut butter cookies in the other hand. She looks good enough to eat. I just might. "Nice dress. You look incredible," I say, staring at her bare shoulders.

"Thanks." She's staring at my package and grinning. She raises the bag of cookies without taking her eyes off my junk. "I brought cookies."

I reach up and take the bag out of her hand. "Thanks, Girl Scout." And then I reach for her other hand. "You should probably come inside and let me ravage you before one of the neighbors catches sight of my boner and calls in the cops for indecent exposure."

She steps in without hesitation.

As soon as the door shuts, she drops her purse and I drop the cookies. My lips are on hers or hers are on mine, I'm not sure which happens first. Our frantic movements are feverish and rushed. I can't get enough of her mouth, these lips.

"I missed you," I say between kisses.

Her fingers are raking my back. "I missed you, too. So much."

I start gathering the bottom of her dress in one hand, inching it up while my other hand cups her breast. She's not wearing a bra and her nipple's already hard when I squeeze it through the fabric. When my hand meets skin underneath her dress, I smile against her lips. "Your panties really are in your purse."

She nods. "I thought it would save time."

I grab her thighs and lift her up onto the small table behind her next to the door. Pushing the material up and out of the way, I'm looking at her spread wide open before me. "Are you on the pill?"

She nods.

"Are you cool doing this bare? I don't have any condoms here."

She nods again.

I don't waste any time in pulling her ass to the front edge of the table and plunging into her.

A near pained gasp surges out of her and she wraps her legs around my back.

I'm holding her hips in place and pounding into her before pulling out almost completely and plunging in again. With each thrust my thighs are slamming the table against the wall. There's definitely going to be damage to the table or the wall, maybe both. The pace is punishing, but she's asking for it. "Harder, Gus."

Her mouth is on my neck, on my chest, and when she tugs at my nipple with her teeth a surge of intense pleasure runs through me. "I need you naked. Now."

She makes quick work of her dress, pulling it easily over her head. She's breathing hard with exertion and passion, and it's so fucking sexy. I slow my hips and lean down, running my tongue around her nipple before taking it in my mouth. I lightly tease the tip before sucking and pressing it to the roof of my mouth and biting down gently.

She moans and her hands find either side of my head holding me in place. I continue my exploration on the right before giving equal attention to her left.

She's squirming on the table, trying to get relief to the ache that's consuming her.

"Are you there, Scout?"

"Almost." Her eyes are closed and her mouth is open slightly. She draws in a deep breath, holds it, and forces it out long and loud. It repeats and each time she does it grows in volume and her features tighten infinitesimally. It's a climax building, and I'm watching the same intense pleasure I'm feeling mirrored in her expression. "*So. Close.*"

I pull back until just the tip of me is still inside her and then I push back in slowly. When I'm all the way in I urge her to lean back slightly, cup her ass in my hands, and tip her hips so I can go even deeper. When I make a final push I gain further access and she sighs. I'm as deep as I can go.

"You feel so damn good," I whisper as I repeat the movement, because *holy hell*.

Her eyes are closed when she responds. "*So damn good,*" which gives way to a low moan that builds and builds to, "Oh, God! Oh my God! So good! God, yes!"

And the next thing I know, my release comes. It's powerful and so fucking satisfying, like I've been storing it up for years. There are so many things I want to say ... to shout. But for some reason I hold it in and all that comes out is a hum from deep in my chest. It amplifies what's going on with every other part of this connection we have.

I never take my eyes off of her, and when she relaxes and finally opens her eyes they are so full of bliss that it takes my breath away.

"Hi," she whispers and smiles. And that smile? I want to look at that smile every day for the rest of my life. It's like a still frame of contentment. "I think I like L.A."

I smile back. "Hi. I miss home, but the sex is fucking *outstanding* here," I add with a wink.

Scout stays for another hour. We sit on my bed and talk and eat her cookies with a big glass of milk that we share for dunking, which should seem boring after a property damaging session, but it's not. I love talking to her. The transformation she's made since I first met her is amazing. She used to hide from the world, living inside herself. It was like she was living dual roles. On the inside she was confident, strong, and self-assured, but on the outside something got lost in translation.

"Tell me about your parents," I say. I don't know if she will or not, but I feel comfortable enough around her now to ask her anything.

Her mouth is full of cookie, so she waits until she swallows to answer. "There's not a lot to tell really. Last time I heard from my mom she was in India. That was a couple years ago. My dad lives in Brooklyn. I haven't seen him in a year or so."

She doesn't sound sad. She tells the story like she's reciting a grocery list. So I press on. "What was your childhood like? I assume your parents are divorced?"

She shakes her head. "My parents were never married. My dad was a musician. He played small bars around Brooklyn and busked to scrape by, still does as far as I know. He's actually not bad, but he has issues living in the real world. You know, where you're required to be sober more than drunk." She raises her eyebrows to drive her point home. "Anyway, I guess my mom was kind of a groupie. They hooked up a few times. She got pregnant. They stayed together until I was born and then my mom split."

My first thought goes to Ma. She's a rabid protector of me and anyone else she sees as her child. I know all moms aren't like her, but I can't fathom a mom abandoning her kid. "She left? Like *left*, left?"

She nods. "Yeah, I've always thought of her as a gypsy. I don't think she's ever had a job. I know she's never had a place of her own. She just drifts through the world. She makes friends and has lovers. They take her in until she gets the itch to move on to the next. I hear from her every couple of years. I've never met her in person, only seen her in a photo my dad has."

"Shit. That's fucked up, Scout."

She shrugs like she agrees and disagrees with me. "It is what it is. I'd rather not have her in my life, than have her and feel like a burden. My dad raised me. It worked out."

"What's your dad like?" I'm almost afraid to ask because I know she said she didn't live with him after the accident.

She blinks a few times like she's trying to remember him. "He loves alcohol. He loves music. And he loves me. In that order."

I know this isn't easy for her to talk about, so I ask her a question to keep her talking. "You grew up in Brooklyn?"

"For the most part, yeah. My dad never had his own place, so we moved around a lot. Stayed with friends of his, girlfriends, sometimes a bar owner would set us up in a room above the bar for a month or two as payment for him playing at night. I never knew any different, so to me it was normal. I was alone a lot, but it forced me to be independent."

"And what about after the accident?"

The look in her eyes is far away. "The accident." She pauses. "My dad got a gig in upstate New York. He borrowed a car and we drove there. I sat backstage while he played ... I remember reading *Little House on the Prairie* while I waited." She smiles faintly at the memory. "He drank for a few hours after he finished playing. I read some more. When he came for me and told me it was time to go home I knew he was drunk." She shrugs. "He was always drunk, so I didn't know I should be scared. We got in the car. It was snowing outside and I remember how cold the backseat was when I lay down on the vinyl. I didn't put my seatbelt on. I didn't even think about it. I'd only ever ridden in a car a few times before. We always rode the subway at home. Anyway, I fell asleep, and woke up in the middle of wreckage and fire." She's staring off into space and her eyes are glassy. Her voice is quiet, but so intense it holds me fast; I have no choice but to listen. "It was *so* hot. That's the thing I remember the most ... even more than the pain ... *the heat*." She licks her lips before she continues. "I was trapped in the car. My dad was outside. I could see him walking around. I screamed and screamed for him, and then I passed out."

"Did he come back for you?"

She nods. "He did. I would've died otherwise. I guess the ambulance and fire truck showed up shortly after and took us both to the hospital. He was unharmed except for a few cuts. I was in intensive care for a few days, due to internal injuries, before I was transferred to the burn unit. I spent weeks there. Lots of surgeries, skin grafts. My dad went to jail: DUI and child endangerment. Social services stepped in and my aunt and uncle stepped up. The rest is history. I went home with them and they were my new family after that."

She's strong. She's so damn strong. I can't imagine the pain and suffering she went through. "Do you ever see your dad?"

"I see him or hear from him about once a year, but it's never planned, always out of the blue. He feels guilty, I know he does. I think it's hard for him to look at me," she points to the scars on her face and neck, and raises her eyebrows. The self-loathing and embarrassment is trying to take hold of her.

I cup her cheek in my hand and turn her head to face me, to look me in the eye. "You're fucking beautiful. Don't let anyone ever make you feel otherwise. And if they do, you tell me and I'll kick their ass."

She smiles and the embarrassment fades. "Thanks, tough

guy."

I kiss her forehead before I drop my hand from her cheek. "Anytime, badass. So you and Pax grew up together then?"

Her smile grows when she talks about Pax. "We did. He was one of the only people who never made me feel like a freak. He never mentioned my scars and he always looked me in the eye when he talked to me. I changed schools when I went to live with my aunt and uncle and I never really made any friends. We lived in Manhattan. Most of the kids came from money. They could be cruel. They teased. Called me names. And as we got older, they just ignored me, which was kind of a relief. I'd much rather be ignored than made fun of. By the time I went to college, I was really good at blending into the background and not being seen. I kept to myself and took as many online classes as I could." She shrugs again, but it's almost like an apology. "It worked for me."

I smile at her because I can't dwell on her past, not when she's finally growing into the person she's supposed to be. "*You* work for me."

She smiles back and raises her eyebrows in question. She's flirting with me now. "Is that so?"

I nod and remove the bag of cookies from the bed between us and set it on the dresser next to the bed. She's half sitting, half lying against a couple of pillows. I pull the pillows out from under her so she's lying flat on the bed. "We're not going to need those." I help her slip her dress off. "Or that." I remove my shorts and underwear. "Or those."

"Gus, I need to go soon. I have to work today." It's just after midnight.

"I know. Just let me make you feel good, one more time before you go."

I settle in between her legs and taste her. And goddamn she tastes amazing.

She trembles once from the pressure of my tongue, and again minutes later when I fill her. Everyone's thoroughly satisfied. Again.

I don't want her to leave, but I know she needs to. I slide into my boxer-briefs as I watch her pull her dress over her head and slip on the panties that were in her purse. I know different things are turn-ons for different people, but watching her take panties out of her purse and put them on? Yeah, that's sexy. "Scout?"

"Yeah?" She answers as she fixes the waist of her lace panties in place and drops the skirt portion of her dress to cover her.

"Can you just start carrying your panties around in your purse?"

She laughs. "Why?"

"I don't think watching you take them out and put them on would ever get old for me. It's fucking hot."

She winks. "I'll remember that."

"You better. Fantasies fulfilled are the best kind of fantasies."

"You're so right. That's what tonight was all about." Her smile is full of mischief.

We're walking to the front door now. "Why didn't you tell me you had a naughty side? I like it."

"I never did until I met you. You're a bad influence." She's walking in front of me and doesn't turn around when she says it, but I can hear her smirking.

I wrap my arms around her waist and kiss her on the back of the head. "I'm the best kind of bad."

She turns when we reach the door and agrees. "The best." And then she kisses me. There's heat behind it, but it's short lived, and too quickly she's turning away and opening the door.

"You sure you're awake enough to drive home?"

When she smiles, I get two answers in one. "I don't think I've ever been more awake. Thank you for tonight." She's talking about more than the sex.

I nod. "Thank you for trusting me with all of you."

She smiles and hugs me one more time.

"Call or text me when you get home so I know you made it."

"I will. Kick ass tomorrow in the studio."

I smile. "That's the plan. Kick ass tomorrow at work."

She laughs as she walks away. "That's the plan. Good night."

"Good night."

I stand at the door and watch her get in her car and drive away before I close it. I decide I need another glass of milk and some more cookies before I go to bed. As I'm walking out of the kitchen the guys walk through the front door. They're laughing. I like seeing them all happy.

Franco's taking off his jacket when he says, "You should've

come with us tonight, scrote. I met a wild little strawberry blond from Northern England named Gemma. She's got a penchant for leopard print, You Me At Six, and gin. She's perfect. Got her number. A good time was had by all."

A good time *was* had by all. Me included.

I smile at the thought and before I can say anything he's sniffing at the air like a fucking bloodhound. "It smells like homemade cookies in here. Why does it smell like homemade cookies in here?" He looks suspicious. And at the same time he says, "Was Scout here? Where're the cookies?" Jamie says, "Holy shit, what happened to the table? And the wall?"

I cringe when I see that the corner of the table has driven into a hole in the drywall. But I can't hide my smile either. I take a drink of my milk before I answer, "Girl Scout may have stopped by tonight to deliver some cookies."

Franco smiles slyly. "That doesn't explain the property damage."

I raise my glass of milk to all of them and shrug as I leave and walk toward my room. "Let's just say they were *really* good cookies. Excellent even. Probably the best cookies I've ever had."

Saturday, January 20
(Gus)

When I woke up this morning, I can't say that I felt sad. It was more like something was missing. I could feel it in my chest, a heaviness. Bright Side died a year ago today. I laid there for several minutes thinking about her. Thinking about growing up with her. I replayed twenty years' worth of memories into a condensed slide show in my mind, accompanied by a violin soundtrack. And by the time I was done I was staring at the tattoo on my arm and smiling. I swear I could hear her saying, "Don't cry for me. When you think of me, be happy."

So I didn't cry. I find myself reaching for my phone and calling Keller instead.

When he answers I hear an out-of-tune piano playing in the background. "Hey, Gus." He sounds good. I'm glad, because I didn't know what to expect.

"What up, Papa Banks? It sounds like a piano's being tortured to give up all its secrets."

He laughs and the piano disappears as I hear a door shut. "I'm at Stella's ballet practice. I don't think it's the piano that's being tortured, so much as the audience. Guess that's why earbuds were invented. How are you doing today, man? I was going to call you when we got home. I know it's still early in California."

"It is early. We're in L.A. and I have to be at the studio in an hour. Working on the second album, it's almost done." I'm relieved. It's been a long couple of weeks, but we've worked hard, I've learned a lot, and I'm so damn proud of what we've created. I've grown up a lot over this past year and half since we did this last. And it shows. Everything's matured, from the music, to the lyrics, to us as a band.

"That's great, Gus. Congratulations. I can't wait to hear it. When will it be out?" He sounds genuinely happy for me. It's strange how we've bonded. It grew out of our mutual love for Bright Side, which should have made us jealous enemies, but like everything else about Bright Side, the impossible just worked and worked out for the best. His friendship means a lot to me.

"They're talking late March and setting up a tour to start in early April." And as soon as I say it out loud it becomes real. I'm actually excited. Excited to get out on the road and play in front of an audience again. Excited to do it right this time. Excited to make the most of it and live it instead of just enduring it like I did the last go around.

"Right on. Are you coming to Minnesota again? I'd love to see another show." He would. I can tell.

"Haven't seen the schedule yet, but I'll put a bug in someone's ear. I know people who know people." I'd love to play Grant again, kind of as a memorial to Bright Side.

He laughs again. "I bet you do."

"What have you been up to, dude?" I need to know he's all right.

"Busy. I graduate in June, assuming I don't crash and burn with the teaching internship I start this week." He sounds a little stressed, but stoked, too.

"Internship? That's awesome. High school, right?"

"Yeah. Teaching English here at Grant High School. I lucked out; it actually couldn't be more perfect. The school's about a mile from our place, and Stella's preschool is on the way. It should be ideal."

"The kids will love you."

"I don't know about that, but I'm ready. *I'm so ready.*" He sounds tired.

Bright Side told me all about Keller. I know his mom wanted him to be a lawyer and she was pretty pissed when he changed his major and followed his heart down the teaching road. I still don't think they talk. Good thing he and his dad are close now. "I bet you are. You'll be done with school soon and this will all be behind you. You should bring Stella to San Diego next fall and get a teaching gig here."

"Oh man. Can you imagine Stella living in San Diego with full-time access to the beach? I'd never get her to come inside. We'd probably just pitch a tent on the beach in front of your house and live there. She'd be perfectly content to be homeless as long as she was surrounded by miles of sand and water for building sandcastles."

"Fine by me. I know Ma wouldn't mind either."

"Damn, with the way things are going with our parents lately, we might be stepbrothers by then."

I laugh because he's right. Ma's been spending a lot of weekends with Doc Banks. She's happy. Hell, I've never really seen her date before, so her relationship with him is monumental. "Did we just become best friends?" I yell at him in my best Will Ferrell voice. I'm quoting the movie, *Step Brothers*. I don't know if he'll get the reference.

But when he enthusiastically answers, "Yup," I continue on quoting the movie, "Do you wanna go do karate in the garage?"

"Yup," he answers, and we both start laughing.

I haven't laughed this hard in a long time and it feels good. "Thanks for that, dude. I needed it."

He's still laughing. "Me too." The laughter settles into a chuckle, but he still sounds happy. "Well, man, I just heard the piano give up the ghost; that means practice is over. I'd better go get Stella. Thanks again for calling today. I miss Katie, Gus. And I'll always love her. Not a day goes by that I don't think about her. But it's different now than it was a few months ago. It's not pain now; it's joy. I'm living my life for her, too. I'm living with purpose, but Stella and I are still having fun along the way. None of this would've been possible if it weren't for her. She taught me how to live. And how to love. I have no intention of wasting it."

I'm nodding my head like he can see. "I'm glad. And ditto. Have a fantastic Saturday, dude. And tell Miss Stella hi for me."

"Will do. Take care, Gus."

"You too. Later."

"Bye."

As soon as I hang up I immediately call Ma. She's on her way to the cemetery with tulips and a Twix bar. And just like Keller, she sounds good. She's handling this anniversary with grace and remembering Bright Side with happiness, which is really the only way Bright Side should be honored. I tell her I just talked to Keller and even share the stepbrother portion of the discussion, to which she laughs but does nothing to discourage rumors. Maybe they are serious; stranger things have happened.

By the time I wrap up my phone calls, there's just enough time to shower and text Scout. *Good morning Girl Scout.*

Three sets of concerned eyes are on me when I walk into the living room to leave for the day. Franco speaks up first. "Morning.

You okay, big man?" He looks worried about me.

I nod. "I'm okay, dude." I know they're wondering if I'm torn up about Bright Side. "I'm always gonna miss her, but she's right here." I pat my chest. "Which has me thinking, I know we're supposed to finish up 'Judgment Day' today, but I think in Bright Side's memory we should just jam. We should just play. See what we come up with. You know that she's been watching us in the studio." I feel her in there with us every day. "So today, let's do something she loved." Bright Side loved to just play. She was so creative. It was like she had all this music bound up within her and every time she wrote something new, she only let a fraction of it out. She was bursting at the seams with new songs.

They're all smiling and nodding their heads. Franco's already at the door. "Let's do this. I'm officially declaring it *Kate Day*." He's holding the door open as we all walk through it to the parking lot. "It's funny that you mention being able to feel Kate in the studio with us. I thought I was the only one. Sometimes when I'm in a groove and everything's just flowing, I swear I hear her whispering in my ear, telling me what a sexy beast I am when I play and how I was always her favorite."

I shake my head and smile because he threw all that out there to make me laugh. "Shut the fuck up, dude. You are a sexy beast when you play, but you were never her favorite."

There's a look of mock hurt on his face as he unlocks his truck and we all pile in. He turns and looks at me in the backseat. "That hurts, fuck nugget. That really fucking hurts." He's grinning by the time he's done trying to make me feel bad. "Who wants coffee?" he says as he backs out of the space. "I say we start *Kate Day* off right with some coffee for Kate."

After we go through the Starbucks drive-thru and spend approximately two hundred dollars on four cups of coffee, we head to the studio. And when we tell MFDM our plans for the day I can tell it's against his better judgment to let us take the day off, but he agrees. He had a place in his heart for Bright Side, too.

I start playing first, just my acoustic guitar, and I notice that MFDM's got tape rolling on me. He's recording. Not all the time, but when he likes what he hears he's capturing it. The wheels are turning, and I really do feel like she's in this room with me. I can hear the intro of a song coming together in my head and trade out my acoustic for my electric. It takes me a minute to adjust my effects pedals and get the delay just right. In my mind, the notes are looping over and over until my fingers catch up and bring them to life.

The intro, even with the delay, is crisp. Each note distinct, but almost lazy. I work through it a few times, and everyone's bobbing their heads; we're all into it. I nod at Franco. "Hey, dude. Rim me out a beat to this. It needs to be rushed though. Downbeat. Don't keep time with me. Push me. I'll lag, but you keep going. It'll work, trust me. Just the rim, no snare."

He does. The first time through we're fighting each other. He's trying to match my tempo, but I don't want him to. He's the timekeeper, but he's leaning on me because he can't hear it yet. We play it a few more times and I talk him through and by the end he's pressing forward and letting me fall behind and it works. *It fucking works.*

Over the next half hour Jamie and I come up with a wicked bassline that would make Bright Side proud. She was always a sucker for a strong, kickass bassline. I've always been guitar driven, but sometimes bass driven is the way to go. Bass resonates; it plays to the core of your physical being, bone deep, like a sonic heartbeat.

With the bassline down, Robbie agrees that he just needs to follow Jamie and let the bass take the lead for the chorus.

Franco's chomping at the bit just to be let loose and go ballistic. He'll get his chance.

I nod at Franco. "You ready?"

He's twirling his drumstick in his hand and stomps his kick bass pedal a few times. He's antsy. He just wants to play, to be unleashed. Franco's a phenomenal drummer and musician, but the best part is his enthusiasm. He motherfucking loves to play. He'd play all day, every day, if he could. "I was born ready, man." He was. No lie.

"Jamie, play that bassline again. Franco, you follow him, all snare and kick bass, no tom. Light cymbal crash at the end of each measure. Robbie you play under Jamie, with him. I'm gonna play over the top. Just ignore me and let me do my thing." I kick the delay down and the distortion up and we play through a few times.

MFDM is leaning back in his chair with a smirk on his face. A smirk is good. A smirk means he likes what's going on. *Really likes it.* He's been quiet, too. That's always a good sign.

"Okay, let's do this, beginning to end. MFDM, will you record? I wanna hear it played back so I can work on some lyrics."

He pairs the smirk with a lazy thumbs up. We're golden. That pairing in producer-speak is *I fucking love it.*

"I'm gonna lead in, give me some space for a few measures Franco, then jump in. Downbeat, rim only. Give us a few measures alone, then everyone joins in on my signal for the chorus. Repeat until I nod you out. That leaves Jamie's bassline and Franco for the second verse. I'll give the transition and we'll repeat the chorus again. Then we'll end with the third verse, which will be a repeat of the second, Jamie and Franco only. We good?"

They all nod. I look at Jamie. "No pressure, but you know how much Bright Side liked a solid bassline. Do her proud, dude."

He raises his forearm tattoo to me and smiles. "I only do epic." He winks. "I've got this."

After I adjust my effects pedals, I strum my guitar twice. It's habit. I do it before I start every song. I look to MFDM. He's got his headphones on and he gives me a thumbs up and hits a button to start recording.

We play through once and it's decent, but the transitions aren't clean. The second time we run through, everyone knows what to expect and it's tight.

When we listen to the recording I get chills. That rarely happens. I love it. Only a few songs have ever done that to me. And I already have lyrics forming in my mind. I look at the clock on the wall. It's just after noon. "Why don't you guys take an hour? Go get some lunch. Give me some time to hammer out these lyrics. I've got most of them. I just need to listen to this a few times and jot them down."

MFDM stands. "You want me to stay?"

I know he's giving me a chance to ask for help if I need it, but that he also trusts me to do it on my own. "I've got this. Do me a favor and bring me back something meatless to eat. I need some fuel. I want to record this and I have a feeling it's gonna be a long day."

He nods, barely containing his smile. "Will do. You're onto

something here. Something great. Follow your instincts, Gus. They haven't failed you yet." He leaves before I can answer him.

None of us leave until two o'clock in the morning, and by that time, we're completely spent. But the song's done. Recorded. Lyrics and all. It's called "Redemption." And the guys don't know it yet, but we just got our album title, too.

Redemption. That's what happened today. Not in the religious sense, but in an I'm-a-better-person-than-I-was-before sense. And it feels so fucking good.

Thursday, January 25
(Scout)

"L.A. misses you, Girl Scout." That's how Gus answers the phone.

"I miss L.A. And you. Happy birthday, Gus."

"Is that today already? How'd you know?" He sounds surprised.

"It's on Audrey's calendar. I'm her assistant. I'm privy to *all* of the important stuff."

"*You certainly are.*" That was a sexual innuendo if I've ever heard one. "Thanks. And speaking of the important stuff, we're all done here Saturday. Would you mind driving Pax up to the studio on Saturday morning? I don't want that kid anywhere near L.A. traffic on his own. We've been texting all month and I've been sending him short videos of what we've been doing, but I know he'd like to see it in person. I still need to record the guitar for the final song and I've saved it for last hoping he could be here for it."

"Of course I'll bring him. He'd love that." Gus is everything to Paxton. I know Gus downplays the influence he has on him, but the truth is that being around Gus is probably the best thing that's ever happened to Paxton. Gus is a father figure, a brother, a teacher, and a best friend. Paxton was always a good kid, but the changes I've seen in him over the past few months are huge. He's more confident. He's more outgoing. He's more engaged in school and more focused on his interests.

"Good. Gracias, muchacha."

"What time do you want us there?"

"I know it's early, but I want to get started at eight o'clock. It shouldn't take me long, maybe an hour or so. Then I'm free and we can head home. Mind if I hitch a ride? Or you could bring cookies and put your panties in your purse and we could go back to the apartment."

"I'd love to bring you cookies and put my panties in my purse, but what about Paxton?"

"Right. When did Pax turn into a cock-blocker? I thought he was my boy?" He's laughing.

And now I'm laughing. "I'd better get to work. I'll talk to you tonight, birthday boy. Have a good day."

"Always. You too, sweetheart." I love it when he calls me that. Every time he says it his voice gets soft, the verbal equivalent of a hug. It makes me feel warm inside and it makes my heart literally flutter in my chest, a physical reaction.

"Bye."

"Adios, amiga."

Saturday, January 27
(Gus)

Scout brought Pax to the studio this morning. The kid was stoked. It fueled me. And now the final guitar track is in the books. And it's epic.

I rode back home with them and we arrived a little after lunch time. Ma had cupcakes and veggie tacos waiting for me. God, I love that woman.

Ma, Scout, Pax, his girlfriend Mason, and I had a low key, belated birthday celebration.

And to cap off a great day, Scout showed me her birthday suit.

And I showed her mine.

And we rocked the hell out of them.

And then she let me hold her all night.

I love being home.

Sunday, January 28
(Scout)

There's a sticky note on the bathroom mirror when I step out of the shower. *San Diego sex is my favorite.*

It has me blushing as I think back to last night.

San Diego sex is my favorite, too.

Sunday, March 4
(Gus)

I've watched Ma and Doc Banks' relationship develop into something solid, loving, and stable over the past several months. Throughout it all I've pretty much kept my mouth shut, but I feel like I need to talk about it with her. And more in depth than just the passing discussion we have when she updates me on trips or travel.

"Hey, Ma."

"Hi, sweetie." She's sitting on the deck reading a book and drinking her morning cup of coffee.

"Can I talk to you for a minute?"

She marks her page and sets her book down on the table. "Of course. What's wrong?" She looks worried. I didn't mean to worry her. Sometimes I forget that even though I'm a grown man, she'll always think of me as her little boy. And when I come to her like this, her mind immediately goes into problem solving, what-can-I-do-to-make-this-better mode.

I shake my head and lean down and kiss her forehead before I take a seat next to her. "Nothing's wrong." And I smile so she knows I'm not lying. "About Doc Banks—"

She interrupts me. "You can call him Eric, you know?" It's a friendly reminder.

I smile at the love in her voice and nod. "I like Doc Banks better. It sounds cooler." She wants to laugh but she's just giving me an amused grin instead. I continue. "About *Eric*. You really like him?"

"I do." She does.

"Do you love him?" Her heart is important to me and I only want someone who truly deserves her to have it.

"I do." She does.

"You're going to marry him, aren't you?"

The light that shines in her eyes is all the answer I need. "We've talked about it." He must deserve her heart, because no one's ever brought this out in her.

I don't know why I'm so fascinated by this. I guess because Ma has always been this force to be reckoned with. The woman can do anything she puts her mind to. She makes things happen.

My entire life she's been this entity unto herself, helping everyone, loving everyone, but always independent. What I always suspected is so clear now—she put her love life aside so she could devote her life to me. To raise me and give me her undivided attention. She's completely and utterly selfless. "Is that what you want?"

She nods. "It is. He's a good man, Gus. I think finding the perfect partner is as much about timing, as it is about the person himself."

"What do you mean?"

"I mean, I think people find each other when they're ready for them. When they need each other the most. And it's in that time of need that the strongest relationships are formed."

My mind drifts to Scout. It always drifts to Scout. I need her. And it's not needy need. Not need that makes my heart ache. It's need that makes me whole. It's need that makes me not only remember who I am, but makes me want to be more. To do more. For me. For her. For us. It's a need that's liberating, because I have no doubt whenever and wherever that need arises, she's there for me. Like Ma said, it's all about timing. We were both at our lowest. Hurting. Grieving. And together we healed each other without even realizing it. I look Ma in the eye. "I think I love her, Ma."

She smiles her knowing smile. "I don't think you do, honey ... I know you do."

Tuesday, March 27
(Scout)

Gus is still sleeping so I leave a few sticky notes on his door before I head out for work. *I downloaded Rook's new album this morning on iTunes. You should check it out. The singer's voice is dead sexy. ;) Seriously, I listened to it on my run. Your talent amazes me. You should be so proud of yourself.*

The truth is my morning run was a walk. Because I was so blown away by what I heard coming through my earbuds that I couldn't run. So I walked. And occasionally I sat down and just listened. A few months ago I listened to him write these songs and play them on his acoustic guitar in his room. It was magical. But today, listening to those quiet songs transformed into tracks with a full band? It floored me. I peeked in on him this morning when I got back from my run. He was lying on his stomach in bed, covered from the waist down by only a sheet, sleeping soundly. I know he was naked because that's how I left him early this morning. The absolute maleness of him is always the first thing that takes hold of me the instant I see him. There's raw attraction that's undeniable. He's absolutely stunning. But when my eyes landed on him this morning, I had an overwhelming feeling of awe. Here's this ungodly handsome man who's funny, and kind, and sweet, and protective, and sexy, and so, so caring. But he's also got this talent that's unimaginable. It's hard to believe a person can possess that kind of a gift. And to be so humble about it. He has no idea how special he is. His humility is every bit as beautiful as he is.

Saturday, March 31
(Gus)

There's a text waiting for me when I check my phone this morning.

CLARE: *Congrats on the new album! Bought it yesterday and listened to it last night, it's phenomenal! Great work!*

ME: *Thanks. You quit smoking yet?*

CLARE: *I did. 2 weeks ago. Didn't want to tell you and jinx it though. It's hard. You quit?*

ME: *Yeah. Agreed, it's fucking hard. Hang in there. And I won't hold you to the bet; keep your money and buy some gum.*

CLARE: *Gum?*

ME: *Yeah. It helps. Don't ask me why but it does.*

CLARE: *I'll give it a try. Take care and good luck.*

ME: *Thanks. You too.*

Thursday, April 5
(Gus)

Our tour starts tomorrow night. I fly to Phoenix in the morning. Eleven o'clock flight. The label car will be at the house to pick me at eight-thirty. My bags are packed and sitting by the front door with my guitars. Scout helped me pack—a week's worth of jeans and T-shirts. She even bought me new socks and chonies—two weeks' worth just in case I can't find a laundromat.

She's lying in bed with me. We're face to face on my pillow. Our bodies are touching, still cherishing the intimacy we shared only minutes ago. Sex with her will never get old. My body fucking craves her. And when we connect, I feel whole. It's an experience that's as emotionally fulfilling as it is physical.

She looks sleepy. It's late. I brush the hair back from her cheek. I love that she doesn't give it a second thought when I touch her scars anymore. She's just an amazingly confident woman. I'm so proud of her.

"Scout?"

"Yeah, babe?" That's the first time she's called me by anything other than my name. I'm pretty sure I just caught fire. This woman fucking slays me.

"I love you." I mean it with everything that I am.

Her lips twitch and then she presses them together tightly. I'm afraid she's going to cry because her eyes are shiny, but as the first tear rolls down her cheek it's paired with the sweetest smile I've ever seen. "You don't know how long I've wanted to hear you say that. I love you, too. So much."

I can't help but kiss her. It's *I love you*. And *thank you*.

"I'm gonna miss you." We'll be gone for five months, US and European tours have been combined. We'll spend three months here before we fly over to Europe for two months. The shows are all at bigger venues than anything we've ever played before, except Grant auditorium. That one we insisted on returning to for Bright Side.

"I'm gonna miss you, too, but I'll visit. I know someone in the band. He's kind of a big deal." She shrugs. "He hooked me up with tickets." I already got her a ticket to every state-side Saturday night show. I gave them to her earlier tonight along with all of the flight reservations I made to get her there. "Thank you. I love that I get to be there to share this with you."

"That album wouldn't have happened without you sitting on the other side of my door."

"I think that's when I fell for you. I'd been falling for a long time, little by little. But that week ... listening to you pouring your soul out? I was yours. I was *so* yours."

"I honestly think you had me from the moment we met. It was such a goddamn battle with you, but looking back now, I think we were meant to be from the very beginning. Maybe it was all the fucking sticky notes."

"You love my sticky notes."

"I do. The tour bus won't be the same without you and your sticky notes."

Friday, April 6
(Gus)

This morning's already been perfect: pre-sunrise sex with Scout, sunrise surfing with some of the best waves I've seen in a long time, and breakfast with Scout, Ma, and Pax. It was a trifecta of serenity that put my head exactly where it needs to be for this journey.

I said good-bye to Scout, Ma, and Pax when they all left for work and school. It was sad, but not the type of sad I was anticipating. They were so excited for me, but more importantly, proud of me. It makes me feel like this time around I've earned it somehow. I've worked my ass off to make this album epic and I'm going to give this tour everything I've got. *Every damn night.*

I'm waiting with my gear in the driveway for the label car to pick me up to drive me to the airport. The sun's warm this morning and I'm soaking it up. When the driver shows up, Franco is already in the car. When he climbs out, he spreads his arms wide. It's a cheesy presentation, like a game show model. And then I see his shirt and I bust out laughing.

He's trying to keep a straight face but he's failing. "It's true, douche canoe. You do. *So fucking moist.*"

His T-shirt reads: *Gus makes me moist.*

"Where in the hell did you get that?" I say as I help the driver put my gear in the trunk.

He shrugs and turns around. "New merch for the tour, dude." Rook's logo and our US tour schedule are on the back.

I can't stop laughing. "This isn't for real, right? This is a one-off?"

"Oh no, it's for real," he confirms.

"What the fuck? How did I not know about this?"

He shakes his head like it's obvious while he climbs back into the car. "Because you would've blocked the idea, Mr. Humble Ass. The chicks dig you. We're doing nothing more than stating the obvious. They know they're moist for you, big man. It's fucking genius. They'll sell like mad."

I climb in behind him. "I need one for Scout."

He rubs his hands together devilishly and grins. "Already on it. They should have hers at the merch table tonight for you. It was

GUS

a special order, one of a kind. Hers says *I make Gus moist.*

I clap my hands and I'm laughing again. "That's fucking brilliant. And true. I'm making her wear that shit to every show."

We pound knuckles. I love this fuckhead.

Saturday, June 23
(Scout)

Paxton and I are standing on the sidewalk outside baggage claim. The local time is nine-thirty in the morning and the Minneapolis air is already hot and sticky.

I text Gus while we wait: *Just landed in MN. Where are you?*

His response is immediate: *We'll be in Grant around noon. You might want to put your panties in your purse now. Just to save time.*

ME: *Already done. I'm efficient. ;)*

GUS: *And horny.*

ME: *Yes.*

GUS: *Moist?*

ME: *That too.*

GUS: *Me too. I love you.*

ME: *I love you too.*

Paxton keeps adjusting the straps on his backpack. He's fidgety and I don't know if he's just excited to see Gus and Rook play tonight, or if he's nervous about seeing his dad again. They haven't talked in months. Paxton won't take his calls anymore.

I hear the labored roar of the engine before I see the old, battered green Suburban pull up to the curb. This must be Duncan. The car is exactly as Keller described it: rusty and beat-up, with one red door. I wave at him so he's knows it's us.

He waves back through the windshield and pulls up to the curb next to us. I ride in the front passenger seat and as I climb in about to introduce myself, Paxton calls out from the backseat, "Right On! Beanbags."

I know I didn't hear that right, so I continue. "You must be Duncan."

He smiles. "I am. And you must be the infamous Scout and Paxton." His shaggy hair and bushy beard are the same deep, vivid red as Stella's.

"We are." It's then that I turn and look at Paxton in the backseat. He hasn't heard a word that either of us has said. He's looking down with a smile on his face that I don't think I've seen since he was seven or eight. And he's not sitting on a seat.

He looks up and the smile grows and he repeats what I didn't think I heard correctly the first time. "Beanbags. This is genius."

"Right?" Duncan comments as he pulls back out into traffic. "Way more comfortable than traditional seating."

Paxton wiggles around in his seat as if to prove the point. "Way more comfortable," he agrees.

The ride to Grant doesn't take long. The conversation is easy between the three of us and before I know it we're parked in front of a coffee shop.

Duncan kills the engine. "Keller won't be home from Stella's ballet practice for another half hour, so we've got a little time to kill. Come on in. I'll buy you guys a cup of coffee."

"I could use some caffeine this morning. Thanks." I don't know if I'm tired because I didn't sleep much last night, or if it's the adrenaline I've been cranked up on all morning that's dragging me down. Either way, I need caffeine.

When Duncan pushes the oversized wooden door open, a bell rings. It's loud and it startles me. "What the hell?" I didn't mean to say that out loud, but Duncan laughs good-naturedly.

"Small town Minnesotans kind of have a thing for bells." He shrugs.

I'm laughing now. It's stunned laughter, because it's impossible that small bell made that much noise. I point to my right ear. "I'm deaf in this ear and I'm pretty sure that registered."

He chuckles by way of introduction. "Welcome to Grounds."

It's cozy. There's a small loveseat sitting in front of fireplace that I bet is great during the winter, and a few small tables and chairs. The building is old and has character. It's inviting. It's the kind of place that makes you want to sit down and hang out. "Cool place."

Duncan nods. "Yeah, it is. Home away from home. Keller works here early mornings and he and Stella live in the room out back."

"Duncan, I see you brought friends." A friendly voice with a thick accent calls out and draws my attention to the man behind the counter.

"Rome, how goes it today?"

The man behind the counter salutes Duncan before he responds. "I am well. And you?"

"Livin' the dream, man. Livin' the dream." And when he says it, I get the idea that he means it. Some people are just so sincere that it's the first thing you notice when you meet them. That's Duncan. He's just a really nice guy. "These are my new friends, Scout and Paxton. They're visiting from California."

"Ah, California. Beautiful. You must be Keller's friends. He said he had company coming in today. I'm Romero."

"It's nice to meet you, Romero. Yeah, we're just here for the concert tonight," I offer.

"Of course. Keller mentioned it. Kate's friend's band, yes?" He's looking at Duncan for confirmation.

He nods. "Yup, they're good, man. You should come check 'em out with us."

Romero smiles sheepishly. "I'm too old for that, niño. But I've heard them. Keller played me some songs. Kate was singing and playing violin. She was something, wasn't she? One of a kind, that girl. Such a tragedy."

Every time someone says something about Kate, it makes me wish I could've known her. So much love surrounds her memory and those that knew her have nothing but the most positive things to say about her. I know her friendship is one of the reasons Gus is the man he is, and for that I couldn't be more grateful.

Duncan nods. "She was. And she had Keller's heart."

Romero smiles lovingly. "That girl changed Keller. Woke him up. I'm so proud of him." He sounds like a father.

Duncan agrees, and it's so nice to hear people supportive of their friends. "Me too, Rome." Duncan looks at us. "Pick your poison. I'm paying. Rome's got the best coffee around. House blend's legendary."

I order a small house blend while Paxton looks over the menu. He settles on a mocha macchiato and looks blissfully happy while he's drinking it. We aren't seated on the loveseat long before Stella comes bounding in from behind the counter. "Where's Gus?" she calls out.

I turn and she's scanning the busy coffee shop. "Hi, Stella. He's not here yet. Soon though."

She runs over and, after she high fives Duncan, crawls up in my lap. "Hi, Scout."

God, she's the cutest little thing I've ever seen. "Hi, Stella. How was ballet?" She's still wearing her pale pink tights and leotard.

"Miss Toler was kind of a grumpy gorilla today because Amy and Ashley didn't have their listening ears on. *Again.*" She rolls her eyes. "It's so much easier for all of us when they just do what they're told."

Duncan's smirking and trying to hold back laughter. "The twins being naughty again, huh?"

It's like watching an adult trapped in a little person's body. "They're so frustrating, Uncle Duncan. I wish they'd just grow up already."

He's still smirking, but he matches her serious tone. "There's always a stinky one in every bunch, Stella. Sometimes two. That's life, big girl. Welcome to the real world."

"Stinky people suck," she mutters as she crawls back down off my lap and takes my hand. "Let's go see Miss Higgins."

I follow her behind the counter and through a door, with Paxton and Duncan trailing after us. Keller's place is on the other side. It's small, but it's homey.

Keller welcomes us with a wave when we walk through the door; he's talking on his phone.

After I meet Miss Higgins and Keller finishes up his phone call, Gus texts me. *We're about 20 minutes away. Meet us at the auditorium?*

I know I saw him only six days ago, but my heart's already racing in my chest thinking about being near him. I answer: *Will do.*

Gus: *I love you.*

Scout: *I love you too.*

I ride with Keller in his car and Stella and Paxton ride with Duncan in the Suburban. And when the bus pulls into the lot I don't know who's more excited to see Gus: me, Stella, Paxton, or Keller.

He's the first one off the bus and Stella is right there to greet him. Seeing him with her in his arms warms my heart. Kids love him and he's so good with them. He's gentle and kind, they gravitate to him. He'll be the best dad someday.

After he sets Stella down, he hugs Paxton. I'm close enough that I can hear part of their conversation. "I've been talking to your dad, dude. I know he's not perfect, but he loves you. You need to talk to him. Hear him out. He knows he fucked up."

Paxton nods before he lets go of Gus.

And now Gus's eyes are on me and he's wearing the smile that he only wears for me. "How's Minnesota treating you, sweetheart?"

I practically curl up into his arms. "Hot. Sticky."

He interrupts me. "Is that a come-on? It's working."

"It's actually pretty wonderful here. Lots of nice people."

He hugs me tight. "You just wait. More nice people to come. Today's gonna be epic."

Keller's next in line for Gus. And when they hug each other it's not your average guy hug. They hold on. It's the kind of hug that's more like a conversation, words passed back and forth, an understanding between two people who share a common bond. And when that bond is love, it makes it even more powerful.

"Traveling in style, I see," Keller says pointing at the bus.

"No complaints, dude. Except that the bunk across the aisle is a little too empty." He looks at me and winks.

"I'm glad you're here. It's good to see you. You guys need anything before we go eat? You need a shower or some coffee? We can stop by my place on the way."

Gus smells his pits. "Nah, fresh as a daisy, dude. Let's go eat. I'm starving."

The band and Paxton ride with Duncan, because the allure of the beanbags is too strong to be ignored. You haven't lived until you've witnessed four grown men absolutely giddy about riding in the back of a moving vehicle on beanbags. I took video. It could go viral.

Jim, Gus, and I ride with Keller and Stella. Gus seems pretty at ease around Jim, which is a nice change from last summer when just being in the same room with both of them at the same time was difficult. Back then, their dislike for each other was so evident it was almost unbearable. I think they've both changed. Jim catches me up on everything that's going on with Jane. When I talk to her these days she doesn't want to talk about her recovery, and I don't pry, so it's nice to get the details I've been worrying about. She's doing better, thanks to intensive therapy and counseling. It gives my heart some peace where she's concerned.

We end up at a bar called Red Lion Road. Keller bartends here on Friday nights so he knows everyone and they already have several tables put together for us in the back.

After the pizza, pitchers of beer, and sodas for me, Paxton, and Stella are ordered, everyone settles into easy conversation.

And then, over the next several hours, the group grows.

The first to join us is a tall woman about my age. When she walks through the door I can't take my eyes off her. She's striking with her black hair, dark eyes, and curvy body, but she's got this presence about her. It's the first thing you notice. It's almost intimidating, like you know you'd better give this woman respect. It's just the way she carries herself.

Duncan stands and meets her before she gets to the table. He kisses her. And when he does she smiles and everything about her softens. This must be his fiancée, Shelly.

Before she takes a seat next to Duncan at the other end of table, she waves. "Hey, everyone." Her voice is low and raspy, and it suits her perfectly.

Gus raises his beer in greeting. "Shelly! Drink up, girl. I've got money on you tonight. Distance. It's *all* about distance."

Her cheeks flame red. "Hey, Gus. I'm limiting the booze intake tonight to manageable levels, dude."

"Well hell. You're no fun anymore. I thought shit was about to get real," he teases.

She smirks. "Oh, I didn't say I wasn't gonna have fun. I'm just gonna have fun that doesn't involve projectile vomiting in the parking lot at the end of the night."

Gus pushes his chair back and holds his beer up. "I'd like to make a toast. Rumor has it a wedding is in the near future. Congrats to Duncan and Shelly."

Everyone raises their glasses and joins in with their congratulations.

Shelly keeps her glass raised. "And congratulations to Rook on the new album. It's freaking sick. You outdid yourselves. Can't wait for the show tonight." She's a fan, that wasn't put on. I like this girl.

And before there's time to make an introduction, two more pairs join us. A small, adorable guy in a quirky outfit and a tall, dark, well-dressed man walk in holding hands. Despite their obvious differences—they look like exact opposites—they work together. They fit together. It makes me smile because they look so comfortable with each other. With them are a conservative looking younger guy and his slightly meek looking girlfriend. They're just normal. Not that normal's a bad thing at all. But in the group of characters I'm surrounded by at the moment, normal stands out. They're both very quiet, but friendly. Introductions are made. Clayton and Morris flew in from L.A. for the show. And Peter and Evelyn go to school here at the college Keller goes to. I learn that Clayton and Peter were roommates and lived across the hall from Kate in the dorms. And Shelly worked with Kate at a flower shop.

And then the stories begin. This day is all about Kate and her memory. Everyone at the table, with the exception of me, Paxton, and Jim, knew her and loved her. It's heartwarming to listen to their stories and amazing to think that some of them only knew her for a few short months, especially Keller. The friendships were deep and meaningful and the love was so real. The laughter is genuine and constant, and the smiles only grow as each person shares their memories. There's no sadness here; it's all positive, all pure joy. She touched so many people.

Time flies and when Jim reluctantly announces that it's four o'clock and time for soundcheck, I'm shocked. He doesn't want to break up the fun everyone is having, I can tell he feels a little bad about it, but it needs to be done. They need to get to work.

Keller lets me, Gus, and the band take his car to the auditorium. Paxton and Jim stay behind to talk. I'm glad, it needs to happen. It's long overdue.

As I sit through soundcheck, I'm regretting the fact that I didn't take advantage of this last summer when I was on tour with them. Now it feels like a missed opportunity.

I don't miss opportunities anymore. Ever. Life is about living every moment. Doing what I want and need to do. No more hiding. No more hesitation. *Just living.*

Gus stops in the middle of a song to answer his phone, which is strange. He talks for only a few seconds and then calls out to me through the microphone. "Scout, there's a VIP at the front door. Can you go ask someone to let him in?"

I nod and jump down from the railing I'm sitting on.

When I get to the front doors and get an employee to unlock it, I find Gustov standing on the other side with a violin case in one hand and a small travel bag in the other.

He sets them down and wraps me in a hug. "Scout. So good to see you again, young lady."

"Hi, Gustov. I didn't know you were coming."

He chuckles. "Well, it was all a bit last minute, but I couldn't say no, now could I? It's going to be a special night."

(Gus)

Seeing Gustov walk up to the stage with his violin case in hand chokes me up a little. Not with sadness, but with the happiness you feel in your chest when you see an old friend. All I can say is, "Thanks for coming, maestro."

He nods his head. "I'm honored, my boy. It's been a long time coming, the two of us playing together. I'll do my best to do her memory proud."

I called Gustov last week and asked him if he'd come to Grant and play violin with us on "Missing You" and "Finish Me." He agreed without hesitation, even though it meant missing a performance tonight in Boston.

He's never played with us before, so we don't waste any time running through both songs a few times. The guy never ceases to amaze me with his playing, he's flawless. I'm humbled to be standing here playing with him.

We're set to go on in five minutes. And I'm nervous. For the first time all tour, I'm nervous. This is a big night. This is by far the smallest crowd we'll play to, only about five hundred people, but they're all amped. It's going to be fun. I'm in the shadows just off stage watching the crowd, mainly looking for Scout. She's standing in the front row with her *I make Gus moist* T-shirt on next to Paxton and surrounded by Keller and all of Bright Side's friends. She hasn't stopped smiling all day. She always smiles these days, which I love. But her smile today is different. She knows how important this is to me and she wants to share it with me. There's not a jealous bone in her body. She knows how much I loved Bright Side, but she also knows that doesn't take away from the love I feel for her. My heart's big enough for both of them. Bright Side helped make me the man I am, and Scout helped me remember who that man was, helping me become my own

331

person. I love her so much.

Someone rests their hand on my shoulder. "You okay, big man?" It's Franco.

I nod. "I'm good, dude. *I'm so good.*"

He sees me looking at Scout. "It's not fair, you know?"

I turn and look at him. "What's not fair?"

He gestures with his chin to Scout. "That a dipshit like you gets all the badass chicks."

I can't help but laugh. "I know, right? I'm one lucky dipshit."

And then he's serious. "You're not a dipshit, Gus. You're my best friend and the best person I know. Badasses attract badasses. You're kinda perfect for each other."

We're interrupted by Jim; I've stopped calling him Hitler now that he's stopped acting like a first-class douche. He's got a lot of shit on his plate and he's trying to do better and I'm trying to support that. "You've got less than a minute before you go on," he says. "Have a great show, guys."

I take my guitar from Slim, one of our roadies. He's wearing a *Gus makes me moist* T-shirt. I think Franco pays him to do it just to embarrass me. "Go show 'em how it's done, Gus." He says it before every show. I like hearing it.

"I'll do my best, dude." It's the same response I give him every time. And I mean it. *Every time.* "Let's do this," I call out to the rest of the band. And we take the stage.

The crowd is raging already. Pumped up from the opening band and ready to party.

As the stage lights come up, the cheers erupt. I scan the front row and see all of the familiar faces lined up and I feel like they've all got my back. When I get to Scout, I wink. And then I address the masses. "What's up, Grant?!" They cheer louder if that's even possible. "It's good to be back. It's been a while. What do you say we make up for lost time and have some fun tonight?"

We lead in with "Redemption." The crowd's into it. They know the song. They're singing along with me. What a great way to kick off the night.

And for the next two hours, we play. Normally our set is about half that length, but tonight's special and we're playing everything we've got, including a few covers that Bright Side loved.

GUS

We saved Gustov for the finale. I motion for the crowd to quiet down. "How many of you were here with us the last time we played this auditorium?" The cheers tell me over half of them. "Well, if you were, you had the privilege of seeing my best friend perform with us. Kate Sedgwick was an unbelievably talented woman. She could sing her ass off and she played violin like nobody I've ever seen. We lost her a year and half ago. Cancer. Which really fucking sucks. I know she's here tonight with us in spirit. She's watching and listening, so I just want to say, we miss you every day, Bright Side. And tonight? This was all for you. All about you. Someone very special flew a very long way this afternoon to play with us on these next two songs. Maestro, come on out."

Gustov walks on from the left side of the stage and takes a seat on the edge of the chair that's been set up for him behind a microphone. He looks composed and professional as always. When he's comfortable, he nods at me and smiles. This feels so right. I'm so glad he's here.

I point at Gustov. "This dude is way out of our league, but we're gonna do our best to keep up with him." I look up. "Bright Side, these are for you. Love you."

The intro to "Finish Me" is all Gustov. It fills the entire stage with an eerie, sorrowful melody. It drives me. I feel like I'm back in the studio with Bright Side when we recorded this song—minus the anguish. I've got my big boy pants on and playing and singing the lyrics are like an out-of-body experience. Inspiration like this is so rare; I give in to it and turn myself over to the music. The song transitions into "Missing You," and Gustov is on fire. He's making that instrument sing with me. It's incredible and draws all of the emotion out of me until I'm happily, and willingly, bleeding out on this stage. When his violin falls silent, and the song is over, I need to take a few deep breaths, both to balance the adrenaline coursing through me and slow my heart rate. He nods first to me and then to the audience. "Thank you for allowing me to be a part of this. Kate was a very special young lady. I hope I did her justice." With that he stands and bows, and the crowd roars.

"Wow." I had to say that out loud, because I'm blown away. The last seven minutes of my life is something I'll never forget. I shake my head to clear it. "Let's give it up again for the motherfucking genius." Gustov bows again and walks offstage. I look back at Franco. I'm still stunned, lost in the dream-like state this performance has taken on. "Did that seriously just happen?"

Franco looks as in awe as I feel. He nods slowly and that gives way to full-on belly laughter and I can't help but join him. You know how sometimes something happens and it's so much more than you ever expected? The type of so much more that leaves you speechless and thinking *what the hell just happened?* And all you can do is laugh because you're so astounded you don't know what else to do? That is exactly what's happening. And I'm glad Franco's in this with me; otherwise I would think I finally lost my mind.

When I stop laughing, I turn back to the audience. "We've got one more song," I say. "We're gonna kill the sun. I need help. I want you all to be as loud as you can and sing with me. Seriously, I want to wake neighboring states. That kind of fucking loud." I look down at Pax and smile. "This one's for you, Pax."

What happens next is five hundred people coming together. The volume is deafening. I think every person in the place is singing along with me. This is, by far, the best crowd of the tour yet, maybe ever. I stretch the guitar solo out to twice its normal length, because I don't want to say good-bye to this night. I'm living the song. Living what it stands for. Wishing I could kill the sun and just hold on to this moment.

The crowd, when we're done, cheers for a solid ten minutes. That's a lot of love.

The Bright Side posse meets us out back by the bus. I thank them all for coming and celebrating with us and say good-bye to each one. It's almost midnight, but our bus isn't leaving until noon. I begged Jim for some extra time here and he's giving it to me. We play Des Moines tomorrow night and it's only a couple hours' drive away.

After I thank Gustov again, I call him a cab and pre-pay to the airport so he can catch his redeye flight back home to Boston.

Keller hugs me last. "Great show, man. Really, I mean it. You guys are the best thing going out there. Katie would be so proud of you."

"Thanks for being here, dude."

He drops his car keys in my hand. "I'm catching a ride back with Dunc. Paxton's coming with us and crashing at my place. I reserved you a room at the Hampton Inn here in Grant. I know you probably haven't had any time alone with Scout in a couple of months. You both need that. Tell her to just come to my place after she drops you off here in the morning. I'll get her and Paxton to the airport."

I'm looking at the keys in my hand and the generous friend standing in front of me. I don't know what to say. There's so much I want to tell him, but no words ... and no time. So I say, "Thank you, dude." And I mean it. *God, do I mean it.*

Scout's confused when we get in Keller's car alone, but she doesn't say anything.

She's even more confused when we arrive at the hotel. She's still not talking.

"Come on, sweetheart. Keller got us a room."

She smiles and it's reluctant hope. Almost like she's afraid to believe it's true, because she wants this so badly.

I check in and get the key card and we head to the room. She looks deep in thought.

Behind closed doors, she finally speaks up. "Gus?"

"Yeah?"

"I've learned a lot about life these past few months. Living life ... *really living it* ... is work. It's exhausting if you're doing it right. If you're out there making the most of every day. Every minute. Every second. Because out there in the middle of the chaos, that's where you find the beauty. That's where you find the reward. And watching you tonight, babe? It was beauty in the middle of chaos. *So damn beautiful.* I was in awe. It was incredible. I mean, you're always amazing, but tonight was special. Everyone felt it."

I smile to myself. "Fuck yeah, it is work. But that's where the beauty comes in. It manifests itself when effort's made. I'm in this, Girl Scout. Totally immersed in life now. Tonight was definitely different, like once-in-a-lifetime different. I'm so stoked you were there." I tip her head back so I can taste her lips. "And just so you know, you're my reward." The kissing escalates quickly, because I can't help myself. But after a few seconds I pull away. "I need to shower. I sweat like a fiend tonight."

335

She smiles against my lips. "You're sexy sweaty."

Which makes me smile. "I'm sexier naked."

She helps me pull my T-shirt up and over my head. "True."

I reach for the hem of her T-shirt and return the favor. "Nice shirt," I say, before pulling it off.

She raises her eyebrows seductively. "They're good. I should probably tell you now that I've got a thing for the lead singer. I took off my panties and put them in my purse just hoping I'd run into him."

I unbutton and unzip her jeans and sure enough, no panties. "Shit. You mean, you've been freebuffing all day and I didn't know? Damn." I slide her jeans down her legs and she steps out of them.

She gives the answer that's become an inside joke between us. "I thought it would save time."

When I'm down to only my underwear and she's standing in front of me in only a sheer ivory bra, I stop and lace my fingers with hers and stare into her eyes. And I speak from my heart. "I love you."

"I love you, too, babe." Every time she calls me "babe" it takes my breath away.

"I want to go slow. I want to enjoy this. Can I just hold you for a few minutes before I get in the shower? I miss you."

I take her arms and wrap them around my neck. And when her body meets mine and her ear comes to rest against my collarbone, everything in the world just feels right. I rest my hands on her hips first, because I just want to touch her. My palms are warm against her skin. The scars on her right side are a different sensation than the smooth skin on her left, but I love them both. It only takes seconds before the smooth skin gives way to goosebumps, and it makes me smile because I know she's not cold; she's reacting to my touch. My hands start their journey to the base of her spine. Once there, my fingertips trace the curve of her ass and she shivers against me. My palms find themselves flat against her skin again and they make their way up her back. When the tips of my fingers meet resistance, I stop. They're brushing the fabric of her bra. I ball my fists and take a deep breath fighting the urge to unclasp it just yet. Unfurling my fingers I glide them under the thin straps and continue upward toward her shoulder blades. I'm restrained by the strap to any further travel north, so I head back down south dragging my palms with added pressure along the way. She's all lean muscle covered by a thin, womanly layer of softness. I rub my hand slowly back and forth across the scarring on her right side, lightly at first but with added intensity as she relaxes into me. I'm trying to show her that every part of her is perfect, without saying a word.

I skim my hands down over her ass, and though they want so badly to hang out there for a long while, they continue down the backs of her thighs until I can get a get a good grasp and hoist her up. Her long legs instinctively wrap around my back.

Once in place, three things happens instantaneously: I wrap my arms around her, one hand holding her ass cheek in my palm, the other cradling the nape of her neck; I'm so fucking hard it's blissfully painful; and she kisses me.

And this kiss ...

Jesus Christ.

Her tongue flirts with my lips before diving in and when it does, she teases me. Licking lightly before retreating, leaving me to chase her. I part her lips and waste no time making my intentions known. I'm going to be hers tonight. Her safe place. Her protector. Her friend. And her lover.

I'm going to be hers.

The possessive strokes of her tongue, the nips at my bottom lip, the gentle kisses followed by the sinful pull of my skin at the crook of my neck in between her lips ... it's heaven. I'm so focused on her mouth and the amazing things it's doing to me that it takes a second for me to catch up when her hips start moving, rolling in and out like the waves.

Damn, she feels good.

Her hands are in my hair now. It was pulled back in a loose ponytail but she slipped the elastic tie off and it's knotted up in her hands now. She knows that's one of my biggest turn-ons. I love it when she winds my hair around her hands like reins and takes charge; it's sexy as all hell.

The pace of everything has notched up. Her breathing. Her hips. Her moaning. Her intensity.

She's so fucking close and I want nothing more than to watch her come undone in my arms.

I shift my hold on her so that one hand is supporting her around her lower back while the other hand slips down from behind. My middle finger splits her and runs back to front, front to back. Back to front, front to back, until she's begging me. "I need to feel you inside me, babe. *Please.*"

I suck at her neck teasingly, before kissing it softly. "Be patient, Impatient. We've got all night."

She's writhing under my touch. She's there, she just won't let go. "Please, Gus."

I'm taking my time because this just got all kinds of sexy. My hair's still reined up in her fists. She's on the cusp of a mind-blowing orgasm. She's pleading for sex as I'm nibbling at her earlobe. And my fingers just slipped inside her. "Better?"

"Oh ... God ... " she pants. Pleasure's set her hand in motion. It's snaking between us, pushing down my underwear until the top few inches of me is exposed against her belly. The sensation of skin on skin ... *damn.*

"*Fuck. Me.*" My fingers are beating out the steady rhythm that her body is demanding.

"No. Fuck me, Gus." That wasn't begging. That was telling. If there's such a thing as verbal fucking, that was just it. The tone, the words, the force, the sound of her voice ...

It was fucking.

Her breasts have my attention now. They're spilling out of her tiny bra. Hiking her up in my arms, I waste no time in taking the triangle of sheer fabric on the left side in my teeth and tugging it up until her breast falls free beneath it. I'm only moments into fondling her tight, hardened nipple with my tongue and teeth when she hits the roof.

Her mouth is open in a scream against my shoulder. And because her lips have formed a seal there's not much noise ... but I feel every sound wave pulse through me. Resonating in me. Reverberating. It's like music.

When she falls still in my arms, she smiles sheepishly. "Was I loud?"

I can only imagine what that scream felt like tearing through her if I felt it tearing through me. I shake my head. "Loud? Nope. Sexy? *Hell. Yes.*" I set her down and drop my underwear to my ankles before removing her bra.

On the way to the bathroom, she says, "I can't believe we get to stay here tonight." It's an innocent, but excited declaration that makes her sound half her age. Totally carefree. It's cute.

"I know, I fucking love sleepovers," I tease. I do love sleepovers with Scout, though.

She laughs at me.

"Especially when there's no sleeping involved."

She laughs again, but it quickly fades and her eyes settle in to that dark, lust-filled space. That space that has my groin throbbing. I turn toward her until our bodies are touching but I don't wrap my arms around her. Instead I lower my mouth to her ear and I talk. I don't whisper. I don't even lower my voice. "I'm going to take you up on your offer now."

"You are? What are you going to do exactly, Mr. Hawthorne?"

Damn, the devil may live inside this woman. That was sexy. "You said you wanted me to fuck you. I'm gonna take you in the shower with me and *we're gonna fuck*. Then I'm gonna make love to you in that bed until the sun comes up."

The side of her mouth tips up. "That sounds exhausting. Good thing I run marathons. Lots of stamina."

I bring her hand to my cock as we step into the shower. "He's got plenty of stamina. Trust me."

While I'm turning on the water she goes down on me, which she's never done before. And *fucking hell*, the things she can do with her mouth. And as good as it feels, I want more. Of her. I pull out and urge her to stand, backing her into the wall while pressing up against her. God, she feels so good.

She wraps her arms around my neck and pulls one leg up and around me, and I'm buried deep within her in seconds. There's absolutely no restraint. We're loud. We're demanding. We're so *fucking* physical. My hair's wound up in her hands again. It's been weeks since we've been together like this, with this kind of privacy. Usually it's a quickie on the bus after the show before she leaves to get back home. But tonight? Tonight I'm going to worship her repeatedly.

Her hips and mine were made for this. She knows my body like no one else. She knows what I like. She pays attention to my reactions when she tries something new and she can make my body fucking sing.

And I'm always doing the same for her.

When we can't hold back anymore, we fall into oblivion together. My final surge is so deep. I'm pulsing into her and she's got me wrapped up tight in her own release.

When we separate, she grins at me, still panting. "I think I just fell in love with Grant."

I can't help but grin back. "I'm still a San Diego boy at heart, but I'm pretty sure Grant's my new favorite place on the planet. I fucking love it here. The shower sex is *phenomenal*. It even comes with oral, added bonus."

After we dry off, I lead her to the bed and kiss her once. The kiss is a promise of what's to come. "Lie down on your belly."

Without hesitation she does. She's so trusting. So open. So confident.

I crawl up the bed until I'm straddling her thighs and I lower myself down on her back. I'm supporting most of my weight with an arm resting on either side of her. "You are so beautiful."

Her cheek's resting on the comforter and she's looking at me out of the corner of her eye through her hair. I brush the hair back from her cheek. "You're nice," she says to accept the compliment.

I grind myself into her backside. "I'm also a beast in the sack."

"Is that a threat or a promise?" The chitchat is over. She means business.

"Oh, it's a promise. Close your eyes. I just want you to feel me, because I'm about to worship you." I kiss her cheek and then I begin the slow process of kissing and massaging every square inch of her back. She keeps her eyes closed and I know she's in the moment. When I lower my body over her again I focus all my attention on her ear and neck. Trailing kisses up and down. Nibbling, sucking, biting. My cock is nestled in the shallow crevice of her ass and I can't stop myself from initiating a little friction because it feels so damn good. In no time, my hips are rocking like I'm buried inside her. I slide my hand under her and she gasps when my fingers find the right spot.

"You're so fucking wet. I love it."

She answers, but not with words. She reaches around behind me and grabs ahold of my upper thigh and squeezes. Her nails dig in with need and desperation, a physical plea.

It's *please.*
And *yes.*
And *now.*
Right now.

I slip my hand out from under her and sit up. I'm planning out my next move and admiring her gorgeous body in the same assessment. Nudging her legs apart at her knees ignites the flame of arousal within me and I can't resist touching her again, slipping my fingers in and out. Her hips lift to meet the penetration. And the act of her engaging in her own pleasure, enhancing it, has me memorizing this visual so I can reference it later when we're apart. It's fantasy material.

"You sure you're ready for this?"

Her eyes are still closed as she rides out the rapture. "Yes," it's breathless.

I slip my fingers out and guide myself to her opening. "Keep your eyes closed." I nudge her with the tip and she moans. "I'm gonna make you feel so good." When I push into her she gasps and all I can say is, "Mmm ... " It's a contented hum deep in my chest. After the initial, crazy good shocking sensation passes I urge her, "Close your legs."

"But, you won't be able to — "

I cut her off before she finishes her counter, "Trust me. Yes, I will."

After I find a slow rhythm that works for both of us, I lie down over her back. I need my skin touching her skin. "I'm gonna go slow, because, *damn* this feels incredible, but when you're close you let me know because we're in this together."

"Okay, babe." It's the breathless answer of a fully engaged, satisfied partner.

We keep up the pace while I kiss her shoulders and back, occasionally telling her what I'm feeling, or how she makes me feel, or how I feel about her. I don't normally hold back, but having sex with her is like truth serum. I'm not censoring anything. It's all out there.

And then she says, "I'm so close, babe."

I reach down for her hands and twine them with mine and I bring them up to rest on the bed on either side of her head. "I've got you, sweetheart. I'm all yours."

She squeezes my hands and the pressure is all the confirmation I need, but she adds, "You're mine."

Everything's ramped up—the need, the passion, the attraction. I'm pounding into her now and she's asking for more. And more. With her legs held together there's so much friction and she's so tight. And everything in my world is so goddamn intense right now. All I want to do is please her. That's all I want. And the moment it happens and she buries her head in the comforter and starts chanting my name, that's all it takes. My name on her lips called out in pure ecstasy. And I'm saying her name like a prayer. "Scout. Scout. You're my world, Scout." And my release is like nothing I've ever experienced, it's like I'm strapped to a rocket and launched into the sky. It's fireworks and satisfaction and need and love.

Love.

So much love.

Wednesday, August 22
(Gus)

Ma answers on the first ring, which is strange. "Hi, honey."

"Hola, Ma. What's the news from the States today?" We're in Budapest. Last night of the tour. We go home early tomorrow. It's been great. The crowds have been great. The music's been great. But I'm ready to go home and rest. And eat some tacos. Lots of tacos.

"Funny you should ask, because I do have some news." She sounds excited.

Which makes me excited. "Well, don't leave me hangin'. What is it?"

"I was going to wait until you're home tomorrow to tell you." I know she's going to tell me or she wouldn't have brought it up.

"Nope. You're not allowed to do that, Ma. You can't tell me you have news and sound so stoked you're ready to burst and then withhold. That's cruel. Spill." She knows I'm only half joking. "Seriously Ma, I won't be able to concentrate on the show tonight if I know you're holding out on me."

"Eric surprised me and showed up here last night."

"That's cool." This is not her news. Ma and Doc Banks and have been spending a lot of time together traveling back and forth to see each other.

"He proposed to me."

"And?" I don't know why I'm holding my breath, but I am.

"I said yes!" she squeals. It's one of the most innocent, insanely happy things I've ever heard.

And now I have tears in my eyes. Happy tears because my mom deserves this. She deserves to be loved and have a partner to grow old with. "Congratulations, Ma." I wipe a tear away that's rolling down my cheek. "I kinda wish you would've waited to tell me in person now, because this doesn't feel right that I can't hug the shit out of you. I'm so happy for you, Ma. Doc Banks is a lucky dude."

"Thank you, Gus. Are you sure you're okay with this? I mean, you like him?"

"Of course I'm okay with this. He's a great guy."

She sighs in relief. "Good."

343

"And besides, I get a kickass brother out of the deal."

She laughs. "And a niece."

I have to pause when she says it. "Damn. I hadn't thought about that. I'll be Stella's uncle. How awesome is that? No offense Ma, but that may be my favorite thing to come out of this whole set-up."

"None taken. She'll be my granddaughter — I get it." She does. Ma loves Stella.

"So, when's the wedding?"

"No date yet, but soon. We'll have a small ceremony here at the house."

"That sounds perfect. So, I assume Doc's moving to San Diego?"

"Yes. He'll be here in two weeks. He got a position at San Diego General in the ER."

"That's great." And now I'm thinking about how different it will be to have another man in the house. And I'm also thinking it's best if I give them some space. They deserve to start their new life together. And I deserve to start mine. It's time.

"Thanks honey."

"Does Keller know?" I feel like I need to call him and welcome him to the family.

"Yes, Eric called him this afternoon. He's happy for us."

"I bet he is. He gets a badass stepmom out of the deal."

She laughs again. "Well honey, I need to let you go. I need to get back to work. Good luck tonight. Can't wait to see you tomorrow. I love you."

"Don't need luck; I've got Franco, Jamie, and Robbie. Can't wait to see you, too. I love you."

"Bye, sweetie."

"Bye, Ma."

I immediately call Keller but it goes to voicemail. I'm sure he's at work. So I text him. *BROTHER!!*

He calls back just as we're getting on the bus after the show to head to the airport.

"Brother!" I answer.

"Hey, bro, crazy isn't it?" He sounds as happy as I am.

"Pretty fucking crazy, yeah. It's a good crazy though."

"Definitely. My dad's a different man since the divorce.

Audrey brings out the best in him. It's great."

"Does your mom know?" I question.

"I doubt it. We're still not talking. I should probably call her one of these days. The resentment's faded. It's time."

"What does Stella think? She does know she's getting the best uncle in the history of uncles, right?"

He laughs. "Baby girl is well aware of that fact. I think that's her favorite part."

"Yes! That's what I said, too."

"I've got some good news, too. I've got a job interview next Monday. I've already had two over the phone and they want me to come in person for the final. I'm ninety-nine percent sure it's in the bag."

That has to be a relief to him. I'm sure he's feeling a lot of pressure to find a job now that's he's graduated. "Right on. Where at? Same school you interned at?"

"No. It's in San Diego." He's smiling. I hear it loud and clear.

"What? Get the fuck out?" How fucking awesome would it be to have Keller and Stella in SoCal with us?

"Yeah. It was kind of a last minute thing that came up. There aren't any positions open around Minneapolis and I'd have to sub this school year, so I started searching the San Diego school district not really expecting to find anything."

"I'll be home tomorrow so I'll be there when you guys come down. I can drive you around. Whatever you need. And I'll take you out and we'll celebrate."

"Sounds good. I'd better let you go, man. I know it's late, or more accurately early, there."

"Okay. See you in a few, bro."

"Okay, bro. Later."

"Peace out."

My entire life changed in the span of a day. And the best part is, I'm totally on board with it. I'm ready. I've got a lot of work to do when I get home.

Thursday, August 23
(Scout)

I hear his sleepy voice before I see him. "If you aren't a sight for sore eyes." When I look up from my desk, Gus is holding a vase of red roses and wearing an exhausted, but content smile.

"I could say the same. Hi, babe." God, even with dark circles under his eyes he's still gorgeous.

He sets the vase down on my desk and then wraps me up in a hug that feels like he's put up walls to the world outside and it's only us inside. My face is pressed into his T-shirt and I close my eyes and inhale him. Not just his manly scent, but ... him. All of him. "I've missed you so much."

He kisses my forehead. "Not as much as I've missed you, sweetheart."

When I look up at him, his eyes meet mine. "You're early."

"Caught an earlier connecting flight in New York. I had someone I couldn't wait to see. I asked the pilot to fly the plane faster, too." The way he's grinning, I have no doubt he really did.

I kiss him once and I have to remind myself that I'm at work, surrounded by people. People that I'm sure are watching us right now.

I whisper in Gus's ear, "Is everyone staring at us?"

He answers, not lowering his voice. "Every move we make. It should be pretty exciting for them by the time I get to third base."

I can't hold it in and burst out laughing.

"I've missed that laugh."

I kiss him just below his ear before I let him go. "You need to get home and sleep."

"With you, yes." He raises his eyebrows for emphasis.

"Did you take a cab here?"

He nods.

"You can take my car home. I'll ride home with Audrey. I'd cut out early and go with you, but we have a meeting with a big client this afternoon."

We're walking out the back door to the parking lot now. "We could have sex in the car."

"The meeting starts in ten minutes."

"I'm killer under pressure." If he didn't look so tired, I'd believe him. Hell, I believe him anyway.

I kiss him at my car.

He grabs my ass.

"Thanks for the flowers. They're beautiful."

He's behind the wheel now, starting the engine. "Like you. I'm gonna go get crazy comatose for a few hours. I'll be all rested up for you tonight. I'm gonna put your marathon running stamina to the test again. Put your panties in your purse before you come home."

I wink. "Already done. Now go home and snuggle Spare Ribs, she's missed you."

My stamina was put to the test. It's one o'clock in the morning. Gus is holding me and I'm lying with my head on his chest.

"I love San Diego sex," he says. He's running his fingertips up and down my arm.

"Me too. I think it's my favorite," I answer.

"Only one thing would make it better."

I take the bait. "What's that?"

"Doing it in our own bed. In our own place."

I pull off his chest and lay my head on the pillow next to him. It's a full moon outside and I can see his face in the light coming in through the window. I think I know what he's getting at, but I want to make sure. I want to hear him to say it.

"I'm moving out. I want you to come with me." He's as serious as I've ever seen him.

"You want to live with me?"

He nods. "Every single day. What do you say?"

I nod. "I say yes."

He kisses me on the tip of my nose. "I say thank you."

Friday, August 31
(Scout)

The past week has been insane. Everything happened at once.

Keller got a teaching job here in San Diego. He starts next week.

Gus flew to Minneapolis and helped Keller and Stella drive his car and a moving truck back here and we helped them get set up in an apartment nearby.

Eric moved in with Audrey and started his job at the hospital.

Paxton moved into the dorms at San Diego State. He starts classes Monday.

And Gus and I moved into a small house on the beach not far from Audrey's. We signed a six month lease. Gus wants to buy a house, but I'm scared to spend the money. I'm not scared of making a commitment with him; I'm just scared of the financial obligation. I'm working on courage in all areas of my life so I know he'll win eventually. He always does. I can't say no to him.

Saturday, October 20
(Scout)

"Remember when we met and you hated me?" he asks. It's dark outside, and we're sitting on a chaise lounge on the deck of our new place. I'm settled comfortably between his legs with my back resting against his chest. We're eating saltines and peanut butter and drinking grape juice.

"I didn't hate you. I just didn't really like anyone back then. It was nothing personal. I didn't know what good men were like."

"We've come a long way, Girl Scout." He's reminiscing. Gus is a deep guy. He thinks through everything with his heart.

"We have." That's an understatement. "I'm a completely different person thanks to you."

"Do you ever step back from your life and ask, *How in the hell did I get here? How did I get so lucky?*"

I rub his thigh with my palm. "Every minute of every day, babe. I never dreamt I'd have someone like you to love. Who'd love me back."

"Scout?" He kisses the back of my head. It's a loving gesture that I feel all the way down to my toes.

"Yeah?"

"I want to make babies with you. Lots of them. Do you want kids?" The sincerity in his voice just made my heart clench in the best way possible. "I mean, I know you lost a baby and I can't imagine how hard that was for you. I don't want to put any pressure on you; I just want you to be honest with me. Would you be willing to try again? With me?"

There are tears in my eyes. And not because I'm thinking about the past ... but because I'm thinking about the future. A future with him. A family with him. I can see it and it's the most perfect life I could imagine. I turn and shift in his embrace so I can look in his eyes.

He reaches up and wipes the tears that are trailing down my cheeks. "Don't cry, sweetheart. I'm sorry. I didn't mean to make you cry."

I smile at the sweetness of this man. "I'm not crying because I'm sad, Gus. I'm crying because I was just wondering how in the hell I got here ... with you. How did I get so lucky?"

349

He smiles. "You're my everything, Scout. *Everything.* I love you with everything that I am. Everything I'll ever be. You're my future, sweetheart."

And the tears continue to fall. "You're my everything, too. You took a broken, scared little girl and turned her into someone I didn't even know I could be. I can't thank you enough. And my love for you? God, it's never-ending, babe. I will love you until the day I die."

He's smiling again. "Does that mean we get to make babies?" He rubs my stomach with his hand. "I want this belly swollen with my little one."

I nod and I'm so emotional I can hardly speak. Having a child with him would make me so happy. Complete. "Yes."

"I'm throwing your pills away when we go inside."

I turn and settle back into to my special spot against his chest. "Okay. Does this mean we're going to have sex a lot?"

He squeezes me. "You better believe it. Morning, noon, and night. You should probably just stop wearing panties altogether. I'll join you in your underwear boycott. Maybe tell Ma you're going on sabbatical and take some time off and we'll just give up clothes entirely and walk around naked until you're prego?"

"I don't think Audrey would give me time off to get knocked up."

He laughs his deep belly laugh. "If she knew she'd get a grandkid out of the deal, hell yes she would. You've seen her with Stella. She's the ultimate G-Ma."

I laugh with him, because he's right. Gus's child would be the most loved grandchild in the history of grandchildren.

We watch the waves come in under the moonlight for several minutes. It's quiet. All I hear is the water crashing against the shore.

"There's something else." His voice has softened. The excitement is gone and all that's left is reverence and adoration.

"Yeah?" I ask. The emotion in his voice has my heart beating double time.

"Will you really love me forever?" He knows I will. He's nuzzling my neck just below my ear with the scruff on his chin.

"And ever," I answer.

His lips press against my neck once before they brush my

earlobe. "I want you to be Mrs. Hawthorne."

I turn quickly and straddle his lap, because I know I didn't hear that right. My hands are trembling when I take his face in my hands. "Can you repeat that?" My eyes are stinging again. "My hearing is *really* bad."

He smiles at me, it's affirming. And then he repeats loudly, "I'm asking you to marry me. I want you to be Mrs. Girl Scout Hawthorne."

I can't hide the bliss that is sweeping through my body. I'm smiling so huge my cheeks already hurt. "You want to marry me?"

He nods and his face looks serious. Impassioned. "Will you marry me, sweetheart?"

(Gus)

She's smiling and crying and nodding all at the same time. It's a full body nod that says without-a-doubt yes. "Yes. *Yes.* Yes, I will marry you."

And I feel it. I'm at peace. If I died right this second, my life would be complete. I won't die of course, which is the best part. I get to live this, for how long I have no idea, but I'm going to live and love the hell out of it.

I kiss her.

It's a promise.

Which leads to sex. Right there on the chaise lounge. On our deck.

It's also a promise.

Scout is already asleep, so I grab the stack of sticky notes and marker we keep on the bathroom counter and I write her a note and stick it to the mirror so she'll see it when she wakes up in the morning. *San Diego, baby making, engaged, I love you forever, deck sex just became my new favorite.*

I'm at the tipping point of a transformation that began months ago, an intentional decision put in motion. And it feels so fucking good. I've come to the full realization that my happiness, my life, falls squarely on my shoulders. No one's gonna do it for it me. I'm the one who makes it or breaks it.

It's a *choice*.

A choice that demands action in exchange for reward. Idleness and complacency lead to mediocrity. Sometimes action is really fucking hard fought, but that's when the payoff's the highest.

That's when great things happen.

Not good things ... but *epic* things.

And I've fallen in love with epic.

It's the only way to live.

Acknowledgments

You can't see me, but I'm smiling and it's huge because this is my favorite part of the book. The part where I get to say thank you to all of the awesome people who helped make this book possible. Sit back and get comfortable because I have a lot of love to spread, this may take a while.

Thank you to my beta readers, who named themselves *The Legion of Moist*. You five incredible women kept me smiling and laughing through the final, tough month of writing and then lovingly and meticulously tore this book apart to help me turn it into something I was proud to hand off to my editor. Your friendship, encouragement, constant humor, intelligence, and love made all the difference in the world. You took me from writer's block to the point where I finally fell in love with this story — I owe you more than you will ever know. So, to Lindsey Burdick, Amy Donnelly, CM Foss, Gemma Hitchen, and BN Toler, I say, thank you. You all make me ...

Thank you to Debbie Clark. You have stood beside me and cheered me on through the past several years of this crazy writing dream I have. Thank you for your constant support and friendship in all things in my life, not just writing.

Thank you to Brandon Hando, crazy talented designer. You created another cover that I am in love with. In. Love. And you are always patient with me and create magic every time I ask for another T-shirt design, or another bookmark, or another sticker, or another ... *anything*. Thank you for always seeing my vision, sometimes even before I do. You have my heart.

Thank you to Monica Parpal, kickass editor. None of my books would have been published without you. Collaborating with you is an honor; you breathe life into my stories. My respect for you grows with every book we work on together (and that's saying something because my respect was through the roof two books ago). And in the case of Gus, you took ownership of this project and committed to it even with your own wedding quickly approaching. I can't thank you enough.

Thank you to Amy Donnelly at Alchemy and Words, kickass editor, formatter and designer. Not only did you beta read, edit, and proofread for me, but you created the most beautiful trailer and teasers for Gus. Not to mention backing me up at every signing event, being an auntie to Phoenix (I'm so glad we adopted you into our family), and letting me bounce anything and everything off you. You. Do. It. All. I don't know what I would do without you. Seriously. I'm bowing down to you right now.

Thank you to Josh Harris at Yerk Design, website designer and general smart dude. You set up my website and have maintained it and added whatever, *whenever* I ask you to, and have offered advice along the way. Thank you for your willingness to always help me out—including proofreading this little book, which was above and beyond the call of duty.

Thank you to Seth King, voice of reason and friend. You talked me off the ledge many times near the end of this project and helped me keep my last, frayed shred of sanity. Aside from writing, I think counseling might be your calling. You're a wise dude. And honest. And caring. And funny. And for all that, I'm eternally grateful.

Thank you to Colleen Hoover, mentor and friend. You are one of the kindest people I've ever met. Thank you for always answering my questions and offering guidance on all things book world related, every time I've needed it, without fail. You'll always be my favorite author, but your heart is what makes you so damn special. Thank you ... for everything.

Thank you to my favorite bands for creating nothing short of pure magic and inspiring me with your music. I wouldn't be able to write without you. And a massive shout out to my very favorite band, Sunset Sons. While I was struggling to wrap up this book, Gemma Hitchen came in literally shouting (IN ALL CAPS) about your band and how you are the real-life Rook. I instantly fell in love HARD with your music and listened nonstop through writing the final chapters and all editing. You were my muse. You are my Gus and Rook. Nothing but love for Sunset Sons.

Thank you to Mom and Dad. For everything over the past forty-two years. I love you.

Thank you to B. and P., my dudes. It's an honor to be your wife and mom – it's what I live for. Period. I love, love, love you both. To the moon and back again.

Thank you to the *Bright Side Support Group* on Facebook. I'm not quite sure how it happened, but hundreds of the nicest and most positive people on the planet all gathered in one spot. We all share a love of good books, but more importantly we all share a love of good people. I am so lucky to be a part of this amazing group. Thank you for being awesome.

And last, but not least, thank you to every reader, author, and blogger who's befriended and supported me. I get to continue to chase this dream and do what I love because of you. That is a gift beyond measure. This book wouldn't be in your hands right now if it wasn't for you. Thank you a million times.

One more thing and then I promise I'm done.
I love you.

That's for everyone mentioned above. Your friendship is a gift. Thank you for being you.

Gus Playlist

The Weekend-Huglife Remix (Coeur de Pirate)
"Wicked Games"
AFI "I Hope You Suffer"
The National "I Need My Girl"
Manchester Orchestra "Cope"
The 1975 "Me"
Sunset Sons "Medicine"
Broods "Killing Me"
Brick + Mortar "Bangs"
Royal Blood "Figure It Out"
Coldplay "The Scientist"
Catfish and the Bottlemen "Homesick"
Sunset Sons "Loa"
Buddy Guy "Baby Please Don't Leave Me"
You Me At Six "Love Me Like You Used To"
Bear Hands "Giants"
Flyleaf "All Around Me"
Balance and Composure "Tiny Raindrops"
Twin Atlantic "Fall Into the Party"
Sunset Sons "On the Road"
Ed Sheeran "Kiss Me"

About the Author

I love reading, writing, traveling, music, coffee, tacos, nice people, my big dude (my husband), and my little dude (my son). And lots of other stuff, too.

I also love to make new friends. Come and find me in one of these spots. We'll hang out. It will be fun.

https://www.facebook.com/kimholdenauthor

https://twitter.com/KimHoldenAuthor

www.kimholdenbooks.com

Other books by Kim Holden

All of It
Bright Side
So Much More

Bonus excerpt from the standalone So Much More by Kim Holden

So Much More
By Kim Holden

Prologue
Love explained...or denied

Ask one hundred people to explain love.
And you'll get one hundred different answers.
Because love is like art, it's subjective.
Fluid.
Ever-changing.
Evolving.

Case in point...

Miranda

Love isn't real.

It's make believe, like Santa Claus or Vegas. All sparkle and fluff, until you look closely, and it's just a sham under the guise of overinflated, wish-granting potential.

Only fools believe in love.

And I am no fool.

Seamus

Love is strange. It comes out of nowhere. There's no logic to it. It's not methodical. It's not scientific. It's pure emotion and passion. And emotion and passion can be dangerous because they fuel love...and hate.

I'm now a reluctant connoisseur of both—an expert through immersion. I know them intimately.

When I fell in love with Miranda, it was swift and blind. We were both young. She was smart, beautiful, witty, and elusive. Rumors surrounded her like a legend that's repeated in hushed whispers for generations based on hearsay and speculation. People said she was cruel, I saw strong willed. People said she was aloof, I saw independent. People said she was cunning, I saw goal-oriented. For every warning I was given, I put on rose-colored glasses and looked at her through my own warped, but discriminating, perspective. That is perhaps my biggest flaw, as well as my saving grace; I tend to only see the best in people. I had visions of grandeur. I didn't want to change her—I didn't think she needed changing. She was the person I'd elevated to mythical status in my head, in my dreams.

Here's the thing about dreams, they're smoke. They're spun as thoughts until they become something we think we want. Something we think we need. That was Miranda. She was smoke. I thought I wanted her. I thought I needed her. Over time reality crept in and slowly dissected and disemboweled my dreams like a predator, leaving behind a rotting carcass.

Reality can be a fierce bitch.
So can Miranda.
And I can be a fool...
who believes in dreams.
And people.
And love.

Faith

There are a lot of things I've done without during my twenty-two years. You can't miss what you never had, right? That holds true for everything in my life, except one. Love.

I miss it, even though we've never met.

It's not something I've idealized into unobtainable perfection. Humans are messy and I'm sure love is too.

I think love is instinct driven, with the heart ruling over mind. It can't be defined. I'll just know it when I feel it, because it will be so bone-jarringly beautiful.

I want that someday, bone-jarringly beautiful.

CPSIA information can be obtained
at www.ICGtesting.com
Printed in the USA
BVHW040651130222
628895BV00002B/10

9 780991 140275